D0765728

27

NOTHING HUMAN

Nancy Kress

Golden Gryphon Press • 2003

This is a work of fiction. All the characters and events portrayed in this novel are either fictitious or are used fictitiously.

LIBRARY OF CONGRESS CATALOGING–IN–PUBLICATION DATA
Kress, Nancy.
Nothing human / Nancy ress. — 1st ed.
p. cm.
ISBN 1-930846-18-5 (hardcover : alk. paper)
1. Global warming—Fiction. 2. Genetic engineering—Fiction.
3. Human-alien encounters—Fiction. I. Title.
PS3561.R46 N68 2003
813'.54—dc21 2002154974

First Edition.

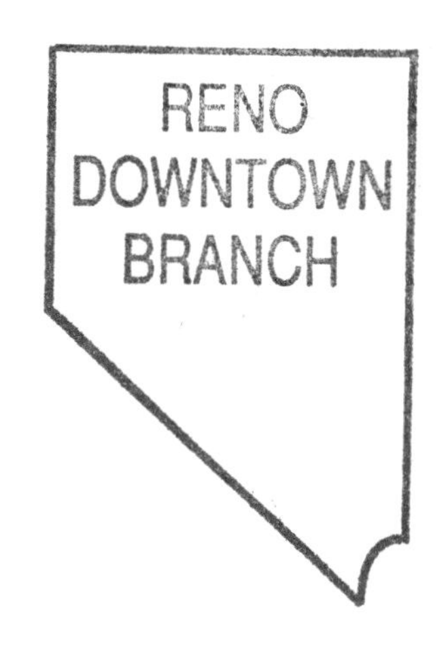

For Charles, Always

NOTHING HUMAN

"I am a man; nothing human is alien to me."
—Terence Africanus, c. 190–159 B.C.

PART I: KEITH

"Some alien blessing
is on its way to us."
—W.S. Merwin, "Midnight in Early Spring"

CHAPTER 1

April 2013

He wrote:

There are things you cannot get your mind around. You go to school, grow up, go to college and law school, get a job. You marry, love, fight, divorce, make partner, marry again, divorce again. People you know have children, or career changes, or deaths. Every change in your life feels enormous at the time, and in the context of your life it is enormous, cataclysmic, life-altering. But not unexpected. Other people around you are experiencing these same things, rich people and poor people, famous and obscure, quietly or with maximum theatrics. Each cataclysm, you see as you get older, is just part of the normal pattern of life. Disappointing or exhilarating, at least what happens to you is universal. Possibly even banal.

Then something happens so far off the expected, outside the pattern, the ordinary turned into the unthinkable, that your mind simply rejects it. It cannot be. It isn't happening. Impossible. No way.

Like the aliens.

Or Lillie.

He looked at the paper, and tore it up. The lame paragraph didn't even come close. What had happened couldn't be expressed in words. There were no words.

Of course, that had been the whole point.

September 1999

"I'm pregnant," Barbara said, and grinned at him like a six-year-old who had just tied her shoelaces for the first time.

Shit.

"Don't look like that, Keith," she said, her voice already trembling. Then, with a sudden show of what passed in her for anger, "Just because you're my brother doesn't give you the power to judge me."

"Of course it does," Keith Anderson said. "Don't spout these mindless slogans at me. Everyone has the right to judge actions according to belief and practicality. It's called 'using good judgment.' "

Her eyes filled with tears, and Keith willed himself to patience. Softly, go softly. Be a good brother. She had always gotten upset too easily, even when they'd been small children. He knew that. Barbara was emotionally fragile.

So how was she going to cope alone with a baby?

He reached for her hand across her tiny kitchen table. Outside the dingy apartment window, someone on Amsterdam Avenue rattled garbage cans and cursed loudly. Cabs honked incessantly. "Tell me about it, Babs," he said gently.

Instantly her tears evaporated. "You know I always wanted children. Then the years somehow went by and things happened and . . . well. You know."

Keith knew. Her first husband the non-working narcissist happened, and her second husband the just-barely-this-side-of-the-law bankrupt happened, and a string of disastrous love affairs happened, and so Barbara was thirty-six and working as an office temp and, apparently, pregnant.

"Who's the father, Babs?"

"That's the best part. There isn't one."

"A virgin birth," he said, before he knew he was going to speak. Once a Catholic, always a Catholic.

Barbara laughed and ran her hand through her short brown hair. It stood up in spikes. "No, an anonymous sperm donor. No man to interfere with us, bully us, upset Lillie and me."

Lillie. Already this fetus was a person to her. Keith braced himself for the argument ahead. But she anticipated him.

"I know what you're thinking, Keithers. But that's taken care of, too. This fertility clinic took five of my eggs and fertilized them all, then chose one that doesn't carry the genetic marker. The baby won't get breast cancer." She and Keith were both carriers; their mother had died of the disease.

When he remained silent she added, "I'm being very careful of Lillie. Yes, I'm positive it's a girl, I had the amnio. I wanted to know."

"How far along are you?"

"Three months already," she said proudly, standing up and turning sideways. "I'm starting to show!"

She wasn't. Skinny as always, impulsive as always, improvident as always. Keith looked around the cramped apartment in the bad neighborhood that was all she could afford. Paint peeled off the walls. He glimpsed a roach crawling in the dim crevice between stove and refrigerator. Outside the grimy window, kids who should have been in school sauntered along Amsterdam Avenue in the mellow sunshine.

"Barbara, how did you afford the *in vitro* fertilization? A woman in my office told me it took her and her husband three tries at nine thousand dollars a pop."

She sat down again. "This clinic, it's called ChildGive IVF Institute, is on a sliding income scale, very cheap. It's because they're part of some test."

"A clinical trial? Who's running it?"

"Oh, Keith, how should I know? And it doesn't matter anyway. Stop sounding like a lawyer!"

"I am a lawyer. How did you learn about the clinic?"

"Ad in the paper. Keithers, please stop."

Again he fought down impatience. "I can't. I care about you. Have you thought how you'll work and take care of the baby, too? Good day care is expensive."

"Something will turn up, it always does. The Lord will provide. You have to trust in Him more."

Keith stared at her helplessly. The Great Divide; they always seemed to run into it sooner or later. But was it really religion, or was it temperament? Trust in God was a great excuse for sloth and lack of planning.

So was the knowledge that you had a hard-working younger brother that wouldn't let you go begging.

It would do no good to say so. Barbara wouldn't hear him; she never did. And Keith was honest enough to admit that he needed her as much as she needed him. His marriage record was no better than hers. Two failures, and he never saw either Stacey or Meg. He was childless, worked fourteen hours a day, would have been wary of trying again with a new woman even if he had had the time. At thirty-four, he was already romantically burned out. Barbara was the only family he had, or probably would have. Barbara and now this child.

He gazed at his sister, with her rumpled-up pixie cut and thin body and hopeful face. She wore jeans from the teen department and a T-shirt with a picture of kittens. A child herself, perpetually.

"Let me show you the baby clothes I bought yesterday . . . they're the most darling things you ever saw!" Barbara said, jumping up from the table so quickly that his tepid coffee sloshed over the rim of his cup. She didn't notice.

Keith mopped up the coffee before she returned from the bedroom with a shopping bag. Then he sat and looked at pink sleepers and a hat with a fuzzy ball on top and impossibly tiny soft white shoes. As she chattered away, he nodded meaninglessly and tried to smile. This was his sister, and she was determined on having this baby no matter what, and the baby would be his only genetic stake in the next generation. His niece.

Lillie.

Barbara had an easy pregnancy, which was good because she had no health insurance and could not have afforded many complications. There was no morning sickness, no bleeding, none of possible worse horrors that Barbara insisted on reading about at the public library. She recited them all to Keith, who would much rather have not heard. He took her to dinner every Tuesday, slashing the time out of his logjammed schedule. He sent her a crib from Bloomingdale's, and he inquired of a tax attorney at Wolf, Pfeiffer about various types of trust funds. The rest of the time he forgot his sister and defended his corporate clients.

He was in court when she went into labor. Turning the case over to his assistant, he drove to St. Vincent's.

"You can go into the labor room but not the delivery room," a harassed nurse told him. Keith hadn't wanted to go into either, but he donned the paper garments and followed her meekly.

Barbara lay on a gurney, her hair plastered wetly to her head and her face sweaty. To his relief, she wasn't screaming. At least not at the moment.

"Keith."

"I'm here, honey." Why didn't she have a girlfriend do this? He tried to look reassuring instead of resentful.

"Talk to me."

"Okay. What about?"

"The trial. What is it about?" All at once her face grew very intent. She gripped the sides of the gurney hard enough to turn her entire hands white. Her features contorted so much that Keith hardly recognized her, but still she made no sound. He began talking very fast, hardly aware of what he was saying, sure she was hearing none of it anyway.

"It's a corporate liability case. I represent the corporation. A worker was cleaning the inside of a mixing machine, which was turned off, of course—"

Barbara gave a long, low sound, less like pain than a weird kind of off-key singing.

"— and he fell asleep. Actually, he was drunk, we've proved that conclusively."

Her face relaxed, became her face again. "Go on, go on, go on." She closed her eyes.

"The allotted time for the cleaning was over," Keith said desperately. He would give anything, anything at all, to be back in court. "And the supervisor, my client, called out loudly that all machinery was going to be turned on again, and—"

Her face contorted and she sounded the long, weird, sliding note.

"Go on, Keith!"

"And so they turned the mixer on." Was this a suitable story to tell a woman in labor? It was not. "The worker was killed. The family is suing."

"Go on!"

"I'll give the summation tomorrow morning. The main point is that for liability you must have negligence on the part of the employer, the standard is that of reasonable care—"

"How are we doing?" the nurse said, rescuing him. She did something to Barbara that Keith didn't watch and, to his intense relief, ordered him back to the crowded waiting room. He sank down gratefully into an orange plastic chair with rips in both arms. People around him jabbered in at least three languages.

It seemed only a few minutes before a doctor appeared, beaming broadly. "Mr. Anderson? You have a daughter!"

Keith felt too wrung out to correct her. He merely nodded and smiled, shuffling his feet like an idiot.

"Your wife is doing fine, she's in Recovery. But if you go to Maternity, you can see the baby. Through this door, down the corridor, take your first left."

"Thank you."

The babies lay behind a big glass window. There were only two of them. Keith pointed to the crib labeled ANDERSON and a masked nurse held up a bundle wrapped in pink. Again Keith pantomimed smiling and nodding until the nurse seemed satisfied.

The baby looked like a baby: reddish, bald, wrinkled, wormlike. All babies looked alike. Keith tried to think what he should do next, and hit on the idea of buying Barbara some flowers. He escaped to the gift shop, breathing deeply with relief.

With any luck, he'd make it back to court before the judge adjourned for the day. With any luck at all.

April 2013

The aide had just left. Lillie lay on her bed in New York-Presbyterian Hospital as she had lain for three weeks now, unmoving. Unseeing, unhearing. Although Keith wasn't sure he believed that last, and so he talked to her whenever he could make himself do it.

"How are you feeling today, Lillie? You look good. Mrs. Kessler put a red ribbon in your hair. I told her red was your favorite color."

He sat down at the little table beside her bedside and pulled out a pack of cards. It helped if his hands were occupied. Helped him, that is. There was no help for her.

Not a conventional coma, the doctor had said. If a nipple was inserted into Lillie's mouth, she sucked. At least that eliminated any need for an IV. She jumped at sounds, closed her eyes at light. But nothing woke her. She didn't use the toilet, didn't respond to anything said to her, didn't move voluntarily. No one had ever seen anything like it. Interns trooped through the room daily. Machines scanned every corner of Lillie. Conferences were held. Lillie harbored no viruses, no bacteria, no parasites, no cancers, no blood anomalies, no nerve or muscular degeneration, no concussion, no endocrine malfunctions. No one could explain anything.

Keith shuffled the cards and began to lay them out. "I used to play solitaire on the computer," he told her companionably. "In law school, when I couldn't stand to study a second longer. I liked seeing those little red and black cards snap into their rows when I clicked on the mouse. Very satisfying."

Lillie lay inert, a physically healthy thirteen-year-old dressed in a blue hospital gown and red hair ribbon.

"Funny, though. Once during a boring weekend at somebody's beach house, a weekend it did nothing but rain, I tried to play with an old deck of cards I found in a dresser drawer. And the game wasn't any fun. It wasn't the solitaire itself I liked, it was the neatness and quickness of the computer moving the cards. Click click."

There was no computer here. Keith could have brought his

handheld, but if he did, he'd probably work. He didn't want to work when he visited Lillie, didn't want to get so absorbed in the law that he forgot about her. If that were possible.

"Red nine on the black ten, Lil."

Someone came into the room. Keith clicked a black eight onto the growing column and looked up. At the expression on Dr. Shoba Asrani's face, Keith got to his feet. Dr. Asrani held a printout in her hand.

"Mr. Anderson, this is a new article from a Net list serve. It describes a patient case, brain scan and PLI and DNA chart. All the same anomalies."

No one had done a brain scan or PLI or DNA chart on Lillie when she was born. No reason: she was a normal healthy infant. And anyway, PLI and DNA charts hadn't been invented yet. The human genome was still being sequenced. Things were different now.

Asrani took a deep breath. "Things are different now. There's another one like Lillie."

August 2001

Keith had the biggest trial case of his career. He'd been working on it with a team of assistants for months, which meant that gradually he'd seen less and less of Barbara.

BioHope Inc. had developed a genetically engineered soya bean with strong pest resistance, good adaptability to soil variety, and dramatically high bean yield. The plant had the potential to thrive in Third World countries. The United Nations had expressed strong interest, the World Health Organization had given the bean its imprimatur, and several governments were interested. Mechanisms were being put in place to distribute seeds free, courtesy of three international charitable trusts, in Africa and Asia. Agriexperts estimated that hundreds of thousands of lives would be saved from starvation.

Then a volunteer in the American clinical trial of the soya bean went into convulsions and died.

The investigation showed that the woman had neglected to tell BioHope that she was allergic to Brazil nuts. A gene from the Brazil nut genome had been spliced into the new soya bean to make methionine, an essential amino acid which soya beans lacked. The dead woman's family sued BioHope.

"I never expected to know this much about Brazil nuts," Keith said to his office friend, Calvin Loesser, when they met in the glossy halls of Wolf, Pfeiffer.

"You lined up good expert witnesses?"

"The best. Did you know that the Brazil nut, technically called *Bertholletia excelsa*, is related to the anchovy pear, which makes good pickles?"

"I didn't know that," Cal said.

"Or that the Brazil nut meat is exceptionally rich in oil?"

"I didn't know that either," Cal said, starting to edge away down the hall.

"Or that less than half the people allergic to nuts in general are allergic to tree nuts like the Brazil nut?"

"Keith . . ."

"The point is," Keith said quietly, "that the genetically engineered soya bean would probably only kill about ten people a year worldwide and would save hundreds of thousands of people from starving. Conservative estimate."

Cal stopped edging down the hall and looked lawyerly alert. "You can't put that in your summation. If you say that even ten people will die, the jury will turn against your client."

"I know. But weigh it out, Cal—ten quick deaths or hundreds of thousands of slow ones? Maybe, over time, millions."

"Too coldly calculating for a jury to respond to."

"I know," Keith said again. "But if it were me, I'd vote in favor of the engineered nut. Ten people is a fair sacrifice to aid millions. What is it, Denise?"

His secretary said apologetically, "I'm sorry to interrupt, but your sister is on the phone and she says it's urgent."

Keith sprinted to his office. "Barbara? Are you all right?"

"No," she said tremulously, "I'm not. Keith, I'm sorry to bother you but I can't . . . I can't do it. I can't!"

"Do what?"

"Any of it! I just can't anymore!" She burst into hysterical weeping.

Keith closed his eyes, calculating rapidly. It wasn't a day heavy with appointments. On the other hand, it was raining hard. Taxis would be hard to get. "Babs, I'll be there as soon as I can. Just sit down and wait for me to . . . where's Lillie? Is she all right?"

"I can't do it anymore!" Barbara cried, and now Keith heard Lillie yelling lustily in the background, screams of rage rather than pain.

"I'll be right over. Just sit down and don't do anything. All right?"

"All . . . right . . ."

At her apartment he found Barbara sobbing on the sofa. Lillie, seventeen months, sat and played with a pile of what looked like broken toys. The apartment reeked. Lillie, dressed in only a diaper and food-stained bib, reeked more. Every surface including the floor was covered with unwashed dishes, baby clothes, pizza cartons, and unopened mail.

Lillie looked up and gave him a beatific smile. Her eyes were gray, flecked with tiny spots of gold.

"I'm sorry, I'm sorry," Barbara sobbed. "I just can't do it anymore."

But somebody had to do it. That much was clear. Keith, well aware that he hadn't the faintest idea how, picked up the phone. Within an hour he had a very expensive Puerto Rican woman from a very expensive temp agency bathing Lillie, clucking disapprovingly at the apartment and murmuring comments in Spanish.

Barbara ignored the cup of tea he made her. "I'm just no good at being a mother, Keith! It's terrible, I'm a complete failure, poor Lillie . . ."

"You're not a failure," Keith said. Was she? He really didn't know if this was normal. He could easily see how it might get overwhelming, a job and a child. . . . But didn't thousands of women all over the city do it every day without collapsing like this? Impatience warred with compassion, both flavored with guilt that he, Keith Anderson, did not have to face this every day.

"I hit her," Barbara said despairingly. "I can't believe it, but Lillie wouldn't stop crying, she *wouldn't* . . ."

"Drink your tea, Babs, while it's hot."

"I can't believe I hit her!"

He stayed until Mrs. Perez had left and Babs was asleep. Then he carried Lillie from her crib in her tiny, stuffy bedroom into the newly cleaned living room. Clumsily Keith undressed his niece. She stirred but didn't wake. He examined Lillie carefully. No bruises, no burns, nothing that looked either painful or suspicious. Grateful, he redressed Lillie and put her back to bed.

He had just returned to the living room when Barbara came out, calmer now, in rumpled blue pajamas. "I'm so sorry, Keith."

"You can't help it, honey," Keith said, not knowing if this was true or not. "It will be easier now. I've hired Mrs. Perez to come twice a week to clean and cook and just sort of take care that things are going smoothly."

"You're so good to me," she said, sitting in a corner of the sagging sofa and tucking her feet under her. Her voice had a softer purr. So this was what she needed: someone to shift the burden onto. She had never been strong enough to carry her life alone, even when that life had been less complicated than it was now.

"So what kind of big case are you working on?" Barbara asked. He heard the envy in her voice. "I know it must be something exciting."

Keith thought of BioHope. Of the genuinely struggling, starving mothers and children the engineered soya bean was supposed to save. Of the American volunteer who had died eating the bean. *"Ten people is a fair sacrifice to aid millions,"* he'd told Cal. But what if one of the ten were Barbara, leaving him with Lillie?

"Keith? What is your case about?"

"Nuts," he said.

April 2013

Dr. Asrani's office was small as a paralegal's cubicle. Keith knew that she had another, more spacious office in the physicians' building adjourning the hospital; this one must be some sort of waystation, a place to leave papers or close her eyes for a moment or talk to patients' relatives in privacy. He sat on the edge of a gray upholstered chair and waited.

"The article was posted by a physician in Pittsburgh," Dr. Asrani said. She had a very faint, musical accent. "He describes a semi-active trance state with no external communication, like Lillie's. And the brain specs . . . here, look."

She hiked her chair closer to Keith's and spread the printout on the arm of his chair. He could see that she took reassurance from the charts and graphs: so verifiable, so unambiguous. She would not have made a good lawyer.

"See, here is the PLI of the Pittsburgh patient, a twelve-year-old boy. Here, in this dark area, is the same anomalous thick growth of nerve cells that Lillie has at the base of the frontal lobe. It's right against the glomeruli, which processes olfactory signals and relays them all over the brain to centers involved in memory, learning, emotion, fear responses—pretty much everything important except muscular control.

"Now here on this page is the boy's neural firing pattern for that region. It is like Lillie's, which is to say, minimal activity in the entire area. Nothing going on in this complex structure. Very odd."

And that was the understatement of the year, Keith thought. An inert, non-malignant, non-functioning but very substantial growth squeezed into Lillie's skull and this boy's, doing nothing.

Dr. Asrani shuffled her printouts. "Now, the DNA chart shows many differences between Lillie and the boy, of course. They have entirely different genetic inheritances. See, Lillie carries the allele for Type AB blood and the boy is A. Lillie has E_2 and E_3 alleles in her APO genes, and the boy has two E_4—a risk of heart disease there in later life. And so on. But look here, Mr. Anderson, on chromosome six. Both children have this very long—almost two million base pairs!—sequence of genes that is utterly unknown. No one has ever seen this in any other human genome. Not ever."

"Of course," Keith said, grasping at a vagrant straw, "you haven't exactly examined every other human genome in the entire world."

Dr. Asrani peered at him as if she thought he might be joking. "Hardly. Genome sequencing is only thirteen years old, after all. There is still much we don't know. In fact, we know hardly anything."

Much as Keith liked her honesty, it didn't help him clarify any feelings about Lillie's genetic anomaly. Which now she apparently shared with an unknown twelve-year-old boy somewhere in Pittsburgh. He gazed helplessly at the abbreviated version of the kid's genetic chart, full of esoteric symbols and swooping lines.

"There is one thing more," Dr. Asrani said, and at her tone he raised his gaze from the printout. "I almost was not going to mention it because it may sound so misleading. But I will say it, after all. Both Lillie and this boy are the products of *in vitro* fertilization."

Keith's mind blanked, then raced. "Where? What clinic?"

"Mr. Anderson, I cannot tell you that. I don't even know it, as the publishing physician has naturally respected patient confidentiality and not included even the boy's name in his article. But I want to caution you that this coincidence is *not* meaningful. No one thirteen years ago—or even today!—could have deliberately altered a fetal genome to somehow lead to Lillie's condition. It is simply not possible. We are far, far too ignorant."

"May I have that printout?" Keith asked, and held out his hand.

She hesitated only a moment. "Of course."

"Thank you," Keith said. "Is there anything more, or shall I return to Lillie?"

She watched him go, her face apprehensive and helpless. She knew what he was going to do: extremely perceptive, Shoba Asrani. She might have made a decent lawyer after all.

CHAPTER 2

July 4, 2010

It was too hot for upstate New York in early July, especially for early evening, especially if you didn't want to be there in the first place. Keith knew he had no right to grumble; summers everywhere were getting hotter and the newspapers said New York City was broiling in its own juices. He longed for his cool sleek apartment on East Sixty-third, acquired only six months ago. He was moving up.

Barbara and Lillie, meanwhile, had moved upstate to Utica. "Beginning a new life," she'd told Keith. "Starting over." To Keith her new life looked quite a bit like the old one.

"Isn't this fun?" Barbara said. "It's so good to see you again, Keith! Lillie, don't go any closer to the water, you hear me?"

Lillie, ten years old, made a face but stopped obediently short of the park "pond" thirty feet across and probably all of two feet deep. Children sailed boats in it. However, since there was no wind moving the sticky, heavy air, this was a losers' game. On her skinny, bony body Lillie wore a halter top and shorts of violent orange. Her dark brown hair hung in sticky tangles.

Barbara and Keith sat on an old blanket spread under a maple tree dying of some slow blight. They'd finished dinner, deli sandwiches and fruit and homemade brownies. At least Barbara hadn't expected him to grill anything. The air was thick with a weird soup of barbecue smoke, portable microwave beeps, pagers, cell phones, Net music, and e-harness alarms shrieking from toddlers or dogs.

"Welcome to a state of nature," Keith said.

"What?"

"Never mind."

"Keith, I've got something to tell you." Barbara lowered her lashes. She looked much as she had when Lillie was born. A forty-six-year-old pixie. "Something I hope you'll be glad to hear."

"Yes?" Keith said neutrally. Her expression, glimpsed through the gathering dusk, made him uneasy.

"It's wonderful, really. A wonder I didn't expect again."

"Spit it out, Babs."

Lillie had come up beside them. She blurted, "Mom is going to get married!"

Barbara looked briefly vexed that Lillie had become the news-giver, but then vexation vanished in enthusiasm. "Yes, and he's the most terrific man in the world! Kind, generous, sexy as hell, fun to be with—"

"You've only been with him three times," Lillie said judiciously, not upset, merely pointing out the facts. "So you don't know if he's all those things."

"I know he's kind because he was so good to you, Miss Smarty Pants," Barbara retorted. "And he's generous because he paid for both our plane tickets to visit him—all three times! And I know he's fun because we laugh a lot, and—"

"You left out 'sexy as hell,'" Lillie said, still without bias.

"Barbara," Keith managed to get out, "how long have you known this guy? And where did you meet him?"

"She met him on-line," Lillie said.

"And what if I did? You can tell a lot about a person on-line, now that I have that live-video feed. Keith, we talk every night, for hours and hours. I've never felt I knew anyone so well, not even you. Bill is the most wonderful—"

Keith interrupted her. "How long ago did you meet on-line?"

"Six weeks and three days ago. And already he's brought Lillie and me to New York three times . . . that's one of the best parts! He lives in Manhattan, in a great old apartment on West End Avenue, bonus witchy, so we'll be near you again!"

Bonus witchy. Keith hated it when his sister used teenage slang. But, then, he hated everything about this setup. Still, he kept his reactions in check, saying carefully, "What does Bill do?"

"Graphic designer for the Net."

Which could mean anything. Barbara rushed on, burbling away about Bill's apartment, the wonderful restaurant he'd taken them to, how he'd consulted Lillie and shown every concern for her opinion, what a great time they'd had. Keith let her run down while he figured out what to say first.

"Barbara, what's Bill's address? West End is long, and pretty varied."

"He's near Seventieth," she said, which also could mean anything. A very mixed neighborhood.

"What's his last name?"

She laughed. "Checking out his ethnicity? It's Brown. Go ahead, counselor, derive clues from that!"

He smiled. "When do I meet him?"

"Whenever you like. We'll be in New York again next week for the wedding, so –"

"Next *week?*"

"Yes, we . . . is that your phone?"

It was. Keith wouldn't have taken the call except it was his investigator's number, with the priority they'd agreed to use only if Jamal found the big evidence they were looking for. The case was complicated. His client was an alternative-energy company who'd lost two workers to an accident that simply wasn't foreseeable. Jamal had indeed found what he was looking for, and Keith's mood climbed as they discussed it.

By the time he'd finished, the fireworks had started. "Oh, look!" Barbara cried as a silver and green pinwheel exploded in the sky. "Isn't it beautiful! Come on, Keith, move out from under the tree so we can see better!"

She hopped forward and plunked herself, laughing, beside the pond. Keith stayed where he was. He was a little surprised that Lillie remained seated sedately beside him.

"Uncle Keith, was that phone call about the trial you told us about? With the new kinds of energy?"

"Yes, it was."

"Our teacher told us about people trying to make new kinds of energy. Safe fusion and solar energy and even that nuclear reactor they're building way out in space. Is your law company connected with that?"

"No. I wish we were."

"Why?"

"Well, lots of money, for one thing. But also it's a fascinating project."

"I think so, too," she said, sounding so grown-up that Keith wanted to laugh. A Roman candle exploded above them. Lillie ignored it.

"Uncle Keith, you said that two people died on your energy case."

"Yes, they did." He was curious to see where this was going.

"Was it worth it? Two people dead, and everybody else gets lots of energy?"

"We don't look at it like that," Keith said, startled by the starkness of her viewpoint. "Although unfortunately new technologies always seem to cost lives at first. Railroads, air travel, heart transplants. Probably even the discovery of fire. Still, it's more a question of whether the energy company could have anticipated that the accidents might happen." Did she know the word "anticipate"? He had no idea what vocabulary a ten-year-old might have.

"I see," she said primly. And then, "I think two deaths is worth it."

He was strangely shocked. Was that normal for a little girl? Weren't children supposed to be sentimental? Peering at Lillie's face through the gloom, he saw her expression: sad and thoughtful. Her gold-flecked gray eyes gave back a reflection of his own face.

"But," she added, "the energy company should give the families of the dead people a lot of money. And medals, too. Hero's medals. Uncle Keith, you're going to have that man you were talking to on the phone, that Jamal, investigate Bill, aren't you?"

"Why, Lillie—"

"That's why you really wanted Bill's name and address."

"I—"

"It's a good idea," Lillie said. "Mom doesn't know him very well. But, Uncle Keith, you shouldn't worry too hard. Because I look out for Mom, you know."

It was that moment, a decade after her birth, that Keith fell in love with his niece. Her serious, half-seen little face, intermittently lit by fireworks, gazed at him with everything Barbara had never had: judgment, reason, sense. She was an amazing little girl. More, she moved at that moment from being an abstract—"my niece"—to being a real, living, individual person. Herself.

But all he said was, "How did you know I was going to have Bill Brown investigated?"

"Because that's what they do in the movies," she said, grinning with ten-year-old glee, and his capture was complete.

"Hey!" Barbara called, ducking under the maple, "come out and watch the fireworks, you two! You're missing everything good!"

April 2013

The Pittsburgh physician's name was Samuel Silverstein. Keith flew to Pittsburgh International and took a cab for the long ride to

Silverstein's office. The office was neither shabby nor luxurious, a solid, reassuring setting located in a new medical building. The door greeted him respectfully by name when he pushed it open, even though he was half an hour early.

"I'm told this is not a medical appointment, Mr. Anderson," Silverstein said. His schedule ran right on time. Silverstein was short, overweight, with intelligent brown eyes.

"No, doctor. I read the article you posted on CaseNet and—"

"You are not a physician."

"No. It was shown to me by my niece's physician, Dr. Shoba Asrani at New York-Presbyterian. My niece Lillie has exactly the same condition as your patient, and exactly the same PLI and DNA charts." He passed Lillie's printouts to Silverstein.

The doctor studied them intently, paging through the stack of papers with methodical attention. When he looked up, Keith said, "Lillie was also the result of *in vitro* fertilization. Like your patient. I would like to know if her fertilization was done at a place called the ChildGive IVF Institute. I don't know where the Institute was located, and no records are available." Barbara had lost all the paperwork. All she had remembered about the location was "some town north of the city."

Silverstein looked at Keith a long time. Then he said quietly, "Give it up, Mr. Anderson. It isn't possible."

"So I'm told," Keith said grimly.

"You're a lawyer, aren't you?"

"Yes. How did you know?"

Silverstein ignored that question, answering instead one that Keith hadn't asked yet. "It *is* against patient confidentiality for me to identify the clinic. Or the patient."

"Can you at least tell me if there are any others? Besides Lillie and this boy?"

Silverstein hesitated. Finally he said, "Yes, there are others. Two more."

"So far. Doctor, I will sign anything you like attesting to the fact that I will not sue the clinic. That's not my aim. I just have to know what happened. Lillie is my niece, my legal ward since her mother died. Anything I can learn, from anyone, might help her physician to understand her condition better, and that of the other three children, too. I'm in a much better position than you to run a discreet investigation, believe me. And I'm prepared to supply you with all sorts of references so you can check me out first."

Silverstein was shaking his head. "Not necessary. I cannot tell you the names, and I wish you could believe that it wouldn't help your niece if I could. I'm sorry."

Keith tried another approach, and then another. Nothing worked, and Silverstein was becoming annoyed. Finally Keith left his card.

So it would have to be an investigation without help. More expensive, longer. But certainly possible.

He flew back to New York.

October 2011

During the year after the July Fourth picnic, Keith saw Lillie often. Barbara married Bill Brown, who turned out to be an ordinary, non-criminal, reasonably solvent guy whom Keith didn't like very much. He was handsome in a thuggish sort of way, with deep-set blue eyes and a heavy beard. Barbara seemed crazy about him. She and Lillie moved into Bill's West Side apartment and Lillie began exploring the city by subway.

"She's too young," Barbara said, running her hand through her short hair and making it stand up in spikes. Barbara had lost even more weight since moving back to New York. "She's only eleven years old!"

"Kids that age go all over by subway," Keith said, "and Lillie's a sensible girl. I'll teach her the ropes."

He did. They went to the Museum of National History, to the ballet at Lincoln Center, for walks in the Park, to overpriced little restaurants in SoHo. Lillie was fun, enough of a child to be impressed by everything and enough of an adult to provide actual companionship. One Saturday just before Halloween they met at an Irish pub for a plowman's lunch. Lately Lillie had insisted on meeting him at their excursion destinations, rather than his picking her up at home. "I like to study the people on the subway," she said. "I'm going to be a film-maker when I grow up, you know."

"Last week it was a diplomat."

She remained unperturbed. "I have lots of time to decide. Uncle Keith, do you believe in angels?"

"No."

"How about ghosts?"

"No."

"Space aliens?"

"Could be. But there's no evidence either way."

"Demons?"

"No. Lillie, what's this all about?"

"Oh," she said, turning her head away, "Mom's on a new kick."

He looked at her harder. "What sort of new kick?"

"She thinks the apartment is haunted."

Keith groaned inwardly. That was all Barbara needed—a "haunting." He said to Lillie, "What does Bill say?"

Lillie's face tightened. "He's not there much anymore."

After barely a year. Keith ran over his schedule: He could maybe go see Barbara Monday night. It was too late today, he had a date tonight. And all day tomorrow he had to work. He took his niece's hand across the wooden table. "Lillie, are you all right? With their . . . their marriage problems?"

"I have to be," she said pragmatically, and with no trace of self-pity. But clearly she didn't want to talk about it. "Uncle Keith, tell me again about SkyPower."

"Well, it's a nuclear reactor in stable orbit, as you know. When it's finished it will generate enormous amounts of energy that will be beamed down to Earth as microwaves. We'll get all the benefits of nuclear power without the contamination risks."

"You mean the owners of it will," Lillie said, and Keith laughed. He enjoyed her shrewdness. She'd pulled her hand away from his; she was getting old enough to feel self-conscious about touching. The day was cold and she wore a bright red jacket. Sometime, he hadn't noticed when, she'd had her ears pierced. Two tiny red hearts nestled in her ear lobes.

She said, "And you're the lawyer for SkyPower."

"Well, one of them." His firm had only recently been named corporate counsel: a coup.

"If anything goes wrong, you defend the company."

"So far nothing has gone wrong. Knock on wood."

She did, rapping on the pub table and saying, "Hello? Come in?" She laughed uproariously. Keith did, too, not because it was funny but because it was so good to see her throw back her head and guffaw. A second later, however, she glanced at the watch he'd given her. "I gotta go. Thanks for lunch!"

"Don't you want dessert?"

"I can't. Mom's getting home soon. Thanks again!"

Home from where? Keith wondered, but Lillie was gone, whirling out the door in a swirl of red. He must call Barbara tomorrow, not wait until Monday, find out what the current crisis was.

But Sunday he had a casual, non-involving date. Monday turned out to be spent putting down brush fires. By the time he called his sister, it was too late.

April 2013

"The same clinic that did your sister did the little boy's mother," Jamal said, "the ChildGive IVF Institute in Croton-on-Hudson. It went out of business in January 2001. Started in May 1999. Eighteen months, and we're looking at some very weird stuff, boss."

Keith nodded. He wasn't going to tell Jamal yet again that Keith disliked being called the semi-mocking "boss." Most investigators were good at one thing: leg work or computer hacking or underworld informants or turning a tiny site clue into an entire trail of reeking spores. Jamal Mahjoub did it all, or at least got it all done by somebody, and if he wanted to call Keith "Rudolph the Red-Nosed Reindeer," he could. Jamal was small, with dark curly hair, glasses, and a face that looked about sixteen.

"The clinic had four employees: a secretary, two nurses, and the doctor. The secretary and nurses check out, working types who just found other jobs when the clinic 'went bankrupt.' The doctor is something else. His name was Timothy—"

"Was?" Keith interrupted.

"He's dead. Coming to that in a moment. Timothy Allen Miller. Born in 1970 and grew up in Siller, Ohio, a small town, mostly farming. Never fit in, the high school yearbook is full of little snide jokes about him. Valedictorian, went to Harvard, did brilliantly in premed but not popular there, either. Arrogant, but also weird in ways other arrogant pre-docs didn't like. Full of conspiracy theories about everything, from the JFK assassination to secret Jewish banking cartels to some sort of black-Catholic alliance to overthrow the government."

"I can see why nobody liked him."

"Big time. He was brilliant at Harvard Med, intern and resident at Mass General, and then they didn't want him on staff. Neither did anybody else."

Keith looked out the window. Ten floors below, two yellow cabs had run into each other on Madison. The drivers stood nose to nose, waving their fists.

"So Miller joins a group practice, and that lasts two years. Then he opens up solo, and in a year he files for bankruptcy. He takes a job as a lab technician in Poughkeepsie."

"Quite a comedown," Keith said.

"And he felt it. Now Miller is bitter as well as arrogant. One of his coworkers said she thought he was the kind of guy who was someday going to come into work with an AK-47 and blow everybody away."

"But he doesn't," Keith said. You had to let Jamal tell it his own way, and he liked audience participation.

"No. Instead, he channels all his weirdness into the Roswell thing. Aliens coming to Earth, all that."

Oh, God. Spare me the nuts. "Roswell is a long way from Poughkeepsie."

"Yeah. But Miller makes the trip, several times. He goes to meetings where UFO types huddle on the highway, waiting to be picked up. And then one night, he is."

Keith grimaced and Jamal laughed.

"Well, all right, he *says* he is. Comes into work and says he has important work to do, aliens have anointed him, blah blah. That same coworker is so creeped out she decides to quit, but the boss saves her the trouble by firing Miller. Miller had been AWOL for a solid month, no word, no excuse."

"Can't blame the boss," Keith said, keeping up his end. His hands felt like ice. Sometime in Jamal's rambling tale, this lunatic medico was going to connect with Lillie.

"No. But Miller just laughs at being fired—my informant was standing right there—and he saunters out, cocky as spaniels. A month later he opens ChildGive in Croton-on-Hudson. Big glossy offices, state-of-the-art equipment, competent personnel."

"Where'd the money come from?" Keith asked.

"Don't know. I couldn't find the trail. But he pays his people well. Even so, none of them like their new boss. He's a son of a bitch to work for. But he's apparently good at what he does. He gets hundreds of couples pregnant *in vitro*, some with the parents' egg and sperm, some with donors. But no shady stuff . . . every time he uses a donor, the parents agree, and all the paperwork dots the legal i's and crosses the legal t's."

"A model citizen."

"Yep. Not only that, but by this time enough genes for hereditary diseases have been identified that Miller picks and chooses his embryos and everybody gets as healthy a kid as possible. No complaints filed with any officials, scores of glowing thank-you letters, money coming in hand over fist. And then, eighteen months later, Miller closes shop."

"Why?"

"He never said. Not to anybody. He waves his hand to make the whole thing go away, and it does. Then Miller himself disappears. No tax returns, no credit cards, no e-mail address, nothing."

"Murdered?"

"You watch too much TV, boss. No, he was alive, but he

changed his name, moved to New Mexico, and worked under the table in a restaurant. For two years, the waiters and restaurant owner and busboys and customers say he's the happiest person they ever met. The original sunshine kid. Then he's killed by a drunk driver while crossing Main Street."

"Did you—"

"Of course. It really was an accident. Fifteen-year-old redneck kid without a license, been arrested for it before, drunk out of his mind. He's still doing time in juvie for vehicular manslaughter. But now hold on, boss. Here it comes."

Keith waited.

"In the last three months, *twenty* of Miller's test-tube babies have gone into trances like your niece's. They're starting to find each other. I have the names, and one of the parents is a doctor. He's actually a stepparent who married the mother of a girl like Lillie years after the kid was born, and he's not a, what do you call it, a geneticist, but he knows enough to know what he's looking at. And he's mad as hell. His name is Dr. Dennis Reeder, and here's his address in Troy, New York. He wouldn't say much to me, but he's raring to talk to you. A physician no less. Doctor, lawyer . . . all you need is an Indian chief."

Keith didn't hire Jamal for his sensitivity. He took the card Jamal handed him and wrote the investigator a large check, plus bonus.

He was going to find out what had been done to Lillie, and why.

CHAPTER 3

October 2012

Barbara hung herself in the bathroom of her apartment the day before Halloween, three days after Bill Brown moved out. Lillie found her. She called 911, then the police, then Keith. By the time he tore over to the West Side, the cops and EMTs were there, filling up the messy space. Lillie had been sent to her room. She sat on the edge of the bed with her hands folded in her lap, and the stoic resignation on her young face broke his heart.

"Uncle Keith, I . . ."

He sat down next to her and put his arm around her shoulder.

". . . I was too late to stop her. I stayed at the library too long."

All the anger at Barbara that he'd never expressed tsunamied over him. Barbara's irresponsibility, her selfish throwing of all her problems onto other people whenever things got tough, her obstinate refusal to consider Lillie instead of making Lillie consider her . . . The strength of his anger frightened Keith. He fought to hold himself steady to Lillie's need.

"Honey, it isn't your fault, not one little part of it is your fault. Your mother was mentally ill, she must have been to do this. Depressed. You aren't to blame, Lillie."

"I should have come home earlier from the library. But it wasn't . . . good here." She closed her lips tightly together and Keith saw that this was all he was ever going to learn about living with Barbara during the last weeks.

Damn her, damn her . . . God, his sister. Babs . . .

He said shakily, "You'll come live with me now, honey. I've got a spare room. We'll move your furniture and things." His mind raced over practicalities, glad to consider moving trucks and dressers instead of considering Babs. Whom he'd failed as badly as Barbara had failed Lillie.

"Thank you," Lillie said. "I think the police want to talk to me before we go."

They did. Awaiting his turn at interrogation, Keith walked out into the hallway, turned a corner, and pounded his fists on the wall. It didn't help.

He arranged for cremation of the body. He moved Lillie into his spare room, first throwing out the treadmill (no space) and emptying the closet of junk he didn't even know he had. Through Lillie's school he found a grief counselor whom Lillie saw every week. He informed Lillie's school and pediatrician and the state of New York that he was now her legal guardian. The paperwork began its slow drift through various bureaucracies.

Lillie turned quieter, more somber. But she didn't collapse into hysterics or start doing crack or run wild in the streets. Keith discovered that it was pleasant, when he turned the key in his lock after work at seven or eight or nine o'clock, to be greeted by Lillie's smile and a warmed-up casserole. On Saturdays (but not Sundays) he conscientiously refrained from work and took her places, unless she was going out with friends. He met her friends. She met the women he casually dated. Gradually they created a routine that satisfied them both.

Quite abruptly, it seemed, Lillie's body went into overdrive. One day she was almost as skinny as Barbara had been. The next day, she was wearing tight jeans and a midriff-baring top over a figure that made him blink. He found a box of tampons in the bathroom and pretended to not see them. Thirteen—was that early or late? There was no one he could ask. And Lillie seemed to be doing fine with her new body. Lipstick tubes appeared on the ornamental shelf under the foyer mirror, tubes with fantastic names: Peach Passion and Ruby Madness and Jelly Slicker. The names amused him.

And then on March 10, 2013, Keith came home and found Lillie lying on the sofa, staring into space, and no amount of shouting or shaking or anything else could bring her out of it. An ambulance arrived within ten minutes, and as the medics carried Lillie on a stretcher out of the apartment, they bumped into the shelves and all the lipsticks clattered to the floor.

April 2013

Troy was an amazingly ugly city enjoying a huge economic boom because of technology invented at Rennselaer Polytechnic Institute and manufactured not far from the campus. Part of that manufactury, Keith knew, was parts for SkyPower, now being assembled in geosynchronous orbit. The Hudson River, a peculiar shade of sludge, flowed through the center of Troy.

Dr. Dennis Reeder lived in a far suburb, away from the factories, surrounded by semi-open fields. Keith had forgotten how beautiful spring could be away from New York. Tulips and daffodils and even daisies foamed around the Reeder house; everything bloomed earlier now that summers had become so long and hot. The driveway where he parked his rented car was littered with plastic toys. A powerscooter, unchained and unlocked, leaned against the garage.

"We keep our daughter at home with us," Reeder told Keith. "My wife is a nurse. She quit working when this . . . happened to Hannah, and we've also hired an aide. Would you like a drink, Mr. Anderson?"

"Keith. Yes, please. Scotch, if you have it."

Reeder did. The large, comfortable house seemed equipped with everything. Hannah's mother, a strikingly pretty blond woman with tired eyes, joined them in the living room but drank nothing.

"Lillie is hospitalized," Keith said. "I'm her only family."

Reeder said bluntly, "You're an attorney. Are you considering some sort of class-action suit?"

"No one to sue. If Miller were still alive, we'd pursue criminal charges. No, I'm here just as a parent."

"So are the rest of us. There are twenty-one kids like Hannah, that we know of so far. We've set up a list serve with—"

"I'd like to be on it."

"Certainly. With a flag program to scan the entire Net continually for news articles, medical references, personal letters, anything that relates to this situation. One of our parents is a programmer. We come from all segments of society, since Miller offered his services nearly free as part of a 'clinical trial.' "

Keith saw Barbara standing sideways, proudly showing off her non-existent stomach bulge. *"This clinic is on a sliding income scale, very cheap. It's because they're part of some test."*

Reeder continued, "The families are wildly different, and so are the kids. Were, I mean. Male, female, good kids, troublemakers, academics, jocks, dropouts, everything. But every single one has that same quiescent growth in the frontal lobe and that same increase in cerebral neurons of as much as twenty percent and the same PLI firing patterns. Plus, of course, all those unknown genes on chromosome six."

"Are they completely unknown? Don't we know what proteins they code for?"

"Yes, in that codons only make twenty amino acids all together," Reeder said patiently. Keith could tell he'd given this speech to non-scientists before. "But how those twenty then combine and fold—folding is the crucial part—can result in thousands of different proteins. Also, multiple alleles at multiple loci can influence gene expression. Hannah's extra genes don't seem to be making any proteins at all at the moment, or none that we can detect in her bloodstream.

"But remember, Keith, that if the brain cells are making proteins to induce the trance Hannah and Lillie are in, the proteins or neurotransmitters or whatever is responsible may be found only in the brain, contained by the blood-brain barrier. Sixty percent of all messenger RNAs are expressed in the brain at some point. However, there's nothing odd that we could detect in Hannah's cerebrospinal fluid, either."

Keith sat quietly, trying to absorb it all.

Reeder poured himself a second drink. "But of course genes do other things as well, including form the fetus. Presumably some of those extra genes are responsible for the anomalies in Hannah's and Lillie's brains."

"So Miller, when he was doing the *in vitro* fertilization, did he—"

"No. Not possible," Reeder said, and that made the third doctor who had said that to Keith. Yet here the impossibilities were, in the form of twenty-one children.

"Inserting specific genes in specific places in the human genome is really difficult," Reeder said. "And thirteen years ago we knew even less. The inserted genes have a way of splicing themselves into unsuitable locations, disrupting other working genes. Also, the transpons and retroviruses that were the means of delivering genes into an embryo twelve years ago could never have carried as big a gene load as this. That Miller could have accomplished that—not to mention designing the genes in the first place!—with identical results for at least twenty-one babies, isn't possible. I don't care how much of a genius he was. The techniques just didn't, and don't, exist."

Keith knew he was going to make a fool of himself. "What if it wasn't Miller's science? What if he got it, spelled out step by step, from elsewhere?"

"From where?"

"I don't know."

Reeder frowned. "No other country is that far ahead of us, if that's what you're thinking. Genetic information is shared internationally."

"Not another country."

Linda Reeder spoke for the first time. "What are you hinting at?"

"I'm not hinting, only speculating. Somebody knew a lot more genetics than we do. Aliens?"

They both stared at him. Linda rose abruptly. "I better check on Hannah." She strode from the room, every line of her body scornful.

"I know how that sounds," Keith said. "I'm not saying I believe it myself. But Miller did tell people he'd been abducted, and he was missing for a month. My investigator, who's the best there is, verified that."

Reeder finished his second drink. "I prefer to stick to facts. There's only one more I haven't given you. In every case I've tested, it looks as if the trance state began with the onset of puberty. There are numerous genes that switch on then, and it's possible they also switched on whatever of the inserted genes are active in the children's brains."

Puberty. Lillie's blossoming body, the box of tampons, the lipsticks clattering to the floor. "I see."

"I'm not sure there's anything more I can tell you," Reeder said. "If you give me your e-mail address, I'll—"

Someone screamed.

Reeder tore out of the room. Keith followed, not caring that it wasn't his house. Reeder ran up a flight of stairs, down a hall to a bedroom.

Linda Reeder stood by a pink-covered bed, her hand to her mouth, eyes wide. On the bed sat a young girl in pink pajamas, looking puzzled and a little scared.

"Mom? What's wrong? What did I say? Dad, what's wrong with Mom?"

Hannah. Looking like a normal thirteen-year-old girl, long blond hair parted in the middle, music cube on the night stand, holographic poster of rock star Jude Careful above the bed. A window framed by white curtains was open to the warm April air.

"Mom? All I said was, the pribir are coming. Well, they are. Mom?

"Dad?"

* * *

By the time Keith drove back to New York, doing ninety miles an hour on Route 87, Lillie had been awake three hours. He'd given his permission over the phone for Dr. Asrani to run whatever tests she wanted as long as Lillie agreed and didn't seem too upset. He could not, in this context, have defined "too upset."

"Uncle Keith!" Lillie said. He hugged her hard, until, blushing, she pushed him away. She was never physically demonstrative. Maybe it reminded her too much of Barbara. Her beautiful gold-flecked eyes looked clear and alert.

"How do you feel?" Such banal, ordinary words! As if she'd had a head cold, or the flu.

"Okay. That doctor said it's April 28 and I've been knocked out for *weeks*. Is that true?"

"Yes."

"How come? Did I get hit by a car or something?"

Shoba Asrani must have told her all this, but he saw that she wanted to hear it from him. "No. You just sort of collapsed in the living room, and I called 911."

"A heart attack?"

"No, sweetie. Nobody knows why you collapsed." God, how much was he supposed to tell her about the extra DNA, the brain structures, Miller, the other kids? How did you discuss what utterly baffled everyone?

"Well, can I go home now?"

"I don't know. I'll ask. Look, I'm going to talk to Dr. Asrani. You get back in bed and wait for me."

"I don't want to get into bed. I'm not tired."

"Then sit in that chair."

"I'm hungry," she said. "Is there a vending machine? In the hall, maybe?"

The sheer normalcy was eerie. Keith gave her money. He found Dr. Asrani in her office, apparently waiting for him. She looked as unsettled as he felt, too unsettled for small talk.

"Keith. We ran tests. The structure in Lillie's frontal lobe and olfactory glomeruli is now active. The PLI isn't like anything we've seen, a totally new firing pattern. Usually neurons fire at intervals of—"

He wasn't yet interested in details. "Is she in danger? Is the growth harming her in any way?"

"Not that we can tell. She checks out fine, and she says she feels fine. Of course, we want to keep her several days to run—"

"No. She wants to go *home*."

Asrani took a step forward, waving one arm. "No, we need to—"

"I'm taking her home. I'll bring her in here every day, if you want and she agrees, or someone will—" How long could he be away from the SkyPower legal work? "—but right now I'm checking her out of the hospital."

Asrani looked extremely unhappy. But she had no legal ground for keeping Lillie, and she and Keith both knew it.

He said, "Something important, doctor. When she woke up, did she say to you, or to anybody, anything peculiar?"

"Peculiar how?"

"Did she happen to mention the word 'pribir'?"

"No. What's a pribir?"

"I don't know. Nothing. Start the paperwork for me to take her home, doctor."

He found Lillie back in her room, looking out the sealed window at a parking lot and eating a bag of corn chips. Two candy bars lay on the windowsill. She'd already found her jeans and sweater in a closet and changed from the hospital gown. "Uncle Keith, I can't find my shoes. Somebody might have stole them."

"We'll get you new ones."

"They were *Kleesons*," she said. "And I had them all broken in just right."

He couldn't think of anything to answer. The situation was too surreal.

The paperwork took longer than Keith thought necessary. Why didn't a modern, on-line hospital have more streamlined systems? Lillie, barefoot, slouched in a chair and read an old movie magazine. The air smelled of chemicals and food and cleaning solvents, a typical hospital smell, but despite the "increased activity in her frontal lobe and olfactory glomeruli," Lillie didn't react.

Finally they walked out of a side entrance toward the car. The sun had just set, replacing the afternoon's warmth with a cool breeze. Warmth didn't last in April, not even an April as hot as this one. Keith shivered and put an arm around Lillie, dressed in her cotton sweater.

She pulled away. "Can we stop at McDonald's on the way home? I'm still hungry."

"Yes, if you want to."

"Good. And oh, Uncle Keith—"

"What?" He was trying to remember where, in his headlong blind haste, he'd parked the car, and if it had been a legal spot.

"The pribir are coming."

CHAPTER 4

By the next day, the Troy *Record* had the story. One of the parents of a newly wakened child had evidently called them, full of joy at the "miracle" that God had brought about in order to return their son. The paper sent a reporter for a human-interest story, but the reporter was less intrigued by the religious angle than by the strange utterance that more than one just-coma-free child had made simultaneously: "The pribir are coming." The reporter only had three names, and Dennis Reeder was furious that the parents had divulged those three, but the parents swore there were seventeen more. The wire services picked up the story, and suddenly it was all over the Net and the papers and the TV news.

'MIRACLE CHILDREN' PREDICT COMING OF ANGELIC HOST!

ARMAGEDDON TO ARRIVE SOON; COMA KIDS AWARDED VISION

ALIENS TO INVADE, SAY MUTANT CHILDREN BACK FROM MYSTERIOUS TRANCES

SPIRITS FROM THE OTHER SIDE CHANNELED BY CHILD MEDIUMS

Nobody knew what the pribir were.

"Well, they're not angels or ghosts," Lillie said with disgust. She had the TV on while she ate a bowl of cereal and a Fun Bun for breakfast. Hers was not one of the names on the Net.

"What are they, Lillie?"

"I told you. I told everybody, at the hospital. They're people coming soon."

"From where?"

"I don't know. We're out of Fun Buns, Uncle Keith."

Her nonchalance was, somehow, the worst part of the whole thing. She was so casual. Some information, some idea (posthypnotic?) had been planted in her brain, and to her it was as ordinary, as much a given, as breakfast cereal and rock music and warm spring weather.

"The anomalous structure is now active," Shoba Asrani had said when Keith took Lillie back to the hospital the next day.

"It happened when we went outside," Keith said.

"That fits with it being olfactory activity," Dr. Asrani said.

"You mean she smelled something?" Keith said incredulously. "And it gave her some hypnotic suggestion? The same thing that kid in Troy smelled?" The open window in the pink bedroom, the sealed one in Lillie's hospital room.

"Not hypnotic," Asrani said. She looked visibly frayed. Keith knew there must be frantic medical conferences going on about this, on- and off-line. How could there not be? He didn't ask, he didn't want to know. Now that he had Lillie back, his previous thirst for information had transmuted to a desire to put the whole thing behind them and have their lives back.

"Sit down, Keith," Asrani said.

"I'd rather stand."

She raised one arm. Let it fall again to her side. He thought he'd never seen such a helpless gesture. "Then listen standing. The usual human nose has fifty million bipolar receptor neurons inside each nostril. Inhaled molecules bind onto those receptor sites and trigger electrical signals. The brain is basically a chemical-electrical machine, you know. Each gets translated into the other all the time.

"The electrical signals travel first to a tangle of nerves called the glomeruli, where undoubtedly selective processing of some sort goes on. Then those signals go out to major portions of the brain involved in memory, learning, emotion, fear responses—pretty much everything important except muscular control. Have you ever seen a dog excited by a scent?"

"Of course," Keith said.

"Well, animals like dogs that rely on smell more than humans do have roughly the same setup as ours, plus an additional structure, the olfactory tubercle, that makes our sense of smell look wishy-washy.

"Lillie's anomalous growth is in the same place as a tubercle would be, at the base of the frontal lobe, but much larger. Her glomeruli are firing in electrical patterns nobody has ever seen before. In each nostril she has not fifty million receptors but closer to five hundred million. Since each receptor site presumably binds a different molecule to it, she could be detecting molecules we have no idea of. And whatever information those molecules give her is going out to both her rational and emotional brain centers."

"Are you saying that Lillie is smelling molecules that tell her these 'pribir' are coming?"

"I don't know what they tell her. Obviously she's not upset by whatever it is, so more than a simple exchange of information is going on. Her emotional centers are being soothed, conditioned to acceptance. She has a high measure of serotonin in her cerebrospinal fluid, much higher than she had before. Serotonin creates equilibrium."

"You mean they're brainwashing her!"

Dr. Asrani did something Keith had never expected: she lost her temper. The serene Indian woman shouted, "Don't you get it? We don't know! We don't know anything!"

After a moment she added, "I'm sorry."

"It's all right. But . . . how did these theoretical molecules get into the air? And how could children scattered over four states smell the same ones?"

"We don't know how they got there. No more than we know how Lillie got to be what she is. But the distance is at least explicable. There are male moths that detect a single molecule of female moth sex pheromone and then zoom to the female moth from six miles away. A model something like that, but even more powerful, might be operating in Lillie and the others."

He couldn't take it in. His mind rejected it. This was Lillie, his Lillie, Babs's daughter . . . He walked over to the window and stared blindly out, seeing nothing.

Dr. Asrani said, "You mentioned 'brainwashing.' There are as many definitions of that as there are so-called 'experts.' But looking at animal models again . . . there are a great many precedents for affecting behavior by manipulating smell. A certain kind of tapeworm in a moose will scent the moose's breath so the breath attracts wolves. The tapeworm needs a wolf to finish its life cycle. So it gets a wolf to eat the moose, and it. And some ants—"

"Enough," Keith said. "I understand."

Which was probably the stupidest thing anyone had said all day. Of course he didn't understand.

He turned to face Dr. Asrani. "The names of all the children won't stay secret long, you know. There have been too many medical people involved. Lillie and the other twenty kids—"

"Eighty," she interrupted him. "We have a fuller roster than Dr. Reeder."

"I'll bet you do. Anyway, what do you recommend I do for Lillie? Bring her here?"

"No," she said, suddenly looking very tired. "Not here. If you want, you can take her to some friend or relative whom you can trust. But frankly, Keith, I don't think it matters where you take her.

"I'm afraid that before long, Lillie may be telling *you* where she has to go."

The first indication anyone had that the pribir did indeed exist came when they blew up SkyPower.

Keith, not knowing what else to do with Lillie, brought her with him to Wolf, Pfeiffer. They arrived by 7:00. He told the hotshots already in and working that his niece had the day off from school and he would be taking her to lunch, so she would spend the day in his office. The assistants and associates looked askance, but he was a partner and nobody objected. The other partners didn't notice. He installed her at his computer, where she promptly began manipulating software he didn't know he had. She found games and programming languages and video feeds and settled in happily.

He watched her a minute from the doorway before leaving for a meeting in the conference room. She sat facing away from him, absorbed in the computer. Her bright brown hair bounced on her shoulders. She wore a pale green sweater in a hideous style currently fashionable with teens, knitted with large holes on both shoulders and stuck all over with what looked to him like dangling yarn braids. Her shoulders, glimpsed through the weird holes, moved slightly as she used the keypad. He could hear her talking to the software in a low, musical voice.

He went to his meeting.

Twenty minutes later, a secretary opened the door, her face disapproving. "Mr. Anderson, your niece wants you. She says it's an emergency." Her tone said that in her opinion there was no emergency at all.

Keith knew Lillie better than the secretary did. He bolted from the meeting.

She stood in the middle of his office, her young face anxious but not frantic. "Uncle Keith, you have to tell all the people to get off SkyPower right away."

"What?" he said stupidly.

"To get off SkyPower right away. It's not the right way for us to go."

He stared at her.

She had opened his office window the six possible inches mandated by the Sick Building Act of 2009.

"Tell me from the beginning, Lillie."

She looked perplexed. "There isn't any beginning. You have to just get all the people off SkyPower right away, before the pribir correct it. That's not the way we should go. It damages genes."

"What do you mean, 'correct it'?"

She glanced out the window. "Make it go away. It damages the right way."

Keith said to his wall screen, "Oliver Wendell, turn on the TV to NewsNet."

"—since eight o'clock this morning. Some of the children themselves have been calling SkyPower Corporation, news outlets such as this one, and the White House. No one knows what to make of this latest—"

"Oliver Wendell, turn the TV off. Lillie . . . how do you know this?"

She looked impatient. "The pribir told all of us, of course. There are people—they don't know how many–on SkyPower and the pribir don't want to hurt them when they correct it. Genes are the right way, Uncle Keith, not power sources or chemicals that damage genes. So you have to get the people off, because the pribir will only wait a little while."

"How long?"

She shrugged. "I don't know. SkyPower is really a bad thing, you know. All the nuclear reactors are. They damage genes."

She looked, sounded, felt like Lillie. She *was* Lillie. But the words were not. For the first time, something deep inside Keith recoiled from her.

Keith called SkyPower Corporation. But he was a secondary legal counsel, and the CEO and her staff had no time for him. They were "in meeting," an assistant informed him neutrally.

"Oliver Wendell, turn the TV on to NewsNet."

"—no more than a silly hoax," someone was saying, a wizened man with an indignant expression. "Elaborately organized, yes. But for a major transnational like SkyPower to listen to a bunch of children would be ridiculous. Nor is SkyPower going to 'damage genes'—anybody's genes. Safety records show—"

Lillie said, "Aren't they going to send the people back to Earth?" She looked troubled. Was that her talking . . . or them?

Did he believe there was a them?

He stayed riveted to the TV, canceling all his meetings. No one disturbed him; evidently the media still did not have Lillie's name. Lillie went back to her computer games. At noon she looked up, frowning.

"Uncle Keith—they mean it about correcting SkyPower. Why are those people still on it?"

He could only shake his head.

"—NASA reporting that, like the Hubble, the Artemis II probe has detected no alien craft anywhere near Earth orbit—"

"Lillie . . . where are the pribir? In a space ship?"

"Yes, of course."

"Where is the ship?"

"I don't know," she said, not looking up from her game.

At 4:00 P.M. Eastern Standard Time, SkyPower blew up. The corporation had not removed its personnel.

Hysteria broke out on the Net. Terrorist acts, international provocation, cleverly obfuscated industrial sabotage . . . theories flew like bullets.

Half an hour later, Keith's secretary stuck a frightened face into his office. "Mr. Anderson . . . the White House is on the phone channel!"

He picked up his phone, already knowing. They wanted Lillie, wanted all of them. As soon as possible, as anonymously as possible. In Washington. Highest national security. FBI agents on the way to his apartment.

Lillie turned off her computer game. "Let's go, Uncle Keith. I need to pack some stuff at home. Where's that red suitcase I took to Kendra's for my last sleep over?"

No one spoke to them as they walked through the office. Everyone stared. Keith put an arm around Lillie.

"It's okay," she told him. "They just don't understand yet. About the right way, I mean. But it's okay. The pribir can explain everything."

NASA announced the position of the spacecraft. Perhaps they'd just located it, perhaps they'd known all along. Keith knew he'd never find out which. The White House press secretary held a tense, almost belligerent session with the press in which he said, essentially, that he wasn't going to say anything. He repeated only that the president would address the nation the following night. Condolences had gone out to the families of the seventy-three SkyPower employees killed in the explosion.

Two FBI agents, male and female, waited at Keith's apartment. Within twenty minutes he and Lillie had packed and been escorted by car to La Guardia. They were shown to a heavily guarded private room in the airport terminal, and for the first time Keith saw some of the other kids that the press was already calling "the pribir puppets."

They looked like any eighth grade class on a field trip.

Seventeen of them had been collected at La Guardia. They were white, black, Hispanic, Asian. The girls appeared about two years older than the boys, although in fact the sexes were distributed evenly throughout ages eleven, twelve, and barely thirteen. Newly pubescent, which had triggered the latent engineered genes. Some of the girls, like Lillie, had lush figures and wore make-up. The boys' voices cracked when they called out to each other. At one side of the room, the parents sat looking shell shocked.

Lillie walked up to a dark-haired girl carrying an e-book. "Hi. I'm Lillie Anderson."

"I'm Theresa Romero. You in eighth grade?"

"Yes. At St. Anselm's in Manhattan. I like your sweater."

"Thanks. I got it at—hey, damn it! Keep away!"

A boy had bounced a basketball off her back. He grinned at her and she scowled. He shrugged and moved away.

"That's Kenny," she said with enormous disgust. "A real bonus. All the brains of a bucket of hair."

"I know some like that," Lillie said, and the two girls moved off, chattering. Lillie gave a little wave back over her shoulder at Keith.

He was drowning in normalcy.

They were loaded, kids and parents both, onto a military plane. Keith recognized the distinctive blue-and-white aircraft of the 89th Operations Group and guessed they were heading for Andrews Air Force Base. That made sense. Close to Washington, easily restricted and guarded, and containing Malcolm Grow Medical Center, the largest Air Force medical facility on the East Coast. Not to mention elite communications for connecting with everything from the White House to the Airforce Space Warfare Center in Colorado. Andrews was the entry point for all Air Force communications satellites, classified and not.

"I demand to know where you're taking us!" a mother said to the Air Force major who, from the moment he appeared, was clearly in charge.

"Of course," the major answered. "We're going to Washington, D.C. If you'll all get comfortable aboard, I'll do a full briefing then."

The woman hesitated, scowled, but shepherded her son aboard

the plane. Probably, Keith thought, others had refused. There were no legal grounds for detention of these people. On the other hand, the military (or the president, or whoever) didn't need all of the kids. They all said the same thing at the same time. That there were so many seemed to be merely deliberate backup.

Maybe. Who knew how these "pribir" thought?

Once everyone was settled, the kids talking or playing handheld games or gazing out the window at clouds, the major stood erect in the center aisle.

"Welcome aboard, ladies and gentlemen. I'm Major Gerald Connington. As some of you already know, our destination is Andrews Air Force Base, just outside Washington, D.C. Let me say right off that the president of the United States personally thanks each and every one of you for your willingness to travel to Washington and assist him in this emergency. It's through working together that this unprecedented situation can be handled most effectively."

Military PR, Keith thought. The major didn't even look uncomfortable.

A mother called out, " 'Unprecedented situation' is quite a euphemism, major. Is blowing up SkyPower going to be seen as an act of war? Are our kids in danger?"

"If war is the result, all of you will be in no more danger at Andrews than in New York," Major Connington said, and Keith's estimate of him rose. Keeping the bullshit to a minimum.

"But are we at *war?*" the mother persisted.

"Madam, I cannot personally declare war all by myself," Connington said, and a few people smiled faintly. "Like everyone else, I have to wait and see what the president and Congress wish to do."

"War is silly! The pribir are helping us!" a boy called out indignantly.

Half the planeload of adults turned to stare at the boy. The other half gazed at their own children, who nodded in agreement, those who were listening, anyway. Keith saw the problem with any in-depth briefing. Parents and children had widely differing perspectives on the pribir. How could you talk war strategy with the enemy's delegates present?

The others seemed to realize this, too. A hush fell over the parents. Into it, Major Connington said, "More parents and children will be joining us at Andrews, coming from different cities in the Northeast. All of you will be housed in on-base military housing that is currently being prepared for you. These are temporary lodging facilities equipped for temporary housekeeping. Each facility will lodge two children plus their parents or guardians. After you are shown to your lodgings, buses will take you all to the Officer's Club for meetings with Pentagon and White House officials."

A boy called, "Will the president be there?"

Connington smiled. "Not this time. Maybe later on."

"Aawwww," the boy whined, and went back to his computer game.

"We cannot, at this time, say exactly how long your stay will be," Connington continued, "but we will do everything in our power to make it a pleasant one. Andrews is equipped with a movie theater, library, bowling alley, picnic area, and a brand-new Youth Center with a full-size gym, dance room, VR lab, and many activities for teens."

"He makes it sound like a fucking resort," a man said loudly somewhere behind Keith, "instead of a lockup."

"Be quiet," someone else hissed. "You'll upset the kids!"

Keith looked at Lillie, sitting across the aisle with Theresa Romero. Both girls had thrown off their light jackets and were combing their hair, sharing a portable lighted mirror. Lillie said something and Theresa rolled her eyes and then giggled.

It wasn't chemically possible to upset the kids.

At Andrews Air Force Base, Lillie and Theresa pleaded to stay together. A harassed housing officer was trying heroically to honor the children's requests about pairing off. Keith introduced himself to the Romeros, a bewildered Hispanic couple. Carlo Romero, who spoke without an accent, was clearly American born, articulate and intelligent. His wife Rosalita, much younger, spoke little English. She was one of the most beautiful women Keith had ever seen, with liquid black eyes, café au lait skin and rippling black hair. She had passed the hair on to Theresa, but not the beauty.

The temporary housing had a living room, a tiny kitchenette, two baths, and three bedrooms, each with twin beds. Theresa and Lillie dumped their stuff into one bedroom. Carlo said to Keith, "Flimsy housing but substantial protection. I think those are Army troops from Fort Meade or Fort Bragg. They're everywhere."

"I noticed," Keith said.

"I'm glad they're here. Your daughter get any death threats?"

"Lillie is my niece; her parents are dead. No, the press hadn't found her yet."

"Lucky you. Those parents who refused to bring their kids here are going to regret it, I think."

"A lot of angry nuts out there," Keith agreed.

Rosalita Romero said something energetic in Spanish. Her husband put his arm around her and drew her close. "She's afraid because Theresa doesn't seem afraid. Rosalita fears . . . well, that Theresa is possessed."

She is, Keith thought. But what did Rosalita mean by "possessed"? Demons? Satan? Was this gorgeous, worried woman going to go in some night and knife Theresa and Lillie in their sleep to set them free from some imagined bargain with the devil?

He glanced at the girls' door. It came with a lock. He would tell Lillie to use it.

He smiled at Carlo and Rosalita. "We're all concerned about our kids."

"Yes," Carlo said neutrally. So he'd seen Keith's glance at the bedroom lock. Wonderful. A bungalowful of mutual suspicion.

Sixty kids and ninety parents thronged the Officer's Club. The kids were divided, seemingly randomly, into five groups and shunted off into five different rooms. All the parents were ushered into the lounge, now set up with rows of gilt chairs. Keith glimpsed the e-board, which apparently no one had thought to change: April 30, 6:00 P.M., DUBOIS/CARTER WEDDING, CONGRATULATIONS SUSAN AND TOM!

He wondered where Susan and Tom were now holding their wedding.

"Ladies and gentlemen, I am Base Commander Brigadier General Harry Richerson." He looked like Keith's idea of a general: tall, sun-beaten, no-nonsense. Not PR.

"I know you're leery about being here, and nervous about what will happen to your children. I don't blame you. Right now they're simply being questioned in groups to see to what extent their experiences are similar. Tomorrow we want to talk to them, and you, individually. We have all the available medical records for each child, but our staff at Malcolm Grow Medical Center would also like to run their own tests. All tests will be with parental permission only, non-invasive, and confidential. Our people will be obtaining permission forms at your individual conferences tomorrow.

"I can't tell you how long you'll be here. Anybody can leave who wants to, but I advise against it. An hour ago one of the so-called 'pribir children' was murdered in Boston by an unknown assailant. Your children and you are much safer here. You are also performing a vital patriotic service. Any questions?"

There was a stunned silence. *Murdered.* Had it been a boy or a girl?

The same mother who'd asked on the plane now called out, "Are we going to war with these aliens?"

"Unknown at this time. The president, his advisors, and the Joint Chiefs of Staff are crafting an appropriate response to the alien act of aggression. Your children's briefing will supply one source of data for that response."

"Have the kids been taken over by some sort of brainwashing? *How?*"

"Unknown at this time. The best medical guess is that communication occurs by very sophisticated pheromones. USAMRIID, the United States Army Medical Research Institute for Infectious Diseases, is involved in determining what molecules have been released into our air. Also involved are the Centers for Disease Control and the Federal Emergency Management Agency, which has responsibility for bioweapon attacks within the United States borders."

"How could they get these so-called molecules into the air?"

"Unknown at this time."

"How in heaven's name could smelling a molecule tell the kids what the aliens want them to *say?*"

"Unknown at this time."

"Is the alien ship in a place where we can shoot it down?"

"Classified. Sorry."

"What if they start blowing up other things of ours, in space or on the ground? What will we do?"

"Unknown at this time."

It went on like that, everything unknown or classified. Keith could see the frustration mounting around him. It was expressed at dinner, a catered buffet served to the parents without their kids. However, everyone was reunited in a large ballroom to watch the president address the nation on TV.

The president essentially said that everything was unknown at this time.

Lillie was sleepy by the time they were bussed back to their temporary housing. Neither she nor Theresa would say much about their briefing.

"What did they ask you?" Carlo Romero said.

Theresa said, "Oh, you know, who the pribir are and why they're here."

"Who are they and why are they here?"

Lillie spoke as if the answer should be obvious but she was being polite anyway. "They're people from another star system who are here to help us with our genes."

"By blowing us up?"

To Keith's surprise, both Lillie's and Theresa's eyes filled with tears. Theresa said, "They didn't want to do that. But you guys wouldn't listen and get the people off! And the genetic good of everybody is more important than a few lives."

Lillie nodded. Keith felt suddenly chilled. He had a sudden vivid memory: Lillie at ten years old, sitting with him under a tree while patriotic fireworks exploded overhead:

"Uncle Keith, you said that two people died on your energy case . . . Was it worth it? Two people dead, and everybody else gets lots of energy?"

"We don't look at it like that. Although unfortunately new technologies always seem to cost lives at first. Railroads, air travel, heart transplants, probably even the first discovery of fire."

"I think two deaths is worth it."

Was that Lillie saying now that the pribir were justified in blowing up SkyPower, or was it the pribir?

Was Lillie herself still in there somewhere?

"Good night, Uncle Keith. Mr. Romero, Mrs. Romero."

"Good night, honey."

The three adults looked at each other. Carlo said suddenly, fiercely, "She's still our daughter!"

Keith nodded. To his own surprise, the nod was genuine. She was still Lillie. He didn't know how he knew, but he did.

And he would do anything to keep her safe.

Life settled, incredibly, into a routine. A schedule was set up for the kids to meet, separately, with both doctors and politicians/military types. Between appointments, youth counselors organized basketball tournaments, library trips, educational software, video-games contests, movies, dances. No child ever left the base and no child was ever unaccompanied outside of the temporary-housing area. The parents went places with their kids, vaguely embarrassing and unwanted presences on the sidelines, or met with "counselors" that Keith suspected were CIA agents.

There was talk of organizing a proper school, but the kids spanned three different grades and forty school systems. Also, no one wanted to admit they would be here long enough to create a separate school. Schooling on base along with the resident "military brats" was not even mentioned.

The pribir did not choose to communicate anything.

The president did not try to shoot down the alien spaceship, assuming that was possible.

Lillie reported to Keith that there was this boy she sort of liked, Alex, and he told his friend Sean who told Donald who told Theresa that Alex sort of liked Lillie, too, but Lillie didn't know that for sure and did Uncle Keith think she should ask him to dance on Friday night or would she look like a fungal bonus?

Hysteria, fanned by the press, mounted throughout the country.

An additional Army unit appeared on base, which now had a totally sealed perimeter.

The pribir did not choose to communicate anything.

Lillie said she was missing too much algebra and would get too far behind and so would Uncle Keith download an algebra program for her at the library, since no kids were allowed at the terminals?

Keith realized the children were not allowed on the Net to protect them from the hate screeds he found there daily.

Theresa broke her thumb bowling and was treated at Malcolm Grow, where medical tests on the kids had shown nothing different from what all the medical tests elsewhere had shown.

The pribir did not choose to communicate anything.

And then, ten days later, they did, and everything changed again.

CHAPTER 5

"I need a big piece of paper," Lillie said, coming inside their temporary housing with a bag of corn chips. PX privileges had been extended to the base visitors.

"Do we have any big sheets of paper?" Theresa asked, bursting in the other door.

Keith and Carlo, who had been using handhelds in vain attempts to do their respective jobs from hundreds of miles away, looked at each other. Rosalita was out shopping.

"Oh, there's this shelf paper your mother bought," Lillie said, rummaging in a kitchen cupboard. "Here, Tess."

Both girls efficiently cleared the bungalow's one table, spread out a hunk of white shelf paper, and began to draw. Keith and Carlo rose at the same time to stand beside them. After a few minutes of silence, Keith risked, "Is what you're both drawing a message from the pribir?"

"Yes," Lillie answered. "Do we have any other color pens besides blue?"

Carlo said, "Do you . . . do you want to use the handheld?"

"No, thanks, Dad," Theresa said. "This is better."

Why? Keith wondered but didn't ask. He found he was holding his breath as he watched the girls draw. They both drew the same thing, although it was obvious that Theresa was the better artist. Lillie's drawing was fairly crude: a human eye. Then she drew a mouse and heavily circled its eye. Then some sort of flying insect, with its eye circled. Underneath she put four symbols: a circle, a square, a triangle, and a short straight line. Then she began to rapidly write a whole string of these, as if they were an alphabet.

When she was done, she stood and stretched. "Tess, want some corn chips?"

"Sure, just a minute, I'm not quite done."

Carlo said, "Theresa, what . . . what are you going to do with that?"

"Take it to Major Fenton. She's leading my group."

"Do you like her?" Lillie asked.

"She's okay. A little staff-assed."

"Yeah, I think so, too. But she's okay."

Keith said, "Do you want me to call her? To give her this . . . thing?"

"No, I'll take it when I have my appointment this afternoon," Lillie said. "But thanks anyway, Uncle Keith. C'mon, Tess, let's eat these chips on the way to basketball."

The girls left the men staring at each other blankly.

"The decision has been made," said a female major—yet someone else Keith hadn't met yet, this project had more personnel than an aircraft carrier—"to pass on to you parents everything we learn about the children's messages from the pribir."

Eighty-three parents sat again in a room at the Officer's Club. Keith counted; evidently seven had gone home. Probably they were from two-parent sets, with other children or critical jobs to see to. He had a critical job, too, and it was going down the toilet, but he couldn't leave.

"We recognize the dangers in this open communication, and hope you do as well," the major continued. "It's much better for everyone if the press receives its information through official government channels, to guarantee both accuracy and security. On the other hand, these are your children." She smiled. The smile came out a bit thin.

She started reading from a prepared statement. "This morning all sixty children produced the same drawing, in most cases immediately after being outdoors. Each child told his or her counselor that the pribir wished to help us with our genes. The four symbols, as you probably guessed—circle, square, triangle, line—correspond to the four bases of DNA, adenine, guanine, cytosine, thymine. The long string of symbols matches the gene that creates the eye in a developing human fetus. Its base sequence is very close to the sequence for the eye gene in mice and fruit flies."

The audience began to buzz. Keith saw that not everybody here understood even the basics about DNA. The major was going to have to get a prepared statement that started genetic education a great deal earlier.

"We think," she continued, "that this message is designed to establish a basic language between pribir and us, in order to communicate future genetic information." She looked up. "Any questions?"

"Are they going to give us the 'genetic information' to understand what was done to our kids?" a man called. It was Carlo Romero.

"We don't know what they're going to say in the future, Mr. Romero, any more than you do. We can only wait."

Keith left the meeting early, as the major struggled to explain concepts so basic to her that she had trouble understanding that her audience didn't all already know them: base pairs, DNA, chromosomes, codons, amino acid formation. Keith had only undergraduate biology, but it was enough for this. So far, anyway.

He caught a base bus back to the bungalow, rather than waiting for designated transport. The bus was filled with military and civilian personnel. A few of them stared at him strangely, and he realized that Andrews Air Force Base knew who had invaded its midst and sealed its perimeters, and not everyone liked the visitors. He stared back.

Lillie and Theresa were in their bedroom, the door half closed. They didn't hear him come in, and he stood in the darkened living room and listened to the conversation he was not supposed to hear.

"Are you scared?" That was Theresa.

"No. I keep thinking I should be, but I'm not," Lillie said.

"It's like it's weird and not weird at the same time."

"I know. But they're such good people," Lillie said.

Who were? The Air Force, the pribir, the parents, the workers who died on SkyPower? Keith scarcely breathed, not wanting to give himself away.

Theresa said, "They *are* good. But my dad says I only think that because the messages are affecting my brain."

"I know. But, Tess, I thought about this. Could the pribir change our emotions about them and not about anything else? I don't think *everything* is good. Or everybody."

"I don't know."

"I still feel like myself. But Uncle Keith looks at me funny sometimes, like he thinks I'm what the assholes call us. Puppets."

Theresa exploded. "You got it easy, Lillie! Your uncle doesn't harass you! My mom . . . if she wasn't leaving tomorrow, I don't know what I'd do. Kill her, maybe. She thinks I'm possessed by the devil!"

Lillie said mischievously, "Well, you did kiss Scott Wilkins at the dance, and open mouth, even . . ."

Both girls giggled and Theresa cried, "You promised to never tell anybody!"

"I won't. But you're amazing, Tess. I wouldn't *dare*."

"Well, it wasn't that great, to tell you the truth. But someday I want to get married and have lots of kids. I love babies. Don't you?"

"Well . . . not especially," Lillie admitted.

"Really? Why not? They're so cute!"

"I don't know. I think I'd rather be an explorer. Or maybe a diplomat. Somebody doing something important for the human race."

"Oh. Well, anyway, I'm glad my mom is leaving. And you know what else? I'm glad the pribir changed me."

"Oh, me, too," Lillie said. "It's like having this really important connection, somehow, who also loves you . . . I can't explain."

Theresa said solemnly, "It's like knowing God."

"I don't believe in God."

"But you believe in the pribir!"

"Oh, yes," Lillie said, and at her tone—fervent, uplifted, religious—Keith crept out of the bungalow and came back in with as much noise as he could. Anything to cut that conversation short. Anything to not hear Lillie sounding like her deluded mother.

There was another "message," leading to another drawing, the next day. Then another the day after that. They came every day, and every one concerned genetics. The Air Force brought in a high school teacher used to basic instruction to explain to the parents in simple terms what was being transmitted by the pribir.

Then a family made a secret deal to sell their story to a Net channel for three million dollars. The secret deal didn't stay secret. Child and parents were sent . . . where? Home would be too dangerous; the full set of violent nuts was still yelling "Death to Mutants." The official sessions passing on communications to the parents stopped. But the drawings didn't, and Keith looked at Lillie's latest sketch and then went to find Dennis Reeder.

The doctor and his daughter Hannah were housed with an older woman and her granddaughter. The grandmother had barely finished the eighth grade. Dennis Reeder was glad to talk to Keith.

"The drawing Hannah did Tuesday was clearly of Sertoli cells. Those are found in the testes. The female equivalent is follicular cells in the ovaries, and Hannah's drawing included those, too."

So that's what that strange pear-shaped object had been. Lillie was no Matisse.

"Remember, I'm not a geneticist," Reeder said, and Keith nodded encouragingly. "But it's pretty obvious that the long strings of base pairs were descriptions of existing genes that the Sertoli cells switches on to make the corresponding proteins."

"What do those proteins do?"

"Sertoli cell proteins do a lot of things. But one of them is make cells kill themselves. Apoptosis."

Keith was startled. "And that's a good thing?"

"Sometimes. There are genes for apoptosis in every cell. They're tumor-suppresser genes, and if the cell starts dividing wildly, they stop it by making it commit suicide. When the tumor-suppresser genes aren't working right, you get cancer."

Cancer. In the last ten years, since the human genome was first mapped, medicine had made some progress toward curing cancer. That is, they could cure some cancers some of the time for some people, which had always pretty much been the situation. Now the success rate was higher, but it was still a long way from even fifty percent.

Reeder said, "Sertoli and follicular cells regulate sperm and eggs. They knock out all the ones whose DNA isn't perfect. A five-month-old female fetus has seven million germ cells—sort of pre-eggs. At birth there are only two million. At puberty, less than a million. Only about five hundred will be allowed to mature."

Keith said, "So these Sertoli proteins are really good at finding the cells with damaged genes and killing them. And if you could somehow apply that to cancer cells . . ."

"Bingo," Reeder said. Then he let himself get excited. "It's been thought of before, but the obstacles are huge. But the drawings Hannah did Wednesday and today . . . I think the pribir are giving us the genetic code to create synthetic proteins that will kill all cancers all the time."

"Well, that should certainly counterbalance the first bad impression they made by killing the SkyPower workers."

He was surprised at his own cynicism. So, apparently was Reeder, who said stiffly, "That seems a pretty trivializing way to view a cure for our major killer of people over forty."

Which only showed how quickly the first impression was being counterbalanced. The pribir obviously knew what they were doing.

Andrews now swarmed with doctors. Keith watched the medvac

helicopters airlift terminally ill patients into Malcolm Grow. Three, four a day. It was too big to muffle; the newsnets had it within a week.

PRIBIR CURE CANCER!!!
ALIENS CHANNEL FORMULAS FOR CANCER CURES THROUGH 'PRIBIR CHILDREN'
BENEFACTORS OR CONTROLLERS?
"OUR LAST HOPE," SAYS TEARFUL DAUGHTER, BRINGS MOM 300 MILES BY GOLF CART

The drawings continued to flow, one or two a day. Someone in Maryland reported seeing a "tiny rocket" descend from the sky and then break open, presumably scattering pribir molecules, but there was no way to confirm or deny this. Air tests at Andrews continued to turn up nothing anomalous in the air. Neither did radar.

A school was finally organized. Lillie resumed algebra.

A few more parents left, forced out by the pressures of ordinary life. Keith had begun spending his free time, of which he had too much, with a psychologist divorcee from Connecticut. Her son was part of the bunch of kids Lillie hung around with. She was warm and funny and pretty, but both of them recognized that the surreal circumstances permitted nothing real to develop between them.

The day she left to go home, she came by the bungalow to say goodbye. "I've left my other son with his father too long, Keith. That bastard's not fit to take care of a gerbil, and Lenny's only seven. David is thirteen, he can fend for himself better, and this place cushions the kids more effectively than I'd dare hope."

"I'll keep an eye on him, Jenna."

"Thank you. I hoped you say that. You know . . ."

"What?"

She smiled wanly. "Anna Freud said something once about motherhood. She said, 'A mother's role is to be left.' I believe that. But not like this, Keith. Not like this."

He kissed her regretfully, not contradicting.

That night one of the doctors—there were so many that he had trouble keeping them straight—made a formal call on Keith. Lillie was at a basketball game at the youth center.

"Mr. Anderson, we'd like your permission to do an experiment with Lillie."

"An experiment on Lillie?"

"Not 'on'—'with.' We asked for volunteers and Lillie immediately raised her hand, but of course we wouldn't go forward without your consent."

Keith didn't like this. Why was Lillie such an adventurer? He said warily, "Go ahead."

"You realize, of course, that the pribir's communication with the children is one-way. They supply inhalant molecules that—"

"Have you captured any of those molecules?" Keith asked. Might as well take advantage of temporarily being sought after.

The doctor hesitated. "Well, no. Olfactory molecules must be dissolved in the lipids in the nose in order to be smelled, so after inhalation they don't last long."

"I see."

"The pribir supply information to the children through the molecules, but there's no way for the kids to supply information back. They're just receptors."

Keith didn't much like this description of Lillie, but he nodded.

"What we'd like to do is take Lillie, and three others, into a negative-pressure room for two days. Air cannot come in from the outside. We want to see if they draw anything, if any drawings still match the kids' outside. Also, see what changes occur in her neural firing patterns."

Keith thought it over. "The things you do to her will be non-invasive?"

"Absolutely."

"Then if Lillie wants to go, I'll give my consent." It couldn't hurt to have her out of the pribir's olfactory clutches for a while.

"Good. Thank you," the doctor said. "We're not publicizing this test, by the way."

"I understand," Keith said.

Lillie and two other children disappeared for two and a half days. Theresa wasn't one of them. In the negative-pressure building, the test subjects drew nothing. Neural activity in Lillie's "anomalous brain area" subsided to nearly quiescent. The children on the outside produced three drawings.

"I'm glad that's done," Lillie told Keith, Theresa, and Carlo when she returned. "It was boring. And I missed the pribir."

"Of course you did," Theresa said.

The media (and probably the FBI) had torn apart the life of Timothy Allen Miller. Reporters found huge numbers of irrelevant details, and no further information than Jamal had about why Miller had been selected by the pribir to create the "pribir children," or how, or to what ultimate end. Depending on the channel, Miller was portrayed as a monster, a traitor, an egomaniac, or a Christ figure. The last came about because the pribir genetic construct derived from Sertoli cells did indeed prove to cure all cancers, all the time.

More drawings, and more genetic knowledge, followed over the next few months. Sometimes a concept took twenty drawings to clarify; apparently cancer had been an easy problem. Huntington's chorea, that terrible loss of brain cells leading to dementia and death, came with a person's genes. The pribir sent detailed directions for how to keep affected brain cells from disintegrating. It involved, as Keith understood it, stimuli to switch on genes that switched other genes on or off that affected more genes making different proteins . . . He couldn't follow the details. The effect was that those genetically fated to get Huntington's would not get it at all.

They identified and rectified the complex chemical imbalance responsible for schizophrenia.

They gave instructions for the Holy Grail of tropical medicine, an immunity to malaria. The World Health Organization set about preparing to save a million lives every year.

"I'll tell you what bothers me about the pribir," Dennis Reeder said to Keith. Reeder was preparing to move back home and resume his medical practice. Hannah, like a growing number of the other "pribir children," would live in a supervised dormitory at Andrews. For Hannah's safety or the medicos' convenience? Probably both.

"What bothers you about the pribir?" Keith asked. A lot about them still bothered him.

"If they wanted to give all these 'genetic gifts' to humanity, and if they did once have Timothy Miller upstairs on some craft to engineer our kids, then why not just give the 'gifts' directly to Miller? He was a geneticist, he would have understood what he was looking at a hell of a lot better than Hannah does."

"I don't know," Keith said.

"It makes me wonder what else the pribir have in store for our children."

Keith didn't answer.

"Are you going home, too, Anderson? You must have a law practice begging for your return."

"Not exactly." He could have gone back, of course. But by now, after months away, his cases had all been reassigned to other attorneys, just as if Keith had died. And for reasons he couldn't explain, reasons connected somehow to his guilt about Barbara, he couldn't leave Lillie.

"Uncle Keith," she said shyly a few weeks later, "do you mind if I move to the dorm with the other girls? Not that I don't love living here with you," she added hastily, "but all my friends are already in the dorm, Emily and Madison and Julie, and Tess and I are missing stuff."

He looked at her hopeful face. How quickly the young could transplant their lives. He remembered doing it himself: for college, for law school, for the job in New York. "No, honey. I don't mind."

"You could stay on base. I'm sure they'd let you." She glanced doubtfully around the three-bedroom bungalow, empty of the Romeroes. "Maybe in a smaller place."

"I'll see."

The Andrews Housing Office assigned him a one-bedroom house across Perimeter Road from the Malcolm Grow Medical Center. He gathered that he was an exception; usually "unaccompanied military personnel" lived in a dormitory and civilian personnel lived off base. Keith knew his life was an exception long before the Housing Office told him so.

He saw Lillie every day, read a lot, hung around Malcolm Grow to learn what he could. The doctor assigned to Lillie, a woman in her sixties named Elena Rice, decided that Keith was both trustworthy and needy. She kept him accurately informed about the information the children were receiving and about medicine's attempts to put it to use.

The media were not accurately informed. Inflated stories spread like the infectious diseases the pribir were curing. The children had been told the secret of immortality. The children had been taught to levitate, to fly, to master telekinesis, to communicate by ESP. The pribir were going to land tomorrow, next week, when humanity had been all remade in their image. The pribir were already here, disguised as humans. The pribir had already left and a mad genius was giving the children the genetic gifts, just before he destroyed us all with a horrific plague.

"People can really be stupid," Lillie said in disgust. She and Keith sat on her dorm steps, shaded from the sultry July sun by a building overhang.

"I didn't know you were allowed to see media stories."

"Oh, they changed the rules a while ago. I guess they decided we weren't going to get too scared or weird or something."

"They were right," Keith said. Lillie didn't look scared or weird. She looked like a normal thirteen-year-old girl. That was what was scary and weird.

"But, you know, Uncle Keith, human people do all this stupid stuff, but pribir people don't."

Something inside Keith tightened. He was going to hear something important.

"That's because the pribir people control their own genes. They made themselves work right, and they got rid of everything on their planet that could damage genes. Like nuclear reactors and chemicals and stuff."

He said carefully, "They control all their own genes?"

"Yes. They go the right way, and that's why they're showing us how to control ours. We're them, you know."

"What do you mean, 'We're them'?"

"They have our DNA and stuff. They're just humans who are way ahead of us on the right way."

Humans. People. That's why she had always, from the start, called them "people."

He said, "Why didn't you tell me—or anybody—this before? That the pribir are human beings far advanced in science?"

"I didn't know it before," she said, as if this should be obvious. She stood. "I'm sorry, I have to find Major Fenton. To tell her this stuff. The pribir need some things done."

"Do you need paper?" Usually the first thing the children did was draw, then hand the drawings to what Keith suspected was a growing cadre of doctors, military intelligence, CIA, and State Department types.

"No, I don't need to draw this. Just to say it. Bye, Uncle Keith, log you later." She ran off across the grass, a long-legged hair-streaming figure somewhere between child and woman.

Keith remained sitting on the shaded steps, sniffing the air. It didn't smell of anything.

CHAPTER 6

After Lillie and the other children explained the "things the pribir need done," the media stories changed again.

"Destroy all our nuclear power plants? Stop using that long list of chemicals in manufacturing?" Carlo demanded, on a visit to Theresa at Andrews. "Who the hell do they think they are?"

"They're the pribir," Theresa said witheringly. "I thought you at least knew that much."

Relations between Theresa and her parents had deteriorated lately. Lillie had insisted that she and Keith accompany Theresa to this lunch at a base restaurant. "She shouldn't have to deal with them all by herself," was Lillie's explanation, which made Keith uneasy. Was he, too, going to move from being Lillie's confidante to being something distasteful to deal with?

Carlo said, "I don't like your tone, young lady!"

"Well, I don't like yours!" Theresa retorted. "The pribir are good people, better than us, and they want to help us on the right way!"

"Why? So we become weak in industry and military and they can take us over easier?"

"You don't know anything, Dad!"

"You watch your mouth, Theresa Victoria Romero!"

Now Rosalita broke in with a long stream of Spanish. Keith, who spoke no Spanish, could nonetheless see that Rosalita's rant was a mixture of anger and grief. Theresa folded her arms across her chest and listened in stony silence.

Lillie said carefully, "Mr. Romero, the pribir really *are* people. They have the same DNA as us, that's how they know what to tell us to do with ours. And they just want us to protect it from the radiation and chemical stuff that damages it, so we can make ourselves strong in the right way."

"So now foreign policy is being set by thirteen-year-olds," Carlo sneered.

Keith said abruptly, "Lillie . . . when you say 'the right way,' is that capitalized?"

The others stared at him dumbly.

"I mean, is it like . . . like 'The Path' of Taoists? Is it a religion the pribir have?"

"No," Lillie said.

"Yes," Theresa said.

The girls looked at each other and broke out laughing. Finally Lillie said, "I guess it depends on the person. How you smell it."

But Carlo had his justification. "A religious war. That fits. Weaken us industrially for a religious war. They had to come here for some goddamn reason."

Theresa stood up so fast her chair clattered backwards. Other diners turned to look.

"You don't know anything!" she yelled at her father, "And you don't want to know! You're ignorant and suspicious and . . . and . . . don't come here anymore!"

In sudden tears, Theresa fled the restaurant. Rosalita started talking rapidly in Spanish to Carlo. Lillie turned apologetically to Keith. "I'm sorry but I have to go, Uncle Keith, she's really upset."

He nodded, and she hurried after Theresa. The three adults were left looking at their half-eaten dinners with nothing to say to each other.

He didn't believe the pribir had come to Earth to wage a holy war. Neither could he quite share Lillie's and Theresa's—and all the other children's—faith that the pribir were interstellar Florence Nightingales, here merely to relieve human suffering. He couldn't forget that they had blown up SkyPower.

Nor could many others. Almost overnight the country erupted in violent groups at such cross-purposes that at times the pribir were reduced almost to irrelevancy, footnotes to pre-existing concerns.

Environmental groups, raging for years against nuclear plants and chemical dumps, gained new legitimacy: Even aliens know we're damaging ourselves! Protests swelled. Protests became activism, and a factory that made tool-and-die equipment in Elizabeth, New Jersey, was bombed. Thirty-two people died.

Groups who had resented America's slow, gradual powering-down of the defense budget seized on both the bombing and the pribir to scream for a military build-up.

Many religious leaders had always been uneasy with the pribir's instructions for gene tampering. Because the engineering instructions had been aimed only at curing diseases, these conservative ministers and priests and rabbis and shaikhs had felt only limited support. It was difficult to persuade an American public that curing disease was against God's wishes. And so far the pribir had not touched inheritable, germ-line genetic changes.

But now it was different. The aliens were preparing to force a new religion on us! All the so-called genetic gifts had merely been a softening up, the honeyed words dripping from the mouth of the Scarlet Whore of Babylon. The pribir were indeed Satan!

Blow it out your ear, indignantly replied America's liberal religious, backed by agnostics and atheists. You guys on the religious right are the ones using this to build your power base! You'd like to brainwash us all against the pribir for your own grandiose ends!

Sometimes it seems as if a religious war was going to occur without involving the pribir at all.

And then, on August 8, a day so hot and humid that after only five minutes outdoors Keith's shirt stuck to both his chest and back, Lillie fired the opening shot of her personal war.

She'd been unusually quiet for a few days. Three days a week, Wednesday-Friday-Sunday, Keith took Lillie to lunch at the base's best restaurant. He jeered at himself for the choice, knowing she'd have been just as happy with hamburgers, but the formal, adult atmosphere was obscurely necessary to Keith.

Lillie wore a pale blue lipstick, matching a dress he hadn't seen before, bare legs, and high-heeled white sandals. Her hair had grown and she'd done it in a complicated arrangement of puffs and braids that he'd noticed on other teenage girls. Her round cheeks looked childlike beside the adult trappings. She ate with gusto, finishing everything, including most of Keith's dessert.

"Sure you're full, honey?" he teased.

"Yes. But why don't you order some . . . some coffee or something."

He never drank coffee at lunch. He saw she wanted more time to say something uncomfortable. Flagging the waiter, he ordered coffee.

"Go ahead and tell me, Lillie. Whatever it is."

She smiled at him with grateful constraint. "Yes. Well, it's the pribir. Something the pribir are going to do."

His stomach made a fist. "What?"

"They've given us so much. All the genetic gifts, and the greater knowledge of ourselves—"

"That's not you talking, Lillie. That's a PR statement. I think I even know which press release."

She grinned at him, a much more honest grin than her previous smile. "Major Connington, right? Okay, I'll tell you straight. The pribir *have* given us a lot, and now they want something in return. They want some of us kids to go up aboard their ship. I want to go."

Whatever he'd vaguely expected, it hadn't been that. Never that. For a moment all he could do was stare, stunned. Her wide gray eyes, gold-flecked, stared back.

"Uncle Keith—"

"No. Absolutely no. Under all circumstances, no."

"Now you sound like Mr. Romero."

"Lillie, you're thirteen years old!"

She said reasonably, "I can't help that."

"*Think.* To go blindly aboard some spacecraft you never saw, to some aliens. . ." He couldn't even finish. They weren't the kinds of words you ever thought you'd have to say in real life. Comic-book words, video-game words. Yet the chair under him was solid as ever, and the ordinary silverware gleamed on the white tablecloth.

"I told you," she said patiently, "they're not aliens. They're people. Humans."

He grasped at anything. "What on Earth makes you think the president, or whoever, would let you go?"

"Well, we don't know that," she admitted.

"What if the military said no? Then what?"

"I don't know."

He had a sudden terrifying thought. The pribir dispensed molecules, undetected by anyone on Earth, to give the children information. Could the pribir just as easily dispense molecules to make Washington agree to this plan? Brainwashing government to release children? No, no one except the children could even smell the pribir's molecules. No one else had the necessary, genetically engineered equipment.

He said, stalling, "What do the ali . . . the pribir allegedly want you there for, anyway?"

"To teach us," she said.

"Teach you *what?*"

"I don't know."

"For what purpose?"

"I don't know."

Fear got the better of him. "You don't know much!"

"I know this," Lillie said. "I'm going."

For once, the press didn't get the story. Keith didn't know how many children the pribir wanted aboard their ship . . . It was too surreal to even think about. No one had ever seen their ship from the inside. It was in orbit around the moon, not the Earth, and although satellites, the Hubble, the International Space Station, and various space shuttles from three countries had of course photographed it when it was visible and they were in position, the photographs were all classified. An entire amateur following had grown up on the Net, posting its orbit with precision accuracy and speculating on its size and composition, but not much could actually be known from Earth.

The two big questions were: How did the pribir get close enough to Earth to drop their "inhalant molecules" over Washington? And was their ship reachable with nuclear missiles, or some equivalently deadly weapon?

Someone might know the answers. Keith didn't.

For the next few days, he and Lillie didn't refer to their discussion at the restaurant. She was pleasant, slightly distant, seemingly absorbed in her schoolwork and friends. But Keith was beginning to suspect that he had simplified Lillie in his mind, and that the Lillie he thought he knew, although genuine, concealed caverns he did not know.

A boy in her group of friends, Mike Franzi, had a birthday. Lillie confided shyly to Keith that she "liked" Mike. His friends at the boys' dorm gave him a raucous party that reportedly went on all night. Some of the girls, including Lillie and Theresa, sneaked into the party. Keith was informed of this transgression and was expected to discipline his niece.

He met with her at a picnic area beside the Youth Center. In the hectic heat, August flowers bloomed in a riot of color: chrysanthemums, asters, black-eyed Susans. Lillie had brought Theresa with her, presumably for moral support.

"You weren't supposed to be in the boys' dorm after hours, Lillie."

"We didn't do anything, Uncle Keith."

"We're not like that," Theresa said, earnestly if vaguely.

Keith felt helpless. What did he know about disciplining teenage girls, even under normal circumstances? The two sat across the picnic table from him, dressed in shorts and brief red tops with strange little mirrors sewn around the necklines. Two pretty young girls with round, unlined faces, their long hair caught back with red leather clips. Both wore hideous purplish lipstick. He had no idea what to say to them.

Lillie helped him out. "I know it was against the rules, Uncle Keith, but we were careful and anyway we won't do it again."

"Well, uh, I believe you."

"Then can I ask you something else?"

"Of course." Now what?

The girls exchanged a glance. Then Lillie said in a rush, "Tess's family has a vacation place in New Mexico!"

"It's not really fancy or anything," Theresa said. "It's just a lot of empty land in the desert. Bare, so my father got it real cheap. But there's a cabin and my mother likes it 'cause she's from New Mexico, so we go there sometimes in October to hike and stuff. Over Columbus Day vacation from school."

"And Tess asked me to go with her! Can I?"

Keith thought rapidly. October. New Mexico. Death threats on the Net. He said, "Well, we can talk about it, at least."

"That's just a delayed 'no,' " Lillie said flatly.

"Not necessarily."

Theresa said shrewdly, "It's really safe out there in the desert, Mr. Anderson. Believe me, there's *nothing* near my folks' property. The cabin doesn't even have a computer."

He said, "You don't even know if you'll be done here at Andrews by October, or if the government will permit you off base by then."

"I know all that," Lillie said. "Of course I'm only hoping to go if we're finished here at Andrews and if I'm back in time from the pribir ship."

Keith felt his temper rise, pushed it back down. "You are not going on a pribir ship."

Lillie stood. The tiny mirrors on her shirt flashed in shards of sunlight. She said calmly but distantly, "I guess you're right, Uncle Keith—we should talk about this some other time."

"I agree. Meanwhile, do you ladies want to go out for a Coke?"

"I'm sorry, I have to study," Lillie said. "But thanks."

"Kind of tough on you keeping school going the whole year around," he said, wanting to keep the conversation going. She seemed so remote.

"I don't mind. But Tess and I have a big French test tomorrow."

French. For children who communicated in an exotic molecular language with aliens.

"Lillie . . . we used to be able to talk to each other."

"We can still talk. What do you want to talk about?"

A polite wall. Did this happen with all teenagers, or was it a product of the situation? He had no way to tell. Theresa stared down at the picnic table, embarrassed.

"Nothing," Keith said. "You better study now."

He watched the two girls walk away.

Two days later a terrorist claiming to act in the name of the pribir struck again, blowing up a DuPont subsidiary in Texas. Four people died.

The pribir went on insisting, through Lillie and Theresa and Mike and Jon and Hannah and DeWayne and the others, that everything which damaged genes be "corrected."

"It's the right way," the children said, and even though they never talked to anyone outside Andrews, many people who weren't there nonetheless heard "The Right Way."

The night of Saturday, August 24, Keith felt restless. He had stayed too long at Andrews. Only a handful of parents were left, mostly mothers with an earning husband and no other children at home. He knew they looked at him askance: Didn't he have a job? The parents that had left visited often. Most of them seemed to have decided that their children were away at the equivalent of boarding school, a feat of self-protective mental gymnastics Keith could not begin to copy.

The night was sultry, but it felt almost cool after the scorching heat of the day. Keith walked past Malcolm Grow, along Perimeter Road. Groups of soldiers headed toward the enlisted men's club, laughing and talking. At the Officer's Club there was some sort of formal event; cars went by carrying women in evening gowns and men in dress uniform or black tie.

He had reached the West Gate when an explosion shattered the sky.

For a moment he couldn't see or hear. Then his vision cleared and he saw the smoke rising from beyond the Headquarters building. Possibly from the Youth Center.

He bolted in that direction, trying frantically to remember where Lillie had said she was going that night with Theresa. A dance? Or to the movies, on the other side of the base? Did she—oh, God, please—stay at the dorm?

Two smaller explosions sent debris flying into the air.

Keith dropped to the ground and covered his head. Nothing hit him. He stumbled upward and ran again, yelling senselessly. "Lillie! Lillie!"

The Youth Center was in flames. Keith heard the fire engines along with the base alert signal. People were running, hollering . . .

an ambulance shrieked to a halt and EMTs leapt out and ran toward the building.

Like so much in Maryland, it was built of red brick. A hole had been blasted in one side but the walls still stood. Flames shot out the window and off the roof. It didn't look as if anyone could be alive inside, but firemen in full fire-fighting suits moved into the building. Keith raced around back. There was less damage here and he saw bodies on the ground, blackened, a few moving.

"Lillie! Lillie!"

"Don't touch her, you moron!" an EMT cried. He shoved Keith out of the way. Keith looked more closely; the charred girl wasn't Lillie.

Sense took over. He ran up to a group of civilians. "Do any of you have a phone? My niece . . . please . . ."

A man stared at him hard, stony: *One of them*. But a woman immediately dug into her purse and pulled out a handheld. Keith punched in the number of the dorm. His hand shook.

All the frequencies were busy. Others had thought more quickly than he.

He keyed in Theresa's handheld, and someone answered. "Lillie? *Lillie?*"

"No, it's Tess," said Theresa's scared young voice. "Lillie's not here. She went out to buy Coke and—"

"Went where? When?"

"The superette. About five minutes ago. Mr. Anderson, what happened?"

"The Youth Center blew up. Listen, Tess, stay where you are. No, wait—are you in the dorm?" They might hit that, too.

"Yes! I am!"

"Then go quietly out the back and down the path to the interfaith chapel, you know where it is. If you see Lillie, take her with you, okay? Do you understand?"

"Y-yes."

He raced toward the superette, still carrying the handheld. The woman cried, "Hey!" and he tossed it on the ground. The superette was a mile away and he was out of shape. Panting, wheezing, he reached it and raced down its aisles. The base alert was still wailing and the store was pandemonium. He couldn't find Lillie.

Why the hell hadn't he kept the handheld?

He stopped to gasp for breath, and a young woman in a waitress uniform walked up to him. "Are you all right? Are you having a heart attack?"

"Handheld . . . please . . ."

She had one. He was barely able to key in Theresa's number. It was answered immediately. "Hello?"

Lillie. She was there.

"Lillie . . ."

"Uncle Keith? Where are you? What should I do?" Scared, but calmer than Tess.

"Stay . . . in chapel . . ."

"We're here. Reverend Duncan is here with us. Are you all right?"

"Yes . . ." He couldn't say more. The waitress took the handheld from him. "Lillie? I'm with your father. He's just out of breath, I think."

"Who are you?"

"I just happened to be in the superette and loaned him my handheld. What happened?"

"He said the Youth Center blew up!"

"Oh, my God."

Keith didn't remember getting to the chapel. The waitress must have walked him there, through the mobilizing soldiers and running civilians. Then she vanished into the night.

He clutched Lillie, who patted his back as if he were the one needing comfort, as if he were the one in danger. Later, that would seem to him the strangest thing of all.

FBI. Military intelligence. Federal Emergency Management Agency. The State Department. Alcohol, Tobacco, Firearms. Protesters. Counter-protesters. Editorials. There appeared to be no one in America not involved in the terrorist attack on the pribir children at supposedly secure Andrews Air Force Base.

The president went on television. "My fellow Americans, an event occurred today which cannot be tolerated in a free democracy. An attack on one of our own military bases, an attack aimed at children. Everything possible is being done to bring the perpetrators to a quick and relentless justice . . ."

It was very quick. The "terrorists" were caught within two hours. They were airmen at Andrews, three young soldiers who believed the pribir were going to destroy America and that her leaders were doing nothing about it. One of them turned out to be a white supremacist, one a generalized hater, one a follower with an IQ of eighty. They had learned to make their easily traced explosives from the Net.

The Youth Center had hosted a dance that night for Andrews dependent children ages fifteen through eighteen, which the attackers had not known. Fifteen "pribir children" were attending a separate bowling tournament in the basement. Nine eighth graders were playing a supervised chess tournament. Eleven boys were playing pick-up basketball in the gym. Three base dependents and one pribir child, Terry Fonseca, survived.

Lillie, pale and red-eyed, insisted on going to the funeral for those whose parents wanted them buried in Arlington. Theresa couldn't face it. It didn't matter; neither of them was permitted to attend. The forty-five remaining pribir children were immediately airlifted to the Marine Corps Base at Quantico and installed in a heavily guarded secure dormitory that looked to Keith like a prison. When Terry Fonseca got out of the hospital, he would go there, too.

The parents who rushed to their kids from all over the Northeast went through checkpoints more stringent than those surrounding the president.

The Justice Department and the Air Force Advocate General jointly announced they would seek Maryland's newly reinstated death penalty for the three airmen.

The pribir, inexplicably, were silent. Of course, they might not have even known about the attack and the deaths. Communication, as far as humans knew, was one-way. The pribir dispensed molecules full of genetic information, the children gave it to the scientists, and nothing went the other way.

Keith didn't believe it.

Lillie sat on her bed at Quantico, fresh from another session with her grief counselor. No barracklike dorms here; each child had a separate room. Some kind adult had tried to make them inviting. Lillie's bed was covered with a red blanket, and a vase of flowers sat on the bureau.

"Uncle Keith, I have to say something."

"What, honey?"

"I want to go up to the pribir ship. I'll be safe there."

He looked at her hopelessly.

"I told Major Fenton. I told everybody. We're going. Not all of us, some people want to stay here."

"The government won't let you go. Now more than ever."

"We're going. But I need to tell you something first. This is necessary sometime, even if it isn't the right way. Genes are the right way."

"What's necessary sometimes? What are you talking about?"

She got off her bed, walked to his chair, and awkwardly kissed the top of his head. It had been nearly a year since Lillie had permitted physical contact; he held her gratefully.

"I love you, Uncle Keith."

"I love you, too."

She moved away from him and pulled something from under her top. A cheap locket on a long chain. Flipping it open, he saw that the two portrait hollows held tiny pictures of him and Barbara, both portraits at least fifteen years old. Barbara smiled radiantly. Keith looked solemn and impressive, still with all his hair. He couldn't remember ever looking that young.

Lillie closed the locket and put it back under her top. All she said was, "They keep the air conditioning too high here, don't you think? Everybody opens the windows at night to let heat *in*."

He nodded, and the moment was over.

When he woke in his room at the Quantico visitors' center the next morning, he was surprised to see how bright out it was. Nine o'clock—he never slept that late! Standing, he was surprised to find himself staggering a little. Quickly he dressed to meet Lillie for breakfast.

She was gone. Twenty of them were gone. Overnight, they had vanished from the middle of Quantico while surrounded by marines, FBI agents, and military police. "They made you fall asleep, and us, too," the remaining twenty-five children explained, over and over. "Everybody around here. With the smell we breathed in. Then the pribir sent another smell to wake us kids up, and they took the ones who wanted to go. It was the right way."

It wasn't possible, screamed everything from White House staff to barstool commentators. No trace of sedative was found in the bloodstream of anyone at Quantico. No ship or shuttle or *anything* irregular had been detected coming in from space, or launching up from Earth. Not by any facility anywhere in the world. Something else must have happened, with or without the complicity of the government. Those children had been taken somewhere by ground, and had been . . . what?

Deprogrammed.

Murdered.

Secured somewhere really safe.

Sent on one of our shuttles to the still uncompleted International Space Station.

Cloned.

Brought to NORAD, under Cheyenne Mountain, where they wouldn't be able to "smell" anything.

Genetically "restored."

Experimented on.

"They made you fall asleep, and us, too," the remaining twenty-five children went on repeating. "But it's okay now. The kids are all with the pribir now. They're fine. From now on, they'll just do the right way."

Keith believed the children. On the evidence, or because he wished to? No way to know.

He wasn't permitted to leave Quantico; from the intensity of questioning going on, it seemed as if no one might ever leave Quantico again. But he was at least allowed outside. That night he stood in the shadow of the dining hall and gazed upward.

The sky, clear, glittered with thousands of stars, although the lights of Quantico dimmed them slightly. The moon was at the quarter. He didn't know enough to tell if it was first quarter or last.

How did you do it? How did anyone do it? Fathers had once sent twelve-year-old sons as midshipmen on three-year sea voyages. Princesses had been sent at fourteen, or twelve, or ten, across oceans to marry distant princes, their parents knowing they would never see their daughters again. Countless mothers had sent young sons to war. In 1914 half the youth of Europe had been sent to die in trenches full of mud. Kids Lillie's age had made up the shameful, futile Children's Crusade. As recently as a century and a half ago, Irish and German and Italian children had emigrated, alone, to America's lush promise. All voluntarily sent away from their homes.

How did any of the parents do it? Lillie wasn't even his child, and yet he felt as if some necessary organ had been ripped from his body. Lung, liver, bowels.

Heart.

"We're going. But I need to tell you something first. This is necessary sometime, even if it isn't the right way. Genes are the right way."

There was no right way for this.

He stood there a long time, staring at the sky, until a young MP, very nervous that nothing questionable should happen on his watch, told Keith to move along.

PART II: LILLIE

"A little more than kin, and less than kind."
—William Shakespeare, *Hamlet*

CHAPTER 7

Uncle Keith didn't understand. He never had, much as he loved her. No one had ever understood her, and Lillie had grown used to that, but still her heart beat faster as she crept along the corridor of the dormitory at Quantico. But the pribir would be different.

"Tess?" she whispered in Theresa's doorway, although there was no need to whisper, "Are you with us or not?"

Theresa materialized from the bed. Her face, surrounded by wild masses of black hair, looked scared. "I . . . I still don't know."

"You have to decide," Lillie said relentlessly. Then, because she knew how scared Theresa was, she added in a softer tone, "You don't have to come, you know. It's all right to stay. The pribir might need people here, too."

Theresa gave a strangled little laugh. "I'm afraid to stay here, too."

"Well, you have to do one or the other."

"I'll . . . I'll come."

She grabbed Lillie's hand. Theresa's was icy. Lillie squeezed her friend's fingers reassuringly. "Get dressed. Something warm."

"Wait for me! Don't go ahead!"

Lillie waited while Theresa pulled on jeans, running shoes, and a Land's End sweater. She threw more clothes, all her make-up, and a plush stuffed turtle into her pillowcase. "Okay, I'm ready."

The two girls slipped down the hallway. In the lounge downstairs most of the others waited. The ones who were going carried suitcases or pillowcases of belongings. The ones who were staying still wore nightclothes.

In the lobby a Marine lay stretched out on the floor, deeply asleep.

"It's like fucking Sleeping Beauty," Jessica Kameny snickered. She was the only one of the girls who had taken time to put on make-up.

Jon Rosinski said, "So how many are going? Stand over here."

Twenty kids moved toward Jon, fourteen girls and six boys. Some, Lillie knew, had only decided in the last fifteen minutes, even though they'd all smelled the plan last evening. She scanned the leavers. Mike Franzi, good, you could always count on Mike. Tess, Amy, Sajelle, Rebecca, Bonnie . . . *Elizabeth?* That could be real trouble. Jason, Susan, the obnoxious Jessica, too bad she didn't stay down here. Madison, Emily, Sam, that was another one she could do without. Hannah, Rafe, Alex, Derek, Sophie, Julie . . . Julie? A major surprise. And Jon, their not-unchallenged organizer, although Lillie wasn't too bad at organization herself.

The kids looked at each other.

Theresa said suddenly to Robin, who was staying, "Tell my dad I said I love him, okay?" Robin nodded.

"Let's go," Jon said.

The twenty-one walked out of the dorm. Another Marine lay asleep outside. The night was warm, but of course they didn't know what weather might come next. *Weather?* Wrong word.

Theresa groped for Lillie's hand and held on tight.

"Well, now what, genius?" Jessica said to Jon. She spoke very loud, as if to challenge the sleep infecting everyone for . . . how many square miles? Lillie didn't know.

"Lay off, Jessie," Bonnie told her. Lillie approved. Jon didn't know what was going to happen, any more than anybody else. The pribir had smelled to them clear pictures of where to wait, but nothing after that.

Jon led them to the empty grassy area. Lillie didn't know what it was for; she'd never been on a Marine base before. A flagpole, now with no flag, they must take it down at night, stood at one end. The pribir had smelled to go to a big open area. They would see the kids if they did. That didn't surprise Lillie; she had learned at school that even humans had space satellites that could read license plates. And these were the pribir.

A long slow tightening started in her belly. She wasn't afraid, exactly. But this was the biggest thing that had ever happened to her. Or anybody! She clutched her red suitcase.

Half an hour passed and nothing happened. Everyone sat down on the grass. People talked in low voices, but not very much. Even

Jessica and Sam weren't harassing anybody. Elizabeth had her rosary out and was saying her beads, but nobody jeered at her. Elizabeth's glasses, thick as pottery, glinted in the moonlight.

A light appeared in the sky. Grew brighter.

As one everybody stood up, even though there was no smell. Somebody whimpered . . . Julie, probably. Julie was afraid of everything. Well, everybody was afraid, why not? But Lillie knew no one would change their mind.

Uncle Keith, plus half the doctors, said that the kids were so accepting of the pribir only because of the chemical cascade in their brains triggered by their extra genes. Lillie knew that wasn't so. She didn't know why the others were going with the pribir—probably each person had their own reasons—but she knew why she was. And it wasn't some chemical in her brain.

The light grew into a ship, soundless and not very big.

Lillie had always felt different. Nobody understood that, not even Uncle Keith. They all thought she was a normal girl, interested in movies and her friends and her grades and her clothes. And she *was*. But underneath, all the time and for as long as she could remember, was this other longing. She thought about things, like death and God and the pointlessness of people being born and living their lives and then dying, over and over through generations, without it meaning anything or going anywhere. What was the point of being alive?

She couldn't accept the religious answers her mother had liked, a different one every week: Catholicism, Buddhism, Wiccans, evangelicals, whatever. In school they learned about evolution, but what good was evolution in giving life any meaning? None. And it was meaning she longed for. Sometimes the longing felt so sharp she couldn't breathe.

She knew from books that she wasn't the first person to feel like that. Over and over she read her favorites: *Of Human Bondage, Steppenwolfe, Time Must Have a Stop*. But Lillie didn't know Somerset Maugham or Hermann Hesse or Aldous Huxley, and none of the people she did know seemed to have this same longing. Certainly not Uncle Keith or her old best friend Jenny, or Theresa, with whom she'd once tried to discuss all this. A mistake. Tess had only talked about babies being life continuing and how that was enough meaning. Lillie wasn't much interested in babies. She wanted more than that.

But nobody else seemed to want—no, *need*—the universe to make sense. Why was that so weird? Why didn't everybody see how important it was? Such as, only the foundation for how you lived your whole life!

The ship floated to the ground, soft as a feather. It was dull metal now, shaped like an egg and as big as a bus, which is what it probably was.

The pribir, Lillie figured, were her last chance.

A part of the egg's side slid up. Jon took a step forward, hesitated, stepped back. Julie hid her face in her hands. Elizabeth's prayers were suddenly audible: "Holy Mary, Mother of God, blessed art thou amongst women—"

Lillie seized Theresa with one hand and Julie with the other. Violently Theresa pulled away.

"I can't!"

"Come on, Tessie, it's just a few steps more."

"No!" And Theresa turned and ran back to the dorm.

Lillie led Julie firmly toward the bus.

Sixty seats, jammed in worse than a Broadway balcony. Well, that made sense. The pribir didn't know how many would be coming. They only had what Major Connington described as "one-way information flow."

"At least the seats are shaped right," Jason said. "Ow, Alex, get off my foot, you dork!"

They had all wondered what the pribir looked like. No pictures had come. That was something Lillie didn't think she'd ever gotten Uncle Keith to understand: that the information the pribir smelled to them was pictures. The pictures formed in the brain somehow; they were just there, in exactly the same way a picture of an ice cream cone would be there if someone told you to think of an ice cream cone. "But what does it smell like?" everybody asked. It didn't smell like anything. "Smelling to" someone wasn't the same as "smelling."

"Everybody strap in," Jon said.

Each seat had straps dangling from its sides. Lillie squeezed into a seat next to Julie, and immediately the seat molded itself to her shape. She jerked up, startled, then settled back down. The straps, which felt like firm jelly, also molded themselves around her.

Rafael, who wanted to be a physicist some day, said, "I wonder how this thing avoided all Earth's radar setups?"

"However they did it, I'll bet the military would like to take this baby apart," Jason said.

Rebecca said severely, "Remember, this isn't the right way. Genes are the right way. This is only dead materials."

"Maybe," said Rafe, "but what materials! Whoooeee!"

Jessica snarled, "Elizabeth, if you don't stop that stupid praying, I'm going to unstrap and come over there and whip your religious ass."

"Don't *anybody* unstrap!" Jon said.

"Jessica, leave her alone," Bonnie said. "God, even on a major occasion you have to be an asshole."

"Better that than a lezzie."

Lillie said, "We're rising!"

There was no abrupt liftoff, no noise, no windows. At first Lillie didn't even know how she knew they were rising. Then she realized breathing was harder. Her chest felt constricted, and everything on her body felt heavier.

"I hope," Rafe said, with difficulty, "that they understand . . . how many gees . . . we can . . . take."

Of course they understood, Lillie thought. They understood everything about human bodies. Their DNA was her DNA, only they had control of theirs, which meant they had control of everything. The right way. She closed her eyes.

The pressure on her chest never became unbearable, and after a while it went away completely. A series of clear images formed in her mind, one after another. She opened her eyes but didn't see the source of the smells. Somewhere in the bus.

She saw a human being, a man, naked except for some cloth around his hips, standing beside an ocean. The only thing weird was that the sky was pink, not blue. Next she saw him looking taller, stronger, *healthier* somehow. Genetics had done that.

Next came a man underwater. Parts of him, legs and arms, looked sort of like a fish, but he was still a man. Lillie understood that he had been genetically changed to live in the ocean.

A woman floated in a spaceship. The ship was vague but the woman clear. She had arms where her arms should be and arms where her legs should be, giving her four hands.

"Gross," someone behind Lillie said.

The next images showed humans changing even more. They didn't look human anymore. They grew tentacles, or shrank to circles, or had hard shells . . . all sorts of weird stuff. Then, quickly, came a series of images showing one of these monsters turned back into a human being. Children trooped up to her. Everyone smiled.

"They've made themselves look like us, just for our sake," Emily said. She sounded cheerful. Lillie felt the same way. The pribir could change their babies' genes to look or do anything they chose. And they had built some to look like Lillie and the others, so their visitors wouldn't feel too scared. It was a nice thing to do, and it reassured Lillie.

Now, was that gratitude or chemical brainwashing? It sure felt like gratitude.

Jason, the clown, growled in a deep voice like General Richerson's, " 'When you push the envelope of technology, you take major risks with personnel. It's inevitable.' " Someone laughed.

All at once they were all light hearted. Even Elizabeth lowered her rosary, and Julie smiled tremulously.

"Everybody ready to walk into the future?" Jon called.

"I'm going be turned into Charlize Theron," Madison said.

"I want Isaac Newton's brain!" Rafe.

"Engineer me a bodacious bod, baby!"

"It's not us . . . it's our *kids*. Make mine geniuses!"

"Make mine rich!"

"Forget the kids . . . I want mine now! Give me sex hormones to kayak night and day!"

"Jason, you'd be lucky to get to kayak once," Derek laughed. "Now *me*. . ."

"Hush your mouth," Sajelle said suddenly. "We here."

The door to the bus opened. The mood changed abruptly.

Lillie unstrapped herself. Julie sat frozen, looking up at her piteously. Lillie said, "Come on, Julie. You can do it. Just stay by me. Emily, help Susan, she's tangled up. Elizabeth, pray to yourself."

Jon went first. Lillie followed, pulling Julie. She stood in a large, empty, completely featureless room with a light source she couldn't identify. There would have been room for three times as many kids. When everyone was in, the door to the bus closed.

For a long sudden moment, Lillie was afraid. What was she doing here, away from her friends and her school and Uncle Keith and even *Earth*? What if she died here? What if the Net postings and the freak channels were right and the pribir wanted to experiment on humans, to torture them . . .

She was being stupid. And anyway, there wasn't anything she could do except face whatever was coming. She was here.

A second door slid upwards at the other end of the room. A man and a woman came through, then stopped. They looked like normal people dressed in normal jeans and T-shirts, except . . . *better*. The woman had a perfect body, high breasts and slim waist and long, long legs. Her shoulder-length hair bounced and shone. The man was hot, with great shoulders and deep brown eyes. Lillie breathed in and suddenly she knew everything they wanted to tell her about themselves.

They had been engineered to match the television broadcasts the pribir had intercepted from Earth. All their lives they had trained for this moment. They knew everything about Earth that it was possible to learn from either TV or high-resolution satellites. They had all the abilities Lillie had, plus more that could be made to fit with these bodies. They would live and die in these bodies, and the purpose of their lives was to bring to Earth genetic gifts—so many genetic gifts!—that would help humans have all the freedom and adaptability and health that they did.

"Fucking A," Jason said softly.

The man and woman came forward. They spoke carefully, as if the language was familiar but the act of speaking by voice was not.

"Hello. I am Pete."

"I am Pam."

Lillie giggled. She couldn't help it. Pete and Pam! Humans finally met aliens and their names were Pete and Pam, like some dorky TV sitcom! She laughed, and Jason laughed, and suddenly nearly all of them were laughing, whooping and hollering, unable to stop. It was so ridiculous, it was such a release from tension, it was just hilarious. Lillie tried to stop laughing, couldn't, and leaned on Emily, weak with hilarity. Only Sam, Elizabeth, and Julie weren't laughing. Sam, Lillie had always suspected, had no sense of humor. Elizabeth was lost in some religious fog. And Julie was too scared to laugh, although how anybody could be scared . . . "Pete" and "Pam"! And she was off again.

Finally she stopped, and was appalled. Impulsively she strode forward and held out her hand. "I'm so sorry . . . we're all sorry. I guess it's the . . . the strain. Please forgive us. We weren't laughing at you, and we're all glad to be here. Really!"

Pam smiled uncertainly. Up close, Lillie could see that her eyes were subtly different. Beautiful, but not . . . just somehow different. What did they see?

"Yes, forgive us," Jon said. "God, we must seem . . . We are glad to meet you guys. It's nice to communicate two ways instead of one."

Murmurs of assent from the others, straggling belatedly toward manners.

"And we're glad you're here," Pete said. "Are you tired? I know we took you from the middle of your sleep cycle."

Emily, the scholarship girl at a brainy private school, said,

"The middle of 'our' sleep cycle? Do you have a different cycle?"

"We don't sleep," Pam said, and it came to Lillie with a jolt that no matter how Pete and Pam looked, no matter how similar the DNA their race had started with, these people were not human in the same way Lillie was human. Once, maybe. Not any more. They were alien.

The thought didn't scare her. In fact, the jolt was more pleasant than not. Alien was new, was interesting. There were great adventures ahead.

Her excitement or their chemical messages affecting her brain?

Shut up, Uncle Keith, she said to her memory. Aloud she added, "I don't think any of us are really tired. At least, I'm not. I'm too excited!"

"God, yes," Rafe said. "What kind of drive does this ship use?"

Pete laughed. It sounded vaguely rehearsed. Poor man, he needed to find more things funny.

"We will answer all your questions," he said, "over time. Maybe you would like to start with a tour of the ship? To see some of the right way?"

"God, yes," Rafe said.

"Then come on!"

It wasn't a tour of the whole ship, and it was going to take a very long time to answer everybody's questions.

Lillie reached these conclusions after just a week aboard the ship. Madison had asked what it was named, and Pam said it didn't have a name. It was just "the ship." She'd lived on it her whole life. Madison thought that was dorky and she and Emily had christened the ship *High Flyer*. Sajelle said that was just as dorky; it sounded like a cheerleading squad. Madison, who'd been a cheerleader, was offended, but gradually everyone began referring to the ship as the *Flyer* simply out of convenience.

It was evident they were being restricted to a small part of it. There were doors Pam and Pete went through that no one else could open. Lillie didn't really mind; what they were given was fascinating.

"This is the most comfortable bed I've ever sat on," Madison said, bouncing on it.

"I think it's creepy," Sophie said, without rancor.

Lillie stood with them in Madison's room. Each person had their own room, but they were all exactly the same, branching off a corridor so featureless that people walked into the wrong room all the time, backing out only when they saw another person's meager possessions. Each room had a plain metal box that opened like a footlocker, a small metal table, two chairs, and a bed that was just a platform jutting out from the wall. The bed and the chairs were made of the same stuff as the seats on the bus; they molded themselves to whoever lay or sat in them. The pillow did the same. Each room had a blanket. Bed, squishy chairs, pillow, and blanket were all the same shade of light tan.

Immediately everyone had tried to personalize the rooms, spreading out whatever stuff they'd brought. Since some people brought more than others, the results differed wildly. Rafe had brought only his handheld, which sat on top of his footlocker. Madison had lugged a big suitcase full of stuff, including clothes, make-up, mirror, a holo poster of her favorite rock band, and a teddy bear dressed in a cheerleading outfit. Lillie hadn't brought much, but she asked Pam for scissors and tacks and cut up her bright blue sweater to make a wall hanging. She didn't need a sweater aboard the *Flyer*. It was never cold, never hot, always comfortable.

At the end of the hall were two bathrooms, boys and girls, and a sealed machine that you stuffed dirty clothes into. A few minutes later they came out a slot, perfectly clean and ironed. Rafe, fascinated, tried to take this apart to see how it worked, but the metal box, as featureless and strong as everything else, wouldn't give.

There was a big common room with more of the tables and chairs. Three times a day the wall disgorged a trolley piled with food and dishes. When they gingerly tasted the food, the kids gazed at each other in astonishment.

"God, this is good!" Susan said, helping herself to more mashed potatoes.

"Pass that salad."

"Give me some first, Jon."

"Greedy box!"

"Like you should talk. How much of that casserole did you eat?"

Lillie had eaten a lot of the pasta casserole, which tasted as wonderful as everything else. Her belly felt full, and warm, and contented. She resented it when Sam began to complain.

"Yeah, it's good, but there's no meat. Future meals better have some meat. I hope Pam and Pete aren't fucking vegetarians."

"If the food stays this good, I won't even miss meat," Susan said.

"You don't need it, Lardball. I want protein."

Madison whispered to Susan, who was overweight and sensitive about it, "Don't mind Sam. He's just a stupid bully."

True, Lillie thought. Although Susan could stand to lose thirty pounds. Madison, despite the perky cheerleader beauty that made some girls distrust her, was a kind person.

Lillie considered the kids. She herself was the tallest girl and, after Madison and Hannah and Sajelle, probably the prettiest. Sajelle was pretty in that way black girls sometimes had, sort of sassy, with her dreads bobbing on her shoulders and her ass all curvy. Rebecca, whose parents came from China or Vietnam or someplace, had gorgeous hair, long and black and shining, but her skin was bad. The other girls looked average except for poor Elizabeth, with her huge chin and squinty eyes and skin as bad as Rebecca's. Of the boys, Jason, who wanted to be an actor, was really hot. Mike and Jon were cute. Sam looked like a thug, but he had a good body. Alex was too skinny, Rafe only about five foot three. Derek, the other African American, was all right but not as cute as DeWayne, the black guy who had stayed behind.

Her mind seized on DeWayne.

That was why she was judging everybody's looks. She could picture DeWayne Freeman. Also the others who stayed behind: Robin Perry and Scott Wilkins and, of course, Theresa. But she couldn't picture the kids who had died in the explosion at the Youth Center. She knew their names. She'd lived with them at Andrews for months. But she couldn't remember what any of them looked like.

In fact, she hardly thought about them at all.

Lillie frowned. That didn't seem right. Some of those kids—Tara, for instance–she'd hung around with a lot. When Lillie's mom died, she couldn't think of anything else for so long, and it hurt so much that sometimes she'd had trouble keeping it from showing. Of course, a mom was different than friends, but still it—

"If you're all done eating, come with me," Pam said. Lillie hadn't even heard her come in. "I have more of the ship to show you. Parts you'll like."

"She always so sure what we going to like," Sajelle grumbled, but she rose along with everybody else.

And they did like it. Pam led them through a door into a huge park. So big . . . how could a park be so big aboard a ship! How large was this spaceship, anyway?

"Wow!" Madison said.

"It's . . . incredible," Sophie said and not even Sam, scornful of everything, disagreed.

They ran through the park, exploring. It was incredible. There was a garden, with the most beautiful flower beds Lillie had ever seen. A big grassy lawn. A woods at one end, thick with trees through which ran narrow winding paths. A *pond*, for God's sake, big enough to swim in. A paved area with a basketball hoop; three balls sat neatly underneath its regulation ten-foot height. A second paved area was furnished with tables and chairs like a little outdoor cafe, surrounded by yet more glorious flower beds.

"This is where I'm going to be," Derek said happily. "Just pull my bed off the wall and put it here."

"No," Pam said. "Another room is where you'll spend most of your time. Come."

It took a while for everyone to obey. Some were in the woods, some inspecting flowers. Jason, the showoff, had actually taken off his running shoes and socks and waded into the pond. Derek and Mike were checking out the basketball court.

Pam waited patiently while Jon, Lillie, and the energetic Madison rounded everyone up.

"This is the most important part of your ship," Pam said, and Lillie noted the wording. *Your ship*. What was their ship? "Follow me. Come."

"She sure is bossy," Sajelle said, but not very loud.

Pam led them to a room reached through a door in the garden wall; Pete waited there. The room looked pretty boring. More metal tables and moldable tan chairs. Two walls were lined with closed cupboards.

Pam said, "This is the school."

Lillie and Jon looked at each other. Derek said with comic exaggeration, "Say what?"

"The school," Pam said.

Madison said, "We're going to *school* here?"

"Yes, of course," Pete said.

Lillie was the first to break a long silence. "What are we going to learn?" Somehow she couldn't imagine Pam and Pete teaching American history or *Great Expectations*.

"You're going to learn the right way. As much of it as you can."

"The right way?" Lillie repeated, sounding to herself like an idiot. "You mean, we're going to learn genetics?"

"Yes. But not until tomorrow. We have made the ship to follow your day-night patterns. In a few hours the lights will dim for sleep. They will come back on eight hours later for washing, breakfast, and then school. You have a great deal to learn, you know. But it will be fun.

"You'll love it."

CHAPTER 8

"No way," Jessica said. "Not me. None of that school shit."

They were all over the garden, in groups of two or three or four. Lillie had thrown herself full length on the grass, which had that wonderful just-mowed smell. Sajelle and Madison lounged with her, and Jessica had barged in.

"So what are you going to do about it?" Madison demanded. "Walk out into space?"

"Not going to do anything about it, just not go. Are you always such a good little follower, Maddy?"

"Don't call me that. It's not my name, Jess-sick."

"I'll call you what I want, bitch."

Lillie sat up. "Stop it, Jessica. We can't fight. We might need each other."

"For what?" Jessica jeered, but she didn't answer Madison.

Sajelle said, "I don't want to go to no school, neither."

"Why not?" Lillie said. Sajelle wasn't usually nasty.

"Just don't want to."

Lillie considered Sajelle. She knew Sajelle had come from what Uncle Keith called "a tough neighborhood." Uncle Keith . . . she had hardly thought about him at all, hardly missed him. Was that right? Again the nagging doubt tugged at her mind, the same that had bothered her when she realized she couldn't picture any of the kids that had died in the bombing.

Jessica said, "Sajelle doesn't want to be bothered with school because she's too busy missing DeWayne."

"You shut up, bitch!"

"Come on, Sajelle. You know you and DeWayne were getting it on back at Andrews."

Sajelle swung on Jessica, who ducked expertly. Instantly Lillie scrambled to her knees and thrust herself between them. "Stop it! We can't afford to fight!"

"Little Mother Superior. You're as bad as Elizabeth," Jessica said, rose to her feet, and strolled toward the basketball court, where all the boys except Rafe, plus Bonnie Carson, had organized a game.

"She's bad news," Madison said. "I don't know why the pribir engineered *her*."

"They didn't engineer her personality," Lillie said. "Not any of our personalities or intelligence or stuff like that. We're too different."

"You can say that again." Madison stood and stretched. "Sajelle, it's none of my business, but *were* you getting it on with DeWayne?"

"You right. It's none of your business."

Madison didn't look offended. "Well, I want a shower before dinner. Anybody coming?"

"Not yet," Lillie said.

When Madison had gone, Lillie looked at Sajelle. "You don't have to tell me if you don't want to, Sajelle, but why don't you want to go to school here? Jessica's just being an asshole, but not you."

"Just don't want to."

"You went at Andrews."

"That different."

"How?"

"Just was."

Lillie knew she was pushing, but something told her Sajelle did want to talk. Sajelle just didn't want to look like she was willing.

"What classes were you in at Andrews? We didn't have any together."

"'Course not!" Sajelle said with sudden energy.

"What do you mean? If you want to talk, I don't blab."

"I know you don't."

"Then what did you mean, of course we didn't have any classes together?"

"Didn't have classes with nobody. They give me a private tutor." Sajelle stared at the grass.

Suddenly Lillie saw it. She said gently, "It's your old school, isn't it? It was probably . . . not too strong academically. So you're a little bit behind."

Sajelle looked up. Lillie was startled by the despair in her brown eyes. "Not that. Derek, he go to school in Harlem and he keep up with the rest of you. It be me."

"What?" Lillie said quietly.

"Something in my brain. I can't hardly even read!"

Dyslexia. Karen, her old best friend Jenny's little sister, had it. Jenny—why didn't Lillie ever think about Jenny any more?

"The tutor help me a lot," Sajelle said, calmer now. "It start to make sense. But this Pam and Pete . . . they *aliens*. They can't help me. And I going to look like an ass in front of everybody."

"They're not really aliens," Lillie said, because she couldn't think what else to say. "They're as human as we are, only more advanced. Maybe you could talk to them about this."

Sajelle snorted. "Would you?"

"No," Lillie had to admit.

Sajelle looked at her. "You honest, Lillie. And you nice. But you not the one going to look stupid tomorrow in front of that bitch Jessica."

"Actually, we're probably all going to look stupid next to Rafe and Emily. They're really brains."

"Huh," Sajelle snorted. She got to her feet and gazed toward the basketball court. Jessica had joined the game.

"She talk about me getting it on. Look at her . . . she going after that sorry ass Sam. That 'ho ain't going to be sleeping alone. Well, she do what she want. Me, too, and I ain't going to no school."

Sajelle walked off across the grass. Lillie lay back down again, troubled. What would Pam or Pete do if Sajelle and Jessica, or anybody else, just refused to go to the school room? Would they *force* them? How?

She thought about this for a while, then raised herself on her elbow to watch the basketball. Jessica *was* going after Sam. Bonnie played like the boys, but Jessica was wrecking the game by "accidentally" falling against Sam and wiggling. Ugh. Why would anybody, even Jessica, want Sam?

And would they really have sex?

God, Jessica was only thirteen, same as Lillie. Lillie had let a boy kiss her once, and at dances they sort of pressed up against each other, but that was all. Did that make her backward? How many of these other girls were virgins?

Well, Elizabeth for sure, she thought, and cheered up. Imagine Elizabeth . . . No, don't. Julie, too, she was too shy to do anything. Madison? Probably. Sex would mess up her hair.

Grinning, Lillie stood up, brushed the sweet-smelling grass off her jeans, and went to join a group of girls inspecting the flower beds.

* * *

The next morning, after a breakfast as delicious as dinner the night before, Lillie headed for the school room. She had slept amazingly well, without dreams. Nobody had talked much at breakfast. Nervous, maybe. Lillie was.

She was the second one in the school room. Elizabeth had beaten her there and now sat hunched at the table in the farthest corner. Suddenly Lillie felt sorry for Elizabeth. Everybody harassed her. Well, she was such a dork . . . but even so. It must hurt. She walked over and sat down next to Elizabeth.

"Good morning, Elizabeth."

"Good morning," she said, sounding startled.

"I wonder what these 'lessons' will be like, don't you?"

Behind her thick glasses Elizabeth's eyes darkened. "If they're about genetics, they're tampering with God's plan."

Lillie should have sat someplace else. "Elizabeth, if you feel that way, why on Earth did you come? Why didn't you stay back at Quantico?"

Elizabeth set her bottom lip stubbornly. "I didn't ask to be made this way. It wasn't my choice. Now God wants me to do everything I can to undo the violation done to me."

"*Undo* it? *How?*"

"That's what I have to learn. God wants me to do this."

She really was crazy, Lillie decided. Lillie rose. "Well, nice talking to you."

"You're here for the same reason," Elizabeth said. "I've watched you."

"What?"

"You sometimes look . . . you're no more like these others than I am. You want something more than this world. I watch your face sometimes when they're talking about sex or basketball or some superficial thing like that, and I see the longing for more. You're like me."

"Not in a million years," Lillie said, and stalked off. God, she shouldn't let Elizabeth get to her like that. The girl was nuts.

It scared her that Elizabeth had seen that about her.

Madison and Emily came in together. "Lillie!" Madison called. "Sit with us!"

Each of the six tables had four chairs. Lillie sat down gratefully. She didn't know Emily very well, but she knew Emily was the smartest girl here. Emily went to a private school as a scholarship student. At Andrews she'd already been taking high school biology and advanced English. Trust Madison to glue herself to a ready-made tutor. Emily, quiet and generous, would help anyone who asked. She was a slight, pale girl with a short bob so blond it was nearly white. Lillie smiled at her. Why should Madison get all the help?

Slowly, following a group of the boys, Sajelle came into the room.

Lillie jumped up. "Sajelle! Sit here!"

Madison complained, "I was saving that seat for Rebecca."

"Well, now you're not. Rebecca can sit someplace else."

Sajelle sat down, frowning, chin raised. Lillie nodded at her encouragingly. From the next table Sam said, "Before Petey and Pammy start asking questions, I got some questions I want to ask *them*."

"Me, too," Rafe said, more quietly.

Pete and Pam entered from another door and stood at the front of the class, smiling. "Good morning. We found from TV broadcasts that this is how you educate your young, so we're going to proceed this way. I hope it's all right."

Sam said, less stridently than before the pribir had entered, "We want to ask some questions. Is *that* all right?"

Pam beamed at them. "Yes, of course!"

"Why did you come to Earth?"

Pam said, "We came to spread the right way. Earth is only one of many, many planets we will go to. Pribir ships are in space for thousands of your years."

There was a stunned silence. Thousands of years!

Madison blurted, "Then how old are you?"

Pete answered this time. "We two are only a few hundred years old, by your measure. As we told you last night, we were born for this visit, engineered for it. Once a person is born, certain things about their bodies are set forever. Other things, of course, are not. You will learn about that. But we will be mostly as we look now for all our lives."

"How long will *that* be?" Madison said.

"Another several hundred years, probably."

Jason said, "Wait a minute. You live hundreds of years and the whole point of your life is this visit to Earth? Of your whole life?"

Pete said, "What's the point of yours?"

Jason looked puzzled. No one answered. They didn't think, Lillie knew, about the point of their lives. Only weirdos like her did that. And Elizabeth. Most kids just lived lives. Maybe most adults did, too.

Pam said, "Our purpose is a great one. Although, we admit, we did expect there to be more of you. Seventy-two were engineered."

What *had* Tara looked like?

"But we can succeed anyway," Pam went on. "The numbers will grow over time."

"The numbers of what?" Jessica called.

Pam smiled. "I'm getting ahead of myself. We need to start at the beginning. Let's take a simple gene, one you already worked with on the planet. You know one protein it can code for. Who can name another one?"

An image formed in Lillie's mind: one of the drawings she had made at Andrews and passed on to one of the constant parade of adults interviewing her. This drawing, like most of them, was a series of meaningless symbols, circles and squares and triangles and short straight lines, repeated in various sequences for anywhere from a hundred to several thousand pairs. The only thing it meant to her was that Pete and Pam could smell images to her just as well aboard the *Flyer* as they could on Earth, which was hardly surprising.

Pam said encouragingly, "What else can this gene encode for besides that protein?"

Lillie looked at Emily, who seemed as clueless as Lillie was.

Pam stopped smiling. "Why aren't you answering?"

Rafe said, "We don't know the answer."

Pete said, "What do you mean? We don't understand."

Jason said, "We don't know! How would we know? We just passed on to doctors the stuff you smelled to us."

Pete and Pam looked at each other. When they weren't talking to the kids, their faces went completely blank. They were smelling to each other, Lillie suddenly realized, in some way the kids couldn't detect. Some genetic receiver they hadn't been engineered to have. Like a secret code.

Pete said, "We know you can't perform the genetic alterations we sent you, of course. Trained people must do that. But surely you understood the information? It's pretty simple."

"Simple my ass," Jessica said.

"What do you think we are?" Sam said.

Sophie stood. "I don't need this shit." She started toward the door.

A babble of voices broke out, arguing with each other. Rebecca grabbed at Sophie's hand to stop her from leaving, and Sophie pulled away angrily. Voices rose higher. Lillie stood and shouted over the din.

"Pam, Pete, you just need to start back farther! So we can understand!"

Mike stood, too. "Lillie's right. Shut up everybody. It's just a misunderstanding."

Slowly everyone quieted. Mike, sensible and low-key, addressed the pribir. "You learned a lot from our TV broadcasts or you couldn't act and talk so human, but—"

"We are human," Pam said, with a tiny spark of something that might have been anger, the first Lillie had seen from either of them.

"If you say so," Mike said. "But the point is that the TV shows don't really tell what kids our age know or don't know. So you guessed. But we don't know as much as you think. You need to start teaching us—" He hesitated, glanced at Sam "—pretty basic stuff. Like, what a gene is. And a chromosome. And . . . what was that thing you said yesterday, Emily?"

Emily, all attention suddenly on her, blushed. "A codon. Or whatever you pri . . . whatever Pam and Pete call a group of three base pairs that codes for an amino acid."

Pam and Pete looked as confused as the kids, and Lillie suddenly saw the problem. TV shows were usually about murders or love affairs or dumb families or sexy dancers. Stuff like genetic information was all over the Net, but it wasn't broadcasted into space. Pam and Pete didn't even have the words Emily was using, not only "codon" (what was a codon?) but even "amino acid," which Lillie had heard of. Vaguely.

However, the pribir caught on quickly. "Yes," Pam said, with one of her smiles that Lillie suddenly realized was also copied from TV shows. "I see. Okay, we'll start with . . . with this."

Lillie smelled another image: a double spiraling staircase with weirdly crooked outsides.

"Big deal," Jessica said. "What the hell is that?"

Pam and Pete looked surprised. *Well*, Lillie thought, *that isn't a facial expression they learned from TV and practiced carefully*. The surprise looked totally genuine. Maybe some expressions were the same even for hundreds-year-old humans from another star.

Rafe said impatiently, "It's a double helix, dummy. DNA."

"You call me 'dummy' again and I'll beat you to mush," Jessica said. No one doubted she could do it.

Lillie and Mike were still standing, although Sophie had sat down again. Mike said calmly, "Look. There's a way to do this. Emily and Rafe, you know this stuff already. The basics, anyway.

You go up there with Pam and Pete and when they smell us something, you explain in our words what it is."

Emily shook her head, red-faced. Rafe said, "Okay," and bounded to the front of the room. Madison shoved Emily until Emily joined him.

"This is good," Pam said, beaming again. "We'll learn your words for concepts. And we can provide the materials."

The tabletops opened. No, not "opened" . . . they sort of *dissolved*. Inside was a bunch of stuff Lillie couldn't identify. Black boxes, thin weird-shaped jars, pieces of what looked like equipment.

"Lab time," Hannah said.

"Yes," Pete agreed. "You will alter a bacteria today."

Jon blurted, "We're going to *do* genetic engineering?"

"Yes, of course," Pete said, surprised again.

"Bonus!" Jason said. "Can I engineer a porno goddess?"

"Like you could do it without giving her three tits," Sam said.

"That'd be okay!"

Rebecca said, "I'm not touching that stuff. Bacteria! How do you know it isn't dangerous?"

"Nothing is dangerous," Pam said earnestly. "And if an error occurs, Pete and I will rebuild it."

"Rebuild Rafe, then," Jason said. "Make him taller than a third-grader."

"Ha ha," Rafe said, from the front of the room.

"Let's begin," Pam said.

It was the strangest lesson Lillie had ever had. Images formed in her mind; Emily and Rafe explained them as well as they could; Pete and Pam instantly learned the vocal terminology from them and explained further. Some images were pictures to remember, and to her surprise Lillie found that now she remembered them easily, without even taking notes. Some images were instructions on how to use the gene-building equipment, and she remembered those, too. The four girls at her table worked together all day, and it felt good.

Sajelle, Lillie realized with amusement, hadn't even needed to read anything.

They discussed it all at dinner, another incredible meal. "They did something to our minds," Jon said. "This time I'm sure."

Rebecca stopped eating. "What do you mean, 'did something to our minds'?"

"I don't like school much," Jon said. "And there's no way I'd do biology all day like that unless I was on something. They put some gas in the room, I bet. So we'd *like* learning genetics."

Madison considered this. "If they did . . . does it matter? Isn't it just like . . . I don't know . . . using fizzies to get a little higher jump for a dance routine?"

Sam snorted. "That's probably the only thing you *did* use fizzies for in your milk-cum school."

Mike, logical, said, "The difference, Madison, is that you chose to use fizzies for dance. This was done without our choice. If it was done at all."

Lillie remembered how contentedly she'd worked for hours and hours at something that didn't ordinarily interest her. And now she remembered everything she'd learned. "It was done *to* us, Mike."

He nodded. "You're probably right."

By now the whole table had stopped eating to listen. Jessica said, "Nobody's going to fuck with my mind! Tomorrow they can just crawl up their own asses. I'm not going back."

"Me either," Sophie said.

A motion at the end of the table caught Lillie's eye. Elizabeth swayed, her face grotesquely distorted. She looked like she was in the worst imaginable pain. A minute later she fainted, crashing off her chair.

Someone screamed. Rafe said importantly, "Let me by! I know CPR!" But Elizabeth didn't need CPR. She revived almost instantly. As she pulled herself off the floor, her limp long hair swung over her face, hiding it, but not before Lillie saw the return of Elizabeth's anguish and her eyes fill with tears. The pain wasn't physical; Elizabeth jumped up and ran out of the commons toward her room.

"Fucking nuts," Sam said.

"Why should she mind having her mind manipulated?" Rebecca said. "It already is by that so-called religion of hers."

"Naw. Four-eyes just can't stand to feel good."

"Feeling good might feel seeexxxxyyyy."

"A sin! God will punish her!"

"That's enough, you morons," Madison said.

People resumed eating, except for a foul-mouthed group at Sam's end of the table who went on riffing about Elizabeth. Madison scowled at them. Julie seemed close to tears.

Lillie put another forkful of spiced carrots in her mouth. It wasn't that Elizabeth minded feeling good. Elizabeth was caught. If she went to class, she'd voluntarily give her mind over to forces of the devil. If she didn't go, she couldn't learn to "undo" the genetic engineering the forces of the devil had already done to her. God wanted her to go to class; it was a sin against God to go to class. Never mind that none of this was true; Elizabeth believed it was true. And was filled with horror and pain.

Lillie felt sorry for Elizabeth. But she didn't go after her. She couldn't think of anything to say.

After dinner everybody except Elizabeth went to the garden, their favorite spot. Lillie was surprised when Mike dropped beside her on the grass. "Lillie, I want to ask you something."

She felt herself color. "Yeah?"

He said, "Remember yesterday? We left Quantico in the middle of the night, and everybody was too excited to sleep, so we got a tour of the *Flyer* and we see our rooms and everything. Then all of a sudden we're being taken to eat dinner, see the garden, and lights out for night. What happened to all the hours of that night and day in between arriving and dinner?"

Lillie was confused. "I don't know. I guess we slept. Yes, we did . . . I woke up in my bed just before we ate dinner."

"But do you remember going to sleep in your bed?"

"Well, I . . . no. I don't. But I must have."

"Or we were put to sleep."

Slowly Lillie nodded.

"Well," Mike said, getting up awkwardly, "I just thought I'd ask." He strolled off toward the basketball court.

Despite herself, Lillie watched him go. He had a nice body. Not as tall as Jason or Jon, a little pudgy in the middle maybe, but nice.

Madison and Rebecca came over. Lillie bent over, pretending to look for four-leaf clovers in the grass so they wouldn't see her blushing.

CHAPTER 9

The next day, everyone was in class right after breakfast, including Jessica, Sophie, and Elizabeth. And the day after that, and the day after that. It took Lillie by surprise to realize that weeks were sliding by.

Three weeks. Four. Seven. Ten. How could it have been ten weeks already? Lillie meant to ask Pam or Pete when they were going back down to Earth. She needed to see . . . who? Oh, Uncle Keith! Of course! She would ask tomorrow.

Tomorrow came, and somehow she forgot.

Twelve weeks. Fourteen. She forgot to keep track.

Each day was exactly the same as the others. Shower, breakfast, class all day, dinner. Evenings in the garden having fun. Pam was teaching three girls plus Rafe to genetically engineer flowers. Games had materialized, after being requested and described: Chess. Cards. Chinese checkers. Hannah had brought a music cube with her, programmed with hit songs. Her favorite was "Don't Matter None to Me," by Printer Scream, and she played it over and over in the "cafe." Basketball remained popular. It was hard to say what they all did, exactly, in the garden every evening, but the time passed and it was all fun. There were arguments but no fights. Even Sam, the bully, and Jessica, the bitch, didn't cause too much trouble.

Lillie hung around mostly with Madison and Sajelle. Sajelle's older sister, fifteen, had already had a baby.

"Last year," she told them matter-of-factly. "My mother really mad. She wanted Dee to finish high school, get herself a decent job. But Dee and Ty . . . you know. And the baby so darling! You should see her."

"What's her name?" Madison asked, not quite able to hide her disapproval.

"Kezia." Sajelle frowned. "You know . . . I miss her, but I . . ." She searched for words, didn't find them, let her hands fall helplessly into her lap.

You miss her but you don't miss her, Lillie said silently. She knew. She still couldn't remember Jenny's face.

But she remembered all the genetics from class.

She knew the location on the human genome of a hundred and sixty genes, what proteins they could express, and how to alter many of them to express something else. She could turn genes on or off by manipulating their promoters, and could then use the results to turn off or on other genes, creating dozens of combinations of different effects. She had custom-built a bacteria capable of learning where she would put out its "food." She had learned to splice in extra copies of genes, cut out copies of genes, locate and replace damaged genes. She understood none of the equipment she used, but she could manipulate it expertly. So could all of them.

Only once did she question what she was doing. Rafe and she happened to be sitting at a table in the garden, drinking glasses of cold water flavored with some delicious plant that Pete had taught Sophie to grow. The others had left. Rafe said abruptly, "It's not new, you know."

"What's not new?" Lillie said, not really interested. Rafe's frenetic energy and hyperintellectualism put her off.

"The genetics we're learning. The Human Genome Project decoded a lot of this stuff over ten years ago, and the Protein Effort found out the rest of it. Well, maybe not how to get proteins to do alternate expression, but everything else. This isn't new genetics they're teaching us."

"It's new to me."

"You don't care, do you, any more than anyone else does. You're the eighth person I've tried to have this conversation with, and nobody cares except Emily that we've been carted up to a spaceship to learn genetics that our scientists on the ground already know."

That got Lillie's attention. "Are you sure, Rafe?"

"Of course I'm sure. I didn't win the Fanshaw National Science Prize without knowing what I'm talking about."

"I thought you were only a state winner, not the national winner."

"Even so. Lillie, why did they bring us here?"

"To learn the right way." She didn't even have to think about the answer; it rose to her lips from the deep well of certainty.

"Well, yes . . . but even so . . ." Rafe seemed to lose his thought. He frowned. "Lillie . . ."

Caught by his uncharacteristic foundering, she looked at him. Really looked. Of course, they were sitting down, but his shoulder seemed to be on a level with hers. "Rafe, stand up."

He did.

"You're taller than you were when we came."

"Yes. Boys get their growth later than girls, my mother always said so. But Lillie . . ."

"No, it's not that." She tried to concentrate. "Look at Rebecca. Over there, with Julie."

"What about her?"

"Her skin is all cleared up. And it was really bad when we came here . . . wasn't it?"

"I don't notice girls' skin. I have better things to think about."

Lillie ignored him. Getting up, she started a slow tour of the garden, looking at everyone. Really looking.

Julie was laughing with Rebecca, a free open laugh. When was the last time Lillie had seen Julie cry? A long time. Julie used to cry at everything.

Susan was no longer overweight. She was still curvy, but a good curvy.

Alex, who used to be so skinny that Sam said you could use him for a fishing pole, had bulked up.

Sam's hair didn't hang lankly over his ears anymore. It was thick and shiny.

And then Lillie came to Elizabeth.

Elizabeth was sitting by the garden pond, braiding rushes together and sticking flowers in them to make a crown. She looked up suspiciously as Lillie approached. "What do you want?"

Still Elizabeth. But definitely not Elizabeth. She was slimmer, too, but the big change was her face. Her features were somehow more . . . what? Regular. Prettier. Her skin was clear. And she wasn't . . .

"Elizabeth, what happened to your glasses?"

She looked briefly puzzled. "I don't need them."

"Why not?"

"I don't know why not. I just don't." She held up the garland she was weaving. "For the feast of Christ the Holy King. It's tomorrow, November 26."

November 26? They had been here for three months?

"How do you know today is November 25?" Lillie demanded.

"I asked Pam," Elizabeth said triumphantly. "She understands that I need to keep the holy days of obligation."

Lillie just stared. Pam understood? But Elizabeth had once told Lillie that Pam and Pete represented the forces of the devil . . . hadn't she? Was Lillie remembering right?

"Hey, Lillie, come dance with us," Rebecca called. "What are you doing talking with that dork?"

Lillie didn't know what she was doing talking to Elizabeth. They'd been discussing something important . . . wait, something about Elizabeth's religion . . . no, her looks . . .

"Come on!" Rebecca called impatiently. She'd gathered six of the girls together for a "dance" to the music on Hannah's cube. "Don't Matter None to Me" pounded its pronounced beat. Lillie hesitated another moment, then ran over to join Rebecca. Bonnie came, too, and Amy, with flowers in her hair.

Lillie did wonder briefly why they never seemed to invite the boys—hadn't Madison and Rebecca, at least, liked boys?—but then she forgot the boys as the dancing started. It was too much fun.

Some uncounted weeks later, Lillie woke up as usual, showered in the girls' bathroom, dressed and went into commons for breakfast. In the doorway she stopped cold. Something was very different.

Nothing looked different. People sitting at the long table, eating the wonderful food, talking . . . No, something *was* different. In the talking, maybe? But she could hear scraps of conversation, it was the same things they always talked about.

"—raising the genemod roses, see, you have to—"

"—and three shots from the foul line, only—"

"—a dance after dinner, would you—"

Something was different. Lillie sat down and said to Jason, "Would you please pass the cereal?" He turned and held the bowl out to her, and something in her chest turned over.

God, he was cute! Of course, everybody knew that, Jason wanted to be an actor and he was the best looking of the boys, but Lillie had never noticed how really handsome he was. His black hair fell across his forehead in a slanting line, and that smile . . .

Their hands brushed when she took the bowl from him, and Lillie felt a little dizzy.

"Lillie," Mike said on the other side of her, "would you like to sit at my table in class today? I don't know why we always sit with the same people. It's boring."

She turned to Mike, and a warm feeling crept up from her belly to her chest, up through her neck . . . She'd never noticed how broad his shoulders were. Broader, really, than Jason's.

"Yeah," Rafe said across the table. "We'd learn more if we changed lab partners and got new perspectives on . . . on the material."

Lillie laughed and looked at him. When had Rafe developed that gleam in his eyes? He was actually witty, sometimes, now that she thought of it. He could be a pain, but he could also be fun.

Breakfast had never tasted so good before.

In class she sat with Mike, Rafe, and Emily. Emily, that pale small brainy shrinking violet, tossed her white-blond hair and teased Rafe.

"That's not the right sequence, Rafaelo. If you don't remove the repressor from that gene, your RNA polymerase isn't ever going to get going."

"I was just going to flex the repressor a bit, not remove it," Rafe said, smiling at Emily.

"You obviously must believe in repression, then."

"Sometimes yes, sometimes no. What about you, Em?"

"Depends on the circumstances," she said, looking at him sideways through half-lowered lashes. "Sometimes repression is a good thing."

"And sometimes you can slip through repressors."

"Can you, Rafe?"

"Well, RNA polymerase can. Just flex the repressor a little . . ."

Mike flexed his biceps. "Like this, Rafe? Or maybe I should ask Emily."

"You can ask me," Lillie said, and instantly thought, *What the hell am I doing?* She felt herself blush.

Mike grinned. "Maybe you are the right one to ask, Lillie. Sensible Lillie."

"That's not very flattering to Lillie," Emily said, laughing.

"Okay," Mike said, "pretty Lillie, then. Beautiful Lillie. Is that better, Lillie?"

"I didn't mind 'sensible,' " Lillie said, with comic primness, and knew she meant it. But he'd also called her "beautiful" . . .

That evening the boys and Bonnie all left their basketball and wandered over to the paved cafe area where the girls usually danced.

Sam was the boldest. "Jessie, wanna dance?"

"Why not?" she said flippantly. Lillie saw that, for the first time in a long time, Jessica had put on the make-up she'd brought with her from Earth. So had Madison.

Maybe Madison would loan Lillie some eyeliner.

"Dance, Lillie?" Mike said. She nodded and he took her in his arms.

The song was slow, "Always and Only You," a big hit by Something Extra. Leaning awkwardly against Mike's chest, Lillie felt waves of warmth roll over her. She didn't want the song to end.

It did, and the next one on the cube was a skurler. Lillie hung back, not knowing the steps, but Alex seized her hand. "Come on, Lillie."

"I don't know how to skurl."

"It's easy. I'll show you."

Skurling required the partners to hold each other's wrists constantly and do as many energetic, rhythmic moves as they could without letting go. Alex was good. Lillie was awful, and once she fell down in a heap. Alex pulled her up, not letting go of her hands, and made her continue. His hand felt warm. She could feel the pulse in his wrist.

She danced a skurler with Rafe, who was better than she expected, a slow dance with Jason, then another with Jon. Then Sam slipped his arm around her waist. "My turn, Lillie."

She didn't want to dance with Sam. She didn't even like him! But his arm pulled her strongly to him, and she didn't pull away. He had a stronger smell than the other boys, a sort of nice smell actually, and the palms of his hands pressed flat against her back. She felt them—oh, yes, she felt them!—even through her T-shirt. But when one palm crept toward the side of her breast, she pushed him away.

"Don't be such a cock-tease, Lillie."

"You leave me alone!" Suddenly she was near tears.

Sam shrugged and walked away. Lillie started out of the garden, but then changed her mind and sat down in a chair to watch the dancing.

Sajelle was dancing, very close, with Alex.

Jason's handsome face was flushed as he clung to Hannah.

Madison was dancing with Rafe, whom she'd always called "that little dork." He was now as tall as she was. Some of her lipstick had come off on his shirt.

Sam had taken Jessica away from Derek, and now Sam was dancing with her. They were pressing the bottom parts of their bodies together and thrusting in unison, and it almost looked like . . . Lillie looked away, embarrassed.

There were more girls than boys, so some of the girls danced together. Sophie danced with Amy and Bonnie with Julie. But it wasn't the same. Sophie and Amy held each other loosely, inches between their bodies, but Bonnie kept pulling Julie toward her. Julie pulled away a bit, smiling, but Bonnie only held her more tightly, and the look on Bonnie's face . . .

They used to call Bonnie "a lezzie." Months ago, when everybody first arrived. Not lately, not for a long time, but—

"My dance," Mike said, looming in front of her. Lillie stood and moved into him, and none of the others she'd danced with, Alex or Jason or Rafe, was the same as Mike. Nobody else felt like this in her arms, nobody else felt so right . . .

She danced with Mike the rest of the evening, which was over so soon that Lillie was shocked. The lights blinked, which meant time to go to their rooms, and it had to be a mistake, the system was off, it couldn't be any later than nine at the most—

Mike and she stared at each other. For a terrifying, exhilarating moment she thought he was going to kiss her. But he stepped back and mumbled awkwardly, "'Night, Lillie."

"Good night, Mike."

She walked back to her room, feeling curiously empty.

Inside, she locked the door, undressed, and lay on the bed. Twenty minutes after blinking, the lights went out for the night, leaving only a faint glow around the doorway and in the corridor leading to the bathrooms.

Lillie stared at that glow, unable to sleep. She heard doors opening, closing again. It was a long time before she could drift off, and her dreams were troubled and strange.

At breakfast the next morning, Sam and Jessica sat very close together and groped each other under the table. "Get a room," Madison muttered. Lillie looked away from Jessie and Sam. It was obvious they'd spent the night together and wanted everybody to know it.

Lillie went back to sitting in class with Emily, Sajelle, and Madison. None of them mentioned it; they just sat together. Lillie felt relieved. Still, she couldn't stop glancing over at the table Mike shared with Derek, Sophie, and Amy. Why was Mike talking so much to Sophie? Sophie had never struck Lillie as that interesting.

Madison said casually, "A few people were talking about another dance tonight."

"I heard that, too," Emily said, too quickly. "Actually, I thought I might put on a dress. I brought one. I just haven't worn it yet."

Lillie hadn't brought any dresses. Suddenly she wanted one. No, she didn't . . . at home she almost never wore dresses. What was the matter with her?

She'd wear her pale blue top. It was the prettiest one she had. And the locket with the pictures of Mom and Uncle Keith, it was really pretty, she'd put it someplace in her footlocker . . .

Uncle Keith. For a minute she saw his face clearly, as shocking as if he'd materialized in front of her. She had to go home, Uncle Keith must miss her so much, he had nobody else . . . She'd always been aware of how much she meant to him . . .

"Lillie, still want to borrow some eyeliner?" Madison said to her, and Uncle Keith's face vanished.

The pale blue top clung to Lillie's body. Maybe it was a bit small, she might have grown some there . . . She left it on anyway. With the locket around her neck, her hair freshly washed, and Madison's eyeliner and lipstick, she decided she looked nice.

All the girls came to the garden later tonight, having taken time to braid or puff hair, trade clothes, borrow jewelry. The boys waited impatiently, not even playing basketball. Tonight they'd agreed on Jason's handheld for the music instead of Hannah's cube. The sound quality on the handheld was worse, but it had more slow songs.

Mike didn't say anything about Lillie's appearance, but that was all right. He didn't have to. She saw it in his eyes.

There wasn't as much switching partners tonight as last night. That caused trouble.

Lillie danced with Mike. Sam and Jessica were dancing so close and moving their pelvises against each other so suggestively that Lillie looked away. Emily danced with Rafe, Sajelle with Alex, Madison with Jon, Hannah with Derek. Only Jason kept changing partners. Unless he was dancing with one of them, the other girls danced with each other.

Elizabeth wasn't at the dance. Well, no surprise there, Lillie thought. But what did Elizabeth do with her evenings?

Bonnie asked Julie to dance. Julie refused. Bonnie then danced with Amy. Lillie wasn't paying any attention to them, lost in dancing with Mike, until Amy shouted, "Get away, you lezzie!"

Everyone stopped moving.

Amy, her face red with embarrassment or anger or both, had shoved Bonnie hard enough that Bonnie fell back against a table. She scrambled up, and tears filled her eyes. For a moment she stood uncertainly, then she made a strangled sound and started to rush away.

Mike squeezed Lillie's hand and let her go. His arm snaked out and caught Bonnie's shoulder. "Bonnie, don't go. Dance with me."

Bonnie stopped, uncertain. Jessica snickered, "You haven't got what she wants, Mike."

Mike ignored Jessica. "Come on, Bonnie, we've always been friends. Dance with me."

Bonnie smiled painfully, then moved toward Mike, keeping several inches between their bodies. They danced. Mike winked at Lillie over Bonnie's shoulder.

"Deserted for a lezzie, Lillie?" Jessica said. Lillie ignored her. She liked what Mike had done. It was kind. Maybe Lillie . . . could she . . .

She did. When Mike's dance with Bonnie was finished, Lillie danced with Bonnie, keeping a good distance away, not looking at the glances of everyone around her. Bonnie was a nice person, even if she was a . . . Why would she want to, with a girl? Well, to each her own. But Bonnie should be included in the group, should feel okay about being here.

She danced the rest of the night with Mike and didn't notice what anybody else was doing. Or care.

He walked her to her door, and kissed her, and said, "Can I come in?"

Sajelle had already disappeared into Alex's room. And, Lillie suspected, Jason wasn't alone either, although she didn't know who he was with. Maybe Sophie, maybe Rebecca. Or Amy.

"No, no," she said to Mike.

"Lillie, please . . . just for a little while . . ."

"No. No, please. I don't want to."

For a second he looked annoyed, but then he sighed. "All right. For now. I guess you're worth waiting for."

He left abruptly. Lillie, shaking, closed her door. She wanted him to come in, but what if he hadn't been willing to stop when she said?

What if he decided to dance and kiss with somebody else?

It was a long time before she fell asleep.

CHAPTER 10

Hannah was having sex with Derek. So were Alex and Sajelle, Emily and Rafe, and of course Sam and Jessica. Jason was having sex with anyone who would agree, but since nobody would admit it, Lillie wasn't sure who that included. The girls who weren't paired off were embarrassed to admit they were sharing Jason. Still, Lillie knew, Rebecca and Sophie were at least spending time alone with him, whether or not they had actual intercourse. Sophie was defiant about this, Rebecca sheepish.

"I don't seem to be able to help myself," Rebecca admitted, looking troubled. But not, Lillie thought, troubled very much. Whatever she and Jason were doing, clearly Rebecca liked it.

That left Madison and Lillie.

"Are you going to?" Madison said.

"I don't know," Lillie said. "I want to. But . . ."

"But we're only fourteen."

Fourteen? Lillie considered. Her birthday was on March 6. Could it be March already? Maybe. It didn't seem important.

Madison continued, looking down at her folded hands. "Still . . . I asked Pam about birth control."

"You did?" Madison was gutsy. Or cautious. Or both. "Did anybody else?"

"I don't know. Not the boys, I'll bet! Anyway, Pam gave me a pill, and she said it would protect me for up to six months. It works with genes . . . what else? She gave me enough for all the girls, and so I passed them out to everybody. Except Elizabeth, of course. You're the last one."

Lillie, immensely curious, said, "Did everybody take them?"

"Yes! Although half of them gave me bullshit about not needing them but if it was a free gift why not blah blah blah. Anyway, here's yours."

Madison passed Lillie a piece of toilet paper. Unfolding it, Lillie found a round green pill. She stared at it, wondering if she was going to use it.

Madison said, "Is Mike pushing you?"

"Yes. No. He doesn't push, he's too nice, but he wants it so bad it's almost like pushing."

"Jon, too. What have you done so far? How much?"

Lillie didn't want to tell Madison that she and Mike had only kissed. She waved her hand vaguely. "Oh, you know."

"Yeah." Madison sighed. "The thing is, I always said I'd wait till college. But when he's playing with my breasts . . . I don't know."

Lillie had a sudden, wholly unwanted image of Jon playing with Madison's breasts. A hot feeling shot up from Lillie's groin through her own breasts. Shocked, she looked away to keep Madison from seeing her face.

Madison was too absorbed in her own dilemma to notice. "The thing is, I never expected to *want* it this much. My cousin Christy told me that when she did it with her boyfriend it was only because he insisted, and they've been doing it a year now and she still doesn't like it."

I'll like it, Lillie knew.

"Well, Christy's a dork anyway," Madison said.

There were no more dances after dinner. Instead, people disappeared in couples or hung around in small groups in the garden. Lillie and Mike had strolled through the little woods and now lay stretched out on the grass under the drooping leaves of a huge tree. It seemed dark to Lillie . . . were the lights lower than she remembered? They seemed to be. The grass had that marvelous just-mowed smell that seemed perpetual in the garden. A little robot mower moved steadily around the lawn. Rafe had wanted to take the robot apart, but Pam wouldn't let him.

"Kiss me, Lillie," Mike whispered.

She did. Her whole body went warm. When Mike put his hands under her T-shirt, she didn't stop him.

Twenty minutes later she said, "Not here. In your room."

"Okay." He was breathing so heavily he could barely get the word out.

Hastily they refastened their clothing. Mike led her by the hand across the grass, around the pond, alongside the cafe. Amy, Sophie, and Julie sat there, sipping drinks. Lillie blushed . . . they *had* to know where she and Mike were going. Amy and Julie pretended not to see them, but Sophie stared at Lillie hard and her look was not friendly.

A little chill ran over Lillie.

It vanished in Mike's room. He groaned and pulled her down on the bed. But almost immediately he sat up again. "Lillie . . . if . . . if you're a virgin, I heard it hurts the first time and I don't want to hurt you . . ."

She laughed. She couldn't help it; nothing else he could have done would have reassured her so much that she was doing the right thing. He was such a nice guy!

"I don't care," she said. A second later she wondered: *Would* it hurt? But Mike had already lain down again and began to move his hands over her breasts, and she forgot everything else.

Madison's cousin Christy *was* a dork. It didn't hurt, and it was wonderful, wonderful, wonderful, and Lillie was in love.

Lillie dreamed. Somewhere in the half-awake recesses of her mind, she was surprised. Since coming aboard the *Flyer*, she'd seldom dreamed. But now she was running, terrified, something was chasing her, a thing she couldn't see . . .

She jerked awake and sat up. She had never taken the green pill Madison had given her.

Mike slept heavily beside her, one leg sprawled over her calves. Carefully she pushed the leg aside and fumbled in the darkness for her clothes, discarded by the bed. Dressed, she fled down the corridor to her own room. It, too, was dark, but by the dim light from the hall she flung open her metal chest and groped in the front left corner for the tiny pill wrapped in toilet paper. When she had it, she moved into the doorway for the better light.

The pill lay in the palm of her hand, as mild-looking as aspirin. Would it still work if you took it after the sex was over? If it didn't . . .

She felt a brief flash of resentment that boys didn't have to worry about this, that the burden fell mostly on girls. But her innate sense of fairness reasserted itself: it wasn't the boys' fault. Wasn't Mike's fault. With a quick swooping motion she brought the green pill to her mouth and swallowed it.

Still, she didn't feel like going back to Mike's room. God, if anything happened . . . Sajelle's sister already had a baby, at *fifteen*. Lillie didn't even much like babies. Oh, they were cute, but when she saw one, she never had the desire that other girls apparently did to cuddle and coo at it.

Still fully dressed except for shoes, she lay down on her own bed, but sleep wouldn't come. She needed to *know*. In the middle of the night? Yes. She needed to know.

Lillie padded into the ghostly corridor and closed her bedroom door. The other doors were all closed. Feeling stupid, she looked up at the ceiling and said softly, "Pam?"

A sudden clear, rare memory came to her: Her mother sitting on Lillie's bed, folding Lillie's small hands, teaching her to kneel and pray.

"Pam? Can you hear me?"

Nothing. Well, maybe that was good. Rafe had always asserted that the kids were constantly spied on by some advanced equipment they couldn't detect. Maybe that wasn't true. Or wasn't true here.

Lillie crept down the corridor to the commons room. The door opened easily, but the room was in total blackness, so nobody ever used it after "night" fell. Lillie let the door close behind her and said, "Pam? Are you there?"

Nothing.

"Pam? I need help. It's an emergency!"

Nothing. God, what if there was a real emergency, if somebody had a heart attack or something? Lillie hadn't realized how much on their own the kids actually were, when they weren't in class. Why?

Why not? Fourteen-year-olds don't have heart attacks. Or maybe Pete and Pam could genetically repair anyone who did. Still, kids were supposed to have adults within call.

Feeling aggrieved, or stubborn, Lillie groped her way in the total darkness to the door to the garden. It took her a while to find it. When she did, it too opened easily.

There was light here. The same dim ghostly glow that suffused the bedroom corridor lit outlines of trees, tall ferns, the tables at the cafe, the basketball hoop. In silhouette they looked scary. Lillie made herself walk several feet into the lawn area before calling. "Pam?"

And then, at a shout, "Pam? Are you there? I need you!"

"Lillie?" Pam's voice came, from nowhere and everywhere. It gave Lillie the creeps.

"Yes, it's Lillie. I—"

"What has happened? Why aren't you asleep?"

Pam's voice held genuine astonishment. Did she and Pete always sleep on an exact schedule, then? No, they'd once told the kids that they didn't sleep at all. But obviously they thought the kids did, every night all night. "I have to talk to you," Lillie said, feeling suddenly ridiculous. But the panic was still there, underneath, and she really didn't think she could go through the rest of the night without easing the roiling inside her.

"I'm coming," Pam said. "Wait."

Lillie shivered, even though the garden was no cooler at "night" than during the "day." The thick grass tickled the soles of her bare feet. Something came toward her, moving fast, and Lillie almost screamed. But then she saw that it was just the lawn-care robot that fascinated Rafe so much, moving much faster than its slow steady pace during the day. It swerved to avoid her. Water, or something like water, sprayed from it onto the grass.

Then Pam was there, hurrying from behind a clump of trees, from a place where Lillie had never seen any kind of door. "Lillie! What has happened? How could you be here?"

What a strange way to put it, Lillie thought. "Pam, I have to ask you a question. Mike and I . . . I mean, Madison gave me one of those pills you gave her. The green birth control pills. But I didn't take it, and then Mike and I . . . we had sex." She felt the fiery color sweep her neck and face. "And I took the pill, but not until much later and so I need to know . . . I was wondering . . . will it still protect me? I can't get pregnant, can I?"

Pam peered at her. Lillie had the sudden impression that Pam was thinking furiously, but Lillie couldn't imagine what.

"No," Pam finally said, "the pill still works, even if you took it later, after sex. You're protected."

"Are you sure?"

"I'm sure," Pam said, and now her voice was gentle, compassionate. She took Lillie's hand. Lillie didn't like that, but it would be rude to say so, after she'd dragged Pam out of bed for a stupid question.

"Lillie, sit down a minute," Pam said.

"The grass is wet."

"Yes. Come to the chairs."

She led Lillie to the cafe. Lillie didn't really want to chat, but what choice was there? She didn't want to be rude. She sat, barely able to make out Pam's face across the table.

"Lillie, I want to tell you something about myself," Pam said. "From the time I was young, I felt this desire for the whole universe to form a coherent algorithm, to have a first premise. I think you would say, 'to make sense.'"

Lillie started.

"I think, after watching you, that you want that, too."

How could Pam know that? *Did* she spy? But Lillie did not have conversations like that with the other girls! Just that one with Elizabeth, but that was so long ago . . .

She said slowly, "You smelled that from me."

Silence. Then Pam said, "Yes. You are very intelligent, Lillie."

"You can . . . you and Pete . . . do you know what everyone is *thinking?* Just from our pheromones?" She'd learned the word in class. Outrage was gathering in her.

"Oh, no," Pam said. "Pheromones tell of emotions, but not thoughts. The sensory molecules that convey images and reasoning . . . you know you can only receive those, not send them."

Which meant Pam and Pete could send them. Of course. They "talked" to each other right in the middle of the Earth kids, and no one else even knew they were communicating. It must be like hearing people talking to each other among a bunch of the deaf.

She said, "But if you can't read my thoughts, how do you know I want . . . what you said? For life to mean something."

"It's hard to answer that," Pam said thoughtfully. "It's partly the . . . taste of your pheromones, combined with which times you answer me or Pete or your friends and the times you don't . . . Lillie, I am human, after all. Our culture is much more advanced than yours, much farther along the right way, but not fundamentally different. Five million years ago, we shared ancestors here on Earth."

"We did?" The pribir had never said that before!

"Yes. We were taken, carried out into space, our evolution accelerated—"

"How? By who?"

"We don't know," Pam said. "Not any more. Maybe the memories were deliberately buried. Anyway, we were evolved, and taught, and now there are many of us in many forms, spreading ourselves throughout the galaxy. We bring the right way. That's our purpose. It permeates everything we do, and it gives our lives the kind of meaning you're talking about. I do understand what you long for, Lillie. It's the quintessential human longing: to matter to the universe. To believe the universe has a design and you're part of it."

Yes. Lillie couldn't breathe.

"We know that we are part of a magnificent design," Pam continued. "If we didn't have that, we would disintegrate. We don't need to strive for anything, not food or travel or health or anything.

The right way provides it all. If we didn't have the right way to strive for, we would be empty. Purposeless. We might do what some other species have done, destroy themselves out of sheer pointlessness. Do you understand what I'm saying, Lillie?"

The odd thing was, Lillie did. No one else she had ever known had thoughts like these. The religious people believed God had a design for them, but Lillie could find no evidence to believe in God. Her mother's crazy beliefs had ensured that. The non-religious people just wanted to have a good time, or make a lot of money, or look good, or maybe raise their kids. Then the kids would grow up to raise theirs, on and on, but without any *point*.

She said shakily, "I think I understand."

"I think you do, too. That's why I told you. I feel very close to you, Lillie. I think in many ways we're very alike."

But that was too much. Pam was a pribir, she came from another planet or ship or something, she whizzed around the galaxy teaching genetics, she smelled what her husband was thinking . . . Pam and Lillie were not alike. Abruptly Lillie stood. She couldn't have said why, but she could not stay sitting down any longer.

"I know," came Pam's voice in the gloom, "it's a strange thought. We're also very different, too. I'm not minimizing that. But I'm glad we talked, Lillie."

And then Lillie was glad, too. In a complete reversal of her precious sudden revulsion, she saw that Pam was wonderful. That Pam understood her as no one else ever had, that Pam had entrusted her with a great idea which made an unbreakable bond between them. Pam was what Lillie wanted to grow up to be, wise and compassionate and centered in herself, and Pam even smelled wonderful, a sudden rush of scent that intoxicated Lillie . . .

"You better go back to your room now, Lillie," Pam said gently.

"Yes. But I . . . you . . ."

"Go back to your room," Pam said, and Lillie went joyfully, making her way through the utter darkness of the common room to the corridor, to her door, to her bed, where she was seized with a tremendous unstoppable desire for sleep.

In the morning, however, she remembered the entire conversation. She thought about it often, while splicing genes and receiving codon images and walking with Madison and Sajelle. Not while having sex with Mike, though. That remained an undivided experience, consuming her, leaving no room for hesitation or reflection or anything else but itself.

* * *

Some days later, Lillie woke feeling ill. At first she didn't even recognize the feeling; she hadn't been sick since coming aboard the *Flyer*. But now her throat felt scratchy and sore and her head ached. She put her fingers to the sides of her neck, as her mother had done so long ago whenever Lillie complained of sickness. The glands in her throat felt swollen and sore.

Mike had already left her bed, probably for the showers. Lillie hadn't heard him go. She swung her feet off the bed and felt the motion ricochet around in her head.

All at once she wanted Uncle Keith, unthought of for . . . how long?

"Lillie? You coming to breakfast?" Sajelle stuck her head in the door. "Mike asking for you."

"I don't . . . feel so good."

Sajelle came into the room. "Oh, girl, you don't look so good. You going to hurl?"

"No. I—"

"I'm getting Pam. Lay right there, baby."

Pam hurried in ahead of Sajelle and Madison. Emily peered from the hallway. It was becoming a parade, Lillie thought irritably, and it seemed even the irritation hurt her head.

Suddenly all she wanted was to go home.

Pam's eyes gleamed. "How interesting! Lillie, you must have a . . . I don't know the word in English."

"A what?" Sajelle demanded. "She got something dangerous?" Madison took a step back from the bed.

"No, no, of course not," Pam said. "You can't get sick on ship. Lillie must have a virus she brought with her, of the kind that can stay dormant inside cells for years and then suddenly go active. But we can deal with that."

"How?" demanded Sajelle, ever practical.

"We'll need to take her into our . . . our hospital. Lillie, we'll give you anesthetic, all right? Nothing will hurt. We'll just fix you up good." Pam was proud of the slang she was learning from them.

"Drugs?" Lillie managed to get out. Her head had never ached like this before. She closed her eyes, but it didn't help. Very rarely had Lillie gotten sick at all, and then she always threw it off quickly. *Good immune system*, Uncle Keith always said.

Uncle Keith . . .

When she opened her eyes, a second bed floated beside hers, and the room was full of people.

"Maglev!" Rafe said, ducking to crawl underneath the floating platform. "Has to be! The floor has superconductors woven into it, right, Pam?"

"Get out from there, Rafe," Pete said. "The floater isn't important. It's not the right way, just a necessary machine. Just relax, Lillie."

"Mike?"

"He's still at breakfast," Madison said. "You want me to go get him?"

Answering was too much effort. Pete easily lifted Lillie from her bed to the platform. Somewhere behind her headache and wheezy breathing, Lillie was glad she was dressed. The platform floated out of the room, Pam and Pete on either side, the others trailing behind in concern or excitement.

"Go eat breakfast," Pam told them irritably.

"Do we still have school?" somebody called.

"Yes! Of course!"

The platform floated Lillie through commons, through the garden, to a far wall. Lillie made herself turn her head to look. The wall was closed seamless metal . . . until Pam touched it. It began to open.

Pam said something sharply to Pete in a language Lillie had never heard. He answered impatiently, "Not outside here!"

Lillie floated through the wall.

She scanned everything, ignoring pain, knowing she would have only a few seconds. Sure enough, the drowsiness struck and she was asleep.

But not before she'd seen a totally alien place, and a monster flowing toward her.

CHAPTER 11

She woke in her own room, Sajelle and Pam beside her. She felt wonderful.

"Hey, baby, you awake?" Sajelle said fondly.

"Yes." Lillie sat up. There was no weakness, no grogginess. She felt she could run a marathon. "What was it?"

"A virus," Pam said warmly. "Acquired, latent until now. We haven't seen it before. We added it to the genetics library."

"You're a library all by yourself," Sajelle said, grinning.

Madison breezed into the room with a huge bunch of yellow and pink flowers. "Lillie! You were right, Pam, she woke up just when you said. These are for you, fresh from the garden."

Lillie took the flowers. They smelled incredibly sweet.

"Mixed the genes myself," Madison said proudly.

Rafe and Jason entered hesitantly. Pam, Lillie noticed, scowled briefly at Rafe, then replaced the scowl with a pleasant smile. Jason said, "The princess awakes!" He made a low sweeping caricature of a bow.

Rafe said, "You okay, Lillie?"

"I'm fine." She swung her feet off the bed. Her body felt bursting with health. "Where's Mike?"

Suddenly nobody looked at her.

A tiny cold chill hit Lillie's spine. "Where's Mike? Is he sick, too? Did I give him my disease?"

"Oh, no, Mike's fine," Madison said, still not looking at her.

Jason said, "He's still in the showers. He was going in when I was coming out."

From Sajelle: "You'll see him in class. Right after breakfast."

Breakfast? Lillie said, "But . . . but you were all going into breakfast when I went into the hospital." A memory tugged at her, something strange and monstrous . . . it was gone. "Pam, did you cure me that fast?"

Pam laughed. Madison said, "She doesn't realize! Lillie, you've been gone ten days!"

Ten days.

Pam saw her face. "It's all right, Lillie," she said reassuringly. "It just took that long to remove every trace of the virus from your body. But you're fine."

Madison added, "And Emily's going to help you catch up on what you missed in class."

Ten days.

Lillie said slowly, "I'd like a shower, too. Before breakfast."

Pam laughed again. "Lillie, we returned you perfectly clean!"

"I'd like one anyway. Sajelle, you, too?" She caught and held Sajelle's eye.

Sajelle understood. "That's where I was going. I'm grubby as hell."

"Well, be quick," Pam said. "Class starts soon. Lillie, we're so glad to have you back."

She left, trailed by everyone except Sajelle. It seemed to Lillie that they were all very eager to leave.

She and Sajelle walked to the showers, undressed, stuffed their clothing into the instant-cleaning slot. Lillie turned on the water hard and said quietly to Sajelle, "What's going on?"

Sajelle said uncomfortably, "Nothing going on."

"Sajelle, please. I need to know."

Sajelle scrubbed herself vigorously, her eyes fixed on a spot on the wall. "You been gone ten days, Lillie. Every day Pam and Pete say you doing fine. And you sure look fine now. But while you gone . . ."

"What?"

"You going to know anyway, I guess," Sajelle said resignedly. "Mike took up with Sophie. They sleeping together."

Such a sharp pain went through her that Lillie was astonished. It actually felt like a physical piercing.

Sajelle said, "I'm sorry, baby. He's just no good."

Lillie said mechanically, "Yes, he is." And then, in anguish, "He couldn't wait for me?"

"Guess not. Aw, Lillie, don't cry."

"I'm not crying." And she wasn't. She didn't feel at all close to tears. Just that sharp, breath-stealing pain in her chest.

Sajelle said, with a transparent effort to distract here, "What did you see in the pribir hospital?"

"Nothing." Only there was a memory, a glimpse of . . . gone.

"You out the whole time, then?"

"Yes."

"We're glad to have you back, girl."

"Yes."

Sajelle shut off the water. "Come on, Lillie. Let's go. You need to eat. He isn't worth it, baby. Get dressed."

Lillie couldn't eat. She put a few spoonfuls of food into her mouth, but the action was as mechanical as dressing had been. She followed Sajelle to class, let Sajelle seat her at a table with herself, Alex, and Bonnie. They were all self-consciously enthusiastic about her return.

At a far table, Mike held hands with Sophie.

It doesn't stop, Lillie marveled. The pain in her chest didn't lessen or increase, it just went on at the same level, swamping everything else. In class Lillie couldn't handle any of the equipment. She just sat, hands folded in her lap, while the images Pete was smelling to them formed, unheeded, in her mind. Pam frowned at her in concern.

It went on the same all day. Every once in a while Lillie thought, *I'm still breathing.* It was an abstract thought, without force. Mike didn't care if she was breathing or not. So neither did she.

After dinner she went to her room instead of to the garden with the others. She sat on the edge of her bed with her hands folded in her lap, staring at nothing. Sajelle and Rebecca came in.

Rebecca said, "Lillie, you have to stop this."

Sajelle snapped, "You ever had your heart broke, Becky? I don't think so."

"But look at her! Lillie, you're not . . . you're barely . . ."

Yes, Lillie thought, but said nothing.

Rebecca started to chatter desperately. "Well, at least let me tell you what's been going on while you were gone, Lillie. You won't believe it! Jason—you know he tomcats around, in a different bed every night, thinks he's God's gift to girls not in couples . . ." She stopped, looking stricken.

"Rebecca, you're a fool!" Sajelle said angrily.

Lillie managed, "What about Jason?" It came out a croak.

Rebecca threw Sajelle a look of triumph. "Well! Guess who Jason finally reached in his sex tour? Elizabeth!"

Even Lillie blinked. "*Elizabeth?*"

"Yes! Rebecca saw him coming out of her room one morning, real early, and Jason just winked and did a cartwheel in the hall!"

Lillie said slowly, "Is Elizabeth okay?"

"Okay? It was probably the best thing that ever happened to that uptight bitch!"

Lillie thought about that. "No. Not Elizabeth. She thinks it's wrong."

"Well, then why did she do it?" Rebecca demanded logically. "And anyway, she doesn't act like she thinks it was wrong. She just goes about her usual praying and whatever."

Lillie fumbled toward a thought. Elizabeth couldn't just be ignoring her sex with Jason . . . if she'd actually had sex with Jason. Elizabeth had too much rooted in her too deeply. If Elizabeth was acting like nothing happened, it must be because . . . because . . .

She couldn't capture the thought. The pain over Mike's betrayal washed over her again, stronger than before, and almost she cried out.

Rebecca went on prattling. "And Rafe—you won't fucking believe what Rafe did. Oh, here's Emily, she can explain it better than I can, the brain. Em! Tell Lillie what Rafe did!"

Emily entered shyly, smiling at Lillie. "*Rafe*. You know how he's been fascinated with the lawn-care machine, Lillie. Well, he snuck into the garden at night—the garden door isn't locked, did you know that? He caught the machine and opened it by force. He says it wasn't built out of very strong metal at all, just flimsy stuff."

Sajelle put in shrewdly, "Nobody never expected anyone to try to take it apart."

"That's right," Emily continued. "But Rafe did. And he says there's no machinery inside, just a mass of living tissue! A blob. He figures that it's a genetically engineered organism created to exude exactly what the lawn needs, the chemicals for it to grow plus water chemically extracted from the air. Anyway, the machine also exudes other microorganisms that eat the grass down to a certain length before they die themselves. Mowing it, sort of."

Lillie tried to pay attention to what Emily was saying. It was hard. All she could think of was Mike. Mike with Sophie. Mike with her. He'd said, he'd promised . . .

"But more than that," Emily said. "Rafe has a theory. He thinks that nearly everything aboard the *Flyer* may be organic, genetically engineered. Not the walls, maybe—"

A wall opening, where there was no door . . . the image slipped away.

Mike with Sophie. Mike with her. He'd said, he'd promised . . .

"—but everything except the walls and some sort of ship's drive. Rafe thinks our food is just genetically engineered molecules to match our taste buds and nutritional needs, not real veggies or pie or whatever—"

"Sam almost slugged Rafe for that one," Sajelle said.

"Rafe thinks that our clothes are cleaned by organic molecules, the beds and chairs are living tissue, the gene splicers and other lab equipment all work by DNA computer, the—"

Sajelle said, "What's that smell?"

"I don't smell anything," Emily said. "Rafe also says that genetically engineered molecules in the air might smell to us not only the images in the classroom, but other ideas, too. It's an interesting theory, I think, given Pam's constant emphasis on 'the right way,' but I'd want to modify it be—"

Lillie wasn't listening. The pain over Mike was gone.

In fact, it had been really stupid of her to get so upset in the first place. Sajelle was right: Mike wasn't worth it. She'd thought he was a nice guy, but a really nice guy would have waited ten days for a girl he said he loved, instead of starting to sleep with somebody else. That was an unpleasant truth—in fact, she hated it—but it was a truth nonetheless. She wouldn't have behaved like that to him. He didn't deserve her.

"That smell is gone now," Sajelle said.

Lillie admitted to herself that she still felt bruised. He'd used her. But bruised wasn't bone-shaking jealousy and unstoppable pain, and what had that been about, anyway? She'd lost her perspective on things. Well, she had it back, now.

"Let's go to the garden," she said abruptly, breaking into Emily's monologue about Rafe's theories.

Sajelle blinked. Emily said uncertainly, "Well, if you want to, Lillie."

"I do." Better to just get it over with.

Mike was dancing with Sophie in the cafe. Lillie, heart pounding but under control, walked past them to a group sitting by the pond. They welcomed her with exaggerated cries, both wary and sympathetic. Jason winked at her.

The wink looked just right to Lillie. He was saying, *Don't let it get to you,* saying it with humor and style. Lillie winked back.

She tried to pretend to be natural, and the more she did, the more natural she actually felt. Also healthy and energetic. She got them all to the basketball court, where Jason, one of the captains, picked her first for his team.

Three nights later, after his persistent and exaggerated gestures that made her laugh, Lillie went with Jason to his room and had sex with him. She felt relief, and desire, and the knowledge that Jason would only be with her a few days before moving on. Sad knowledge, irrelevant knowledge. What mattered was the sex. In fact, it seemed to Lillie she wanted it more with Jason than she had ever with Mike. It was as if she was driven toward Jason, hungry and eager, and couldn't help herself. But, then, why would she want to?

"Sajelle! Wake up!" Lillie stood by Sajelle's bed, barefooted, shivering in a room that shouldn't have been cold.

"Wake up! Now!"

Sajelle stirred sleepily beside Alex, opened her eyes, sat up quickly.

"Something's happening," Lillie said. "I don't know what. Please . . . come."

Sajelle climbed over Alex and followed Lillie into the corridor. By the time they closed the door behind them, Sajelle was already frowning. "What is it?"

"I don't know," Lillie said helplessly. "I just woke up knowing something's . . . wrong."

Sajelle said slowly, "Yeah. It is."

Relief washed over Lillie. She wasn't the only one with this sense of doom. Not just doom, either. Anger, fear, shame, a flood of nasty emotions that made her feel terrible. What was she doing on the ship so long? God, poor Uncle Keith must think she was dead! And then Jason . . . and before him Mike . . . how had she acted like such a slut? She, Lillie! She didn't behave like that! And she'd been here—they'd all been here—how long? What month was it, anyway? Why had they stayed, learning genetics from aliens, while their families below must not even know what happened to them!

"God," Sajelle said, "those . . . *aliens*. What have I been doing here? How long has it been?"

"I don't know. I lost track."

"They not even human!"

"Well . . ." Lillie said, her native fairness asserting itself. But then an image came to her, sharp and horrifying: Pam taking her through the garden wall into the rest of the ship, and flowing toward her a thing, a blob, of living tissue . . . How had she forgotten that terrible picture? She clutched Sajelle's arm.

"Don't you go clinging to me!" Sajelle snapped. Then, "I'm sorry, Lillie. It's just . . ."

"I know," Lillie said. She felt on edge herself, anxious, almost sorry she'd woken Sajelle. "What's *happening?*"

"We ourselves again," Sajelle said grimly.

Yes. But how, and why? And who had Lillie been before? All of a sudden she wanted to cry, or kick something, or find Pam and Pete and demand explanations, reasons.

The door to commons opened and Rafe came through, very pale. "I did it."

"Did what?" Sajelle snapped. "What your sorry ass doing now?"

"I took out the scent-organism complex."

The girls stared at him. He said impatiently, "Don't be stupid, you two! If the lawn machine was organic, then don't you see that the scent-producing mechanism must be, too? It's the 'right way.' Genetically engineer everything you can, and regard the rest with disdain. Olfactory molecules have been coming at us day and night, incredibly complex molecules, controlling our behavior. Probably acting on the emotional areas of the brain just the way the learning molecules act on the cortex."

Lillie struggled to take it in. "You mean . . . Pam and Pete have been controlling our behavior? With engineered molecules? Getting us to . . ." She couldn't finish.

"You got it," Rafe said grimly. "Getting us to like school, and be happy here on ship, and not worry about what we left down below, and fuck like minks."

"You wrong!" Sajelle yelled. "Nobody controls me!"

"Wanna bet?"

Sajelle swung on him. She connected. Rafe was taller than he had been but still slightly built; he went down, staggering up a moment later with a bloody nose.

"I'm sorry," Sajelle whispered.

"Yeah, I'll bet you are." Rafe looked on the verge of tears. "Listen, Sajelle, would you have done that if I hadn't poisoned the scent organisms? I don't think so. Face facts for once in your unintellectual life, why don't you."

Lillie cried, "How did you do it, Rafe?"

"Not hard. I found the opening in commons—apparently it does our whole area—made some strong acid in the school, and poured it in."

"We weren't taught to make any acid."

He looked disgusted. "Not by Pam and Pete. But unlike you, I knew some chemistry before I arrived here. I had some other priorities than clothes and sports and sex."

"You and Emily done your share of fucking since you got here," Sajelle jeered. "Or did you two just talk about chemistry all them nights?"

Lillie said, "We have to go back. To Earth. My Uncle Keith . . . how long have we *been* here?"

Rafe said, blood still streaming from his nose, "Seven months and twelve days. It's April 10."

April 10! God, how had so much time passed? She hadn't known, hadn't even remembered, hadn't been herself. Who had she been? The things she'd done with Jason and Mike . . .

Lillie said to Rafe, "They didn't control us completely, or we'd all have been the same. But we weren't! Sam was still a bully, and you were still interested in science stuff, and Elizabeth was still religious, and—"

"You're right," Rafe said sulkily. "Basic personality remained. Like Sajelle being an idiot. But olfactory molecules controlled our moods, made us happy here no matter what, took away missing people and wanting to go home and sexual inhibitions and any emotional pain."

Any emotional pain. Her jealousy and betrayal over Mike, and then all at once it vanished. Just like that. And Sajelle saying "What's that smell?" And the talk with Pam in the garden, Lillie thinking Pam was wonderful, so warm and caring.

Sajelle said, "You crazy, Rafe. Why would Pam and Pete want us fucking like that?"

"I don't know." He'd succeeded in stopping the blood flow from his nose. He looked a mess, bloody and dirty and angry.

A door flew open and Rebecca rushed out. "Hey! I woke up and . . . what is this?"

"Tell them, Rafe," Sajelle said, and even under her roil of painful emotions Lillie could see that Sajelle was trying to make amends to Rafe, trying to let him shine.

Rafe began his explanation again. In the middle of it Sam and Jessica bolted out of Jessie's room, and Rafe had to begin a third time. When Julie appeared, Rafe said in disgust, "I'm not going to keep doing this! Wake up everybody and get them into commons so I can tell everybody at once!"

"You better watch who you're ordering around," Sam said

threateningly. He waved a fist in Rafe's bloody face. Rebecca scowled at Sam. Julie, cowering against a wall, began to cry silently, tears sliding down her frightened face.

They were all themselves again, Lillie realized. They'd been themselves all along, but only partly, the rest of their selves controlled and manipulated and tamed. And now they were themselves again completely. And so was she, and she was scared and angry, and she wanted to go home.

She fought down the feelings. "Becky, start waking up people. You, too, Jessie. Try to be gentle. Julie, stop bawling! It isn't going to help. We need to get everybody into the commons room."

Elizabeth ran out of her room. Lillie caught sight of Elizabeth's face and the thought flashed across her mind: None of the rest of us are *that* terrified! But there was no time for Elizabeth. Lillie got the others set at waking people up, and then she went with Rafe to the commons.

"Here, put this on your nose, it's bleeding again." She handed him the sash from her pants.

"The effect is in here, too, do you feel it? Or, rather, the lack of effect." His voice was unsteady.

"Rafe, do you think that by poisoning those . . . organisms, you might have poisoned our air, too? Is it safe to breathe, long term?"

"As far as I know."

"Okay," Lillie said.

"Do you think we should call Pam and Pete? If that's even possible."

It was possible, Lillie knew. Standing in her bare feet on the thick garden grass, bleating for Pam, who had reassured her about the birth-control pill and told her she was different and special, that Lillie and she were the same because they wanted, needed, meaning in their lives. Wonderful, caring Pam, who had turned Lillie into a puppet for seven and a half months. Who had used pheromones to make her forget Uncle Keith, and stay mindlessly on the *Flyer*, and have sex with Mike and then Jason, and . . .

"No," she told Rafe. "Don't call Pam or Pete. Some of the others might kill them. Sam or Jessica, for instance." *And me.*

"Yeah, you're right," Rafe said. "Fuck."

When they were all there, Rafe explained again what he'd done. He showed them the slit, a small horizontal slash high near the ceiling, into which he'd poured the acid. Shouting and tears and horror followed, a pandemonium until Jon out-shouted everybody else and got them listening again.

Proof, Lillie thought through her own anger and fear, that there were no surveillance cameras in commons. If Pam and Pete knew what was going on, wouldn't they be there?

"The question is," Jon said, "what are we going to do?"

"Kill the fuckers!"

"Sam, *think*," Jon said curtly. "Even if we could do that, what good would it do? We want to go home."

"Make them send us home!" Sophie called.

"How?"

More argument, everyone jumping up and talking at once, no one listening. But what good would listening do? Nobody, as far as Lillie could tell, had any real ideas. Finally, in a lull resulting not from agreement so much as exhaustion, Lillie said, "We have to *ask* Pam and Pete to send us home."

"Ask them? You think they care what we want?"

"They sure didn't ask us before!"

"Break down the fucking door! The door they took Lillie through when she was sick! Beat the shit out of them until they scream!" Sam, yelling again. Lillie looked at him, dressed only in jeans, fists clenched, stubble on his chin. Looking demented, like something from a bad video game. She looked at all her friends, these people she'd spent seven and a half months with, now furious and terrified and helpless.

Julie, crouching in her chair, bent over so that her straight fine hair hid her tearful face.

Sajelle, naked under the long T-shirt that had been the only thing on her when Lillie woke her. Her dark face set in stubborn lines, lip pushed out, black liquid eyes scared.

Jason, not clowning now, his handsome face shocked into immobility like stone.

Madison, breathing fast with her mouth open, as if she couldn't get enough air.

Rafe, sulky and fearful and triumphant, holding Lillie's sash to his bloody nose.

Elizabeth . . . Elizabeth wasn't here.

Lillie frowned. Had Elizabeth gone back to her room, to cower and pray? Lillie hadn't seen her leave commons. But she remembered the look on Elizabeth's face in the hall, a look of revulsion so much deeper than anything the others showed that it had made Lillie pause. Revulsion and horror and . . .

The door to the garden flew open and Pam and Pete strode into the room. But . . . was that them? It actually took Lillie a moment to recognize them, Pam's smooth face was so contorted. Pete's teeth were bared, perfect white teeth.

"You . . . you . . ." Pam couldn't get words out. *Pam.*

"It wasn't bad enough that there were only twenty of you here!" Pete screamed. "Now you have to reduce the number more . . . stupid stupid raw genetic . . . All the effort! All the time! And you think you can destroy our carefully . . . *you!* You!"

The kids had all stopped dead, staring. Lillie shrank back against a wall. What had happened, why were Pam and Pete like this, she hadn't known they could be like this—

"Our whole lives!" Pete shrieked. "To benefit you stupid ungrateful—"

Pam let loose a sound no human voice could make, a roar that rose into a steep wail.

"—don't deserve all we've done for you, all we're trying to do . . . our whole *lives*—" Pete ran into the room and struck Alex, closest to the garden door, full in the stomach. Alex went down, bent double.

"Get 'em!" Sam cried. "They'll kill us!"

He rushed Pete. After a shocked moment, Mike and Jason joined him. The three boys hit Pete together, and he went down.

"No, no, it's all a mistake!" Pam cried. "We won't hurt you! You're our—" She didn't get to finish. Derek and Bonnie jumped her, knocking her down, and Sophie immediately sat on Pam's chest.

"Stop!" Jon called. "Stop! Let them explain! They're not—"

Lillie didn't hear more. She had run to Alex, crumpled by the garden door. He gasped for breath, clutching his stomach. He was turning blue. Something inside him must be injured, Pete had killed him . . .

"Alex! Alex!"

Slowly his gasps began to bring air into his lungs. Color returned to his face. But he continued to clutch his stomach, moaning. "Hurts . . ."

"Don't try to talk," Lillie said. She knew CPR, but Alex didn't need it now. She watched, panicky, for signs of shock. Elevate the feet, keep him warm . . . but it didn't look like shock. Pete had injured something inside Alex, some organ . . . what if Alex were bleeding inside? Lillie wouldn't have any idea what to do.

She turned her head to the fight behind her. Pam down, Pete down, Sam's fist raised over Pete's face . . . Lillie saw it all as a frozen image, a single-moment snapshot. Her head whipped back to Alex, and the motion swept her line of sight through the door into the garden, and she saw it.

Elizabeth. Hanging by the neck from a big tree. Dead.

The look on Elizabeth's face in the hall, a look of revulsion so much deeper than anything the others showed. Elizabeth, who believed in a God that would punish her if she didn't undo her genetic modifications. Who would also punish her if she herself learned Satan's art. Who punished sex if you weren't married. Rafe's words: "*Olfactory molecules controlled our moods, made us happy here no matter what.*"

The olfactory molecules Rafe had killed with his homemade acid.

Lillie opened her mouth to say something, or call somebody, or scream, but whatever it was never came out. Dizziness hit her like a hammer and everything vanished.

CHAPTER 12

She woke in a small space filled with people. Immediately she recognized it, from months and months ago: the shuttle. She was strapped securely into a seat. The other eighteen kids woke at the same time. Pam and Pete, calm again, stood in the open doorway of the shuttle, behind them a huge empty room.

"You can't speak yet," Pam said wearily, "so don't try. It's only temporary. By the time you get back on Earth the speech inhibitor will have worn off. Yes, you're going home. We've done as much work with your kind as we can. If there had been as many of you as there were supposed to be, or if you could understand more—"

Pete interrupted. It came to Lillie, even through her dazed incomprehension, that Pete sounded apologetic. "It was our first assignment," he said.

"Just do the best you can, especially you girls. Lillie, Emily . . . well, we tried," Pam said, still wearily. "We'll be back." She and Pete stepped outside the shuttle and the door closed.

The shuttle moved. Acceleration pushed Lillie against the back of her seat. She closed her eyes, her mind whirling.

The ride seemed very short. Lillie made a few attempts to speak, but they didn't work. She saw the others do the same. By the time the shuttle came gently to rest, she could talk again. The straps holding her automatically fell away, and the shuttle door opened.

A blast of hot air blew in.

"Where are we?" Rebecca said, to no one. Sophie whimpered. Lillie felt someone grab her hand: Julie. Julie held on tight.

"I'll check it out," said Jon, their natural leader. He rose and walked cautiously to the open door. "Well, it *looks* like Earth. I just don't know where."

There was a general stampede outside.

The sun was just rising. They stood in a red glow on a deserted plain, with the hazy outlines of mountains in the distance. A highway ran beside the shuttle, two lanes, straight and utterly empty. A tumbleweed blew by. The rest of the plants that Lillie could see were low and dry and thorny, colored faded greens and browns.

"Looks like a high desert," Alex said, and Lillie turned to him in surprise.

"Alex! Are you all right? Your stomach—"

"Yeah." He felt his midriff, looking puzzled. "I'm fine now."

"How long were we unconscious?" Emily demanded. No one answered. It could have been days, Lillie realized. It had been days for her, before. Pam and Pete had fixed up Alex.

There was nothing they could do for Elizabeth.

"Stand well away from the shuttle," the shuttle suddenly said. Lillie jumped; Julie cried out. "Stand well away from the shuttle. You will be in danger otherwise. Move now. Stand well away from the shuttle—"

"Move!" Jon said.

They all followed him, running down the road. Lillie looked behind her. The shuttle suddenly collapsed. One minute it was there, the next it was not.

Everyone stopped, uncertain. Jon said tentatively, "Well, I guess this is far enough . . . Rafe, don't go back! It said not to!"

Rafe hesitated, stopped.

"Now what?" Bonnie said.

"I don't feel well," Sophie said. She turned away and threw up beside the highway.

"Hey, Sophie, hold it together," Bonnie said softly. "It'll be all right."

"I'm not afraid, you moron," Sophie snapped. "I just threw up, is all."

Sajelle was staring at Sophie strangely.

"Something's coming!" Jason said.

The nineteen kids moved closer together. Should they run, hide, wait? Nobody knew. They did nothing.

The thing Jason had spotted grew larger, resolved itself into a bus barreling down the highway. A small blue bus. Jon stepped into the road and raised his arm to flag it down. He didn't have to. The bus skidded to a stop, and Lillie saw that it was old and patched, the metal almost rusted through in places. The door opened and a man and a woman climbed out.

Jon said bravely, "Can you help us? We were . . . were camping, and we're lost and we need—" He stopped dead, staring at the man.

Lillie peered at him. The man didn't look familiar. But the woman did. She gazed unbelievingly at Lillie. A short, dark woman with a sun-wrinkled face and chopped-off black-gray hair. Old, maybe even in her fifties.

Jon said, choking on the word, "*Scott?*"

"It's me," the man said. He sounded dazed, too.

The woman stepped forward. "You don't recognize me, Lillie," she said.

Lillie shook her head.

"It's Theresa Romero."

Lillie stared. A black swooping wave passed over her mind, receded. Theresa? "But . . . but . . ."

"We didn't expect you to be this age, either," the man got out. "I'm Scott Wilkins, people. Don't you remember me from Andrews Air Force Base?"

It was Jason who got the words out, "But . . . you're old!"

"And you're not," Scott said. Lillie remembered him as a runty, brash kid always running to keep up with the bigger boys. Now he was tall, a little fat, old.

Rafe blurted, "What year is this?"

Theresa answered, her eyes still on Lillie. "It's July 8, 2053."

Again Lillie felt the black faintness brush her, and again she succeeded in pushing it away. 2053. Forty years since she'd left Quantico . . . not possible . . .

"Time dilation," Rafe said. "Oh, wow!"

Julie whimpered. Sam advanced, fists clenched. "If this is some fucking joke—"

"Still the same old Sam," said the man claiming to be Scott Wilkins. "It's not a joke, Sam. You people have been gone forty years. Everyone assumed you were dead, or at least weren't coming back. And Rafe is right, or at least I think he must be right. Your . . . the pribir must have accelerated into space and then come back, going so fast that time aboard the ship is different. Forty years passed for us, and . . . whatever time for you."

Jon said, "Seven and a half months."

"That we were awake for," Rafe said. "We don't know how long we were out. But how . . . you . . ."

"They contacted us," Theresa said. "The old way. They *smelled* to us, three days ago. Come to this place at this time, pick up the travelers." She shook her head, as if to clear it. "But they didn't bother to tell us about 'time dilation,' the bastards. Or to tell you, it looks like."

"No," Lillie got out. She couldn't stop staring. Theresa? Theresa fifty-four years old, her voice raspy, her face sagging. *Old* . . . "Theresa? My Uncle Keith! Is he . . ." She couldn't say it.

Theresa said, "I e-mailed him while Scott was getting the bus going, if you don't think that was a bitch . . . Yes, he's alive. Eighty-seven, but still breathing. He's in a nursing home in Amarillo."

"My mom and dad?" Madison demanded, and then everyone was shouting names except Julie, crying hopelessly, and Sam, frozen with fists clenched and no one to hit. Theresa held up her hand.

"No use asking, I didn't check on anybody else's family. I only know about Lillie's uncle because we've kept in touch, Lillie and I were friends—" She stopped.

Friends. Girl buddies. But Lillie was fourteen and Theresa was fifty-four. Suddenly Lillie couldn't take any more. She felt her stomach rising, and, like Sophie, she barely turned away before throwing up beside the road.

When she had finished, Scott Wilkins stood beside her, laying a hand on her stomach. Indignantly she pushed him away.

"It's all right, Lillie, I'm a doctor."

A doctor? Runty, tag-along Scott?

He felt her belly, then squatted to lay his head against it. Lillie saw Sajelle watching her with the same strange look Sajelle had given Sophie.

Scott straightened, pulled Sajelle toward him, felt her belly. She submitted, very unlike Sajelle, without protest. Why? Did they all have some awful worm or virus in their stomachs? Were they seriously sick?

Scott said somberly, "The time dilation wasn't the only thing the pribir didn't tell you. Lillie and Sajelle are pregnant. I'll have to examine the rest of you girls, but my hunch is that you all are."

Madison blurted, "Oh, no. We had birth control." Then she blushed crimson.

Scott—Dr. Wilkins—said gently, "I don't think any birth control you were given was meant to work."

"You!" Madison cried, glaring at Jon. Lillie's head swam. Mike? Jason? Oh, God, how could she even know which—

"Madison, don't blame Jon," Dr. Wilkins said. "I don't think your baby, if you're carrying one, is his. Or not completely. The pribir are master geneticists, you know. And they used all of us for whatever their purpose really is. Your baby was probably very carefully engineered *in vitro* and implanted in you."

"We bring the right way. That's our purpose. It permeates everything we do, and it gives our lives meaning . . . You're our first assignment."

"I want an abortion!" Madison cried, and Dr. Wilkins's face showed something like pain. "We'll talk about it, Madison. Things are different now."

"Different how?" Madison demanded, but he didn't answer.

Pregnant. She, Lillie. Carrying a baby inside her. A genetically engineered baby—

She cried, not knowing what words would come out, "The pribir said they'd be back!"

No one answered her. Silence fell. Even Julie, stunned, had stopped crying. The only sound was the wind, rising violently with the sun, hurling tumbleweeds across the dry ground.

PART III: THERESA

"The dictates of the heart are the voice of fate."
—Johan Schiller, *The Death of Wallenstein*

CHAPTER 13

In the old days, Theresa thought, they'd have brought in crisis counselors, child psychologists, what all. But these weren't the old days. They had only themselves.

"Where will I go?" Lillie had asked, after the initial crying and shouting had subsided a bit. The infernal wind had begun the way it did every morning, hot and violent, and Scott had herded everyone into the shelter of the bus, which was already heating up like the furnace it was.

Theresa and Scott looked at each other. Scott said, "Lillie, all of you, it's been a long time. Things are . . . different. Nobody knows you're back, and probably only your families will care. And they—"

Sajelle said, "We back from an alien spaceship, pregnant, and *nobody* going to *care?*"

"I'm afraid not," Scott said. "Since you left . . ." He trailed off and Theresa saw that he didn't know where to begin describing the world they had returned to. How did you compress forty violent years into a few sentences for fourteen-year-olds?

Madison clung to the main point. "Our families . . . how can we get to them? Will you take us?"

Sam said, without a trace of the obnoxious bluster Theresa remembered, "If our families are still alive."

The point was truer than he knew. Nearly a third of the United States population had died in the war ten years ago. Theresa had heard that in Africa, the rate was eighty percent. She didn't know if the figure was correct or if it was, like so much else, inflated rumor. Anything on the Net was suspect, even the news sites, and there was no other source of information any more.

She said to Madison, "To get you to your families, we'll have to find them first. A lot of people have been dislocated. Scott, it's dangerous to stay here, they're predicting another storm. I'm going to drive back to the farm." *And leave you to explain.* He gave her a look that would wither a cactus.

Theresa slipped behind the wheel. They were going to be lucky to have Scott: a doctor, a good man. He had shown up at the farm last night, the only one to respond to the pribir's message. Well, maybe the others, now scattered God knew where, had never smelled it. Theresa had happened to live close to the landing area. What would have happened to these children if she and Scott hadn't come? They would have died out here, that's what.

These children. Who had been part of her own childhood, long ago in a different world.

The bus was noisy. Modified to run on methanol, it was anachronistic, inefficient, falling apart, and highly illegal. But the fuel-cell-powered electric car, also falling apart, could not carry twenty-one people. The bus's tires were so patched it was a miracle they held together. God knew how much unlawful emission they were putting out this very minute.

Theresa couldn't hear Scott over the engine noise. What was he saying? How could he possibly explain?

Global warming took off, Scott could tell them, *and accelerated in a feedback loop, more than anyone ever imagined. We reached a tipping point, where even a tiny additional increase could throw the system into violent change. And it did.* He could tell them that, but how could they understand what it had meant?

The Earth's temperature had risen fifteen degrees Fahrenheit in forty years. Peat bogs and Arctic permafrost had released their stored methane, trapping yet more heat in the atmosphere. Polar caps melted, coastal areas flooded, farmland became dustbowls, deserts became farmland. Entire island archipelagos disappeared under water. The weather became the enemy: crazy storms, wildfires covering half a state. Tropical diseases spread as fast as famine. People migrated, people died, people dug into places that were still livable and shot refugees who tried to move in. Governments collapsed. Technology slid backward, except among the rich in defended enclaves that have somehow kept the Net going through aging satellites. Conservative backlashes developed, and weird religions, and a dozen other means for people to make sense of the senseless. And then, in rational response to all of this, we had a biowar with China and nobody won.

Somewhere behind her, one of the kids cried out.

Where were they all going to go? Trains still ran, sometimes, if no eco-groups sabotaged. The Net might be able to track down these kids' relatives, or it might not. The farm couldn't feed nineteen more people, twelve of them probably pregnant.

Behind her, the bus had fallen deadly quiet.

Two hours later, Theresa stopped the bus, which had—miracle, miracle!—held together, in the space between the barn and the farm wellhouse. Her practiced eye ran over the farm; everything looked all right. Her three sons were out with the cattle, following them around on summer forage to check that their GPS collars still worked, and to make sure nobody stole a cow. Her daughter Senni had shifted the garden-guards against the hot wind. The huge rain cisterns were still half full; the windmills whirred frantically. Behind the chicken coop, their current and temporary farmhand, Ramon, was slaughtering a chicken.

Senni came out of the house onto the porch, expressionless, as the kids got off the bus. The hot wind whipped Senni's short hair into a dirty froth. Hurriedly, squinting, the pribir children covered the distance from the bus to the doorway.

"The pribir children." How long since Theresa had said that phrase? Or even thought it?

Inside, they looked around at the large adobe-walled great room, as wind-tight as Theresa could make it, lit at this hour only by light from the small windows. Some of the kids looked bewildered, some angry, a few in shock. Well, Theresa couldn't blame them.

"Sit on the floor," she said gently. "We don't have enough chairs. This is my daughter Senni and my granddaughter Dolly, who's almost two."

Lillie's face turned slowly toward the baby.

"I guess the next thing is food," Theresa continued. "Are you hungry? Senni, did you make that soup?"

"Yes," Senni said sullenly. They'd argued about it before Theresa left. Silently Senni ladled out steaming bowls. Lillie got up and passed a bowl to each kid. She'd always been sensible, Lillie had. Solid. A few children started eating, but most did not.

Scott said, "Where's your computer, Tess?"

Senni started. No one had called Theresa "Tess" for forty years.

"I'll get it," she told Scott, and fetched the ancient thing from the bedroom. Carlo kept it running, the only techie among her four children. She put the computer on the long wooden table.

"Good God," Scott said, "does it work?"

"Not for me," Theresa said. "You any good at tech, Scott?"

"I can manage. Voice control?"

"Only Three-A. You'd best use the keyboard except for simple stuff."

Scott sat on a chair and turned the computer on. Abruptly Rafe rose from the floor and stood beside Scott. That's right, Rafe had always been interested in machines. Theresa watched them, the sun-wrinkled middle-aged man (there was no other kind, now) and the young boy, who had been born in the same year.

Scott linked the computer to the wireless Net. Rafe said, "Basic information search. Rafael Domingo Fernando," and Scott looked up at him.

"Not your name, Rafe," he said gently. "You'll be listed as dead. Your parents' names."

Rafe said, "Angela Santos Fernando and Carlos Juan Fernando."

Scott entered the names. Theresa saw that he was trying to shield the screen from Rafe, who saw it anyway. Rafe said in a flat voice, "Both dead."

"Do you have any siblings?"

"An older brother. Maximilliano Fernando."

"Do you know his citizen I.D. number?"

"No."

"Birthday?"

"September 7, 1996."

"Okay. This is him . . . he's living in Durham, North Carolina. There's an e-mail address listed. Do you want to mail him?"

And say what? Theresa thought. Here I am, back from the dead, a fourteen-year-old kid?

Rafe said, his voice finally unsteady, "In . . . in a minute. Do someone else first."

Theresa couldn't stand it. All right, she was a coward, she couldn't watch. She picked up Dolly. "Her diaper's dirty. I better change it." She carried the baby into the bedroom.

Senni followed her. "Mom, what the hell are you doing? Where are these kids supposed to go?"

Theresa turned on her daughter, glad to have someone to yell at. "I don't know! But I couldn't just leave them out there! These are—were—my friends! Lillie . . ." But there was no way to explain to Senni what she and Lillie had once been to each other, in those extraordinary circumstances that could never come again. "Senni, whatever the others do, Lillie at least is staying here. I know she hasn't got anywhere else to go."

Senni flounced out of the room. She, too, was pregnant, with her dead husband's last legacy. Theresa sighed.

She lingered over Dolly, playing with her, rocking her to sleep, fussing with the blanket in the crib that Senni had made out of a dresser drawer.

When Theresa went back into the room, three girls were crying. Two boys yelled at Scott, who was showing superhuman patience. Sophie, whom Theresa had never liked, strode up to her and demanded, "Can you take me to the train today? Train to New York?"

"No, not today," Theresa answered. She understood, as she had not forty years ago, that Sophie's belligerence sprang from insecurity and youth. But Sophie didn't understand that winds and storms made day travel on the plains risky; that a train all the way to New York was equally risky; that Theresa didn't have the money for tickets for everybody; what New York would be like even if Sophie could get there.

"You won't help me?" Sophie demanded. "You always were a bitch!" And then Lillie was there, taking Sophie's arm, soothing her, and Sophie unexpectedly turned and buried her face in Lillie's shoulder.

Theresa met Lillie's eyes. Lillie smiled sadly.

"You must be scared, too," Theresa said, out of the old, never-admitted antagonism that her friend could cope better, adapt quicker, control herself more.

"I am," Lillie said, so softly that Theresa wasn't sure of the words. But, then, she didn't have to be. She understood, and her momentary resentment evaporated, never to return. Lillie was a child, still. And she, Theresa, was not.

The moon shone high and clear as Theresa drove the horse cart to town. They had a few more hours before dawn, before the winds began. Night on the high plains was still cool, even in July. Theresa and Lillie sat wrapped in blankets.

"Is the horse old?" Lillie asked.

"No," Theresa said, "just malnourished. Like most everything else, except you."

Immediately she regretted her words. She'd intended them to be jocular, but they hadn't come out that way. It wasn't Lillie's fault she was healthy when nothing else seemed to be. God, think how much worse it would be if sick kids had been dumped on the farm! By way of apology, she said to Lillie, "Are you feeling all right?"

"Yes," the girl said. "Why are we taking a horse, Tess, instead of the bus or that little car?"

"The bus is illegal. Greenhouse emissions. The car is all right, it uses fuel cells to make electricity and gives off only water, but the car is old and I want to save it as much as I can."

Lillie was quiet. So much of this must be strange to her. Tess said, "We have pre-war solar panels on the roof, too, you probably noticed them. They're getting old as well. They mostly fuel the water pumps, while the wind power—" But Lillie wasn't listening.

"Tess, this is your parents' land in the New Mexico desert, isn't it? We were going to come here once to hike."

"We were?" Theresa said.

"Don't you remember? We said that after we left Andrews Air Force Base to go home, we'd come here with your parents for a vacation. Together we asked Uncle Keith to let me go."

Theresa didn't remember. It was forty years ago. But not to Lillie.

The land had changed as much as she had, Theresa thought. She could recall it as she'd seen it at thirteen: a forsaken tract in the Chihuahuan shrub desert, bare of everything but mesquite, creosote, and yucca. Dry playas and arroyos. Nothing moving until you looked close enough to see the scorpions, lizards, and diamondbacks.

But all over the Earth, warming had brought climate shifts. Georgia now looked like Guatemala, Alberta like Iowa, Iowa like the edges of the Sahara. None of the computer models to predict warming consequences had been accurate, except to say that everything would get warmer. New Mexico was supposed to get a temperature increase of three degrees in spring, four degrees in winter and summer, with increased spring precipitation, decreased summer soil moisture, and spreading deserts.

It hadn't worked out that way.

Her parents' remote, worthless land bloomed. Its average annual rainfall had been fourteen inches in 2000, ninety percent of it between July and October, with an annual average evaporation rate of forty inches. But temperatures rose, wind patterns shifted violently, and El Nino events proliferated in the all-important Pacific, thousands of miles away. The beautiful clear desert air contained few pollutant particles to block sunlight and provide countering cooling, and so the temperature rose even more. Runaway greenhouses gases let plants use water in the soil ever more efficiently. Year by year, the average rainfall increased and the average evaporation decreased, until the numbers passed each other going in opposite directions.

The mesquite and yucca gave way to blue grama grasses and

yellow columbines. The desert had always had the odd cottonwood or cedar growing along its intermittent waterways, but now these dusty trees were joined by young groves of oak, juniper, and pinion. The arroyos and playas, most of them anyway, stayed wet year-round, and in some years of heavy winter runoff the ranch even developed a temporary through-flowing river, running south down the tilted face of New Mexico toward the border. This past May, Theresa had found a wild rose bush, unheard of here, its delicate pink flowers perfuming the warm air. Antelope moved in from the faraway hills, and bobcats and wild Angora goats.

Carlo and Rosalita Romero were dead by then. Theresa and Cole brought their young family from the East twenty years ago, when times were dangerous and the desert still not arable. It had been safer than the East because it was more remote. Over time, they bought cattle, built outbuildings, expanded the house, planted peanuts and corn and beans and potatoes, some of it even without irrigation. The growing season now extended from April to November. When the biowar ten years ago reduced the Earth's population to less than two billion, about what it had been in 1900, Tess's farm had not been reached by any of the blowing, deadly, bioengineered microorganisms.

Patches of desert remained; there was a wide swatch of empty scrub to the south of the ranch. And there were still the flash floods, the terrifying thunderstorms, the wildfires and the infernal daily wind, rising at dawn and dying at dusk like some diurnal atmospheric tantrum. But Theresa knew she had been one of the lucky ones in the unpredictable climate sweepstakes. Their high-tech machinery was breaking down year by year and the world was not manufacturing much by way of replacements, but the farm was making do and increasing its productivity. The United States slowly recovered from the war, putting together some sort of replacement civilization. Nuclear energy, once anathema, powered cities. Theresa Romero and her family were part of that effort. Survivors. Contributors.

None of this would have meant anything at all to Lillie, of course. That young grove of oak over there, strong straight saplings silvery in the moonlight, was not a symbol of anything to her. No reason why it should be. She didn't know that the fields of wildflowers, vervain and blue gila and sweet alyssium, were, in this place, a miracle.

Still, hard times were difficult to relinquish. They were all so accustomed, she and Senni and her sons, to scrimping and saving and going without! The little edge they'd achieved for themselves, the food stored on the ranch and the credit stored in the rebuilt on-line banks, could so easily vanish again. That was why Senni hadn't wanted Theresa to make this trip. A waste of resources, of time, of precious money, Senni said, her mouth drawn in a tight hard line. Her brothers would be back anytime with the cattle; Mother should be here when they arrived. Jody and Spring and Carlo had a right in this decision to feed so many extra mouths.

The remaining pribir kids, too, had looked sullenly at Lillie, the only one given free train tickets. The days immediately following the kids' arrival had been hard on everyone (there was an understatement!) Things had sorted themselves out, but not without tears and anger and threats.

Eleven kids contacted relatives on the Net. Only one, Amy, had a parent still alive, but the other nine found brothers or sisters. Susan, Amy, Rebecca, and Jon had train tickets booked for them, and Hannah had an actual airline ticket, worth more than the entire farm income for a year. Scott had driven them in the bus to the train station at Wenton, and they had disappeared into the vast disorganized mess that was the United States transport system. Theresa hoped they would each reach his or her destination, that they would stay in touch as long as the farm computer held out, and that she would never see any of them again.

The other six—Julie, Bonnie, Sophie, Jason, Mike, and Derek —had located siblings that could not afford to send for them. Theresa had already explained that there was not enough money to buy them train tickets. She had found them all jobs, the boys as laborers and the pregnant girls as clerks in town. They would work a few months in return for room, board, and a train ticket "home." They, too, had gone on the bus to Wenton.

That left eight kids with nowhere to go: Madison, Sajelle, Jessica, Emily, Alex, Rafe (whose older brother had recently died), and Sam. And Lillie.

The boys weren't really a problem; they could bring more land under cultivation, free Theresa's sons for more skilled work. Strong young backs would earn their own keep, and then some. It was the five pregnant girls that Theresa and Senni had argued about. "Five now, and how many later?" Senni demanded. Her lusterless hair straggled around her thin face. "Scott Wilkins says each of those girls is carrying triplets!"

"What do you want me to do, Senni? Abandon them on the range to die?"

"Find them jobs in Wenton, like the others!"

"It was tough enough finding town jobs for the other three girls. I had to call in every favor we owe."

"On *their* behalf. Strangers."

"Not to me."

"What do you think the boys are going to say when they find five pregnant teenagers here? Eating our food and whelping God-knows-what . . . what do you think the people in Wenton are going to say?"

Theresa went silent. Bonnie, Julie, and Sophie would all have left Wenton before their pregnancies began to show. That was part of the bargain that Theresa, hating herself for having to negotiate with bewildered and frightened children, had insisted on. Wenton, like most small towns now, was pretty conservative. It was a survival trait. People supported each other, helped each other, protected each other. The other side of that was conformity, provincialism, distrust of anything strange. Nothing could be stranger than Madison, Sajelle, Jessica, Emily, and Lillie. Unless it was their fetuses.

"Senni," Theresa said, and merely saying her daughter's name brought welling up all the love and frustration Theresa felt for this most difficult of her four living children. All her life, Senni had hurled herself against circumstances. Almost always, she'd lost. Theresa's heart ached for her.

"Senni, I know what people in Wenton are going to say. Even if Madison and Jessie . . . you know. But I can't help it. Don't you see . . . there's nothing I can do. All my choices are bad. I can't send them someplace else because there is no other place for them. I can't throw them out to die. I can't do anything but keep them and try to muddle on. All of us, getting through."

"And I don't have a vote."

It always came down to this, with Senni. "No," Theresa said wearily, "you don't. I still run this farm, which means I still make the decisions. Not you, not the boys. That's the way it is."

"Fine," Senni said, with the triumphant coldness of having forced her mother into the role of bully. Which of course left Senni as the innocent victim. "You get your way, Mother. They stay."

Theresa let Senni have the last word. God, she was grateful that her sons all had more easy-going temperaments. They might not like having the kids here, especially Carlo, given to fits of religion. But they wouldn't fight her.

That left only the fight with Madison and Jessica, which also took place in the barn. The old horse dozed in his stall, and the half-feral cat, Pablum (never was a cat more inappropriately named) toyed with a maimed rat in the corner. Theresa hoped that Madison, fastidious, didn't notice the rat.

Madison said, "Tess, I mean it. I want an abortion."

"Me, too," said Jessica.

"I told you, it's not that simple," Theresa said patiently. "One more time . . . *this is not the world you left*. Abortion is illegal again. Too many Christians decided that all our troubles were caused by Godless practices, starting with Roe v. Wade."

"With who?" Jessica said.

Madison said, "You also told us that laws don't count for much any more, because there's nobody to enforce them."

True enough. Theresa, Senni, and the boys had learned to defend what was theirs. All of them could shoot. Ammunition was a high priority on her yearly budget. And as arable land shifted in their favor, there could only be more "refugees" to defend against.

She heard Senni's voice jeering in her head: "*So why shoot them and not this lot? Same thing*."

"Yes, Madison, there's nobody to enforce laws. Mostly. But there's also nobody to perform abortions. You already argued with Scott, and he absolutely refuses."

"He's too interested in the monsters we're supposed to give birth to," Jessica sneered. "Wants to take apart their genes. No way. Not me. Let Emily and Sajelle and Lillie be his own private genetic experiments. Shit, Sajelle probably will love having his wrinkled old hands on her."

Madison ignored Jessica. "I don't believe there's no place in Wenton or Amarillo to get an abortion! I just don't believe it! My mother told me that abortions were illegal when *her* mother was a girl and people got them anyway!"

When Madison's grandmother was a girl. A hundred and ten years ago.

Jessica said, "If you don't help us, Theresa, I'll do it to myself."

"You'd kill yourself."

"Maybe." Jessica smirked. The girl knew there was no way Theresa would let her do it to herself, or to Madison.

"*I wish you weren't so damn maternal!*" Cole had once yelled at Theresa when they'd been fighting about how little time she gave him since Jody and Carlo were born. It hadn't been a happy marriage.

"Please, Tess," Madison whispered, her eyes filling with tears. "I can't go through with this birth. I just can't."

And Theresa had given in, out of God-knew-what twisted reasons. Pity. Friendship. Jealousy. Practicality. Fear. So now she sat on the hard bench of the primitive cart Spring had made, behind a wheezing horse, going to the train at Wenton and then on to Amarillo to find Lillie an uncle and Madison an abortionist.

"Why is the town called 'Wenton'?" Lillie asked. The sun was rising, gold and pink, above the endless plains.

"Because we just 'went on'," Theresa said. "It's not a real town, just a stop on the railroad that was routed through here after the climate shifts made these parts of New Mexico and west Texas better for ranching and farming. The global warming—" She saw that Lillie again wasn't listening.

Just in time, Theresa stopped the cart. Lillie leaned over the side and threw up.

Only she and Emily had morning sickness. Lillie's was worse. Scott said it was normal (Theresa had never been sick during her pregnancies, except for Carlo) and might go away after the first trimester. The fetuses, as far as he could tell with the equipment with him, were all healthy and thriving. Jessica was right about one thing: Scott was intensely interested in the pribir children's children. It was the reason he stayed on. Not even Senni objected to that. Already townspeople had heard there was a doctor in the area. Three people had come for treatment, paying Scott (and the farm) in livestock or Net credit.

When Lillie had finished retching, she swiped her hand across her mouth. "Sorry, Tess."

"Don't apologize. You can't help it."

"No. Will I recognize him?"

"No. He's eighty-seven years old. But he'll recognize you," Theresa said. Lillie was only seven and a half months older than when Keith had seen her last.

"Tess, did you go on to college?"

Theresa remembered, now, how direct Lillie had always been, how intense about finding out all she could about everything she could. "Yes, I went to college."

"Where?"

"Saint Lucia's. A small Catholic college for girls." Her mother's choice.

"What did you study?"

"Elementary education. I didn't finish."

"Why not?" Lillie said.

"A lot of reasons. I wasn't very academic, you probably remember that. And then my father lost a lot of money. And I met my husband and got married."

"What was his name? What was he like?"

"Lillie, I'd rather not talk about that."

"Okay. I . . . pull over again, Tess!"

This bout of retching lasted longer. Probably the jouncing cart wasn't helping. Theresa waited, watching the light grow on the eastern horizon. It would be best to reach Wenton before dawn.

"Just one more question," Lillie said when they'd started forward again. "When you went back home after Quantico, and then to high school and college and everything, was it hard? Did people still stalk you and threaten you and point you out as a pribir kid?"

Theresa thought about how to answer. "At first, yes. My parents had me home-schooled for the rest of high school. I entered college under a different name, nobody but the admissions committee knew who I was. And later . . . well, the world had more important things to think about. We were pretty much forgotten." *Not even Cole knew, when I married him. And when I told him, it helped destroy our marriage.*

"But," Lillie said, "didn't doctors and geneticists and everybody want to keep examining your genome?"

"Lillie, you don't understand. I keep telling you, but you're not listening. *Everything changed.* Climate, government, economics. And then the war. Nobody funded scientific research. Nobody cared."

Lillie was silent for a long time. Then she said, "I don't believe that. Somewhere there are scientists still investigating genetics. In one of those rich enclaves, maybe. Scientists don't give up."

She was probably right. "Then you better hope they don't discover you kids are back. Or about your babies."

Wenton grew on the horizon, its one-story buildings lower than the oldest cottonwoods and level with the newer oak and juniper.

"Tess," Lillie said in a different voice, "will it hurt? The birth?"

Tess glanced at the girl. God, so young. She said gently, "Yes, it will hurt. I won't lie to you. But when you hold your baby in your arms, it's all worth it. The day Jody was born was the happiest day of my life."

"I don't feel that way."

"Not yet," Tess said. "Wait."

Lillie didn't answer. The wind was definitely picking up, but they'd reached Wenton. Theresa saw it suddenly through Lillie's eyes, a weird mixture of time periods. Buildings with traditionally thick walls to keep out the murderous heat, but made of foamcast and topped with microwave rods like tall slender poles. No street paving, almost no vehicles, but a VR bar with garish holo-ads projecting onto the boards that acted as a sidewalk. No school (kids learned off the Net, if at all), no supermarket, no drugstore, no drycleaners—what else had existed in the past which Lillie remembered? No books or music stores or movie theaters, all that came on the Net if it came at all. And the train tracks winding away across the mixed mesquite and new green. No, she couldn't imagine what Lillie thought of Wenton.

They stabled the horse in the foamcast building run by old Tom Carter to protect anything from dust and storms, for a reasonable fee. The windowless building smelled of animals, and Theresa saw Lillie gulp hard and leave quickly. Theresa remembered. With Carlo, nearly anything made her throw up.

She put her arm around Lillie against the wind. Bent almost double, they reached the train station and gratefully ducked inside. Open at both ends for the train to pull through, the building was hot but at least sheltered.

"Does the train run on diesel?" Lillie asked. "I thought all that was illegal now because of emissions."

"Yes, but an exception was made for trains, in order to get food to cities. Also, there's some form of superconductivity involved, I don't understand what but it was one of the last things built before the war. Partly built. We're lucky to have it."

Or maybe not. Theresa watched as people—too many people, too badly dressed, carrying too many bundles—got off the train. Refugees. Had to be. Well, if they were willing to work, there was work digging more irrigation systems and wells, bringing more land under cultivation, channeling the new-found water. However, not all refugees could or would do manual labor. Those were the dangerous ones.

So far, the farm had been lucky. This southeast corner of New Mexico was still very remote and the world population as a whole was much less than it had once been. Wenton, despite its growing prosperity, had received few visitors. Neither had the farm, miles out on the once-desert.

But nothing stayed hidden forever.

CHAPTER 14

Lillie fell asleep on the train. At Amarillo, Theresa woke her and they set out on foot through the city. It was quite a walk but bicycle cabs were exorbitant and anyway Lillie, except for morning sickness, seemed to be in superb physical shape. What had the pribir done to her?

Better not to know.

At the nursing home, Lillie pressed her lips tight together. Theresa's heart went out to her. Such an adult gesture for a child.

Keith Anderson had dealt shrewdly with his money. Unlike most very old people, who were cared for by often grudging families or not at all, he had been able to buy life-long care in this decent, if shabby, for-profit home. Theresa had been here once before. She led Lillie to the tiny third-floor room where Keith lay in bed. At the threshold she paused, wanting to say something to prepare Lillie . . . stupid. Nothing would prepare her.

"Lillie!" The thin voice cracked and the easy tears of the old slid down Keith's wrinkled cheeks. Lillie stopped dead, collected herself, moved forward. Theresa thought, *She was always brave.*

"Hello, Uncle Keith. I'm back."

"Lillie . . ."

She sat on the edge of his bed. Theresa saw him wince slightly, his bones disturbed. Lillie, unused to the old, didn't notice. She took his hand. "Are you all right, Uncle Keith? Is this a good place for you to live?"

"Yes. Oh, Lillie, it's so good to see you. I thought . . ."

"You thought I was dead. But I've just been aboard the pribir ship for seven and a half months. I mean, forty years. Do you know about time dilation?"

"Yes. Oh, Lillie . . . you look so much like your mother."

Once, at Andrews Air Force Base, Theresa had seen a picture of Lillie's dead mother. Lillie looked nothing like her.

"Once," Keith quavered, "when we were young . . . Barbara was only four or five . . ."

Theresa slipped out. Keith wanted to live in the past. A past where he was young and fresh, maybe a later past where Lillie was a little girl. Theresa went down the steps to the living room. Several old people in deep chairs sat expressionlessly watching something on the Net. A stale smell hung in the air. Outside, the wind howled around the edges of Amarillo's shabby buildings.

"Is there a terminal I can use?" Theresa asked a woman who might have been a nurse, or a cleaning lady, or a murderer. Government regulatory agencies had all but disappeared. Ordinarily Theresa never thought about this; it was a given. But now she was seeing things through Lillie's eyes.

The terminal was even older than the one at the farm, and slower. Theresa had few contacts on the local Net site, and none in the UnderNet, that shadowy information reached only through secret data atolls that changed constantly. But Scott had told her what to do, although he wouldn't do it from the farm computer. "Too dangerous," he'd said, without explaining.

"There's no one to enforce laws," Theresa had told Madison, but that wasn't strictly true. There were organizations as shadowy as the UnderNet, vigilantes and religious groups and supremacist groups and anti-science groups and God-knew-what-all. The religious groups were the least vicious but the most pervasive. A vindictive God was apparently a great comfort to some when the planet itself seemed to turn vindictive. Theresa didn't understand the reasoning, but it was widespread enough to earn respectful caution.

Nonetheless, she found an abortionist in Amarillo, messaged with her, and set up an appointment for Madison and Jessie. More credit spent, plus three more train tickets. Although only Theresa's would be round-trip. Still, facing Senni would be no fun.

Theresa walked back to the living room. None of the old people had changed position or expression. She took a chair and pulled out the sewing she'd brought. They couldn't start back until sunset, when the wind would die down. Trips away from the farm were usually measured in day-long units.

Maybe Lillie would want to stay here with Keith. Work for room and board, one less mouth to feed at the farm . . . until the triplets were born. If Keith lasted that long.

She started sewing a maternity dress for Emily.

"I asked to stay there," Lillie said on the way home. The sky had clouded over, and Theresa was pushing the horse to make the farm before all light faded. She had a halogen torch but hoped to save it. They had spent a few hours in Wenton, checking on the kids working there to earn tickets home: Bonnie, Sophie, Julie, Jason, Derek, Mike. Julie had cried when Lillie and Theresa left.

Theresa said, "Why didn't you stay in Amarillo, then?"

"Uncle Keith said no."

"Did he say why?"

"He wants me with you and Scott. He said he can't help me if anything goes even a little bit wrong, and you can."

"That's sensible."

"I won't see him again, I don't think," Lillie said. "He's close to dying."

Theresa didn't deny it. "You can keep in touch on the Net."

"It isn't the same."

Of course not. Nothing was the same. The horse plodded through the pearly, inadequate light.

"Tess," Lillie said after a long while, "I don't want to be a mother."

Not Lillie, too. "Are you saying you want an abortion?"

"No. I talked it over with Uncle Keith and . . . no. He said I don't understand now how precious the continuing of life is, but I will someday."

Theresa thought of Jody, Carlo, Spring, and her dead daughter. Of Senni and Dolly and the child Senni carried. *Yes*.

"Maybe he's right," Lillie said, with her odd mix of measured judiciousness and child's complaint, "but I don't want to be a mother anyway. I'm not interested in babies. And I don't think . . . I don't think I can love them like Uncle Keith loved me."

Theresa suddenly saw that this was true. Lillie was too detached, or too young, or too something. She was many good qualities, but not tender.

"We'll all help you," Theresa said, inwardly groaning. More work.

"Thank you. And I'll do the best I can. For Uncle Keith."

The light was gone. Theresa switched on the torch. A sudden breeze brought a faint, pungent odor, and she gave a cry of pleasure. Cattle. Her sons were home!

Her heart lifted, and the night seemed much brighter.

* * *

The abortionist operated in a clean, windowless basement divided by curtains into "rooms." Theresa brought Jessica, defiant, and Madison, scared, on the Wednesday train. "If you would help, we wouldn't have to do this," she told Scott accusingly before they left.

He didn't meet her eyes. "I can't. I know you don't understand, Theresa."

"Fucking right I don't. This woman isn't even an M.D. And you of all people should know that a bunch of genes aren't sacred!"

Scott lost his temper. "It's because I know how temporary a 'bunch of genes,' as you disparagingly call it, can be that I believe what I do! Those are people those girls are carrying, damn it, no matter what you say! If those engineered babies aren't people, then neither are you or me!"

"Shut up, they'll hear you in there. So what are you going to do, Scott, alert a vigilante religious group? Abortions in progress! Murder the killers so they can't murder a bunch of non-breathing tissue!"

Scott turned away. "Let me be, Theresa. You know damn well I won't say anything to anybody. But let me have my beliefs. You have yours."

"Mine don't make two frightened girls spread their legs for an unlicensed stranger."

"Let me be!"

"Okay, Scott," Theresa said wearily. "I'll let you be. I need you. The other girls need you. Just so long as you know that you're clinging to a selfish, irrational, superstitious belief for your own comfort, no matter who else suffers."

Scott strode away, toward the open range. Almost sunrise—he shouldn't go too far. Fuck it. Let him get lost and roast in the sun that was as unrelenting as he was.

In Amarillo, Theresa waited upstairs with Madison while the abortionist took Jessica downstairs. Jessica, her bravado stretched thin, scowled and tossed her head. Madison sat completely still, saying nothing, eyes wide and frozen.

"Maddy," Theresa said, the old name rising, unbidden, from some well of memory, "it won't hurt. She has good equipment and reasonable pharms." Which was why it cost so much.

Madison didn't answer.

Half an hour later they were called down. Jessica lay on a mattress on the floor, covered with a light blanket. She was smiling. "I'm all right."

"Yes," Theresa said, wondering what she was feeling. She had borne five children, all joyously. Even Spring, born in such a hard time that the season he was named for had been the only good thing happening anywhere around Theresa.

"And I'm not pregnant," Jessie said, without ambivalence.

"It went very well," the woman said crisply. "She can travel in a few hours, I think. Do you want the tissue?"

"No!" Theresa said.

The woman shrugged. "Some people do. Now you, young lady. This way."

"Wait," Theresa said, "I do want it." She needed to look. She knew what a three-month fetus looked like; this was her only chance to see if what the girls carried was indeed normal, or if it was some sort of . . . what?

The woman pointed to another curtain and led Madison away.

Theresa made herself go through the curtain. A dark blue plastic box sat on a table, its cover beside it. She peered in, and her eyes filled with relieved tears. Normal.

She should take one of the fetuses for Scott, she realized belatedly. He would want the genes. No, he wouldn't, not this way . . . not Scott. Or would he? Which was stronger, the religious or the scientist?

Suddenly she knew that whatever Scott wanted, she couldn't carry this thing back with her on the train. She just couldn't. This clump of genetically engineered tissue, this dead baby.

She went back to sit by Jessica, who had fallen back asleep. Theresa studied the young face smoothed into blankness by sleep. Forty years ago she had been afraid of Jessica. Jessica the bully, quick with her fists, sarcastic about everything, dangerous and despicable. Forty years ago. Theresa reached out and smoothed a few stray hairs back from Jessica's forehead.

Time passed. Too much time—Madison was taking much longer than Jessie had. Theresa got up and made her way through the maze of curtains. At the end she found an actual door, wood set into the foamcast wall, and went through it.

"Use the calatal!" cried a woman Theresa hadn't seen before. She and the abortionist were applying various pieces of equipment to Madison, unconscious on a table. There was blood everywhere, way too much blood. The smell of it, metallic and hot, hung in the air.

"Get out!" the second woman yelled at Theresa. "You're not sterile!"

Theresa blundered back out the door. She stood there, not breathing, for what seemed like hours. When the door finally opened, Theresa already knew.

"Unexpected tearing," the abortionist said unsteadily. "It's never happened before, I couldn't stop it, I tried and tried . . . I'm so *sorry* . . ."

A sound behind her. Theresa turned to see Jessica leaning against the wall. "Madison's dead, isn't she?" Jessica said, and when no one answered, Jessica—the bully, the truculent—cried and cried, and would not be comforted.

The rest of the summer brought many good things. It didn't matter. Every night Theresa dreamed of Madison's face. Not even the birth of Senni's child in October made a difference to Theresa's mood, which made no sense. Senni was her daughter, the new child her granddaughter. Madison was only someone Theresa had known a long time ago, in another time and place.

Senni had an easy birth. The baby was healthy, perfect, strong despite being three weeks premature. Senni named her Clari, after nothing in particular.

Patients came to Scott from towns up to fifty miles away. It turned out he had bought a small ad on the Net. By the beginning of November he was going into Wenton three days a week to hold "office hours" at a tiny rented room. He bought a horse for this trip, helped by Jody, who also taught him to ride. Fortunately, Scott was a natural. There was a lot of work: the warming and increased rain had had brought malaria and dengue fever this far north. Simple diseases to treat, even to vaccinate against—if you had the knowledge and the drugs.

The delivery of drugs was only intermittently reliable. There was no Post Office anymore. Information went by the Net; packages went by the few struggling private companies that exploited the rail circuit. Scott ordered double amounts in staggered deliveries; some got through. Eventually.

He charged patients according to what he learned about them on the Net. Often the fee was paid in welcome foodstuffs or livestock. As his reputation spread, Scott began to get rich people from the enclave outside of Ruidoso. Except for buying drugs, Scott turned every credit he made over to Theresa for the farm.

The crops flourished in the summer heat and new rain, despite the punishing daily wind and violent storms. The harvest was rich. Theresa was now beyond subsistence farming, and ten years ago that had been a glittering goal. The warming had killed billions of people, one way or another: geographic dislocation, epidemic diseases, political collapse, random violence. The war had killed billions more. But Theresa was going to have her best year ever.

Winners and losers, she thought, and her mood did not improve.

At the beginning of October, Bonnie Carson and Julie Cunningham arrived back at the farm, brought by old Tom Carter from Wenton.

"Theresa, these girls would rather be with you," Tom said, his ancient, pale blue eyes giving away nothing.

"Come in, Tom," Theresa said. She stood in the cool dawn, already dressed, and bit off her questions until she was alone with the girls. You didn't burden outsiders with family troubles.

"Got to get back," Tom said.

Theresa glanced at the brightening sky. "You can't now. Not in that open cart."

"I'll spend the day at the Graham place," Tom said, not looking at her. The Grahams owned the next homestead; Tom could make it there before the punishing wind began. Theresa understood. Tom didn't want to be around whatever was going to happen next any more than Theresa did. She, however, didn't have a choice.

Julie helped Bonnie out of the back of the cart. Bonnie could hardly walk. She held her left arm cradled in her right. Her strong-planed face was covered with bruises, the lip split open. Jody, Theresa's oldest son, appeared at her side, casually armed. When Tom had left, Julie quavered, "She was in a fight. She—"

"I can see she was in a fight," Theresa snapped. "Bring her inside. Jody, go find Scott and tell him to bring his medical stuff. Julie, stop sniffling. Did Bonnie miscarry? Any show of blood?"

"I don't think so," Julie sniffed.

"I'm . . . okay," Bonnie muttered.

Her arm was broken. Scott sedated Bonnie and set the arm. Bonnie lay on Lillie's bed; God, they were going to have to jam two more beds in here somewhere. The farm house had only three small bedrooms. Theresa, Senni, and the two babies were in one; Rafe, Alex, Sam, and Scott in another; Lillie, Emily, and Sajelle in the third. Theresa's sons, having ceded their mattresses to pregnant girls, now slept in the barn with the migrant laborers who drifted through. And there were no more extra mattresses. Well, Rafe or Alex or Sam, any two, could give up theirs. Although five mattresses would never fit in this tiny space . . .

She was pondering housekeeping to avoid thinking about anything else.

Scott frowned. "Bonnie will be fine. In fact, the break is already healing much faster than it should, and her injuries are much lighter than they should be for the kind of beating she took. The pribir did something to her, Tess. Boosted her immune system somehow."

"Too bad they didn't give her more muscles so she could have kicked the hell out of those bastards."

Scott wasn't listening. Probably he was running over medical possibilities in his head. Theresa went into the great room.

Fifteen people and two babies awaited her. Infant Clari nursed at Senni's breast; little Dolly wandered around, whimpering for her breakfast. Sajelle got Dolly a piece of bread. Everybody else looked expectantly at Theresa.

"What?" she snapped. Irritation as cover for feeling burdened beyond bearing.

Jody spoke up. "Mom, we've been talking. Julie told us why that girl was beat up. She's . . . somebody thought she liked girls instead of boys." He said it with distaste, and Theresa sighed. Her children had grown up in a world they didn't choose, a frightened world backsliding into protective conservatism. Not what she would have chosen for them, but there it was.

"All right, listen up," she told everyone. "I don't care if Bonnie likes boys, girls, or roadrunners, and that means nobody here is going to care, either. She's one of us—"

Senni opened her mouth, closed it again, scowled.

"—because she was with me and the others at Andrews Air Force Base. I've told you about it, and that telling is all I need to do. I still run this place. Bonnie is a scared, pregnant kid, just like the others. She stays here. Julie, too. Now, is anybody going to fight me on this? Jody?"

"No." Promptly. Bless her oldest, he had always been her ally.

"Carlo?"

Hesitation. Carlo, she knew, dabbled in religion. Then, "No, Mom."

"Spring?"

"Not at all." Her sweet-tempered boy.

"Senni?"

Senni said coldly, "You haven't left much choice, have you? This hardly seems a time to bring in more dependents, with what happened on that farm near Hobbs. But naturally I'll go along with whatever you say."

"Good," Theresa said. They were all nervous about the other farm, forty miles away. Its owners had disappeared from the Net, and Wenton rumor was that refugees had attacked, killing the owners. There was no law enforcement to check up on the farm, and so far no one else had either, probably from fear. The same thing had happened eighty miles east, in Texas, and there the investigating neighbors had also disappeared.

Theresa said, "Now, about rooms—"

Spring interrupted her. "Mom, we need an extension on the house. Harvest is over. The herd is here for the winter—anyway, six more GPS collars broke and we can't just keep track of the herd remotely any more, so they have to be here. Work is slack enough right now that Alex, Rafe, Sam, and I can build it in a week." Alex and Rafe, both slight boys next to Theresa's hulking sons, looked startled. Sam scowled. "All right?"

"Yes," Theresa said, "good. Now let's get breakfast."

Five mothers-to-be, all carrying triplets. It was going to have be a hell of an extension.

For the first time since Madison's death, she felt better.

CHAPTER 15

Keith died two weeks later. Theresa, amazed that he had hung on this long, got the news on the Net. The computer had been moved into the new part of the building, which had four more tiny bedrooms and a smaller gathering room that Scott called grandly "the den."

She found Lillie on her knees, weeding the winter herb garden in the relatively calm air after sunset. The girl, seven and a half months along, looked up over the massive curve of her belly.

"Lillie, should you be doing that?"

"Sure. I'm fine."

"You look like a beach ball."

Lillie laughed. Theresa could say things like that to Lillie. None of her own kids had ever seen a beach. Lillie's morning sickness had ended after four months and, like the other five pregnant girls, she was healthy, strong, and active still.

"Lillie, I have something to tell you. It's going to be hard. Your Uncle Keith died this morning."

"I'm glad," Lillie said simply.

Theresa stared at her, then slowly nodded. Lillie was right. Keith had been lingering too long in weakness and pain. And how like Lillie not to cry or wail, but to accept. Julie would have needed emotional attention for days.

Lillie said, "Do I need to do anything? Go to Amarillo?"

"No." Funerals were simple now; you put the body in a sheet or box and buried it as soon as possible. Embalming, viewings, waterproof caskets, funeral directors . . . all gone. And by Theresa at least, not missed. "I made the arrangements on the Net."

Lillie nodded. Sweat stuck tendrils of brown hair to her forehead and nape. The armpits of her maternity smock, a basic tent, were stained dark. Even in November the days, if not the nights, were warm. "I'd like to be alone for a bit, Tess. To walk out a ways."

"Just don't go too far." Theresa would have Jody keep an eye on her.

Lillie hauled herself to her feet and waddled off, her bulky figure silhouetted against the fiery sky.

Theresa sighed and went to find Jody. Instead she found Spring and Julie, sitting in the seclusion of a drooping cottonwood tree. Julie's head was nestled on Spring's shoulder. He put his hand under her chin, lifted it, and kissed her.

Oh my dear Lord.

They hadn't seen her. Theresa crept silently away. She hadn't seen it coming. Not at all, not at all. Julie was heavily pregnant, and fourteen years old! Spring was twenty-four. And Julie, timid and weepy—why couldn't Spring at least have chosen Lillie instead?

Theresa sat on the ground behind the barn and laughed at herself. A mother, choosing among pregnant fourteen-year-olds for her son! And it was inevitable that her boys choose somebody, sooner or later. Already she suspected Carlo was visiting a girl in Wenton. And for Spring, that tender-hearted rescuer of wounded rabbits and broken-winged birds, Julie was probably inevitable. Get used to it, Theresa.

It was full dark when she went back to the house, its candles gleaming through the small windows. Jody met her on the porch. "Where's Lillie?"

Theresa felt her stomach sink. "Isn't she here?"

"We thought she was with you."

"No, I was going to . . . but I forgot because . . . she went for a walk, she said. Her Uncle Keith finally died, and she wanted to be alone."

"Which way?"

"West. But you can't . . ." Jody was already gone toward the barn to saddle his horse. A half moon, stars . . . all her boys could ride at night if they had to. Heart hammering, Theresa went inside.

How long?

They were back in an hour, Lillie seated on the horse, clutching the pommel desperately. Lillie, child of New York subways and a spaceship, had never learned to ride. Jody walked alongside, leading the horse. Theresa couldn't help her image: Joseph and the pregnant Mary. None of her kids except Carlo would even recognize the icon.

"She's fine," Jody called. "But, Mom, we've got trouble."

Inside, he told them: a large band of refugees camped by the arroyo a mile to the west. Lillie had seen them before they'd seen her, and had caught the glint of moonlight on guns. She'd been starting back when Jody found her. He'd taken a closer look with night-vision binoculars.

"They have at least one shoulder-mounted missile launcher. Military, looks like. About thirty men and women, no kids that I saw. Military tents. This is no ragtag bunch of migrants, Mom."

No. Theresa knew what it was. How had they escaped it this long, so many years, with the land growing more arable and desirable and prosperous? Dumb luck, she guessed.

She said quietly, "Lillie, take the other girls into the bedroom. You go, too, Sam and Alex and Rafe."

"No," Rafe said.

Theresa looked at him. She remembered him as a skinny, intrusive, intelligent nerd, and he still was. She almost tended to forget that he and Alex (but not Sam, noisy as ever) were around, so completely had they become her sons' responsibility.

Rafe said, "We're in this together. You said so over and over, Theresa. Whatever you're going to do, tell us."

"All right!" Theresa snapped. Rafe wasn't the problem, anyway. Scott was.

She continued, "We have a few guns and ammunition and five people who can shoot. Nowhere near enough to stand against what Jody and Lillie saw. We've known that for a while. But we also have something else, something left over from before you came back, Rafe. A bioweapon."

Scott jerked in his chair, rose to his feet.

"It's an engineered virus," Theresa said steadily. "Ten built-in replications after release before the terminator gene kicks in. Airborne. Lethal within five minutes."

"Jesus God, Theresa!"

"Scott, don't lecture me. Just don't. I knew this day would come eventually, and when I had the chance to buy this stuff left over from the war, I did. I'm not letting all of you die because I'm too squeamish. That would be like being presented with a choice and choosing them to live, not us."

Her knees trembled. Yes, she'd known this day would come, but she'd dreaded its coming, too. Thirty men and women . . . who would kill without any trembling. Remember that. At least there were no children with them. She hoped.

Theresa looked at the faces around the room. The rains had tapered off and the solar panels generated every clear day, but she tended to store the power or use it for farm needs. Candlelight flickered shadows around the room so that she saw a cheekbone here, a chin there. But it seemed to Theresa that she could see all their eyes, every pair. Shocked, frightened, impassive, angry.

"You can't," Scott said. "You don't even know that those refugees are going to attack here!"

"I know. And so do you. They're camped closest to us, we're on a line from the other two attacks, people don't carry around missile-launchers for fun. And anyway," she said, her voice rising in fury, "what if the attack isn't on us? What if it's on the Graham farm, or even on Wenton? Is it the moral high ground to let those people die because we're not the direct target?"

Scott said, "You're going to kill—"

"Yes! Would you rather sacrifice these kids and unborn babies and my sons and daughter and grandchildren? Would you, Scott? Because if the answer is no, you better not judge what I'm doing."

"You're not the law, Tess!"

Abruptly the fury went out of her. "Yes. I am. Out here, now, I am."

She put her hands over her face. Jody took them down, gently. "I'll do it, Mom. Tell me where the canister is."

She gazed at her first-born. Yes, he was the right person. Spring was too sweet-natured, Carlo too entangled in religious conflict. Carlo sat in a corner, his face gray. Well, she couldn't talk to him now. At least he wasn't interfering.

She led Jody out to the porch. Scott took a step as if to follow her, then didn't. Outside, the infernal wind howled around the barn, blew her hair into her mouth, sent a chair carelessly left outside flying across the yard. Night wind, hot angry breath of the violated land. Well, the wind was her ally now.

"You'll have to circle around the far side of the arroyo to get downwind of them," she told Jody. "The dispersion distance is supposed to be only a mile, but I don't trust it. Some micro might reach here. I only have six masks. I think I better take everybody in the bus, maybe three miles out into the desert."

"All right," Jody said neutrally.

"If they catch you—"

"They won't catch me."

They walked hand-in-hand to the barn, Jody keeping Theresa upright against the wind and her own trembling. She showed him where the canister was buried and gave him the code to activate it. His horse was already saddled from looking for Lillie. In ten minutes he was gone.

Theresa fought her way back to the house. "All right, everybody, into the bus. Now. We need to get out past the dispersion distance.

Come on, we don't have time to waste." She didn't look at any of them directly.

They crowded into the ancient bus, eerily silent. The only noise was the wind. Theresa drove until she reached the start of a patch of desert, a reverse oasis in the greening land. When she turned off the engine, it was pitch dark.

Julie sobbed softly.

Someone cleared his throat.

The baby, carried in Senni's arms, woke and whimpered for the breast.

Then she heard Lillie's clear voice. "How long before we can return, Tess?"

"I'm going to give it five hours." Twenty minutes per replication, ten replications. After that, even if remnants did reach the house, the virus would be inactive.

They would all have to endure five hours here. So they would.

Maybe a few of the kids would be able to fall asleep.

When they returned to the farm, Jody was there. He nodded at her. Carlo pushed past his brother and headed for the barn. Scott went directly to his room, looking suddenly much older than his fifty-three years.

Jody and Spring sat with her, drinking coffee, saying nothing, until Theresa told them she could sleep now, from sheer exhaustion.

When she woke late the next morning, all three of her sons were gone, plus, surprisingly, Sam. They'd taken the cart and the decrepit horse that drew it. Carlo must have been driving; Jody's and Spring's horses were gone but Carlo's bay snorted in its stall. Theresa thought of saddling him, but she was at best an indifferent rider and the wind blew at its full force. She returned to the house.

They came in after sunset, filthy and silent. She had already brought the well hose to the back shed and filled the two oversize plastic garbage cans sometimes used as vertical bathtubs. When the men were washed, she had their dinner ready. She'd sent everyone else to their rooms or the "den," damn if she cared how cramped they were in there for an entire evening. Scott had left a day early to do his doctoring in Wenton, leaving word with Senni that he'd spend several nights there. Just as well.

After he'd eaten ferociously, Jody said, "We buried them all. Mass grave. The weapons, plus anything else I thought we could use, we brought back on the cart. It's all in the barn. You can look it over tomorrow."

Theresa nodded. Slowly she said, "I never wanted this for my children. Not for any of you."

"We know," Spring said. He smiled. "Stop feeling guilty, Mom. You're not responsible for every single bad thing that happens to us for our entire lives, you know."

Jody said, "Motherhood is powerful."

"But not that powerful," Spring added.

"I want to say," Jody added, "that Sam was an enormous help to us. He more than carried his share."

Sam flushed with pleasure. He was sunburned, a whole day spent in that dangerous high-UV sun. Not good. But his angry, sullen look was gone. He'd been needed, and praised.

She said, "Carlo?"

He looked at her directly. Seeing the pain in his eyes, she could have wept. Carlo said, "We did what we had to. But I don't have to pretend it wasn't a mortal sin." Abruptly he pushed his chair from the table, stood, and strode out.

Spring said, "He had a funeral. A mass, or whatever you call it, over the grave. Prayers and crosses in the air. I thought he'd never get done."

"Let him have it, if it helps him," Theresa said.

"Mom, he's going into Wenton to that priest's church, Father What's-His-Name, spending the entire day with him, every Sunday. Did you know?"

She hadn't. "I thought he was seeing some girl."

"Carlo?" Jody laughed. "No. But I am."

She was caught by surprise. "Well, you certainly took time for it that I didn't notice. Who?"

He said defiantly, "Her name is Carolina Mendoza."

Mexican. From the new encampment, growing larger every month, a few miles beyond Wenton. The source of migrant labor, especially at harvest . . . but of brides? How had Jody even met her? The Mexicans guarded their women zealously. Theresa didn't ask. She said carefully, "Do her people mind you seeing her?"

"She doesn't have any people," Jody said. "Just a cousin. She's been knocked around a lot. But she's sweet and good and beautiful and very soon I'm going to marry her and bring her here."

Careful, be careful. "Have you thought this through, Jody? Are you sure?"

"I'm sure. I've thought."

But about what? Theresa wanted to say. Jody had been a teenager during the war with Mexico, which had been a confused and misbegotten side conflict to the global biowar. The warming, the depression, the greenhouse gases, the UV exposure—all of it had been harder on Mexico than on the United States. More people had starved, had died of diseases, had died of floods and storms and wildfires, had died period. Mexico had been desperate. Mexicans had flooded over the border in numbers too big to stop, or to economically tolerate. The state of Texas had gone to war, using illegal bioweapons in defiance of Congress and the entire federal government, and in a week the war was over. The anger and fear, on both sides, were not.

The bioweapon Jody had just used at the arroyo came from that war.

He said tightly, "Say it, Mom."

"Say what?"

"Whatever you're thinking. No, just answer one question. Is Carolina welcome here?"

Even brief hesitation would be fatal. She said, "Of course."

The relief that flooded Jody's eyes made her chest tighten.

Spring said, "Of course she's welcome, if you're marrying her. But Senni won't like it."

"Senni never likes anything," Jody said.

Spring grinned. "Well, tell her that if we can have five pregnant genetically engineered girls carrying fifteen mutated babies, then we can have one senorita. But I have something to say, too, Mom."

Theresa groaned. "No, Spring, no. She's only fourteen years old!"

"Fifteen last month. And I want to marry her, Mom."

"Who?" Jody demanded, and despite herself, Theresa laughed.

"Jody, you've been so wrapped up in your own girl that you haven't even noticed your brother falling all over Julie."

"*Julie?* She's fourteen!"

"Fifteen. You going to give me a hard time, big brother?"

Jody shook his head.

"Well, then," Spring said, "we can go to Wenton together and have a double wedding. I hear Father What's-His-Name is back in the marrying business. And that will please Carlo. Hey, maybe Carlo can marry Emily or Sajelle!"

"Ha ha," Theresa said. "Now get to bed. It's back to the cows in the morning."

Somehow they had moved from murder to marriage. Theresa shook her head to disperse the sense of unreality. It didn't go away. But, then, she was getting used to that.

CHAPTER 16

Lillie went into labor the second week in December, in the aftermath of a storm so severe it knocked down the wellhouse. Flash flood in the arroyo carried off and killed two head of cattle. The men, plus Senni and Carolina, were all out on the farm, repairing damage. Theresa was minding her grandchildren, Dolly and baby Clari. Lillie, Emily, Sajelle, Bonnie, and Julie all worked at tasks near the house, so Theresa could keep an eye on them, too.

Lillie looked up from making tortillas at the wooden table. "Oh!"

"What is it, Lil?" Bonnie said.

"I think it's starting. A sort of sharp pain in my gut, here."

Theresa said, "You can't be up to sharp pains yet, Lillie. Your water hasn't even broken."

"It just did. And we don't know what the pribir did to change labor," Lillie said logically, then doubled over with a look of surprise that was half comical, half pain.

Theresa got her into bed. Eight months, shouldn't be a problem. Eight months was perfectly viable. Everything was ready. Except maybe Theresa and Lillie.

"Get that sheet of plastic on the bed first, Emily, there's going to be blood and I want to save as many sheets as possible. Bonnie, heat water and boil the scissors and the string. Sajelle, warm blankets and line three of those baskets I bought in Wenton. Keep the blankets warm. Julie, watch Dolly and Clari. If Lillie starts screaming, take the kids out to the barn."

"I'm not going to scream," Lillie said.

"You don't know that."

"I don't scream," Lillie said.

And she didn't, although at one point she bit her bottom lip almost through. Labor lasted only thirty minutes. Theresa couldn't believe it; she'd been twenty-seven hours with Jody.

Sajelle turned out to be invaluable. Steady, quick, unsqueamish. Theresa sent Emily and Bonnie away; no use cluttering up the tiny room with more people than necessary.

"You doing good, Lillie," Sajelle said.

"Talk to me," Lillie said, her face horribly contorted.

"Remember the garden on the ship?" Sajelle said. The pribir seemed a strange subject for Sajelle to choose, until Theresa realized that the aliens were the only experience the two girls had in common. "Them gorgeous flowers by the pool, yellow and red, smelling like heaven? Remember that music cube of Hannah's that we played over and over? 'Don't Matter None to Me.' " She began to hum.

"Keep talking," Lillie grunted.

"Okay. Remember the day we all swapped make-up and tried on different colors? Or the time Rafe took apart the lawn robot thing and Pam was so mad? Lillie?"

"Keep *talking*," Lillie gasped, and Sajelle did, talking her friend through it, talking her on, talking her down from the bad heights and the worse depths, until it was over and three babies lay in the warmed baskets, two boys and a girl.

"They're human," Sajelle said, and Theresa looked up, startled at the deep relief in Sajelle's voice. Sajelle cradled her own belly.

"Lillie," Theresa said, "you have three beautiful children." But Lillie was already asleep, her face turned toward the wall.

Lillie named the babies Keith, Cord, and Kella. She nursed them with a puzzled look on her face. "What is it, Lillie?" Theresa said.

"They don't really seem like mine."

Theresa noticed that Lillie was conscientious in keeping the infants fed, dry, and warm. But she didn't play with them, or make cooing noises at them, or cuddle them. The two people most interested in the triplets were Carolina and Scott.

Carolina spoke no English, a fact Jody had neglected to mention. How much Spanish did Jody know? Enough, apparently. She was too thin but nonetheless buxom, with masses of dark hair and the prettiest face Theresa had ever seen, prettier even than Madison had been, except for a long wide scar that started at the right side of her chin and disappeared into her dress. Theresa wondered how far the scar extended and what it was from. She didn't ask.

At first Carolina seemed afraid of all of them. But when that wore off, she turned out to have an exuberant nature. Well, she'd have to be adventurous to meet and marry Jody. So far Theresa had seen no reaction in Wenton to news of the marriage, although that didn't mean the reaction wasn't there. Carolina fell instantly in love with Dolly and Clari, which won over Senni. The girl loved babies. She gave Lillie's triplets all the hectic affection that Lillie did not, chattering away at them in Spanish.

Scott, on the other hand, was all science. The very day of their birth he brought home from Wenton a piece of equipment the size of a small chair. "It came on the train yesterday. Finally. I thought it wasn't going to get through, which would be a genuine loss considering how much credit I gave for it."

"What is it?" Spring said.

"A Sparks-Markham genetic analyzer."

Senni said suspiciously, "I don't know what that is but it looks like it cost a lot of credit."

Theresa intervened. "It's Scott's credit to spend. Scott, what do you need?"

"Just the stem cells from the umbilical cords, which I have. For now, anyway. And a place to work."

"Take the den," Theresa said. Lowering her voice so only he could hear, she added, "And Scott—talk to me first about whatever you find."

"Of course," he said quietly.

Several hours later he emerged from the den, looking dazed. The great room was full of people, exclamations, babies. Theresa caught Scott's eye and motioned toward the door.

It was after sunset and the wind had softened to a hot breeze. They walked to the creek down the slope from the house, once more flowing decorously between its banks after its rampage during the storm. Debris it had left behind scattered the ground: mud, branches, rocks, a dead coyote. The creek had made its appearance, a gift of the increased mountain runoff plus more frequent rain, about five years ago, and had grown steadily since. It flowed past a grove of old cottonwoods. The cottonwoods had once drawn all the moisture available in the dell at the bottom of the little hill. Now juniper and oak saplings grew beside the cottonwoods. Spring had nailed a sturdy wooden bench to the largest tree, and the bench hadn't been washed away in the storm, although it was still too wet to sit on.

Theresa had a sudden visceral memory. This was how her stomach had felt when she and Lillie had gone to the picnic grove at

Andrews Air Force Base to be bawled out by Lillie's Uncle Keith, the day after the girls had crashed a party in the boys' dorm. A lifetime ago. Yet for a moment, she'd felt again the Maryland sunlight, smelled the honeysuckle, heard the roar of jets taking off and landing.

"I don't know where to begin," Scott said. "The children's genome is . . . is what? Is ours, and isn't. As far as I can tell from the preliminary scan, they possess the same forty-six chromosomes we do, and all the genes we have on those chromosomes. But every chromosome except the X and Y have extra genes spliced in, because . . . I still can't believe this. It can't be true."

"Tell me, damn it!"

"There's no junk DNA. You remember, Tess, from what we learned at Andrews, that the—"

"I don't remember anything of what I learned at Andrews. I don't have that sort of mind. Start at the beginning."

"Okay. The human genome is about seventy-five percent non-functioning base pairs. Some is fossilized virus genomes that spliced themselves in hundreds of millions of years ago. Some are stray scattered fragments of DNA that don't do anything, just get themselves replicated over and over whenever a cell divides. Some are—"

"I get the picture. Get on with it, Scott." His eyes still had that dazed bemusement.

He licked his lips. "The babies' genome, it doesn't have any of those introns at all. None. They've all been cut out."

"Three-quarters of their genome is *gone?*"

"Yes. It's an amazing job. And more . . . there are new genes added in place of the excised base pairs. Tens of thousands of them."

"What do the new genes do?"

"How the hell should I know? They make proteins, or regulate protein making, because that's what genes *do*. But until I see them in action, I don't know what proteins or what regulation or . . . or anything."

Theresa fell silent. Night insects sang around them in the dark. From somewhere blew the sweet sharp smell of mint.

"Scott . . . are they human?"

"No. Yes. I don't know . . . how are you defining human? They share twenty-five percent of our time-damaged genome. Hell, *chimps* share ninety-eight percent!"

"They look human. They look like human babies."

"I know."

Theresa jumped up. "They are human babies. Lillie's babies. Listen, this is very important. Don't say to anyone what you've said to me. Don't lie. Just say . . . say that the babies have all our genes. That's true, isn't it?"

"Yes."

"If you say more, if you tell—"

He said irritably, "I know what the consequences would be, Tess. I can't even publish in what's left of the Net scientific journals. If anyone knew even that you and I and Lillie are pribir kids, there would be people from Wenton unhappy about our presence. Some folk there don't even like Carolina being here. And if I published this genome, either I'd be dismissed as a crackpot or . . . or I wouldn't."

Theresa said, "They're just little babies. Let them have a chance at a normal life. God, I can't believe I just called how we live now 'normal.' "

"Kids think whatever they grow up with is normal. But, Tess, I want to go on gathering data from the kids. How do I explain that if I say their genome is identical to ours?"

She considered, chewing on her lip. "Say they have six extra genes."

"*Six?* Why six?"

"Twenty-six, then. Do you think anybody here knows enough about genetics to interpret that?"

"Yes. All the kids who went to the ship. Especially Rafe and Emily."

"Well, they're not going to broadcast it. Just say there's a small difference from us, enough so it's plausible you'd study it but not enough to make the babies seem too different."

"All right," Scott said. "You know, when the wind dies down, it's pleasant here."

Theresa said, "When the wind dies down, and we're not having a hugely destructive storm, and the sun has set, and no toxins happen to be carried on the breeze, and the tropical diseases that have come north aren't infecting, and the UV damage hasn't caused too much cancer . . . then, yes, it's pleasant here."

He said, "Do you ever wish you'd gone, that night at Quantico? Gone up to the pribir ship instead of staying behind?"

"And have missed out on all the excitement of the last forty years? No."

"Ha," he laughed mirthlessly.

Theresa stood. "We should get back to the house."

"Wait a minute more. Now that I've got the analyzer, I'd like to scan your genome, too. And Jody and Carlo and Spring and Senni. Plus Senni's children. I'd like to see if the modifications we carry are dominant."

"You mean . . ." God, she'd never considered this before! "You mean, my kids and grandkids might be able to smell pribir messages? Like we did?"

"If there were any pribir to send. Which there aren't. Can I scan them, Tess?"

"If they let you."

"Okay. You go on in, I want to sit here and think for a while."

She was glad to leave him. She didn't want any more information to confuse her actions. Besides, her arms ached to hold a newborn baby: that helpless warmth against her chest, those rosy sucking little lips screwing themselves into yawns and cries and, eventually, smiles. Why should Carolina get all the cuddle time?

Theresa ran back to the farm house in the fragrant dusk, feeling light as a young girl, light as air.

Emily also had an easy birth, bearing three bald, round, blue-eyed girls. Bonnie had two boys and a girl. Sajelle bore two girls and a boy, chocolate-brown infants with huge brown eyes. Only Julie had a difficult time. One of her triplets, a girl, died soon after birth. The other two, a boy and girl, were healthy and strong.

"We're awash in babies," Bonnie said. She gazed lovingly at her three infants, miraculously all asleep at the same time in baskets lined up in her room. Yet another addition had been hastily put on the farm house, which now looked like a crazily growing organism of some kind. Each mother shared a tiny bedroom with her children. Jody and Carolina had a room but the other men had moved, with relief, to the barn. All the babies were remarkably good: no colic, no projectile vomiting, no prolonged crying. Theresa, sleeping on a pallet in the great room, silently thanked the pribir.

Carolina was invaluable. From dawn till bedtime she tirelessly tended children, cooing endearments at them in Spanish. "*Mi corazon, mi carino, primito* . . ." Then she disappeared one day in the cart, returning with two other Mexican girls and a boy of about twelve.

Jody translated. "These are Carolina's cousins, Lupe and Rosalita and Juan. They can help with the babies." Jody looked defiant and embarrassed; clearly he had not authorized this.

Theresa looked at the newcomers. Skinny, malnourished,

hopeful, clinging desperately to each other's hands. Carolina said pleadingly, "Rosalita, Lupe, Juan work much. Very much."

Theresa said to Jody, "Can we feed all these people? The babies won't be on breast milk forever, you know."

"I think so. We're doing pretty well, Mom. Cattle prices are a little up now that things are returning to normal, and we're going to unload twenty more head at Wenton."

Normal? This was normal? And how would Jody, living in a crashing world his entire life, know?

She looked again at the Mexican "cousins." In the house, two babies began to wail simultaneously. Maybe three.

"Okay," she said, and the girls fell to their knees and kissed her hands, which embarrassed her. She saw a louse crawling on the top of Lupe's head.

"Get them scrubbed and deloused before they go anywhere near the babies! Also, Scott should check them out for diseases. And, Jody—no more Mexicans. Tell Carolina."

"I will."

"None of the triplets are identical," Scott said, after running days of gene scans. "I guess the pribir wanted as wide a gene pool as possible."

"Do they all have . . . are they all . . ." Theresa asked.

"They all have the same scan as Lillie's babies. Introns completely excised. Thousands of extra genes."

"And you still don't know what any of them do."

"Not a one. Blood chemistry is completely normal, no unknown proteins. So is urine, tissue samples, everything I can think of to test." He almost sounded disappointed.

Theresa wasn't disappointed. There were already rumors in Wenton of odd occurrences at the farm, and on trips to town Theresa had felt the drawing back by people who had known her for fifteen years.

The news from the Net, however, distracted everyone. The United States's economy might slowly be returning to "normal," but much of the rest of the world was not. A national news network now operated via ancient satellites. It didn't go as far as sending actual reporters to China, but it picked up and translated China's own broadcasts.

"They're talking about *war*," said Sam, who didn't remember the last one. During that war horrifying bioweapons, some with and some without terminator genes, had been swept by the warming winds around the globe. Some places were still unlivable. Bacteria or viruses lurked in the ground, in the water. No one knew what micros the survivors still harbored in their livers, in their bones, in their blood.

"They can't," she said. *War.* "Not again . . . they can't."

"Do you really believe that?" Scott said grimly.

"Are there any bioweapons even left? In China? Here?"

"Of course there are," Scott said. "And new ones have probably been invented. Never, in all of history, have hard times prevented war."

"But *why?* What do the Chinese want? They don't even have transport to get here and take over the country after they destroy it!"

"I guess they think they do," Scott said. "Enough transport, anyway."

An unspoken arrangement developed in the house. After dark, the people who wanted to hear the news gathered in the "den" around the computer, now upgraded with parts that had only recently appeared for sale in Wenton, part of the town's growing prosperity. The news listeners were Scott, Jody, Carlo, Senni, Rafe, and Lillie. The others stayed with the children in the great room, asking no questions when grim faces emerged from the den.

One night, however, the faces were not grim. Lillie raced from the den into the great room, where Theresa was changing the diaper on Lillie's son Cord. "Tess! Come here! DeWayne is on the Net!"

"Who?"

"DeWayne Freeman! From Andrews!"

From Andrews Air Force Base, which for Lillie was eighteen months ago and for Theresa, forty-one years. She barely remembered DeWayne Freeman. "You talk to him, Lillie. I can't leave Cord. But don't tell him anything about— "

"I know," Lillie said. She and Alex talked to DeWayne. A week later DeWayne turned up at the farm, driving a new fuel-celled electric car that immediately brought gawkers streaming out onto the porch. "Wow," Rafe said. "Look at that!"

A tall, well-dressed black man climbed out of the car. He carried an expensive suitcase. Theresa said quickly, "Everybody go inside. *Now.* I want to talk to him alone." She hadn't heard from DeWayne in forty years; he could be an anti-genetics nut for all she knew.

The family vanished inside. DeWayne climbed the porch steps. "Theresa Romero?"

"Hello, DeWayne."

"I wouldn't have known you, Theresa."

"And I wouldn't have known you."

"I want to talk to you. Can we go inside?"

"I don't think so. I really have a lot to do. Let's talk out here." She knew she sounded ungracious, as well as peculiar, but she couldn't help it.

DeWayne didn't waste words. "Rafe told me how a bunch of you have gathered here—a bunch of us from the old days. Friends. My wife and children are dead. They . . . never mind. I don't have anyone. But I have a lot of credits in the Net, and more each day. I develop Net prosi . . . what used to be called software. I can do it from anywhere. I'm rich, Theresa, and I'll share it all with the farm if I can live here with you and the rest."

Theresa said, "How rich?"

He smiled. "Six billion international credits."

Theresa sat down on the nearest porch chair, nailed down to keep it from blowing away. Six billion credits. Even with inflation what it had been, that was a fortune. She said bluntly, "Why, DeWayne? With that kind of money, you could buy yourself another wife. Hell, you could buy pretty much anything. Why here?"

"I haven't ever felt at home anywhere, Theresa. Not since I came out of that trance in a Queens hospital forty-one years ago and learned what I was. And nobody's been at home with me, either. Andrews was the only time I ever belonged. We're getting older. I want to settle somewhere."

Theresa studied him. There were people, she knew, who made their own alienations in life. Maybe DeWayne was one of those. Maybe he'd never belonged because, feeling so different, he never let himself belong. Like, she thought, her throat closing with the old anxiety, like Carlo. DeWayne didn't look like a man who made emotional revelations easily. Talking to her like this, on her porch long since wind-scoured of any paint, had cost him. Was he telling the truth? Well, Scott and Rafe could check that out on the Net. Could he be trusted? That was a much tougher question.

And then he said, not looking at her, "Rafe said Sajelle is here. And that she isn't married."

Oh, God. Damn Rafe! "DeWayne . . . I have to talk to my sons and daughter about this. Could you come back tomorrow? I'm afraid I can't let you stay here, but there's a sort of inn in Wenton . . . who's that sitting in your car?"

"Bodyguard. But he won't be staying. I'll send him back to the enclave, he—" DeWayne stopped dead.

Sajelle was hurrying up the path from the chicken coop, carrying a basket of fresh eggs clutched against her chest against the wind. Her dreadlocks tossed wildly. Bent over the eggs, she didn't notice DeWayne until she'd rushed into the comparative shelter of the porch and nearly run into him. Sajelle looked confused to see a stranger, a black man, on the porch. DeWayne hadn't recognized Theresa right away. Not so now.

He said dazedly, "Sajelle?"

Theresa thought of saying this was Sajelle's daughter. But Sajelle herself recognized something in his voice or manner. "DeWayne? DeWayne Freeman?"

He seemed unable to speak. Theresa said, "You might as well come in, DeWayne. There are a few little things we're going to have to explain to you."

CHAPTER 17

DeWayne stayed, and many things became possible.

In the late spring, Rafe, Emily, and Lillie waylaid Theresa in the barn, pitching hay to the horses. "Tess, we need to talk to you."

"So talk. But if you're going to tell me more bad news about the Chinese, forget it. I don't want to hear it until I have to."

"It's not about the Chinese," Lillie said. "We have a proposition. We want to convince you so you can convince the others."

Theresa put down her pitchfork and looked at Lillie, who stood a little in front of the others and was clearly their designated spokesman. Lillie had regained her figure after the triplets' birth more quickly than the other girls. She stood slim and young, direct, her gaze meeting Theresa's squarely. Lillie's babies, Theresa knew, were right now being bathed by Carolina and Lupe. Whenever Lillie looked at her children there was a faintly puzzled look in her gray eyes: *Mine?* Theresa did not understand.

"You know that we learned a lot of genetics aboard the pribir ship," Lillie said. "We only know how to use pribir equipment, though. But Scott has been teaching Rafe and Emily how to use his Sparks-Markham, plus all the new stuff DeWayne bought, and they've been teaching Scott what the pribir taught us. They remember a lot, unlike me and the rest."

"Yes," Theresa said neutrally. Why didn't Lillie feel more involved with her babies? They were adorable, especially little Cord. He had Lillie's eyes, gray with gold flecks.

"Rafe and Emily put some of the hay genes through the scanner. Also rice from the sacks Carlo bought in Wenton. They experimented with the splicer, and they think they can create hay that will have three times the yield on the same plot of land, and rice that will grow here in the summer rains."

Three times the yield. They could run more cattle, lots more. The range grew more vegetation than ever, but there was still not enough to sustain her herd year-round without feed. The amount of hay had been the limiting factor on how much cattle she could run. And if rice, which had never in the history of the world grown here, could be raised as a cash crop, the market for it would be large and close. Cheap transportation costs . . .

Suddenly it hit her. "'Create.' You mean genetically engineered crops."

"Yes," Rafe said eagerly over Lillie's shoulder.

"Anything to do with genetically engineered crops is illegal. You know that. Anything to do with genetically engineered anything —that's why we've been so careful!"

"And we'll go on being careful," Lillie said. "No one will know, anymore than they know about us, or about the babies. And anyway you said there's no law to—"

"There's vigilantes," Theresa said harshly. "God, you three don't remember. You weren't here during the war." The labs and corporations that had been the targets of mob rage during and right after the biowar. The CEO of Monsanto had been disemboweled alive. Theresa had seen a Net video.

"That was eleven years ago," Lillie said logically. "And anyway, no one will know. Wenton doesn't have any gene-analyzing equipment. We'll just say DeWayne bought a different kind of seed from back East, and we'll offer to share planting seeds for the hay with anyone who wants them. Look, Tess, I've done some figures."

Lillie held out a piece of DeWayne's grayish paper, another new luxury, and began to go over the numbers for Tess. Costs, needed labor, projected market price, possible profit range. The handwriting was the round unformed hand of a schoolgirl.

"Lillie, who taught you to do this?"

Lillie looked surprised. "Nobody taught me. It's just common sense."

And Lillie had always had a lot of that. No maternal feelings, but a direct pragmatism even greater than Theresa's own. She said, "Does Scott know all this?"

"No," Lillie said.

Rafe said transparently, "We thought you, as boss, were entitled to see it first."

"No, it wasn't that," Lillie said. "Scott isn't going to like it. He wants us to keep as much out of public notice as possible. We're showing it to you first so you can change his mind."

Emily said eagerly, "We know it will work!" Unlike Lillie, she had baby-food stains all down the front of her maternity smock, which she was still wearing because she hadn't lost all her pregnancy weight.

Theresa looked at the three young faces: Rafe excited, Emily hopeful, Lillie coolly considering. It *was* an interesting idea. Rice . . . Theresa could almost see the low green plants growing in the flat land below the cottongrove, where the creek flooded regularly. Regularly enough? Maybe they could build a little dam . . .

"I'll talk to Scott," she said, "and Jody, Senni, Carlo, and Spring. We'll see."

"We can increase farm income by about twenty percent, not counting DeWayne's contribution," Lillie said. "That's a lot of flour and cloth and ammunition."

Not, Theresa noticed, "a lot of diapers." Oh, Lillie.

After much argument, they planted a test crop of the genetically engineered crops. Both hay and rice flourished. It was only a few inconspicuous square yards of land under cultivation this year, but next year . . .

Sajelle married DeWayne in July. She was fifteen, he was fifty-four. Senni thought it was "obscene," but Theresa only shrugged. Things were different now. Statutory rape laws belonged to another life. DeWayne was good to Sajelle, she made him happy, and her children's future was assured. Within two months Sajelle was pregnant again.

The babies turned eight months old. With Senni's nine-month Clari, there were fifteen babies crawling around the great room, pulling themselves up on furniture, throwing around food, babbling at each other. Without the three Mexican girls, caring for them would have been impossible. All of the children were beautiful. None had ever had as much as a cold. Scott could find nothing abnormal in any of their physiology.

That summer Carlo married Rosalita. Theresa, who was afraid that Carlo would someday announce he wanted to be a priest, was relieved. Everyone pitched in to expand housing, and eventually there was a compound of four houses, one large and three smaller, and everyone had more room.

Another group of refugees attacked, but they were ill-equipped and easily driven off with guns. Only one was killed. Theresa didn't ask where Jody, Bonnie, and Sam buried him.

The Chinese threat abated, presumably due to some mysterious cycle of political fluctuation. Maybe the Chinese were also becoming more prosperous, less desperate. Maybe not. Theresa didn't care just so long as the word "war" disappeared from farm conversations.

That summer, the horrendous storms leveled off. Net news said the global warming seemed to have stabilized, perhaps due to the drastic cutback of greenhouse gases since the war. Theresa's land remained fertile, and the range was better watered than ever before. She allowed herself to be hopeful, then grateful, then happy. They were going to make it.

Just after she'd decided this, the delegation from Wenton arrived.

"Come in," Theresa said, because she couldn't keep them standing on the porch. There were six of them, arriving in the early afternoon, an indication of how far the weather had softened. The wind still blew till sundown, but it had less force, less grit, less unrelenting howl. The delegation came in a car, as new as DeWayne's but larger and very simple, a closed metal box on a slow-moving, fuel-cell-driven base. Still, the fact that new, non-luxury cars were available in a place like Wenton felt significant to Theresa.

She studied them as they filed into the great room. Three of the babies crawled around under Carolina's watchful eye. The rest were either in the smaller houses or napping. Everyone else who could be was out harvesting.

Old Tom Carter, who used to run the storage building that was no longer needed. Rachel Monaghan, a woman Theresa's age, who kept a cloth and clothing store. Lucy Tetrino from the train station. Bill Walewski, the grain buyer. Two hard-faced men she didn't recognize. She saw Rachel's lips purse at the sight of Carolina.

"Carolina," Theresa said pleasantly, "take the babies down to Senni's, please. Everyone, sit down anywhere you like."

Carolina cast one frightened look at the Wenton delegation, then piled all three babies into a huge basket and hoisted it to her hip. She was much stronger than she looked. The children gurgled delightedly. Carolina hurried outside.

"My daughter-in-law, Jody's wife," Theresa said. A pre-emptive strike.

"So we heard," Lucy Tetrino said, and from her tone Theresa knew that Wenton didn't like having the Mexican girls and Juan here but that they weren't the reason for this visit. The delegation scanned the great room, with its litter of baby clothes, leftover beans and rice on the table, guns high on the wall where the children couldn't reach. The room smelled of candles and diapers and food and the vase of wild roses Sajelle had picked by the creek.

"Theresa," Bill Walewski said, "I guess I better start, since I'm the new mayor of Wenton."

"Congratulations," Theresa said. She hadn't even known there'd been an election.

"Thanks. The reason we're here is that there've been some pretty strange rumors going around town about you this last year."

"Really." Bill didn't meet her eyes. Whatever was going on, he wasn't fully behind it.

"Yes. People are saying . . . people are wondering how you could have got all these teenage girls, all pregnant at the same time, all having twins or triplets or even quads. Pretty peculiar."

"There are no quads," Theresa said.

"But there are twins and triplets," Lucy put in.

"Yes." She didn't explain that there would have been only triplets if one of Julie's infants hadn't died.

"Well, don't you think that's a little weird?" Lucy said.

"More than 'weird,'" said one of the strangers. "It's obscene," and Theresa knew the source of the delegation.

"I'm afraid I didn't get your name, sir." Courtesy just this side of insolence.

"Matt Campion. I represent America Restored." He didn't smile.

Theresa said, "Restored to what?"

"To livability. To respect for the natural ecology of this great country. To decent acknowledgment of human limitations, so that we don't destroy ourselves by mucking around with forces beyond our ability to understand or control."

An anti-science league. Well, Wenton had escaped longer than many places. "I see."

"I doubt it," Campion said.

Old Tom said hastily, "We've all known you a long time, Theresa, and—"

"Yes, you have, Tom. Rachel, I've been buying cloth from you for sixteen years now. Bill, you've been buying grain from me for . . . how long?"

"Nine years," Bill said unhappily.

"Right. And Lucy, we've ridden the train and shipped supplies on it since my husband and I came to this state."

"None of that is relevant," Campion said harshly. "We're here to find out what's going on at this farm, Ms. Romero. How come you have all these girls simultaneously giving birth to triplets?"

"That's not hard to explain," Theresa said. The explanation had been ready for a year. "You know that Dr. Wilkins boards here.

We're old friends, from before the war. After his wife died, he came here to practice because I told him there was no doctor anywhere around and he was both needed and could build a good practice here."

"That's true," Tom put in, nodding vigorously. "Dr. Wilkins came about a year and a half ago."

"Yes," Theresa continued. "Before that, he practiced in Illinois. He did *pro bono* work there, too. One of his projects was a home for unwed mothers." Briefly Theresa remembered the flamboyant, loose sexual atmosphere of her youth. All that had been swept away; homes for unwed mothers were plausible again. "The home was going to close. No credit. Five of the girls had no place to go. I said Scott could bring them here."

"Why?" Campion demanded.

Theresa opened her eyes wide. "Humanitarian reasons, Mr. Campion. I'm sure any organization that, like yours, values decency and respect can understand humanitarian purposes."

Rachel Monaghan narrowed her eyes, and Theresa told herself to watch it. Ruffling Campion wasn't worth losing any lurking support from her long-time neighbors.

"So that explains why the girls came here," said the other stranger. Quieter, milder, his expression gave away nothing. "But it doesn't explain the multiple births."

"No," Theresa said.

"Well, what about that? Isn't it a little unusual? I'm the Reverend James Beslor, incidentally."

"How do you do. Yes, it is unusual. We were all surprised at so many babies."

Campion said in exasperation, "Well, what caused it?"

"I have no idea," Theresa said.

They all stared at her.

"Neither does Scott Wilkins. Nor the girls. Nobody even has a theory. All we know is that since the girls came to us pregnant, and my daughter hasn't had twins or triplets, whatever happened didn't happen on this farm. And, of course, the babies are all completely normal. You're welcome to examine them, if you like."

Campion said, "We most certainly want to do that."

"Now? I can wake them up."

"No, not now," Campion said, flushing in annoyance. "When I get a doctor out here!"

"Any time that's convenient," Theresa said. Scott had assured her that no one short of a geneticist with expensive analyzers would find anything odd about the children, and it was unlikely this delegation could produce anything like that. Although, if this organization "America Restored" was big enough and funded well enough . . . she felt a thrill of fear.

Campion said slowly, "There's something else going on here. There is. Even if those girls came to you pregnant and you had nothing to do with it, the girls are still *wrong*. Unnatural. Dangerous. We don't ever want another repeat of the ecological disasters that almost destroyed us. Never again."

Theresa made herself look bewildered. "I don't know what more I can do, Mr. Campion. I've said you can examine the children, and their mothers, too, if you like. They're just normal people. Statistical flukes do happen, you know, including multiple births. If you can't prove anything else . . . I can tell that your belief in this country is too great to undermine the Constitutional requirement for proof before finding anyone guilty. Of anything."

Campion looked at her with open dislike. But Lucy said eagerly, "It's true, Matt. Theresa has agreed to cooperate completely, nothing happened here at the farm, and there's not any proof anything wrong ever happened at all."

"That's so," Tom said.

Theresa stood. "Can I get you some chicory coffee? Or sumac tea?"

Bill said abruptly, "Theresa, where did that fancy truck come from? The one Jody was driving the other day?"

"Oh, that was recently purchased in Amarillo by a new member of our farm co-op. DeWayne Freeman. He's a Net developer, you should look him up. Impressive guy."

"What's he doing here?"

"He married another of our co-op members."

Bill nodded, satisfied. Theresa showed them out. Matt Campion gave her a hard stare. When they were out the door, Theresa closed it and leaned against it, breathing hard.

The children were two, three, four. Nothing changed, everything changed. Carlo and his wife Rosalita left the farm, almost breaking Theresa's heart. Carlo, ever restless, searching for something he couldn't name, wanted to go to a religious community he'd heard about in Colorado. Theresa only hoped they would be back some day.

Sajelle had two children with DeWayne. Carolina and Jody had a son, Angel. Scott ran genome analyses on each child minutes after the birth. The results were always the same: the frontal lobe included the dense structure connected to the huge number of receptors in the nose. The genes were dominant. The babies would be able to smell information molecules, if anyone had been able to send them.

The genetically altered rice and hay flourished, although out of prudence Theresa insisted the entire crop be consumed on the farm rather than sold. Lillie was disappointed, but she managed production costs and quantities so well that the net savings to the farm was large. Lillie, and the others, turned sixteen, seventeen, twenty-one. Gradually Lillie began to share with Theresa and DeWayne the financial management of the farm, which Theresa had never enjoyed. The federal government resuscitated both itself and the income tax.

Lillie had grown lean, hard-bodied, briskly capable. She and Alex were the only two of the pribir kids who learned to ride. "Pribir kids"—it had been years since Theresa had thought that phrase. There was nothing about the farm that did not look and feel totally normal, except for the large number of children the same age. Everyone looked and acted no different from their neighbors.

Unless you counted Lillie's attitude toward her children.

As the years rolled by, Theresa became more troubled by this. Lillie was kind to Cord, Keith, and Kella. It was the wary, impersonal kindness of a childless boarder. It reminded Theresa, as nothing else could, of the days at Andrews Air Force Base, when both she and Lillie had been on the receiving end of wary consideration from doctors and intelligence agents and security chiefs.

"It's not right, Lillie. They need you."

"I know it's not right," Lillie said with her habitual honesty. "But I can't help it. Although they don't need me while they have you and Carolina."

"You're their mother!"

"I know."

"Cord, especially, needs you. Haven't you seen how he follows you around, hoping for your attention?" Kella, Lillie's daughter, had fastened herself onto Carolina. Keith seemed to have a temperament like Lillie's, adventurous and self-sufficient. But the look in Cord's eyes when they followed his mother tore at Theresa's heart. The only time the little boy seemed happy was with Clari, Senni's little girl. The two were inseparable. Just a few months apart in age, they shared secrets and games far more than did Cord and his siblings.

Lillie said, in a rare moment of overt emotion, "I can't . . . can't seem to love them, Tess."

"Why the hell not?"

"I don't know."

Theresa gazed at Lillie. Theresa didn't understand, wouldn't ever understand. Cord—all the children—were beautiful, bright, good-natured. Sometimes Theresa felt guilty because she preferred Cord to her own blood granddaughter, Senni's older girl, Dolly. Dolly was a whiner, and she had a selfish streak not shared by her younger sister, Clari. Cord was a wonderful child. How could Lillie not feel—

"I don't know," Lillie repeated and turned away, her face once more a composed, competent, pleasant mask.

CHAPTER 18

The drought began in the summer of 2064.

At first, no one worried. For years the climate in southeast New Mexico had been improving, increasingly favorable for agriculture, ranching, and shade trees. The farm barely needed to irrigate anymore. Theresa and her "farm co-op" had learned to take their good luck for granted. They were in the right place, during the right years. In the vast planetary climatic lottery, they'd drawn a winning number.

However, after the drought had continued for an entire year, Theresa began to get nervous. The farm had been sustained through the year by savings, by DeWayne, and by good management. But the herd had been reduced in size and the harvest was largely a failure. If the land began to revert to its former aridity, both water and plant life drying up, she would be ruined. There were too many people, too many cows, too much diverse activity to go back to what the farm had been twenty years ago.

It was the same in other places, but not everywhere. With mixed feelings Theresa heard on Net news that the northeast coast, that part of it not under water, continued to rise in productivity, population, and malaria. The Canadian plains also continued to enjoy its gains of the last decades. But the southwest, along with large portions of China, were shifting in weather yet again.

International tensions with China again worsened.

Let it be temporary, Theresa prayed to nothing. Not a dangerous shift, just a few bad years. Farmers and ranchers have always had bad years. Nothing new in that, nothing terrifying.

Jody and Spring decided to end the hog operation. Lillie, studying the figures, agreed. They also stopped growing the genetically altered rice. The creek was not delivering enough floodwater.

She was too old for this, Theresa thought. She and Scott and DeWayne, all sixty-four years old. Arthritis was starting to make it painful to turn her neck. She could no longer eat raw vegetables without stomach distress. She was too old to hunker down and then spring up to start over.

Autumn still didn't bring rain. In December, Lillie's children would turn eleven. Theresa decided to have a party. Everyone needed cheering up. She would hold a massive party for all fourteen kids on December 10, Cord's birth date. The look in his eyes when they followed Lillie had changed. Wistfulness had been replaced by bewildered anger. Theresa was worried about him. He played, worked, and studied almost exclusively with Clari, his gentle shadow. She worshipped him, much to Senni's annoyance.

"Let's have party hats," Julie said, from some memory at least a half century old. "I know how to fold them out of newspapers."

"There aren't any newspapers," Sajelle pointed out.

"Well, any paper. And candles."

"That we can get," Theresa said, making a list. Lillie could go to Wenton and pick up the supplies for the party. It was probably the most involved Lillie would get.

"Carolina said she'd bake three of those Spanish cakes with the prickly-pear jelly inside," Emily said. "They were soooooo good."

"What about presents?" Bonnie said. "The same thing for everybody? Or each mother buys her own?"

"There shouldn't be a large difference in cost, though," Emily said, not looking at Sajelle, who thanks to DeWayne had so much more than the rest of them. Although Sajelle never flaunted it.

Bonnie said, "I heard Angie talk about a doll in Lucy Tertino's store. Some woman in Wenton sews them by hand, with little outfits, too."

Emily laughed. "Bonnie, your daughter is such a girly girl."

Bonnie smiled. "You saying that's ironic, Em?"

"Never."

"I know!" Julie said. "Water balloons!"

Theresa listened to them plan, joke, enjoy, four young women of twenty-five, her school friends and contemporaries as she faced her sixty-fifth birthday. It would be a good party. And for a day at least, nobody would think about the drought. Maybe.

As the day grew closer, the children became frantic with excitement. Studies were neglected, chores left undone, sleep interrupted. Even obedient Clari forgot to water the winter herb garden because she was out playing with Cord, and after two days, when Theresa discovered this, the cooking herbs were nearly dead in their pots under the relentless sun.

"I'm sorry!" Clari sobbed, and Theresa wouldn't have had the heart to punish her. But Senni did.

"You were off playing with Cord, weren't you! You irresponsible brat! If you'd pay attention to your chores instead of that spoiled kid, everybody would be better off!"

"I'm sorry, Mommy, I'm sorry . . ."

"I'll make you sorry, all right, Clari Marie. I'll make sure you don't forget again!" She took a bridle strap from its peg on the barn wall.

Theresa didn't hear about this scene until the next day. By that time, Cord was gone.

"Who saw him last?" Theresa demanded. His brother Keith said, "Not me. We woke up this morning and Cord wasn't in his bunk and the blankets were still all smooth." For the last year, the bedrooms had been shuffled yet again to make separate bunkrooms for boys and girls. This wasn't observed much; the kids slept wherever they chose, at whatever house they chose, in whatever groups the evening's play had dictated to them.

Theresa looked at the people assembled in the great room: seven ten-year-old children, Lupe, Carolina, and a clutter of younger children. The others were already busy elsewhere. Lillie had left for town before dawn. Theresa said to Keith, "Was Cord around when you went to bed last night?"

"No," volunteered Gavin, Bonnie's son. "We looked for him and Clari to play Hot Rocks, but they weren't around."

"Clari's missing, too? Carolina?"

"No, no, Clari, she here. She come breakfast, eat nothing. I say, 'eat,' but she no eat. She cry and cry."

"Where is Clari now?"

"In the girl room. Not in her mother's house, I say Clari no do chores today. Senni hit Clari." Carolina's dark eyes flashed; she didn't approve of Senni's child-raising methods. Her and Jody's son Angel was never hit, and he was very well behaved.

Theresa said, "Senni hit Clari? For neglecting the herb garden?"

Carolina nodded, her lips pursed.

"All right, kids, everybody get to work. You, too, Lupe. I'll take care of this."

She knocked on the door to the girls' bunkroom. There was no answer, but she pushed in anyway.

Clari lay rumpled in a dark corner of a bottom bunk. Theresa looked at the child's miserable, tear-stained face and inwardly cursed Senni. Her daughter was a hard woman. Why Senni, when Jody and Spring were so sweet-tempered? Even moody Carlo would never have hit a child. And Clari herself was the gentlest kid on the farm. Genes were so strange.

"Clari, it's Grandma. I want to talk to you, honey. Come out."

Ever obedient, Clari crept from the bunk. She was taller than Cord but smaller-boned, with short brown curls and blue eyes. Theresa said, "Where did your mother hit you? Never mind, I can see from the way you're moving. Take off your pants, honey."

Painfully, Clari wiggled out of her pants. Red welts striped the backs of her thighs. Something turned over in Theresa's chest: anger and fear and a painful love for Senni, who was alienating those who should love her. Carefully she took Clari on her lap.

"Tell Grandma what happened. Don't leave anything out."

Every child at the farm and most of the adults obeyed that tone in Theresa's voice. Clari said, "We were playing, me and Cord and Kella and Susie and Angel. Monday and Tuesday, a long game of Hot Rocks, it lasted three days and I forgot to take care of the herb garden in the evenings."

Theresa had never asked the rules for Hot Rocks, an enormously complicated game the kids had invented and, apparently, kept adding to. She said, "Go on."

"Mommy hit me and Cord found out 'cause I was crying. He got really mad. He threw the Ender Rock so hard it broke, Grandma. Then he said him and me should run away and that would show Mom."

"Run away? Where? How?"

"To our secret place. On Uncle Scott's old horse."

Cold seeped up Theresa's spine. She hadn't thought to check the horses. Scott's bay, the one he'd first used when he came here, was too old for real use, but Scott let the children ride him for short periods and short distances. Cord wasn't a very good rider.

"Did Cord go to your secret place on Uncle Scott's horse?"

"I don't know. I couldn't go with him, Mommy would have been really really mad. I came here and slept in Angie's bed. Is Cord gone?" Clari looked scared.

"Yes, but I'm going to get him back right now. Where is your secret place, Clari?"

"Where all the dead bad men are buried. It has ghosts."

Theresa closed her eyes. She should monitor the stuff the kids watched on the Net more carefully. There was never time. The "bad dead men" were the refugees that Jody had killed with the bioweapon and buried in the arroyo, once again dry in the year-and-a-half drought. How had Clari even known about that incident?

She didn't ask. "Clari, I want you to go ask Carolina for some breakfast, eat it, and do two units of school software. It's your turn." DeWayne had bought school software and computers for all the kids to share.

"Is Cord okay?"

"Of course he is. Now go do as I told you."

Scott's nag wasn't in the barn. No one had noticed, since all the other horses were in use out on the range. DeWayne's truck, which he had purchased in lieu of the fancy little car he'd arrived in, had gone to Wenton. The bus was finally dead, and the new one Lillie had ordered last year had had to be sold as the farm funds dwindled.

Theresa smacked her fist against the barn wall in frustration. She could have gone back to the house and Net-paged Jody out on the range, the pagers being another innovation due to DeWayne. But God knew where Jody was. He could be halfway to the El Capitan mountains with their cattle. The arroyo was only a little over a mile away. She put on the wide-brimmed hat with neck curtains that the high UV made necessary, filled a canteen, and started to walk.

By the time she reached the arroyo, Theresa's legs felt wobbly. She didn't walk much anymore on the open range. She had a canteen with her but wanted to save the water for Cord. The arroyo was completely dry, and the gray rough bark of the cottonwoods looked tired and dusty. Cord wasn't there.

She sat in the welcome shade, panting. Hoof tracks led away from the arroyo. But there was nothing in that direction but desert. Desert that a year ago had just begun to be prairie, its greening now cut off like an execution.

Theresa took three long swallows of water and started walking. If Cord hadn't thought to bring a hat . . . it had been night when he'd run off. And he'd been too angry to think straight or he wouldn't have started this stupid trek in the first place.

A few miles out, Theresa came across Scott's horse. It had found a semi-living green bush and was chomping at it eagerly. The saddle was empty.

Now she was genuinely afraid. How far had Cord gotten before he fell off, or let the horse wander away, or whatever had happened? The child could be laying injured in the hot sun, dehydrated, alone . . .

Theresa took two more swallows of water—her last, she promised herself—and kept on walking. How soon before someone followed her? They would, of course. Senni would have the sense (and the remorse) to Net-page Jody or Spring. Lillie and DeWayne would come home from town. Someone would come.

Meanwhile, she kept walking, kept calling. "Cord! Cord, can you hear me? Cord, answer me! Cord!" Her throat grew hoarse.

The wind was picking up. Sand started to blow against her face, into her eyes. Oh, God, no, not a dust storm, no one would ever find Cord or her, and alone out here in a dust storm . . . "Cord! Cord!"

The wind blew harder.

Was that him? She ran forward, her legs aching, but it was only an unusually large prickly pear, vaguely shaped like a prone boy.

She was sobbing from frustration and fear when she finally spotted Cord. Lurching, stumbling forward, she fell on her knees beside his crumpled little body, lying beside a clump of thorny mesquite.

She gasped, inhaling a mouthful of dust.

It was Cord . . . and it wasn't. He crouched on his stomach, head tucked forward as much under his chest as possible, facing away from the wind. His arms and legs were drawn under him. His thin shirt had torn, and Theresa could see that over his back and neck and head had grown a sort of . . . *shell*. A thin membrane, tough and flexible as plastic when she touched it.

Water. He had grown a temporary shell to keep water from evaporating.

The sand was blowing harder now. Theresa closed her eyes against its sting and groped for Cord's pulse along his neck. She found it through the membrane and counted: ten pulses per minute, slow and even. Her fingers groped underneath the boy, and touched something hard and thin at his belly. She felt it, dug with her nails where it entered the soil. She knew what it was, had encountered it her whole life on the range. All cacti had them. A taproot, sent deep into the soil to tap whatever water might be buried far down.

Behind the membrane, Cord's eyes were closed. His child's face had evened out in his deep sleep, hibernation, estivation, whatever the right word was. Or maybe there was no right word for this.

The storm was building fiercely now. Theresa drank the last of her water, feeling it mix with the grit in her mouth and scrape down her throat, knowing it wouldn't make much difference. Everything depended now on how long and hard the wind blew, obscuring visibility, accelerating dehydration. She lay down beside Cord and put her arms around him.

Scott, I know what all the extra genes are for. They're for adapting to whatever we do to fuck up the planet.

She squeezed her eyes shut. Grit ground under the lids, making her gasp with pain and open them. A mistake. Now she could barely see the mesquite a foot away.

Was Cord human? Yes, yes, yes, her fading mind said. She didn't know why or how she knew, but she did. Cord, all of the children engineered on that alien ship, were human. She would bet her life on it.

Which was pretty funny, actually—

The wind mounted in fury. Theresa's arms loosened, unable to hold their grip.

Her last thought was for Cord: *Pribir, wherever you are, thank you.*

The storm blew till night fell. The winds brought clouds in their wake, fierce black clouds like a tarp under the sky. Clouds, but no rain. It was twenty-four hours before they could find and retrieve Theresa's body. By that time, there wasn't much left of it. Weather and coyotes.

Lillie spent the twenty-four convinced that both Cord and Theresa were dead. Theresa, who had been first a friend and then a mother to Lillie, far more of a mother than Barbara had ever been. Theresa, who had taken Uncle Keith's place so naturally, so unobtrusively that Lillie had hardly even noticed.

For those two days Keith and Kella had clung to her, crying for their brother. Awkwardly she held them to her, struggling with her own pain. Cord, dead out on the range somewhere in this terrible storm. Cord, her little boy . . . oh, God, at least let them be together. Let him have Theresa in his last hours. He'd never had his mother.

Keith and Kella slept with her, for the few hours she could sleep. Lying in the narrow bed with a child pressed up close to her on either side, clutching at her even in sleep, Lillie realized for the first time the terrible burden of being a real parent. It was not that she didn't love her children, but that she did. She was hostage to their fortune, her life's outcome dependent on theirs, as Keith's had been on Lillie's. She had never known. She had never understood, not any of it.

Theresa had known. Theresa had always known.

When Spring found Cord, he was still "dormant." That's what Scott called it. Scott, fascinated and grateful and appalled, took cells from all of Cord's adaptations, including the "taproot" that Spring had sliced through because it went too deep to pull up. Then, holding his breath, he'd poured water over Cord.

As Scott and Lillie watched, the membrane around the child dissolved. The base of the taproot fell off as easily as an outgrown umbilical. Cord's breathing quickened. He opened his eyes, saw his mother's face, and started to cry.

Lillie gathered him into her arms, wet and filthy and smelling of what Scott would later determine was a skin repellent against predators. She held him tightly against her, and for the first time in years she cried, too. Scott left the room with his collected samples, softly closing the door. Lillie cradled her pribir-created son and knew for the first time not only what he was, but also that through him she, too, was becoming, finally, fully human.

PART IV: CORD

"If this is the best of all possible worlds,
then where are the others?"
—Voltaire, *Candide*

CHAPTER 19

After his grandmother died, nothing was the same for Cord, except Clari. Everything else turned itself inside out, like a sock.

"Tell me about the pribir," he demanded of Dr. Wilkins. It seemed all Cord could do lately was demand, as if he were a three-year-old like Aunt Julie's newest baby. He knew it, and regretted it, and couldn't stop it.

Dr. Wilkins, gray-haired and a bit stooped, said, "What do you want to know?"

"Everything. Grandma didn't talk to me about them. All she said was they changed the genes for my mother and then for all us kids."

"All of you born to the girls—women—who went up to the spaceship. Not Dolly or Clari or . . ."

"I *know* that. But what did they do on the ship?"

Dr. Wilkins said gently, "I wasn't there, Cord. I stayed behind, like your grandmother."

"But—"

"You should ask your mother."

"Okay," Cord said. "But you're the one who can tell me about genetics."

Dr. Wilkins looked startled. He was really old, as old as Grandma had been. But he knew things, and Cord wanted to learn them.

"Cord, you never showed any interest in genetics before."

"Well, I am now," he said stubbornly. But when Dr. Wilkins started to explain messenger RNA and transcription and protein formation, Cord's mind wandered. This wasn't what he thirsted for, after all. Even he could see that. Bobby and Angie and Taneesha were much more interested, working at the school software in biology, clustering around Dr. Wilkins and Uncle Rafe to learn to use the complicated, expensive engineering equipment.

Cord turned instead to his mother. That was another thing that had changed. His mother used to mostly ignore him, busy with the farm's bills and income and boring stuff like that. But now she was home for dinner every night, listening to Cord and Keith and Kella, asking about their day, touching them on the arm or cheek. It made Cord uncomfortable. He didn't know why she was behaving like this, like all of a sudden she was Grandma. Well, she wasn't. Grandma was dead. Nobody else was Grandma and he wasn't going to pretend otherwise.

Still, she was the one to ask about the pribir. He waited until late afternoon on a hot, dry, June day. June was supposed to bring rain, Uncle Jody said. That was the old way for this country; the new way was rain all year long. But now they didn't have either way. The drought continued, and every night his mother walked out to watch the sunset with her face calm and hard.

On the porch Cord passed Clari coming up to the big house. "Cord? Where are you going?"

"I want to ask my mother about the pribir."

"Can I come?"

"Sure." As far as Cord was concerned, Clari could go anywhere he did. She was quiet, and she listened carefully, not like his pesky sister Kella, who interrupted everybody all the time.

The two children started toward the cottonwood stand by the creek, where a long time ago somebody had built a wide bench facing west. It was the prettiest place on the farm, the only place wildflowers bloomed often, even though the creek was only a trickle. Lillie sat there, gazing at the sky flaming red and gold above the long stretch of gray land. "There goes a jackrabbit," Clari said, but Cord had more important things on his mind than jackrabbits.

"Hi, Cord, Clari," Lillie said. "Look at that sky."

"Yeah, it's pretty. Mom—"

"It would be much prettier with rain clouds in it."

"Sure. Mom, tell me about the pribir." Cord flushed in embarrassment. He was demanding again, and anyway it never felt easy to talk to his mother.

But she tried to make it easy. "Okay, what do you want to know?"

"Everything. I heard you talk about Andrews Air Force Base with Grandma. What's an Air Force Base? Were the pribir there?"

"No. Sit down."

Cord and Clari sat. The wooden bench felt smooth under his rump. Somewhere above him an owl hooted softly.

His mother began slowly, as if searching for the right words. "Andrews Air Force Base was—maybe is again—a big camp for soldiers and planes. After doctors discovered that Grandma and Dr. Wilkins and I were genetically engineered, we were taken there."

"Why? How did they find out?"

"They found out because we all, all sixty of us, started to smell things. Smell information."

Clari said timidly, "I don't understand, Aunt Lillie."

His mother smiled. "Well, that's reasonable, because neither did we. All at once all of us just started to have . . . images in our head. Ideas and pictures and information, all about genetics. We were smelling special complex molecules that the pribir were secretly releasing into the air to send learning to humans on Earth."

Cord demanded, "How come you kids could smell the molecules and no one else could?"

"We were genetically engineered to do it, before we were born, by a doctor working for the pribir."

"Why didn't the pribir just give humans the information themselves? Why use a bunch of kids?" Cord said logically. This roundabout transmission route seemed dumb.

"They didn't want to risk coming to Earth. A lot of people didn't like the idea of genetic engineering."

Well, that made sense. As long as Cord could remember, he'd been told over and over to never mention genetics to anybody from Wenton.

"Also," his mother continued, "the pribir had something else in mind. Eventually they sent a shuttle—a small spaceship—to pick up all the engineered kids who wanted to go up to the ship. Twenty of us went, including me. Your grandmother Theresa stayed behind."

Clari asked, "Why did you go?"

His mother hesitated. "I'm not sure. I think partly for the adventure, partly because the pribir were making us smell molecules that made us want to go."

Cord considered this. "They couldn't be very strong molecules. Some people didn't go. Like Grandma."

"True."

"What happened on the ship?" Cord said.

Again his mother hesitated. The colors in the western sky were fading now and the stars were coming out, one by one. Finally she said, "A lot happened on the ship. The main thing was that the pribir engineered the babies we girls were all pregnant with. Including you, Cord. They gave you many different genes. Dr.

Wilkins thinks a lot of them are designed to let you survive on Earth no matter what changes the planet undergoes, or what environment you find yourself in."

Like the sandstorm that had killed Grandma. Cord had been told how he'd survived that.

Clari said, "How many pribir were on the ship, Aunt Lillie?"

"Probably a lot. But we only saw two."

Cord hadn't known that. "Two? Only two? The whole time?"

"Only two."

Clari breathed, "What did they look like?"

His mother smiled, but it wasn't a good smile. "They looked exactly like us. They said they'd been made that way deliberately. Their names were Pam and Pete."

Cord peered at his mother through the gloom to see if she was joking. She didn't seem to be. But . . . "Pam" and "Pete"? Those were names on old, stupid Net shows, not names for pribir. He said harshly, "Then did the pribir put you back on Earth? Why?"

"We didn't know. To have our babies here, I guess. But, Cord . . ." The longest hesitation yet. Cord waited. This was going to be important, he could tell from her voice. "Cord, you should probably know this. You're old enough, and anyway I think Dr. Wilkins already told Bobby and the other kids that hang around with him. The last thing the pribir said to us was that they would be back."

Cord sat very still. His mother put her arm around him, and for once he didn't pull away. He hardly felt the arm. Gladness was flooding through him. They were coming back!

Clari said fearfully, "When?"

"We don't know."

"Soon, I want it to be soon!" Cord burst out.

His mother pulled her arm away. "Why?"

It seemed to Cord a stupid question. The pribir were clearly heroes, a word he'd learned in school software. They had tremendous powers . . . imagine sending information through smells! They had made all the kids at the farm, practically . . . why, without them he wouldn't even exist! And they had saved his life by giving him the genes that had protected him during the sandstorm. More, they represented something Cord couldn't name, didn't have words for. He knew only that it was larger than the farm, the drought, the falling price of cattle that seemed to occupy the adults so much. Something large, and mysterious, and glorious.

But all he said to his mother was, "They're wonderful!"

His mother's voice turned cold. It was full dark now and Cord couldn't see her face, but he didn't need to. That voice was enough.

"'Wonderful'? You call it wonderful that they designed unborn babies with no regard to anything except pribir needs? That they kidnapped us kids and used smelled chemicals to manipulate our minds? That on the ship they made us . . . never mind that. That the pribir designed and engineered our babies and impregnated us without so much as asking permission, so that you and Keith and Kella and all the others never even had a recognizable father. You call that wonderful?"

Floundering under this attack, all Cord could think of to say was, "I don't need a father! I have Uncle Jody and Uncle Spring and Uncle Rafe and—"

"Every child should have a father."

"Clari doesn't!"

Clari, who had shrunk against the cottonwood trunk at the first hint of conflict, nodded loyally.

"But Clari did have a father," his mother said, more softly. "He just died before she was born. But she had him."

If Clari's father had been dead for Clari's whole life, Cord didn't see what good having a father had done her. Cord was angry now. "The pribir *are* wonderful! You just don't understand!"

"Oh, Cord," she said, and now her voice was completely soft, as soft as Clari's. He was not going to be won that easily.

"You don't understand, Mom. The pribir gave you everything, even me! And Keith and Kella!" He'd always known his mother didn't really want her kids. Now here was proof.

"I know," she said. "But, Cord, honey, they still did it through manipulation, tyranny, for their own reasons, not for our good."

"I don't care! Come on, Clari, the mosquitoes are out."

"Cord, please don't go, I want to talk more . . ."

But he grabbed Clari's hand and pulled her up off the bench and toward the house. Halfway there he turned back to face the cottonwoods and shouted, "The pribir *are* wonderful!" before running the rest of the way inside, dragging Clari with him.

He learned more from the other children. At various times, their respective mothers had dropped bits of information about the pribir. Aunt Bonnie's daughter Angie said that when she and her two brothers were born, their mother had had a very easy labor. This was important because recently Aunt Julie and Uncle Spring had had another baby, and Aunt Julie had screamed so much that

Dr. Wilkins gave her a drug. Cord didn't see why that was a problem, but Angie said importantly that Aunt Julie had wanted to do without drugs because they could be bad for the baby. Also, added Angie, who seemed to be a gush of information on birthing, Aunt Senni had had a very bad time with both Dolly and Clari.

"So the pribir made birthing easier with the babies they engineered. Less painful," Cord said. He was very glad he was a boy and would never have to birth anybody at all.

"Yeah," Angie said. "They sound like good people."

"I think so, too," said Taneesha, Aunt Sajelle's daughter, who was listening in. Taneesha, Kezia, and Jason had a father, Uncle DeWayne. But he wasn't their genetic father; the triplets had been engineered inside Aunt Sajelle, just like Cord had been. Cord thought Taneesha was the prettiest girl at the farm, not counting Clari. She had light brown skin and black curly hair and the biggest brown eyes Cord had ever seen. It made him uncomfortable, though, to think that Taneesha was so pretty. It seemed unfair to Clari.

But Taneesha was a good source of information. Aunt Sajelle apparently spoke to her kids much more frankly than anybody else's mother. "The pribir messed with my mama's genes, too. Not as much as with ours, of course. But Mama—and your mother, too, Cord—doesn't get sick. You ever noticed that? The pribir did something to them so they don't catch colds and stuff like Dolly and Clari and Angel do."

It was true, Cord realized. Clari had had something just last month that made her head ache and her muscles hurt, and Dolly and Angel got it, too, but nobody else.

"*And*," Taneesha said, leaning in close to the other kids huddled together behind the barn, "the pribir put the babies inside my mama and the other women without any sex!"

Cord flushed. He'd only been told about sex a few months ago, and the whole idea made him uncomfortable.

Dakota, Julie's son, was logical. "If there wasn't any sex, then how did the babies get made? You need an egg and a sperm."

Taneesha said triumphantly, "The pribir had a whole supply of sperm and eggs, and they just snipped out whatever genes they wanted from any of them and sewed them back together however they wanted."

This explanation seemed lacking to Cord—no sperm or egg anywhere had genes for what he'd grown during the sandstorm. So the pribir had also built brand-new genes from scratch, or taken them from some other . . . thing. If so, that made the pribir more powerful than ever. And smart: They'd known what he might need to survive. And kind, because they wanted him to survive. Probably if she hadn't already been a grown-up when she went to that Andrews place, they might have engineered his grandmother Theresa to survive the sandstorm, too.

Dakota said solemnly to Cord, "They saved your life, you know."

"I know."

"Well, I can't wait till they come back." This piece of Cord's information had electrified them all.

"Me, neither," said Kendra and Taneesha, simultaneously. Taneesha added kindly, "I'm sorry you're not genetically engineered, too, Clari."

Clari looked down at the ground and said nothing.

By summer of 2067 it still hadn't rained much. Three years of drought. Wenton, which had over the years grown to look almost prosperous, didn't look that way any more. Some people left. Others, from even more desperate places, arrived on the one train per day still arriving at the decaying station. One Thursday in April, two women, one man, and six children got off the train. They stood staring past the shrunken edge of Wenton to the flat, parched plains, stretching for miles and miles of nothing.

Cord, in town with Uncle DeWayne and Taneesha to buy cloth, spied the starers, skinny and battered-looking. *City people*, he thought. He knew cities from the Net shows and Net news, which was the way he knew about anything more than ten miles from the farm. Well, these people wouldn't find whatever they were looking for, work or food or a new start, in Wenton.

Uncle DeWayne stopped walking.

"Daddy?" Taneesha said. But Uncle DeWayne ignored her, walking toward the strangers and leaving her and Cord behind.

"Oh oh," Taneesha said.

"What?"

"Haven't you got eyes, Cord? Six kids, two women—they're more of *us*. Daddy must recognize one of them."

Of course. Cord and Taneesha ran after Uncle DeWayne.

Uncle DeWayne said to the man, "Mike? Mike Franzi?"

The man said nothing, studying this well-dressed black man. One of the little girls shrank behind him.

Uncle DeWayne grinned hugely. "Sure it is. Mike Franzi, and you've forgotten all those basketball games at Andrews where I whipped your white ass. DeWayne Freeman!"

The stranger seized Uncle DeWayne's hand. One of the women started to cry.

Taneesha said in a low voice to Cord, "Here's trouble."

"What? Who?"

Taneesha didn't answer, but she stared back without flinching at one of the girls, who was giving her the finger.

It was another of those weird relationships. Two of the strangers, Mike Franzi and Hannah Reeder, were twenty-seven. They had been at Andrews Air Force Base with Uncle DeWayne and Dr. Wilkins, who were sixty-seven. So had the other woman, Robin Perry, but she hadn't gone up to the pribir ship and so she was sixty-seven, too. Three of the kids were "Aunt Hannah's," as Cord was instructed to call her. The other three belonged to some woman named Sophie, who was dead, but now old "Aunt Robin" was taking care of her kids.

When he was a child, thought thirteen-and-a-half-year-old Cord, all this seemed normal. It was just the way things were. Now, after watching the Net, he saw how abnormal it was. Well, that was good! He and his "family" were abnormal because they were special, made that way by the pribir.

The strange thing was the way his mother reacted when they all went back to the farm in Uncle DeWayne's truck.

Lillie—lately Cord had begun thinking of her that way, although he wasn't sure why—took one look at Mike Franzi and stopped dead. Then a slow, long blush spread up from her neck over her face, turning it red as sunset. Lillie, who never blushed!

"Hello, Mike."

"Hello, Lillie. Long time."

"How many years? Twelve."

"You look wonderful," he said. Cord scowled. His mother looking 'wonderful'? She was just his mother.

Lillie said, "Tell me what happened."

He smiled. "Direct as always. All right, the short version is, Hannah and I were in Philadelphia. It got impossible, food riots and burning. We found Robin and Sophie on the Net, living together with their kids in Denver. We went there because it sounded better, and for a while it was. But then it got as dangerous and hungry as Philly, no jobs. Two weeks ago Sophie was killed in a riot. By that time I recognized Rafe's message on the Net, and here we are."

Cord knew that message, although he didn't understand it. It went: *Do you remember Andrew? How about Pam and Pete? They're still gone, of course, but their legacy remains. Sometimes it seems I can still smell them. So much is gone, but we're here.*

Dr. Wilkins said, "Why didn't you Net us that you were coming?"

Mike didn't answer. After a moment the girl who had given Taneesha the finger said defiantly, "We were afraid you wouldn't take us in."

Uncle Jody said, "We will. My mother would have wanted it."

Lillie added, "If we didn't want you, why would Rafe have posted that message? You're welcome, all of you, as long as you're willing to work. Times are tougher than they were—but I guess I don't have to tell you that."

The old woman, "Robin," said bitterly, "Lillie, you don't know about tough times. You missed the war. Don't try to tell me about tough times."

Lillie looked startled, and then her eyes met Mike's, and something passed between them. All Cord saw was a tiny smile and an even tinier shake of his head, but once more his mother—his mother!—blushed. And then she looked at the younger woman, Hannah, and looked away.

Mike said, "These are Sophie's children, Roy, Patty, and Ashley." Ashley and Taneesha stared each other down. *Trouble*, Taneesha had said, and Cord believed it. Ashley was as skinny as the rest but taller and muscled. Her insolent look around the cluttered great room said she didn't think much of it. As if she was used to better.

Hannah said in a high, strained voice, "These are my children. Frank and Bruce and Loni."

"Hi," a few of the farm kids said shyly. The rest of the introductions were made. The new people would never remember all the names, Cord thought. He couldn't even remember all of theirs, and there were only nine. Which one was Bruce?

Aunt Sajelle said, "Let's get you all fed and settled." Since Grandma's death, Aunt Sajelle had taken over running the big house, with Aunt Carolina's help.

Clari, at Cord's elbow said, "They look so hungry."

"They probably are," Cord said. Clari was always kind, so sweet. The other boys, especially his brother Keith, teased Cord about having a girl for a best friend, but he didn't care. There was no one like Clari.

CHAPTER 20

Ashley Vogel was the only kid at the farm who hated the pribir. "They wrecked my life," she said. "Fuck them."

"No," Taneesha said, "they gave you your life. They wrecked our lives by sending you here. Why don't you just go back where you came from."

"Fuck you," Ashley said.

A ring of kids surrounded the two at Dead Men's Arroyo. Ashley had wanted to see where the refugees who once attacked the farm were buried, because Dolly had told her it was haunted. Nine of them had hiked out in the late afternoon, when the sun wasn't too dangerous, on the half-day a week they were allowed off from chores and studies. The hike out was tense. Dolly, the only person who liked Ashley, walked ahead with her, whispering together and jeering over their shoulders at the others.

Cord had gone because he was both bored and strangely keyed up. The new kids had upset the balance at the farm. New friendships formed, old alliances shifted, among both children and adults. No one liked Aunt Robin. She was the same age as Uncle DeWayne and Dr. Wilkins, but she seemed older, nastier. Her hip hurt her, her gut ached, she was always complaining. Aunt Hannah was all right and her kids didn't cause any trouble, but something wasn't right there, either. Something about Aunt Hannah and Cord's mother. He didn't like to think about it. It was partly to avoid thinking about it that he'd hiked down to the arroyo with Dolly, Ashley, Taneesha, Jason, Keith, Kella, Gavin, Dakota, and Bobby. Clari had another one of her colds and her mother made her stay in bed.

Walking over the land, following his own lengthening shadow, Cord remembered how it used to be. Greener, with bushes and little low flowers everywhere and even some cottonwood saplings starting to take growth. Now, except where the farm irrigated with windpower, the ground stretched gray and bleached, dust devils rising in yellow funnels on the wind. The new saplings had all withered. Tumbleweed rolled across his path.

At the arroyo, studying the marker stone for the mass grave, Ashley said, "Let's dig them up."

Kella was shocked. "You can't do that! You're not supposed to disturb the dead. Besides, what if some of the micros from the bioweapon are still active? We could die!"

"The micros aren't still active," Dakota said authoritatively. He was one of the kids that studied with Dr. Wilkins. "They had a terminator gene built in for only twelve replications."

"Too bad," Ashley said coolly. "We could all die. That would be so bonus."

Cord gaped at her. He knew that Ashley was showing off, but something about her disturbed him. Not just her meanness . . . something else he couldn't name.

Kella said, "But you don't want to die, Ashley!"

"Why not? End this misery."

Cord found himself saying, "I don't want to hear that kind of talk."

"Yeah," Bobby said. "And anyway, what misery? You're here now, the farm is going to take care of you, what's so miserable?"

"We are," Ashley said. "All of us. Miserable abominations because that what the fucking pribir made us."

"Stop it, Ashley," Kella said. "I know you're just showing off."

"I was never more serious in my life," Ashley said, and again Cord glimpsed that something he couldn't name. It was almost as if Ashley . . . meant it.

"The pribir did an incredible job of creating us," Dakota said, and began a technical recital of genetic engineering. Dakota, Cord saw, was also showing off.

"Fuck that," Ashley said. "The pribir made us so we're not human and regular humans spit on us and hate us, and I hate the pribir for doing that. If they come back the way they said, I'll kill them myself. Personally."

Complete silence.

"I'll sneak up on them from behind with the scythe in the barn," Ashley embellished, "and one smack to the head will cut them in two. I'll dance in the blood. I'll—"

"That's enough," Taneesha said. Until now she'd been quiet,

sitting expressionless on a boulder. Now she stood, and Cord saw that she was outraged, and afraid, and eager. "Shut your mouth, Ashley."

"Don't tell me what to do, you bitch."

The two girls started to circle each other. Everyone else drew back. Cord suddenly realized that this was why Ashley and Taneesha had come to the dry arroyo, and maybe the others, too, or at least some of them. This fight that had been building for weeks now, for reasons he couldn't begin to state.

Cord didn't want to see it. He wanted Taneesha to win, of course. Ashley's words had genuinely sickened him. The pribir were heroes, Cord couldn't wait for their promised return, and for Ashley to say what she had was like . . . well, like pissing on food. Nonetheless, he still didn't want to see the fight.

Taneesha, taller and better nourished, got in the first punch, hard and quick to Ashley's stomach. Ashley bent over in pain and Cord thought the fight had ended right there. But Ashley straightened up and after that she attacked like a wounded bear. Cord had never seen this sort of fight. Ashley screamed, she gouged at Taneesha's eyes, she kicked and scratched and bit. Was *that* the way kids fought in the city?

After a stunned moment, four people rushed forward to pull the girls apart. Ashley would not let go. Cord stayed only long enough to make sure that the others had the wildcat under control and that Taneesha was being taken care of. Then he turned and started back to the farm. He was disgusted.

Clari would never behave that way.

No, it was more than that. He didn't want to see blood dripping down Taneesha's pretty face.

No, it was more than *that*. If Taneesha hadn't fought Ashley, Cord might have done it himself, for what she'd said about the pribir. It filled him with a deep rage that he didn't know what to do with. He took the rage away from the others, out on the plain, alone.

But that wasn't a good idea, either. Days were longer than in winter, but not all that long, and being caught alone on the desert at night wasn't a good idea. He'd learned that at eleven years old.

So he stalked the mile-and-then-some back to the farm, knotting and unknotting his fists, circling a very long way around the outbuildings and cattle pens and cottonwood grove to give himself more time alone, and that was how he happened upon his mother and Uncle Mike.

They sat on the ground under a lone cottonwood farther down the creek than the grove with the bench. This tree's low branches drooped almost, but not quite, over the two adults. They didn't touch. But the way they sat so close together, the tension in both figures, caught at Cord. He crept closer and crouched behind a boulder. It didn't hide him completely and if they turned they would see him, but both were too absorbed to turn.

"—too mixed up to tell," Mike said.

"I know," Lillie answered. "They just took whatever they needed from whoever's sperm. Any of them could have anybody's genes."

The pribir. They were talking about the pribir. Cord strained to hear.

"Still," Mike said, "Kella and Cord look like me. A little. But with your eyes."

"Well . . . a little," Lillie said. "But then, so does Bonnie's Angie, sort of. We'll never know."

"Scott can't—"

"No. He says the mixing is just too complete. The usual markers simply don't apply. The pribir apparently built almost from scratch."

"Still," Mike said, "it was you and I who slept together on the ship."

"Plus you and Sophie," Lillie said. After a moment she added, "Not that it matters any more, Mike. We both know what was being done to drive us. If I blamed you at the time, it was because I was a lovesick child."

"I know. But, Lillie—"

"Don't say it. Please."

"No, I'm going to. It has to be said. We're not children now."

"You're with Hannah now," Lillie said. "Since how long?"

"Two years. But Lillie . . . be fair. She was desperate, she and later Sophie, and I've never risked being with anyone else who wasn't one of us, afraid of what genes I'd pass on—"

"Oh, God, I know," Lillie said. "Some nights I've ached. For you, Mike. Only for you."

"Then we should—"

"No! What are you going to do, tell Hannah to leave the farm? You told me what it was like out there for her, for the kids. Or are you thinking you can just switch wives while we're both here? What will that do to Hannah?"

"She's not my wife. We never married. Oh, damn it, Lillie, I know you're right. We can't . . ."

"We can't even talk about it again," Lillie said.

"Then if that's so, give me one kiss. Surely one kiss isn't too big a booby prize for never having you again."

Slowly, like a rock slide starting small, Cord saw his mother lean toward Mike and his arms go around her hard.

His rage broke. At Ashley, at Taneesha, at Clari for being sick in bed, at the loss of the pribir who'd said they would come back and hadn't, at everything. He exploded from behind the rock and shouted, "Stop it, you whore! Stop it, you, get away from my mother!" And then stopped dead because no one spoke like that except in Net shows, he had said the unforgivable no he hadn't but he was wrong wrong wrong. Now his mother would kill him.

She didn't. She detached herself from Mike's arms and walked over to him. A pulse beat in her neck, above her open shirt, and her face was flushed, but her voice was calm. "You're very angry, Cord. But even angry, you aren't allowed to behave like this. Apologize, please."

"I'm sorry," Cord mumbled, and then he was sorry, sorrier than he'd ever been in his life. He raised his hand, dropped it, hid his face in the crook of his arm. Lillie's arms went around him and her voice sounded close to his ear, low and sweet and sad.

"I know, Cord. I know, honey. But it's all right, and no one will ever mention this again."

Cord knew it was the truth. She never would, and she would make sure Mike didn't, and she wouldn't treat him as anything less because of this. Overcome, he said, "I love you, Mom," and felt her arms tighten and her face grow wet against his ear.

Ashley and Taneesha both came home bloody, and Taneesha's arm was broken. Dr. Wilkins set it, muttering about childhood stupidity. Aunt Robin, who was supposed to be in charge of Ashley, wanted to whip her but Uncle DeWayne, who along with Lillie and Aunt Sajelle and Uncle Jody was more or less in charge of everybody, refused to allow it. The girls were punished by extra chores and no time outside for two weeks. Both of them healed so fast that Dr. Wilkins took more tissue samples and spent three more days crouched over his gene equipment, trying once again to map all the immune system activity in Ashley and Sajelle.

For days the kids talked about the fight, whispering about what Ashley had said and done, why she could possibly have done it. Her brother and sister, Roy and Patty, were consulted about things that had happened to them all before they came to the farm. Roy and Patty were reluctant to talk. Both quieter and more cooperative than Ashley, they seemed to want only to put the past out of their minds. Gavin, who had begun to read old psychology books on the Net, said that Ashley showed "self-hatred," but this was deemed silly by the others. Why would anyone hate themselves?

Five of them were whispering about this in the den at the big house, with Cord trying to ignore them and do his schoolwork on the computer, when Dr. Wilkins walked in. "Come to the great room. Now," he said, and walked out again. The five kids looked at each other. Dr. Wilkins was old and wrinkled and tired, but his face didn't usually look that gray. Something had happened.

Cord sat on the floor next to Clari and whispered, "What's going on?"

"I don't know. More people are coming."

When nearly everyone had squeezed into the great room, Dr. Wilkins said, "China and European Federation are at war. They're using bioweapons. We're too far away for viable micros to affect us here, but I don't have any idea what the weapons are. There are micros that can encyst and then vitiate after they're breathed in. Also, if China decides to include us in the war—either because they're winning and can or are losing and are desperate—or even to include Mexico, we could have a problem. I want everybody to be completely alert to any changes in your physical functioning. And I mean anything: diarrhea, constipation, a cough, a pain, a headache, a muscle twitch, anything. Tell me or Emily." Dr. Wilkins was training Emily in medicine.

Spring said, "Hell, if I reported every muscle spasm, I'd never have time to get on a horse. Hey—what about the horse's muscle spasms?"

"It isn't funny, Spring," Dr. Wilkins said, which wasn't fair because Spring was probably serious. Sometime it was hard to tell. "You and other non-engineered are at special risk. I think."

Cord took Clari's hand. She wasn't engineered. Lillie was, sort of, like the others in the first generation the pribir had helped. Could Cord himself withstand all bioweapons? Nobody knew. That was probably another reason that Dr. Wilkins wanted to hear about any symptoms. He could learn more about what all Cord's extra genes were supposed to do.

But that wouldn't be as good as learning it from the pribir themselves. Aunt Sajelle had said that the last two pribir visits were forty years apart. God, he wasn't going to have to wait another twenty-nine years, was he?

"Cord," Dr. Wilkins said, "are you listening?"

"Yes," he lied. Across the room, Taneesha made a face at him, her eye still half closed and her lip swollen from the fight. Cord smiled despite himself. She was healing very fast, Emily said. Taneesha would be all right. Everyone would be all right. China and Europe were an unthinkable distance away.

Finally, three and a half years after the drought began, the rains returned. All that spring and summer majestic thunder clouds formed over the high plain, towering black piles that sometimes let down moisture and sometimes didn't. "Much better than before the warming or the last three years," Uncle DeWayne said, "but not as good as the best years."

The following summer, Cord abruptly grew four inches. His voice cracked. He spent a lot of time in the fields, since he didn't like to ride, and the work turned him strong and, even with precautions against UV, brown. When he looked in the mirror, he frowned. Was that him? "You look wonderful," his mother said, and he felt himself go hot with embarrassment and pleasure.

The kids all seemed to fly apart that summer. Instead of spending their time together playing Hot Rocks, each of them began to spend more time with adults, working hard. Dr. Wilkins was training Emily in science and genetics. Keith spent more and more time with Uncle Jody and the cattle. Kendra started learning poetry by heart—why would anybody want to do that? Kezia and Roy hung around the hot cookhouse, and Roy learned to make a chili stew that was better than Aunt Sajelle's or Aunt Carolina's. He wouldn't tell anybody what he put into it.

Aunt Hannah had brought an old music cube with her, and her kids played it over and over. Ashley's favorite song was "Don't Matter None to Me." The first time Cord's mother heard the cube play that song, she froze, a strange look on her face. But the look passed, and Cord forgot about it.

Small biowars went on breaking out over the globe, but Cord didn't pay much attention. Nobody in New Mexico got sick, and that was all he really cared about.

The pribir did not come.

Later, it seemed to him that the three years between Grandma Theresa's death and Cord's fourteenth birthday had passed in one long, unbroken, monotonous, peaceful stretch. Nothing seemed to have happened, even though he could recite events that had. But he walked through them half-conscious, maybe, or encased in some sort of childish membrane. Nothing got through unfiltered, undiluted. Nothing upset his internal chemistry.

In December 2067, Cord and the others turned fourteen.

CHAPTER 21

Cord awoke abruptly, his heart pounding. Second time tonight! He could take care of it in the usual way . . . but he didn't want to. He wanted to go outside. Why? He just did. Damn it, did he have to have a reason for everything he did?

Throwing on his clothes, he left the room where Keith, Bobby, and Gavin slept fitfully in their bunks. Jason, Roy, and Dakota had gone on the cattle drive, along with some of the girls, Kendra and Kella and maybe Felicity.

At the thought of girls, the problem got worse.

The night was cool and starry, moonless. An owl hooted in the dark. Cord smelled sage and mint on the fresh breeze. Maddened by the sweetness, he paced restlessly out to the barn, didn't go inside, paced back. He didn't want to go in. He headed for the bench under the cottonwood grove by the creek, stumbling and cursing in the dark.

Two figures sat there, wrapped in each other's arms.

Cord couldn't tell who they were, not even by straining his eyesight. Suddenly he was ashamed of himself for even trying. Not his business. Only . . . why would any of the married couples be kissing outside at two in the morning? They could be warm in their beds, touching each other in comfort and . . .

He ached with envy.

Cord turned toward the smaller houses set up the slope. At Senni's place, he stopped. Clari was in there. God, to sit with Clari under that tree and do what that couple were doing! He would wake Clari.

He couldn't wake Clari. She would be upset and if Aunt Senni ever found out . . . Cord shuddered.

Totally frustrated, he smacked his fist into the side of his head and again started toward the big house. He hadn't even put shoes on, his feet were freezing, he was the world's biggest idiot . . .

Someone stood in the shadows on the porch, a dark figure in a white nightdress. Cord moved cautiously closer. He had to practically walk into her before he could see who it was. Taneesha.

The two stared at each other, inches apart. Cord could hear himself breathing. Finally Taneesha said, "I couldn't sleep."

"Me neither." His voice came out ragged.

"Cord, I . . ." She took a step toward him.

Cord couldn't help himself. As if propelled by some sort of motor, a will-less machine, he reached for her. She lunged toward him with a sort of small hop, and then they were kissing and his hands were on her breasts through her thin nightdress and nothing else existed in the world.

"Where . . . can we go?" Taneesha breathed when he pulled his mouth away from hers to breathe. "Oh, Cord . . ."

She was as driven as he was. He gasped, "Wait here a minute," went back inside and pulled the blankets off his bunk. He thought Gavin opened his eyes but Cord wasn't sure and he didn't care.

They took the blankets to the wellhouse and threw them on the floor of hard-packed dirt. It was even colder in here, plus damp; neither noticed. They went at each other with a fierceness beyond control. Not even breaking Taneesha's hymen, and her brief cry of pain, stopped either one of them. Afterward, they both fell asleep, only to wake sometime in the predawn and do it again.

It wasn't until he woke for the second time, shivering under the inadequate blanket with Taneesha rumpled beside him, that Cord thought in anguish: *Clari*.

Sex happened to all of them at once. That was how Cord thought of it: "Sex happened." Like thunderstorms or earthquakes.

Keith and Loni, Bobby and Maya, Gavin and Susie, Frank and Patty, Bruce and Ashley. Kezia, unpaired, looked angry and desperate. She asked often when the range crew was returning.

It took the adults twenty-four hours to notice what was happening. Work was neglected, couples disappeared, all the kids looked dazed and wobbly. Dr. Wilkins was appalled. "They're not even using birth control!"

"Then give them some," Sajelle said wearily. "Scott, you don't know. They can't help it."

"Of course they can help it!" snapped Robin, old and outraged. "They're not animals!"

"Robin, you weren't on the ship," Emily said. "You don't know.

For us the pribir did it with olfactory molecules. For this generation, it's apparently built in."

"I don't believe—"

"I don't care what you believe, Robin," Lillie said, and Cord, who overheard this and knew he was not supposed to, was surprised at the rare anger in his mother's voice. Why?

Keith, Lillie's son, was having sex with Loni, Mike's daughter. Was that it? That whole episode with Lillie and Mike under the cottonwood three years ago looked entirely different now. Had his mother and Mike felt like he did with Taneesha? Don't think about it.

Lillie added, still angry, "Scott, give them some birth control."

Emily said, "I'm not sure it will do any good. I can run some tests, but the pribir knew their genetics. My guess is that the girls' Fallopian tubes are designed to counteract any birth control we can manage."

Bonnie said, appalled, "You mean the girls . . . my Angie . . . she's going to get pregnant no matter what we do?"

"We did," Lillie said, still angry.

Julie—quiet, timid Julie!—said, "Damn the pribir all to hell forever," and Cord crept away. He didn't want to hear that.

And he had to find Clari.

She was in the washhouse, doing laundry. The wind-powered generator made limited amounts of non-emission electricity, which powered select machines in order of necessity. The washing machine was not a high priority, but nothing else was running right now and Clari, Dolly, and Aunt Carolina's eight-year-old, Elena, were doing laundry. Dolly looked up as soon as Cord blundered in.

"Come to help, Cord?" she sneered. "You haven't been much use otherwise lately."

"Clari," he said humbly, "can I talk to you?" Her nose was red and swollen; she'd been crying.

Dolly said, "Leave her alone. We know where you've been and what you've been doing!"

"What was he doing?" said little Elena with interest.

"Please, Clari," Cord begged.

She put down sopping clothes and followed him outside. Glaring sun cast stunted shadows.

"Come under the trees, Clari." He led her to a nearby stand of young juniper that had been carefully nurtured through the long drought. "I . . . I . . ."

She looked at him miserably, and his words burst out.

"Oh, Clari, I'm so sorry. It was you I wanted, not Taneesha, but you were asleep in the middle of the night and . . . Clari, I heard the grown-ups talking. Aunt Emily said we've been engineered to do this, to be driven to sex right now so the girls will get pregnant—" At the look on her face he stopped.

She said, "Engineered? To have sex and get pregnant, and you can't help it?"

"Yes! I mean, no!"

"That's evil, Cord! That's genuinely evil. To use people like that."

Cord didn't feel used. Looking at her swollen, dear face, he felt more lust. His groin swelled and all he wanted was to—

"Come with me," he said desperately. "To the barn. Or someplace. It's you I want, not Taneesha, but if I can't have you I will do it again with her. I know it. Oh, please, Clari, we belong together, we always have, I want to marry you . . ."

He didn't know what he was saying. Marry? Now, at fourteen? But he dimly realized that he would say anything, anything at all, to get Clari to go with him to the barn.

She looked scared. "Cord, I . . . don't want to. Not yet. Someday—"

"I can't wait until someday!"

"Then you don't love me very much, if you won't wait for me," she said sadly, and walked away.

Cord stood there, wretched and angry and ashamed and driven, and after a minute he went to find Taneesha.

For forty-eight hours he avoided Clari and had sex with Taneesha every chance he could. The range crew came in, or rather part of them did. Alex said, "I brought the kids back. They were no use. They . . ."

"I know," Lillie said.

"Me, too," Alex said, not looking at her. "I remember. Jody is upset and angry."

"He doesn't have to be, Alex. His and Carolina's kids aren't engineered."

"What about Julie's kids with Spring, when they're older? Will they inherit it? The sex drive could be dominant."

"I hadn't thought of that," Lillie said slowly.

"I'll bet Scott has. Lillie . . . I'm going to ask you because you're the most level-headed woman here. There are more girls than boys. Do you think Kezia . . . I mean, does it have to be one of their own . . . God, Lillie, it's been so long!"

"She's fourteen, Alex."

"I know. So were we."

"You're twenty-eight."

"I know!"

"It's up to you and her," Lillie said wearily. "And, I guess, to Sajelle. Sajelle's her mother. You can ask. Sajelle's always been clear-eyed."

Alex said, "I hate this. But in Wenton now there are mostly . . . I'd be good to Kezia, Lillie."

"I believe it," Lillie said.

The next day Kezia left to go back with Alex to the cattle on the range.

Cord said to Taneesha, "Tannie . . . I'm sorry. You're great, and beautiful, and I always liked you. But me and Clari—"

Taneesha's dark eyes flashed. "Yeah? You and Clari? It's Clari you want to have sex with, not me?"

Cord said nothing, staring at his stupid goddamn feet in their stupid goddamn boots.

Taneesha was Sajelle's daughter, clear-eyed. She sighed. "Okay, Cord. I guess I knew that. I just . . . I just . . ."

"Don't cry!" he begged.

"I don't ever cry, Cord Anderson, and don't you forget it! You aren't the only male in the whole sorry world, you know! Anyway," she said, changing mood again, "does Clari want to?"

"No."

"Then why are you—"

"I don't know!" he shouted, and to his surprise, she actually chuckled.

"I know. You love her, you always did. Go find Clari and talk her into it, Cord. I'll be fine."

She was. The next time Cord saw her, she was with Rafe, who looked just as embarrassed and uneasy and pleased as Alex.

Cord found Clari and pleaded and coaxed until Clari said yes. But it wasn't like with Taneesha. Clari didn't seem to enjoy it and the first time hurt her a lot. Cord hated himself, and couldn't stop, and vowed in his heart that he would make it up to Clari. He would get for her anything, everything, she might ever want. If it took the whole rest of his life, he would make it up to her.

By year's end, all eleven of the girls engineered aboard the pribir ship, plus Clari, were pregnant. On January 7, war was declared with China. Within the first hour, missiles delivered bioweapons into the atmosphere over forty-seven targets in the United States.

The U.S. defense system, more obsolete than the government had even realized, shot down only eight. The Defense Department retaliated with bioweapons of their own.

Net news reported deaths in the millions, then the tens of millions. The camvids on the Net, the posted recordings of the dying, the roboviews of entire cities, were horrifying.

Then the Net sites, one by one, ceased to record, or post, or move from the frozen agony of whatever they'd been displaying last.

"It's a mixed lot, from the little definitive information I can get on the medical list serves still running," Uncle Scott said. "It's possible not all the bioweapons are Chinese. There's anthrax and Ebola, for sure, possibly modified. The Ebola may have been made airborne. There are also engineered bacteria and viruses and even spores, which present a special problem because they remain viable so long. One in particular we want to watch out for—it induces your cells to produce TP53 in enormous quantities, and that in turn induces apoptosis."

"What's that?" Sajelle said.

"It makes your cells commit suicide."

Emily, very pale, added, "We want more samples from each of you."

Cord had already given so many samples of blood and tissue that he felt like he'd run into a cactus. Poke here, pierce there, scrape somewhere else. Not that there was much choice.

Kendra said, "What about the babies? How can you tell if they're going to be all right?"

"We're going to take amniotic samples from each of you," Emily said.

Cord put his arm around Clari. Guilt, a constant cloud, settled into his bones. Unlike the other pregnant girls, Clari hadn't sought the sex that led to this. And unlike the other pregnant girls, she wasn't engineered for a super-boosted immune system. Julie and Sajelle, pribir-blessed women married to normal men, had passed on their lesser protection to their new babies. But would it work for Cord to pass on his unfathomable genes to Clari's children? Was his total engineering, like the previous generation's milder version, dominant? Nobody knew.

By summer, the only people transmitting live on the Net lived in isolated pockets in rural areas. Rafe monitored every waking hour. Grimly he reported that some of those people were falling ill, too, from a dozen different diseases.

"The winds go everywhere," Clari said. She was having a very bad pregnancy, morning sickness and anemia and edema and half a dozen other things Cord couldn't name. He wanted to spend every minute with her, and he wanted, from guilt, to never see her at all. Fortunately, the decision was not his. Every person on the farm was working as hard as possible all day, every day, to make the place self-sufficient. There were a lot of things they were going to have to do without, but right now the aim was simple survival.

Taneesha said, "You mean . . . everybody in the world might die?"

"Except us," Emily said. She was too thin. She hadn't eaten more than snatched mouthfuls in days. Neither had Dr. Wilkins, who was much older and looked much worse.

Clari said, "How would we know if anybody else survives?"

Lillie said, "Rafe will hang onto the Net until nobody at all posts or until the satellites fall out of the sky. But there might be really isolated groups that survive who don't have Net access. Inuit or Laplanders or someone."

Cord didn't know who those people were, and he didn't ask. It wouldn't help anything. And the truth was, he didn't really care.

Uncle Scott cared. He said somberly, "When I was born, the world held six billion people. After the first biowar there were two billion left, about the same as there had been in 1900. Today there's maybe two hundred million people on Earth. I'm estimating, of course, extrapolating from what few figures I have. Two hundred million is the same number as when Christ was born. And the number is going down."

Emily said gently, "Scott, the changed ecosystems probably can't support many more than that, anyway."

"And who changed them? Us. Humans. We're all as guilty of these deaths as the people who fired those bioweapons."

To Cord, that was just silly. He and Uncle Scott and Aunt Emily hadn't killed anybody. Somebody in one of the back bedrooms began to play the music cube: "Don't Matter None to Me."

"Population projections for this year," Uncle Scott said, "once were ten billion people. Instead, we have suigenocide." He walked heavily to his room and closed the door.

Cord didn't know what "suigenocide" was. He didn't ask Aunt Emily. She and Uncle Scott were talking about the past, and the past was over and gone. Cord honestly couldn't see the point. "*We've lost so much,*" Aunt Robin constantly whined. But Cord couldn't see that, either.

Everything that mattered to him was here, now.

Then, in April, the cattle suddenly began to die.

CHAPTER 22

"Oh, God," Lillie said. "Scott, what can we do?"

"Nothing until we figure out what's killing them," Scott said testily. "Send the range crew out for blood and tissue samples. Mark each cow carefully so we know what came from whom. Emily and I will get to work as soon as you bring the samples back."

"No," Emily said.

It was another farm meeting in the great room. As usual, only about half were present; the rest couldn't be spared from vital work, or were grabbing a few hours of sleep, or, in the case of Clari and Felicity, were throwing up from pregnancy. Another meeting, but different, Cord thought. He could remember when farm meetings had announced new income, new cattle purchases, new gains in water supplies. Now all the news was bad.

The room even looked different. The windows were closed tightly, a minor effort to keep out windborne micros. Alex and Dakota had built a series of entryways with shallow pans of chemicals in each to wash off your boots. People kept their outdoor clothes there, and only there, stripping to light inner layers and washing their hands before they came into the big house. The house had acquired an unaired, stale smell. And hot; this was July. Not even the thick walls could keep the house cool.

Dr. Wilkins said harshly, "What do you mean, 'no'? Don't go difficult on me, Emily!"

The young woman, her blond hair dirty and lank, faced the old man who had been born the same year she had. With difficulty she said, "Scott, listen. The people who never went up to the pribir ship . . . all that you got for genetic modifications was the olfactory alterations. You remember, at Andrews no doctors could find any other expressed alterations, and you and I haven't found any either.

That means you and Uncle DeWayne and Aunt Robin don't have enhanced immune systems. Yours are no better than Jody's or Carolina's, and you're much older. I don't think you should handle any of the cattle samples, in order to avoid infection. I can do it all."

"You can't! You don't know enough to—"

"Yes," Emily said. "I do."

Dr. Wilkins looked at her for a long time. Finally he nodded, saying nothing. Then he turned and walked slowly out of the room, closing the door. Cord thought of a cow he'd once seen, old and unable to keep up with the herd, lumbering away from the herd to lie down in shade.

Emily said, "I—" and stopped.

Cord's mother said clearly, "You did the right thing, Em. Now everybody get back to work. DeWayne, Robin, you stay indoors, just in case."

Ashley muttered, "Like anybody cares if that old bag Robin gets infected."

"Shut up," Taneesha said. The two girls glared at each other. At least, Cord thought, they couldn't have another fight. Both their bulging bellies would keep them from getting close enough to each other to swing.

The cattle samples showed an engineered virus that Emily had never seen before. She took printouts in to Scott, who hadn't seen them either. Scott chafed at not being able to work with the live samples, but Lillie, DeWayne, and Emily remained firm. Scott never left the big house to go anywhere, especially not down to the small house taken over as Emily's laboratory.

"It kills bovine cells, all right," Emily said, "but I think it's species specific. Look, here—"

Scott listened. "I think you're right."

Jody, hovering in the doorway, said, "How many head are we going to lose?"

Emily answered. "All of them."

"*All?* The entire herd?"

"Yes." Her thin face looked pinched. She knew what it meant. They were all going to have to survive on corn, chickens, and hunted game . . . unless that went, too. What then? There was enough food stored for maybe six months, but no more than that. The corn, genetically enhanced, gave a high yield as long as it was irrigated constantly. But no more food was going to come in to Wenton for trade.

Jody said, "It's almost calving time. Will the calves—"

"I don't know," Emily said. "Isolate the calves as soon as they're born, and wash each with dip right away. Keep them from contamination from their mothers."

He stared at her. "Emily, how the hell can we do that? You've never done a calving. There's blood and what you'd call 'tissues' all over the place. You can't keep the calves from 'contamination by the mothers.' And even if they could, the calves have to nurse, for God's sake. How can we—"

"I don't know how!" Emily shouted. "That's your job! Just do it!"

Emily never lost her temper. Dr. Wilkins put a hand on her arm. Emily shook it off. Cord, listening, went to find Keith and Spring, to tell them the herd was going to die and the calves had to be isolated from the milk that would maybe have kept them from dying, too.

Both range crews worked night and day at calving, and they pulled in people who usually had other tasks. Cord, so exhausted that if he stopped moving he fell asleep standing up, had never seen a calving like this. Even Spring, perpetually cheerful, went grimly about the grim business. They were shorthanded because all the female teenagers who usually worked range crew were pregnant. The only women were Lillie, Senni, and Bonnie. Twice Cord caught Bobby, who had a sensitive stomach, vomiting.

Cows, pre-delivery, post-delivery, and not pregnant at all, died constantly. First the animal began to tremble as its nervous system was affected. A few hours later it lay down, lowing in pain. Half an hour after that the cow thrashed on the ground, desperately gasping for air, often breaking its legs in the process. A few minutes later it died.

Dakota and Keith, both good riders, tried to cut the trembling cows out of the herd and drive the animals away from the rest. It seemed to hurt them to walk, but the men kept at it anyway. They forced the cows as far away as possible, then shot them to spare the animals their inevitable agony. The rifle shots terrified the others, as did the smell of the rotting carcasses of the dead.

If the cow was pregnant, Jody and his crew induced labor, trying to get the calf out before the mother started to tremble. Sometimes they succeeded, sometimes not. A few cows died, thrashing, with calves halfway born, and most of these calves died, too. Cord saw his mother stick her hand up a cow whose induced-labor calf hadn't turned properly and turn it by sheer force. He looked away.

The surviving calves were carried, bleating for their dying mothers, to the antiseptic dip. There was no time to clean up anything. The ground was slippery with blood, placentas, death. The reek and noise were indescribable.

Cord, covered with blood, finally could work no longer. Jody said roughly, "Go lie down, Cord. Now."

"I can't, the—"

"Do it!" He pushed Cord toward the bedrolls set upwind. "I'll wake you in two hours."

Cord collapsed onto the blankets, not washing first, and was asleep instantly, the smell of dead cattle in his nostrils.

When Lillie woke him, he put out his hand to ward her off, unsure where he was, who she was. "Cord, wake up. We need you to take charge of getting the surviving calves onto the truck and back to the barn."

He nodded, stumbled upright, lurched back to the pens. The sky had clouded over, low angry clouds, and Cord didn't know if it was morning or afternoon, or of what day. He set to work. The small, slippery calves, some premature from the induced labor, bleated piteously. One died on the way, falling to the truck bed where the others, packed in, crushed it with their tiny, deadly hoofs. At the barn, taking the calves off the truck and finding the dead one staring at him with open eyes, Cord succumbed. Ashamed of himself, he cried.

Emily, Sajelle, Julie, Carolina, Hannah, and Lupe waited at the barn. Emily showed them how to wash the calves again with the brew she'd concocted, and Cord showed them how to grasp the animals to carry them inside.

"Cord, you smell *awful*," Hannah said distastefully, and he was too tired to feel his own anger.

Lupe had learned somewhere how to feel calves. She'd prepared bottles of warm solution designed by Emily for maximum nutrition. Under Lupe's instruction, the women awkwardly began to hold bottles for the calves, two at a time, while Emily efficiently gave each a shot in the neck from prepared syringes.

"This is a gene sequence delivered by a bovine version of an adeno-type viral vector," she said to Cord. "It's tailored to this specific pathogen. It'll splice in genes to create T-cells with receptors for the pathogenic virus. There's also expo molecules to drastically increase the frequency of gene expression so that—Cord, are you listening to me?"

"Yes," said Cord, who wasn't. He couldn't focus enough to understand her.

"Never mind," she said kindly. "Go in and sleep. But wash first. Do you hear me? Don't go in like that."

He fell asleep in the yard, beside the outside pump, before he even had his clothes off. Somebody rigged a tarp over him to shield from UV, and he slept.

They saved only twenty calves. Three of those died despite attempts to nurse them. The others fought off the bioweapon micro even when they contracted it. There were seven bulls and ten cows. Eventually they castrated three of the males. Four bulls were a lot, but Jody and Spring didn't want to risk being without any sperm for the next generation.

That decision was, Emily said, an act of pure unjustified faith that there would be a next generation.

Cord wondered about that. Staring at the surviving calves, he remembered the huge herd of his early childhood, when Grandma Theresa had been alive. It had seemed to Cord then, held firmly on the front of Uncle Jody's saddle, that the world had been full of living, breathing cattle. All gone.

He turned away from the pen and stumbled toward the house.

CHAPTER 23

Sajelle, thinking ahead to winter, put everyone on rationing, the calories carefully worked out for men, women, pregnant women, children. Cord always felt slightly hungry. He assumed that everyone else did, too, but not even Dolly complained. Even the youngest children understood how close to the edge the farm might be balanced. But there were still—for now, anyway—enough game to trap, enough plants to gather. Wild onion, chicory for coffee, salad greens, agave to make the sweet syrup that Cord loved. Plus, this year's harvest would be good, thanks to careful irrigation. The chickens, mercifully, didn't contract any diseases from bioweapons.

"Well, that makes sense," Emily said. "You start fooling around with avian pathogens, you could infect all birds and really ruin the ecology." She fell silent, realizing that it was she who was not making sense.

"Aunt Emily, how many other people are left alive near us?" Kezia asked plaintively.

Uncle DeWayne said, "There are still some groups posting. A large one in Colorado, one in east Texas, one in the Arizona mountains. A few more, farther away. Then there are groups in the East, plus a few overseas. But there are fewer every month."

Dr. Wilkins said, "Nobody else has the enhanced immune systems of our people."

But not all enhanced equally, Cord thought. His generation, built genetically by the pribir, could probably survive in ways they didn't even know about, as he had during the sandstorm four years ago. The men and women who had gone up to the pribir ship, including his mother, at least never got sick with anything. But DeWayne, Robin, and Dr. Wilkins had no engineered protection. Neither did Grandma Theresa's children, Senni and Jody and

Spring. Spring's kids had boosted immune systems from their mother, Julie, but Jody's and Senni's children were vulnerable. Including Clari.

Cord went into their bedroom. Clari wasn't there.

She, like Uncle DeWayne and Dr. Wilkins and Aunt Robin, wasn't supposed to go outside. But sometimes she did anyway, dressed in a plastic rig Sajelle had created, with a mask over her face. Cord knew where to look for her.

The sun was setting in the west, fanning theatrical rays of gold and orange over a purple sky. A full moon shone gloriously on the eastern horizon. Over it passed momentarily the silent silhouette of a hawk. With the return of rain, some of the plants new since the warming had revived. Cord smelled the cool fragrance of sage, the stronger odor of cedars brought to him on a shifting breeze. Grandma Theresa had been buried under a stand of cedars, a quarter mile from the house.

Clari, in her weird plastic covering, stood in the shadow of the cedars, gazing at the stone marker. The bulge of her pregnancy made her look even more grotesque. How much longer? Two months, unless the baby came early. Clari, unlike the girls engineered by the pribir, carried only one child. Cord's son.

He didn't feel like a father. He felt like a boy looking at the girl he loved, who inexplicably was carrying around a hay bale under her smock.

"Clari," he said softly.

"Hey, Cord."

"Are you cold?"

"In this plastic? No." She laughed, without pleasure.

"Are you . . . can I do anything for you?"

"Yes," she said, which surprised him. He asked, often and helplessly, and the answer was always no.

"What? Anything, Clari, you know that."

She didn't answer. He peered at the semi-transparent face mask, but couldn't make out her expression. Finally she said, "It's going to sound terrible. I don't mean to be gloomy or to upset you, but if . . . if anything happens . . ."

"What?"

"If anything happens while I'm in labor, would you please bury me and the baby here, next to Grandma?"

He didn't understand why he felt anger. "Nothing is going to happen to you or the baby!"

"You don't know that. It might. I'm not made like the other girls.

And sometimes—" She dropped her voice so low he could hardly hear her, "—sometimes I hope it does."

"Don't say that! What's wrong with you, to say that? I don't want you to die!"

She clutched at his hand. "Don't be mad, Cord. Please don't be mad. It's just that I don't believe . . . everybody is so optimistic. They say we'll get through this. But, Cord, almost everybody in the world is dead! Everybody! Don't you think about that . . . a whole planetful of people just gone?"

Cord didn't usually think about that, although he knew that others did. What good did thinking about it do?

She rushed on. "I have trouble believing this farm is going to make it when no one else did. And sometimes I think that if we're all going to die anyway, I'd rather it happened to the baby now, before he's properly born, so he doesn't suffer. I don't want him to suffer, Cord."

So many conflicting feelings swamped Cord that he couldn't answer. He didn't have to. A figure came running toward them from the big house, calling, "Cord! Cord!"

"Who is it?"

"It's Keith." His brother tore up to Cord and Clari, and at the look on Keith's face in the moonlight Cord's chest tightened.

"Cord, come quick. It's Mom. She's sick!"

Lillie? Sick? They were none of them sick, that generation! "You're lying!"

Keith didn't even counterattack. "Come quick! Now!" And he was off, back to the house.

Cord ran after him, remembered Clari, stopped and turned.

"Go, go," she said. "I'm coming."

He raced away, leaving her lumbering after.

Lillie sat on the bed in her room at the big house. She didn't look sick to Cord. Emily, masked, had just handed her a homemade plastic suit like the one Clari wore. Even through the mask Cord could see Emily's fear. If Lillie could get sick, then any of her generation could.

"Mom?" Cord said from the doorway.

"Get out, Cord, and close the door," Emily said. "I'm taking your mother down to my lab, in quarantine. You can talk to her there if you wear a mask."

"I'm not going to get sick," Cord said, before he thought. "I'm pribir-engineered from scratch!"

"Good for you," Emily said acidly. "But it doesn't look like the pribir knew what they were doing after all, does it? Lillie's supposed to have a much boosted immune system, too."

Not like mine, Cord didn't say, because he was too worried about his mother. She smiled at him.

"I'm all right, Cord. Get out now and I'll see you and Keith at the lab. Don't let Kella come, though, or any of the pregnant girls."

"They're not coming, Lillie," Emily said. "Cord, close the door."

He did, feeling relieved. His mother didn't look sick at all. Whatever it was, the pribir would have guarded against it. They wouldn't let Lillie die. They were too good for that.

For the next two weeks, it looked as if Cord were right. Lillie started with merely a headache, which wouldn't have even been noticed except that none of that group, the twenty-nine-year-olds, ever got headaches. And she couldn't seem to sleep, not even fitfully. A few days later those symptoms disappeared, and Emily would have let Lillie out of quarantine if she and Scott hadn't already discovered the problem.

"Oh my dear God," Scott said.

"I found it on the Net medical library, what's still functioning of the Net medical library, but I hoped I was wrong," Emily said, white as bleached bone.

"No. You're not wrong."

"Can we—"

"No. I don't know how to fight this in the brain, Emily. No one does. We'll have to rely on Lillie's own immune system."

"What is it?" Kella demanded. "Tell me!"

Lillie's two sons had waited outside Emily's lab. They insisted on going with her to Dr. Wilkins in the big house where Kella, eight months pregnant, had joined them. The five people crowded into Dr. Wilkins's little room, crushing each other between bed and crude dresser, knocking elbows into the enormous curve of Kella's belly.

Dr. Wilkins said, "It's an induced variant of a prion disease."

Cord and Keith looked blank. Kella, visibly dredging her memory, said, "That's . . . wait a minute . . . that's a disease where a protein changes its form and it . . . does what?"

Emily said, "Clumps together in sticky, aggregate lumps that disrupt cell structure. And resists all efforts to destroy it. Lillie's prion changes are in the brain, uninduced by her genes. Something else caused it."

"Wait," Kella repeated. "Prion disease . . . I remember now. That's no choice for a bioweapon! It takes months to kill, sometimes even years!"

Dr. Wilkins said, "Ordinarily, yes. But whatever is inducing Lillie's proteins to refold, it's designed to act fast. The only reason she isn't dying now is her boosted immune system. Whatever the pribir did to it, it's fighting like hell now."

Keith, always direct, said, "Well, find whatever's causing the protein refolds and kill it!"

Emily said gently, "That's just it, Keith. There's nothing there, now. Whatever the agent was, it's gone, destroyed by Lillie's immune system. It just left this process going on."

"Then stop the process!"

"We don't know how," Emily said, and Cord heard the frustration and anger in her voice.

Cord stared hard at the rough wooden surface of Dr. Wilkins's dresser. There wasn't anything on the dresser, not even a hairbrush. Barren. Knotty-grained. Splintery.

"She's not contagious, at least," Dr. Wilkins said wearily. "You can see her. She can come out."

"But what's going to happen to her?" Cord burst out. "No, damn it, tell us! Don't give me that shit about protecting us!"

"I wouldn't do that," Emily said. "Lillie's prions are forming in her thalamus. She'll get more headaches. Have increasing insomnia. Eventually dementia will set in. If we're lucky, coma."

And then death. Cord pushed his way to the door.

"Cord!" Kella said angrily, because she needed to be angry at someone. "Aren't you even going to—"

"Tell Mom I'll see her later," Cord said. He had to get out of that room, that house. Lillie would understand. That he was sure of, in a world where nothing else was any longer sure: his mother would understand.

Lillie couldn't sleep. At night Cord, lying sleepless himself in the room in the big house where he'd moved Clari to be near Dr. Wilkins, heard Lillie moving around the great room. It didn't matter what hour he woke; she was there. She would walk restlessly, sometimes stumbling. As August wore on, she stumbled more often. By day she looked dazed, pale, and filmy-eyed from lack of sleep. She never complained.

One night he heard her cry out. Cord leapt up from his pallet and tore into the room. She gazed at him wild-eyed. "Uncle Keith!"

"It's me, Mom. Cord."

"Uncle Keith, Mom's killed herself!"

Cord didn't know what to do. He tried to put his arms around her, but she pushed him away, stronger than he could have imagined. "Get away! Don't drug my mind, Pam! I'm not part of your mission!"

"Mom . . ."

"Get away!" she screamed, so loud that Cord thought half the house would rush in. But no one else awoke. Lillie started to moan. "Uncle Keith, help me, she didn't mean it, Mom didn't mean it . . ."

Again Cord tried to approach her, and again she shoved him off with that startling strength.

"Tess, Tess, don't let Pam make me . . . don't let . . ."

"Mom!" Cord said, his despair dwarfed by horror. This wasn't his mother. Her body, her face, her voice, and not his mother *not his mother*. . . .

"Okay, Lillie," another voice said behind him, deep and soothing, and Cord spun around. Mike Franzi. Cord hadn't even heard the man come in.

"It's all right, Cord, I'll take it from here," Mike said. He reached for Lillie.

"Get away!" she shrieked.

Mike ignored her, folding her close to his chest. "Lillie, it's all right. You're safe now, nobody will mess with your mind. I've got you now, it's all right . . ."

"Mike? They're inside the walls, they took me there, I saw . . . I saw . . ."

"I know." To Cord, over Lillie's shoulder, he said, "She's back aboard the ship. Go back to bed, Cord. I'm here."

And Hannah? Cord didn't say. His jumbled feelings of relief, rage, and guilt left him no room for speech. He went back to bed, creeping in beside Clari. She moaned softly in her sleep and he turned away, his face toward the wall.

When it happened, it all happened at once.

Two days later, when Lillie seemed again to have rallied, Angie went into labor. "Not quite eight months," Dr. Wilkins said. "Come on down to the birthing house. You can walk."

"Of course I can," Angie said. "Who said I couldn't?"

"Nobody, dear. Come on."

Dr. Wilkins sent Carolina's son Angel to find Emily. Gently

Dr. Wilkins took Angie's arm and walked her to the small house that Emily had cleared out and prepared as a maternity ward. Halfway down the well-worn dirt path, Angie suddenly pulled away from the old man. "You're not supposed to be outside!"

"I'm not missing this," Dr. Wilkins said. "Don't baby me, you baby. And anyway, Emily may very well have her hands full and need help. When you lot were born, all the girls went into labor at once."

"But . . . even so . . . if *you* got a micro . . ." A sudden pain hit Angie and she bent over, straightened up, put a hand on her swollen belly, her face a sculpture of comic surprise.

"Come on, Angie, almost there . . ."

"What is it?" Cord called, coming out of the barn and running toward them when he saw Dr. Wilkins outdoors.

"Angie's going to have her triplets," Dr. Wilkins said. "Go get Sajelle, she's the steadiest for this sort of thing."

But instead Cord went to check on Clari. She stood at the wood stove, boiling down agave syrup, a shapeless mound with the moody face of the woman he thought he'd loved.

"Oh, leave me alone, Cord, I'm not going into labor just because the others are. I'm only carrying one child, remember, and it's only been eight months." She stirred the syrup harder.

Cord hastily withdrew and went to find Sajelle. She was walking Loni toward the birthing house. Loni, unlike Angie, looked panicked. Her round face, still not shed of all its own baby fat, jerked around to scan the farm.

"Where's Mother? I want Mother!"

Sajelle said to Cord, "Go find Hannah." When he didn't move, she snapped, "Don't just stand there! Find Loni's mother!"

Everybody was telling him to find somebody else! Well, he didn't know where Hannah was. Cord had never been comfortable with Hannah, and after the scene with Mike and the raving Lillie in the middle of the night, he'd avoided Hannah altogether.

Loni cried out and Cord suddenly found himself willing to look for Hannah. Anything rather than listen to that animal cry. Anything rather than spend the day around girls giving birth.

He ran back to the barn, even though he knew Hannah wasn't there. Next he checked the vegetable gardens, with their system of irrigation ditches to bring water from the increasingly sparse creek. Bonnie, Sam, and Lupe were weeding the vegetables. Cord remembered to call to them, "Angie and Loni are having babies!" before he took off for the spring house.

Hannah wasn't there. Carolina was putting eggs into the half-buried plastic boxes used as coolers. Cord paused a moment, grateful for the damp coolness under the thick adobe walls. "Carolina . . . where's Hannah?"

Carolina answered with a burst of Spanish in which Cord discerned "eggs" and "broken" and "clumsy child."

"Carolina—where's Hannah? Loni's in labor!"

Now he had her full attention. A smile like spring sunlight broke over her face. "Babies? Now?"

"Yes, and she wants her mother! Where's Hannah?"

"I don't know," Carolina said. "Here, put these eggs in, I am need!" And Carolina was off, leaving Cord with the eggs.

He shoved them into the box, breaking only two, and pushed the lid on. Where the hell *was* Hannah? Not with the pitifully reduced range crew; Hannah was afraid of cattle.

He looked in the smokehouse, the privies, the windmills, everywhere he could think of. Finally he turned toward the cottonwood grove. It wasn't likely she'd be here, in the middle of a workday. Over the long months that generation had gone outside more and more, simply because the work there needed to be done. But they didn't just sit outside by choice.

Hannah wasn't on the bench in the grove. Cord stood still, listening to the creek murmur over its bleached stones. A jackrabbit broke cover and streaked past him. He had looked everywhere possible. No one went to town anymore; no one went anywhere, for fear of infection. So where was she?

A tiny flash of blue across the creek caught his eye. The flat land there, once thick with pine saplings and wildflowers, was reverting to mesquite and yucca. He waded through the water and bent down.

A bit of blue cloth, snagged on mesquite. Silky blue cloth, cloth such as it wasn't possible to make anymore. A durable microfiber synthetic, his mother had told him the first time he'd seen the beautiful blue-and-pink scarf around Hannah's neck, the colors shading into each other so subtly that the fluttering scarf looked to him like a piece of sky. A piece of Hannah's old life, like her music cube and silver hair brush, that life she'd shared with Lillie and Mike and Emily and the others long ago. Cord held the piece of silky material clenched in his fist and shouted Hannah's name. No answer. He waded into the mesquite, under the grilling sun.

It took him an hour to find the next fragment of cloth, but after that it was easy. The buzzards circled the place.

Cord scared them away. He took off his jacket, long-sleeved and high-necked to keep the dangerous UV at bay, and wrapped it around Hannah's torso. She was heavier than he expected. Too late, he realized that he shouldn't be exposing himself to whatever she had died of. Well, fuck that. He had survived the sandstorm on the desert that had killed Grandmother Theresa, his immune system could probably handle this bioweapon. It was Lillie who was sick, Hannah who was dead, not anyone from his generation. His generation had the durable, subtle, silky genetic alterations from the pribir.

Halfway to the big house, Hannah a boulder in his arms and the sun beating down on his head, Cord began to cry.

He couldn't brush away the tears. He let them run, along with his nose, finally stumbling clear of the mesquite when he returned to the creek. He lay Hannah down for a minute on the rough grass. He had to; his arms ached. Then, as he straightened, swiping at the snot on his face, something happened.

A picture. In his mind. Clear as if he'd seen it out a window, accepted as matter-of-factly as the day's work schedule. There could be no doubt, no mistake. The picture in his mind was a message.

The pribir were coming.

CHAPTER 24

Frank, Loni's brother, stood outside the birthing house with Keith, the father of Loni's babies. Jason, the father of Angie's children, was out on the range. Frank and Keith looked at Cord, and he saw from their faces that they'd received the image, too.

Frank said simply, "The pribir are coming."

Cord nodded. What he had to say next tore at him. Frank was Hannah's son. Cord had left Hannah's body, still wrapped in his jacket, on the bench under the cottonwood grove. Frank and Keith didn't even notice that Cord was without his jacket, or that he had blood on his light undershirt. They were too bemused.

A baby's cry shrilled into the air.

Keith jumped as if he'd been shot. Against orders, he flung open the door of the birthing house. "Loni!"

"She good, she fine, go away," Carolina yelled, and shut the door again. Another baby cried, or the same baby again.

Cord looked at Frank, and he couldn't do it. He couldn't say, *Your mother died of a bioweapon and buzzards have been at her and somebody has to go bring her body up from the creek before other scavengers find it.* He couldn't do it.

Emily was the doctor. Dr. Wilkins and Uncle DeWayne were in charge of the farm. This was their job. All Cord had to do was tell Dr. Wilkins and Emily and the whole burden would be shifted to them, who would at least know what to do. They would know how to find out what micro had killed Hannah, what to do with the body, how to tell Hannah's children and Mike. This was their job, babies or no babies. And the pribir was coming—he had to tell them that, too!

Cord pushed open the door and did not let Carolina close it until he was inside.

The room smelled of blood and sweat. It was infernally hot, the windows shut tight against infection. At a far bed Sajelle bent over Angie, who was panting like a coyote in August desert. Emily waited at Angie's feet. At a table Dr. Wilkins stood over a newborn baby, collecting stem cells from its umbilical cord. Carolina put something in a basket, and Sajelle fussed over more baskets. Thin high wails pierced the fetid air. In a bed closer to the door Loni lay, evidently finished. Her hair stuck to her scalp in sweaty coils. A bloody sheet had been thrown over her, and her eyes were closed.

A gust of air blew in with Cord, hot dry high-plains air but not as hot as this terrible room. Instantly Loni opened her eyes. Feebly she tried to raise her head, let it drop back to the bed, sniffed the air. She looked straight at Cord.

"The pribir are coming," she said.

Six beautiful infants. Two boys and four girls, born with minimal labor of mothers who immediately fell into deep, healing sleep. Two sets of perfect triplets, and the adults hardly mentioned the children. The pribir were coming.

They had all smelled it, Cord's generation and their parents and even the white-haired Dr. Wilkins and Uncle DeWayne and Aunt Robin. "It's like the first time," DeWayne said quietly, holding Sajelle's hand.

Emily held one of the new babies against her shoulder, patting the baby's back. "Only we didn't know if you young ones would smell it, too."

"'Young ones,'" spat Aunt Robin. "You're what, twenty-nine yourself, Emily? Why shouldn't the 'young ones' be able to smell the pribir? They're the ones that got everything, all the fancy genemods to survive."

Nobody answered her. Instead they looked at each other, glanced away, were drawn back to stare again into each other's eyes. The pribir were coming. They were really coming.

"I wish they'd just stay away," Alex said in a low voice, and there it was, out in the open, filling up all the space in the great room. The older generations thought the pribir would bring only more trouble. "Controlling our minds, slicing into our bodies . . . they better not try that shit again," Alex added, still in that quiet, menacing tone. Sam and Bonnie and Sajelle nodded. Emily looked fearfully into the infant's face.

Everyone of Cord's generation, except the perverse Ashley, was filled with eagerness and hope.

They knew better than to say so. Not even Taneesha or Bobby, usually so scrappy, did anything but let their eyes meet, wide and wondering. All rejoicing had to be silent. Hannah had been hastily buried under the cedars beside Grandmother Theresa. Dr. Wilkins, gray-faced, had done a quick blood analysis and identified the engineered virus that killed her. Hannah's sons and Mike were absent from this meeting, grieving privately, remembering years no one else had shared. Lillie, worse again and given a sedative by Emily, slept heavily in a back room.

"So what are we going to do about the bastards?" Sam said.

Uncle DeWayne said, "You're kidding yourself if you think you can do anything. You should know that even better than I. You were aboard their ship."

"I won't let them use us again! Not us, not the kids, not these new babies! Not any humans!"

Sajelle said sharply, "How you going to stop them, Sam? You got a plan, hmmm? You going to just develop ways to block out those smells that control our minds?"

"I can at least wear a filter!"

"Yes," Emily said thoughtfully. "And perhaps stay outside. Their most concentrated effects were in the ship, a closed system. Out here the winds will dilute the olfactory molecules."

"Oh, yeah, like they did fifteen years ago at Andrews," Bonnie said sarcastically. "The pribir had no trouble getting their message through then, and they can do it now."

"Still," Emily said, "filter masks might help."

Sam said, "The only thing that's going to help is to kill them the second they step off their shuttle."

Kella gasped. And Cord, unable to contain himself any longer, burst out, "Don't you touch them!"

Deep silence fell over the room.

Cord looked at the faces. Keith, his brother, nodding slightly. Kella, with Lillie's gold-flecked gray eyes, creasing her forehead in anxiety. The bitter downturning curves of Aunt Robin's mouth. Rafe, his face clouded, remembering some past event unimaginable to Cord. Jody, who neither had known the pribir nor was their product, warily waiting. Emily, her pale skin mottled with suppressed emotion. And Dr. Wilkins, tired, his neck marred by the start of still another purplish skin cancer that he hadn't yet had time to inject.

Spring, their eternal peacemaker, had the last word. "Maybe the aliens won't come down, after all." But no one believed him.

* * *

One day, two days, and the pribir didn't come down. Cord could no longer smell their image. Felicity gave birth to triplets, all girls. An easy birth, said Carolina, smiling hugely. Not even the threat of aliens could overcome her delight in babies. "*Primita*," she crooned over one of the small wailing bundles. Little cousin.

Kella had two boys and a girl in the middle of the night. Cord hadn't even known his sister was in labor.

"Bring Mom to see them," Kella said to her brothers. She'd already left the birthing house and was sharing one of the small, shifting-occupant houses with Carolina, Jody, and their children, none of whom were present just now. Kella sat up in bed, surrounded by infants. One was asleep, one was nursing, and one lay at the foot of the bed gazing up at Cord from enormous blue eyes exactly like Dakota's. Cord gazed back because he didn't want to stare at his sister's exposed breast. Keith, never modest, said, "I didn't know you had such great bulbs, sis."

"Shut up," Kella said. "Bring Mom."

"Kella," Cord said, "we can't. She's sedated again. Dr. Wilkins says she might . . . last longer that way."

Until the pribir can get here, they all understood.

Keith said, "Which kid is named after me?"

"None of them, buttlips. This is Sage, that's Wild Pink, and he's Dakkie. After his father. Cord, Clari says you're neglecting her."

Cord said coldly, "Is that any of your business?"

"Yes. I like Clari. I thought you did, too."

Cord was silenced. It was hard to be around Clari. Cord couldn't feel any connection with this new pregnant person Clari had become: weepy, frightened, sometimes even irritable. Clari, who was never irritable. Worse, Cord couldn't feel any connection with the baby that was supposedly his. Although in truth all the babies seemed to pretty much belong to everybody. The older generation all assumed equal care and interest and responsibility as the infants' mothers. Kella acted as if her triplets should be just as exciting to Cord and Keith, to Susie and Gavin, as to Dakota. Cord looked resentfully at his sister, in her newfound happy maternal bossiness, and felt more like an outsider than ever.

Keith said, "Not to change the subject, but what's going on with Mike? Jody says he's no help with the work because he's always running off to check on Mom."

Cord felt warmth flood his face. He'd never told Keith or Kella about their mother and Mike. They both turned to him. "What is it? Cord, you know something!"

"No, I don't."

Kella bit her lip critically. "Yes, you do. What's wrong with you lately? You don't sit with Clari, you blush about Mike, you skulk around here like a wounded coyote. What's wrong?"

Cord couldn't help it; he laughed. "'*What's wrong?*' The pribir aren't arriving, Hannah died of some micro that could still be around, the farm is failing, Sam's group is ready to shoot the only people who can help us, and Lillie is dying! What's *wrong?*"

Kella said hotly, "I meant with you!"

Keith, in a rare moment of social observance, said, "Cord, why do you always call Mom 'Lillie'? Like she's not your mother?"

Cord didn't answer. He didn't know why. It had something to do with her remoteness when he was small, or their special understanding after that, or Clari, or something. Before Keith could press him, Emily burst into the room.

"Keith! Shut that window!"

"Why?" Kella demanded. "It's hot as hell in here already. The babies—"

"The babies are my concern," Emily said grimly. "And you. We miscalculated. Your generation isn't safe after all, and . . . and . . ." She broke down, gasped for air, pulled herself together.

"One of Angie's babies just died of a micro. Mutated from the war, Scott says. A micro that must have just blown in on yesterday's shift in the wind."

Cord moved slowly to the window and closed it.

If a mutated micro could kill one of Angie's babies, a baby that had inherited all the protection built into her pribir-designed genes, then it could kill any one of them. Any one of them at all.

"Clari," he said aloud, and pushed past his brother toward the door. It was blocked by Taneesha, still widely pregnant, her brown eyes opened so wide the whites glittered against her dark skin.

"Cord," she said, and then stopped.

"What? Get out of my way!"

But she gripped his sleeve, and something in her face stopped him from shaking her off. Her eyes slid sideways toward Emily.

"Let me past!" Emily snapped. "I have to get everybody else inside with closed windows!"

When she was gone, Taneesha clumsily kicked the door closed. "Cord," she said hoarsely, "they're here. Down by Dead Men's Arroyo. A space ship, Gavin saw it come down. They're here."

Cord went, and Keith, and Dakota, the only other one of their generation they could instantly find who wasn't having babies. He'd been on his way to see Kella. Gavin had whispered the news to Taneesha and immediately gone back to the arroyo, to watch the ship. None of the older ones knew yet.

"Just a minute, I have to get something at the big house," Keith said.

"What? You don't need anything!" Dakota snapped.

"Just go ahead, I'm right behind you."

Cord and Dakota slipped away from the farm and raced the mile to the arroyo. Late afternoon shadows slanted purple over the ground. The wind had picked up, and Cord felt it blow hot against his face, stinging skin with bits of grit. Keith, a fast runner, caught up with them at the edge of the arroyo.

The ship sat on the far side, motionless. Cord gaped. Used to rough wood, stone, adobe, with small machines hoarded carefully and cared for devotedly, he had never seen so much metal in one place. It was beautiful. Dull silver, or maybe more of a pewter color. Hannah had had pewter candlesticks, heirlooms brought with her from the cities. They were Loni's now. This ship would make a million candlesticks, Cord thought. As large as the big house, it had what was clearly a door on the side facing away from the farm.

"How did it get down without us seeing it?" Dakota whispered. Cord understood. He felt like whispering, himself.

Gavin said, "It didn't. It came in . . . sideways. Riding low over the ground from the east, I don't know from how far away. It came in so *fast*." His voice held awe.

Cord slid down into the dry arroyo and started to climb up the opposite side. After a moment, the others followed him. Hesitantly he put one hand on the ship. It felt warm, but no warmer than saddle fittings got from the sun. But this wasn't saddle fittings, this was a space ship, and it had come from somewhere out there among the stars. He was the first human being to touch it.

If Keith hadn't dragged him to see Kella's babies . . . if Gavin hadn't encountered Taneesha first in his mad rush to inform somebody, anybody, at the farm . . . if Emily hadn't rounded up everybody to go inside and shut the windows . . .

Inside. They would all be in the big house now, and they'd have already noticed the four boys were missing. They'd make Taneesha tell. Or Spring would track them to the arroyo; Spring could track anything.

"We have to make the pribir come out!" he said. "Or go inside ourselves. We have to warn them the others are mad at them and might—"

"Shit, yes," Dakota breathed. "How?"

Cord looked at the pewter ship. He walked around to the door and knocked, feeling an absolute fool. Well, the pribir were human, weren't they? That's what Dr. Wilkins had said: human DNA. So would they recognize knocking?

"Pam! Pete!" Keith bawled. "We're here! Can you guys come out a minute?"

"Shit, Keith!" Dakota said. "They're not kids!"

Keith wasn't deterred. "Miss Pam! Mr. Pete! Can you come out here a minute? We got something you should know!"

Cord held his breath. Nothing happened.

Keith yelled, "We got sick people who need your gene help! Hannah died, and my mother is sick. Lillie . . . you remember Lillie, she was on your ship before!"

"And she isn't going in there again," another voice said.

Cord whipped around. Sam stood across the arroyo, holding a gun. Behind him were Alex, Bonnie, and Rafe.

Time seemed to stop. Cord took a step forward, then didn't know what to do. But Sam did. He led the others down the arroyo and up the other side. Unerringly he walked to the side of the ship with the door. Dakota, Cord, and Gavin looked at each other. Keith had disappeared.

"Go back home, you boys," Sam said.

"We—"

"Go! This hasn't got a damn thing to do with you. You weren't even born when those aliens . . . go home."

Cord had never liked Sam. Rafe and Alex were all right. Mike—Cord's feelings about Mike were complicated. But he'd always considered Sam a loudmouth, a bully if anyone would have let him be one, and not even very smart. Cord caught Gavin's and then Dakota's eyes, and Gavin started talking.

"Rafe, Alex, Bonnie . . . you don't want to hurt the pribir. You know you don't. Whatever they did before, they might be able to cure Lillie. And maybe prevent another baby dying, like Angie's baby did. And anyway, do you really think a gun could hurt them? They came all the way from the stars in a ship that twists time! Do you think a Smith & Wesson can stop people like that? You'll only get yourself killed, maybe."

Bonnie said, "He's right, Sam. Rafe and I told you this isn't the way. We—"

Sam fired at the ship, an obscenely loud sound in the gathering dusk. The bullet ricocheted, not even denting the metal, and flew out over the mesquite. Rafe shouted, "You crazy son of a bitch!" and the door of the ship began to open.

Sam stepped back and prepared to fire again. Before he could, another shot sounded and Sam screamed. He dropped the gun and clutched his right arm. Keith stepped from behind a boulder, holding Jody's cherished Braunhausen. At the same time a cloud of blue gas jetted out of the ship into Sam's face. Instantly he crumpled to the ground. Rafe, standing closest to him, swayed and also fell. The door finished opening and two people, a young man and young woman dressed in khaki pants and yellow T-shirts, stepped out. They completely ignored Sam and Rafe on the ground, and Keith holding the gun.

"What have you people been doing!" Pam screamed. "How could you have ruined everything in only fifteen fucking years?"

CHAPTER 25

They were people, Cord would think later. They were humans, or made in the shape of humans, with human brains and human feelings. And they were young, Lillie had said so, said that this was their first job of engineering. Human, young, furious that their work was being ruined. Like little kids when a fort was destroyed by the wind, branches and mesquite and an old blanket all blown and scattered over the ground. So they got mad, they . . . they had a tantrum. The pribir had a tantrum. They were alien kids.

Cord didn't think this while he stood gaping at Pam and Pete. He couldn't think anything. Pam looked in her twenties, maybe, her beautiful face a light brown color framed by soft brown hair parted in the middle and falling to her shoulders. Her skin was flawless: no purplish skin cancers, no lines from squinting into the sun, no windburn, no rough patches from harsh soap. Pete, too. Their clothes looked like something on Net shows from decades ago. They carried nothing.

None of it felt real.

Keith recovered first. He walked straight over to Sam and stood over the body. Cord saw his brother's lip tremble. Keith said, "Is Sam dead?" He still held Jody's gun.

Pete snapped, "Of course he's not dead. Neither of them are. They'll revive in a few minutes. Give me that ridiculous weapon, please!"

After a moment Keith handed Pete the gun. Where did his brother get the courage? Or maybe Keith just didn't want to end up on the ground like Sam and Rafe. Pam, still scowling and glaring, held out her hand to Gavin and hesitantly he put Sam's pistol into it.

Cord heard himself say, "Sam didn't mean to . . ." Stupid! Of course Sam meant to. "I mean, he just wasn't sure about . . . you."

Dakota said in a sudden burst, "None of them are. The ones who were on your ship before. They say you manipulated them and used them. But we young ones don't think that. We've been waiting for you!"

"You have?" Pam's face softened. Was she that easy to flatter? Cord thought dazedly. And yet Dakota had only spoken the truth. It was just that this whole thing was not at all what Cord had expected.

Pete said, "Well, of course we would plan to come for the birth of the next generation, next month. You must have known that."

They knew when the girls would all get pregnant. Which meant they'd known exactly when those temporarily unstoppable sexual feelings would overwhelm the farm. They'd designed all that frantic, driven sex into Cord's *genes*. He felt his face grow hot.

Dakota said, "Most of the babies are already born."

Gavin added, "And one already died."

Pam's face darkened again. She was moodier than Ashley, even. "Born? Died? Your gestation period is supposed to be nine months!"

"Yeah, well," Dakota mumbled.

Gavin added, more helpfully, "Dr. Wilkins says they come early when there's three at a time."

Pam and Pete looked at each other. Cord saw that they hadn't known that. Doubt hit him like a blast of hot air. They were supposed to know all about humans! What else didn't they know?

Pete said, "One offspring died? Of what?"

"Of this perversion of the right way!" Pam said. She was back to full anger. "This fucking 'war'! How dare you misuse the right way!"

Keith, now also riled, said, "*We* didn't! We're just trying to survive it!"

"Oh," Pam said, and subsided again. After a moment she seemed to remember. "You said Lillie was sick?"

Cord nodded, unable to speak. Keith said eagerly, "You remember our mother? Lillie?"

"Of course," Pam said, "we've only been gone a few months. Now let's go to your home base. Get in the ship."

Nothing was like Cord imagined it would be. Nothing.

He was the only one who would ride to the farm in the ship. Keith, Dakota, and Gavin refused. Instead they ran home. "Should we tell everybody you're here?" Gavin asked uncertainly.

"Of course," Pete said.

Keith said, "But . . . they might try to kill you again."

"Oh, don't worry about that," Pete said.

Keith's eyes narrowed. "Why not? What are you going to do?"

The pribir didn't answer. Cord looked again at their healthy human good looks, their casual old-fashioned clothing, and a kind of dizziness came over him. It was like a dream, or a Net show. It wasn't real.

Pam said, "We'll just smell to them before we open the ship."

Cord finally had to say something. "Miss Pam, Mr. Pete—"

"Just 'Pam' and 'Pete,'" Pam said smiling, and she reminded Cord of Spring's ten-year-old daughter, Terri, playing grown-up. The thought horrified him.

He tried again. "If you drug our families . . . the people at the farm . . . they're going to be even madder and want even more to hurt you back. They resent you fooling around with their feelings."

"Really?" Pete said. He sounded genuinely interested. "Why?"

Cord stared at him, dumbfounded. He had championed the pribir, believed in them . . . he still believed in them! But even he understood their parents' objections to what Dr. Wilkins called "mood manipulation."

Keith said shortly, "They'll resent it because their feelings are their own."

Pam said thoughtfully, "But it would be all right to smell information to them? Why is that different? Surely their ideas are just as much their own as their feelings."

The boys were silent.

"You can't explain it?" Pam said, and Cord heard triumph in her voice. "See, Pete? They don't understand their own irrationality any better than we do!"

Keith said hotly, "It's not irrationality! It's . . . it's . . ." But he couldn't explain what it was.

Neither could Cord. He said, "Send them just information, not feelings. Send them information that you can cure my mother and you can stop more babies from dying. Then they'll accept you."

Pete said, "At least they can understand that much of the right way. Do you humans even realize how perverted your misuse of it has been?"

Pam said, more practically, "What if we can't cure Lillie or save more babies? Pete's right, you know. You people exceeded all genetic perversions that we'd planned for. I'm not even sure you're worth this much trouble at all. We have other planets we're working on, you know."

Other planets. Cord clung desperately to the here and now. He repeated, "Just send them information. Say you can cure my mother and you can stop more babies from dying."

"Well, all right, if you insist," Pam said sulkily.

Sam and Rafe stirred on the ground. Pete said, "Do you want to dump those two in the ship? We can bring them."

"I think," Gavin said quickly, "they'd rather walk."

"All right. Come on, Lillie's offspring . . . what's your name?"

"Cord," he said, and his voice came out strangled. The ship door opened.

Nothing was like Cord imagined it would be.

The inside of the ship was small and blank. He was bewildered until he realized this was only one small section, even though he saw nothing that could be called a door. Pete spoke some high-pitched sounds no human throat could ever make, and the ship lifted slightly. A window appeared—just appeared!—in the front and Cord saw they were following Keith and Dakota, moving toward the farm at a fast jog. Gavin must be waiting for Rafe and Sam to wake up. How was Keith going to explain to Jody that the pribir were now in possession of Jody's cherished gun?

Pam was studying Cord intently. "So you're Lillie's offspring."

"I'm her son, yes. So is Keith."

She didn't ask which one was Keith. "You're the child I built with her eye genes, that gray with gold flecks. And the girl, your . . . sister? Has she had her offspring yet?"

"Yes."

"Oh, I wanted to be there for the birth. I was very close to your mother, you know. She admired me intensely. We had a special relationship, aboard our ship."

Fifteen years ago. Didn't they realized how much that generation had changed in ways that weren't physical?

Pam continued, "What is she sickening of?"

"A micro. One genetically engineered to kill people in the war. Airborne."

"Well, I guessed that much. What is the micro's genome? I wish you could smell me its prabisirks."

Cord had no idea what a "prabisirk" was. He said helplessly, "You need to ask Dr. Wilkins. Or Emily. They're our geneticists."

"I remember Emily," Pam said. "An intelligent girl. But who is Dr. Wilkins?"

"Scott Wilkins. He was . . . was one of the kids at Andrews Air Force Base but he didn't go with my mother and the rest on your ship."

"Oh, one of those," Pam said, clearly losing interest in Scott Wilkins. "They don't matter."

Cord had to ask. "Don't matter how?"

"They're not carrying the engineered genes, the right way," Pam asked, clearly surprised by the question. "Like you and your children."

"But . . ." He couldn't find words for what he wanted to say. The best he could do was, "But my mother doesn't have my engineered genes, either. All she got was that she can smell your information. And a boosted immune system." *But not boosted enough.*

"Well, that's true," Pam said judiciously. "Lillie was only one of the vessel generation, but I became fond of her. Still, you're right. She doesn't really matter, either."

He couldn't manage an answer. Lillie, Dr. Wilkins, Grandmother Theresa, who had died trying to save Cord's life . . .*"They don't matter."*

Nothing was like he imagined it would be.

The pribir had another tantrum inside the big house.

Cord had been right; Dr. Wilkins had convinced everyone to let the aliens in without violence. Cord had still been on the ship, but he could easily imagine the arguments Dr. Wilkins used: Angie's dead baby, Lillie, Hannah, maybe even the dead cattle. He could imagine, too, who had lined up against Dr. Wilkins, who for. Keith and Dakota would have been asked to tell their story over and over. When Sam and Rafe and Gavin straggled in from the arroyo, an arrival that Cord saw on the ship's monitor, they would have added their voices. In all, the pribir sat waiting for an hour.

It didn't seem to bother them. Pete had disappeared through a "door" that was there one moment, gone the next. Pam sat doing something incomprehensible with a small piece of machinery she held on her lap. She sat on a low chair, while Cord stood tensely by the monitor.

Cord ventured, "What's that?"

"An analyzer." She looked up, scowling. "You people really have created some perversions. What's wrong with you? Ship plucked this micro-organism out of the air right here, by your dwelling, and it's packed with enough genetic monstrosities to kill every cow on half this continent."

"It did," Cord said. "Well, not all. Dr. Wilkins and Emily identified it and made something to cure it, so we saved twenty head of cattle. Out of a herd of three hundred."

Pam didn't seem impressed. "Yes, the righter wouldn't be that difficult."

"The what?"

"The righter. The organism to destroy the perversion and return the planetary genome to the right way."

Cord left the window and squatted by her chair. It seemed important to meet her eyes directly, on the same level. "Miss . . . I mean, Pam, do you know that nearly the entire planet was killed in the last war?"

"Oh, yes. We know. Ship monitors thermal signatures from orbit."

Cord didn't know what a thermal signature was, but he was staggered by her casual unconcern. She must not have understood. He tried again. "I mean, did you know that almost all humans everywhere are dead?"

"Yes," she said absently, turning back to her machine. "Oh, look, this allele is at least interesting."

Something in Cord's stillness finally caught her attention. She gazed at him with impersonal kindness. "You're bothered, aren't you, by all those deaths. Don't be. Do you know what the right way really is, Cord? It's what you've named 'evolution.' The organisms that can best adapt and breed survive, and others disappear. If they disappear, it means they weren't fit to survive in the first place. Every species eventually gets to the point of directing their own evolution, and our mission is to help species get there faster. That inevitably means that lesser species disappear faster. But it's nothing to mourn over, no more than was the disappearance of those big reptiles, I don't remember the word for them."

"Billions of people died! Billions!" What was happening here? This was the same argument Cord had had with Dr. Wilkins, only then it was Cord who hadn't cared. But that was before he'd seen how indifference looked on somebody else.

"Yes, billions died," Pam said with a brilliant smile, "but you won't, nor your children. We've returned in time to ensure that, I think, even with the perversions that have been added to the environment. You and your children will survive and evolve."

He could scarcely get words out. "And . . . and my mother . . ."

"Oh, yes, we'll save her and any other remnants of the old species that we come across, anybody that gets to this 'farm.' At least, we'll save them to the extent that non-germ-line alteration is possible. We'll rehabilitate their genes so they don't join the billions of obsolete dead. Yet. Of course we'll do that." Her voice took on tones of reproach.

"After all, Cord, we're human, too."

Uncle DeWayne eventually came out of the big house. It was full dark now, and he carried a powerful flashlight. These hoarded relics were usually saved for emergencies. DeWayne illuminated the ship, a straight-backed dignified black man with gray hair, and spoke without raising his voice. "My name is DeWayne Freeman. I'm addressing the pribir in the ship. You're welcome at this farm. Come out of the ship and inside, please. No one will try to harm you if you don't harm us, and everyone will be grateful for your help."

"It's about time," Pete said. He'd returned fifteen minutes ago from wherever he'd been. Cord had the impression that he and Pam were communicating furiously, although they neither spoke nor looked at each other.

Pam made unreplicable sounds at the door and it opened. Cord emerged behind them.

The flashlight caught them full in the eyes and DeWayne courteously lowered it. The upward light cast weird shadows on DeWayne's lined face, so that to Cord he suddenly looked more alien than the pribir. Cord looked away.

The only people in the great room were Dr. Wilkins, Emily, and Jody. How had Uncle DeWayne persuaded the others to retreat to the back rooms or the other houses? Or maybe Jody had, he was supposed to be the boss of the farm. Jody, who had never seen a pribir, never been smelled to by one, looked both apprehensive and curious. Emily, who had been aboard the ship, looked as if she was trying hard not to glare. Dr. Wilkins was expressionless.

"Hello, Emily," Pam said. "You haven't changed very much, dear."

Emily scowled.

Pete said genially, "You must be Scott Wilkins." He held out his hand and Dr. Wilkins took it. Pete looked expectantly at Jody.

Dr. Wilkins said, "This is Jody Romero Ridley, the son of Theresa Romero, who was at Andrews Air Force Base with me. Jody runs this farm."

Pete and Pam smiled at Jody without interest. Pam said, "Where's Lillie, Scott? Cord says she's contracted one of your perverse bioweapons." She pronounced the word with distaste.

How strange, Cord thought somewhere in the depths of his dazed mind. She can't stand the thought of bioweapons, but she doesn't care at all about the billions they killed.

"Yes," Dr. Wilkins said, "Lillie is sick. The micro is out of her system. It started prion conversion to cause an accelerated form of fatal familial insomnia. It—"

"'Prions'?" Pam said. "We didn't learn that word from Rafe or Emily. We'll do our own analysis. Bring Lillie aboard the ship."

"No," Emily said, and Cord saw that she hadn't been able to help herself. Were the memories of pribir ship that bad? For his mother, too? Emily pressed her lips together tightly and looked at the wall.

"Jody," Dr. Wilkins said, "tell Mike to bring Lillie out."

"Oh, Mike is here, too," Pete said, sounding pleased. "You really must give us a complete list of our old friends."

Emily started to leave the room.

"Emily," Dr. Wilkins said, "come back. We both have to go aboard, too. To learn."

Pam said doubtfully, "It'll be very crowded."

Pete added, "And you won't learn anything, anyway. You couldn't possibly build our equipment. That's why we're building the alterations right into your genes, to compensate for your ignorance. You know that."

Emily slammed the door behind her.

Mike appeared, carrying Lillie. Cord felt tears prick his eyelids. Lillie was so thin her elbows were visible knobs. Much of her hair had fallen out. She was asleep, or drugged.

"Well, good heavens," Pam said.

Pete added, "It appears our immune engineering was inadequate."

Pam turned on him. "Who expected them to fuck up the environment this badly? The only genetic thing they *are* good at is perversions. All right, Mike, bring her along." She stamped out, followed by Pete, Mike, and Dr. Wilkins.

Cord went with them. He couldn't help himself. The procession went into darkness thick as mud, without DeWayne's flashlight. Pete made a noise and the ship began to glow, guiding them. The door opened.

This time they went through the blank room and into one that made Cord blink. Machines lined all the walls—or were they machines? No, they were the actual walls, studded with projections and indentations, and as Cord watched, *the walls slithered.*

Not slithering. Breathing.

Not breathing. Some other movement, unnamable but unmistakable. The walls were alive.

Pete made another sound and a wall indentation grew longer, higher, deeper. "There," Pete said to Mike.

Mike stood unmoving.

"Oh, for—" Pam said, and effortlessly took Lillie from Mike's arms. He tightened his grip for a moment, then let Lillie go. Pam laid her in the indentation and its back wall began to mold itself around her.

Cord broke and ran. *This was not right.* This was not human. As he fled through the blank outer room to the outdoors, he knew that he was being watched. He exploded into the darkness—the ship had stopped glowing—and bent over, gasping.

A moment later he was ashamed of himself. He was a coward. It was only technology, just machines using genetics instead of motors, just the right way, what did he fucking expect . . .

Not this. Not this.

How did Mike and Dr. Wilkins stay? Of course, they were older, they were more used to the pribir . . .

They were brave. He was a coward.

For the first time, Cord understood why Emily, Lillie, all that generation hated the pribir. They had done this sort of thing to them aboard the first ship, without the humans' consent, without telling them what would happen to them. The pribir had even made the girls pregnant, had taken sperm from the boys . . . that was *rape*.

He'd never seen it before. If anyone had done that to Clari, had handled her body and put babies in her that weren't Cord's . . .

Cord straightened in the darkness. He knew he wasn't going to go back into that ship. Neither was he going to tell the pribir to leave his mother alone . . . not that the aliens would obey him! But the point was that he wasn't going to do it. He was going to go along with whatever Pam and Pete did, and don't fool yourself, Cord: it's not like with the older generation. They'd had no choice. His going along was a choice. He, Cord Anderson, was choosing to let aliens rape his people.

He couldn't go back inside. Shivering even though it wasn't cold, he blundered in the dark toward the bench under the cottonwoods and sat there, hearing the creek trickle over stones, staring anywhere except at the ship he couldn't see anyway through the thick night.

Twenty-four hours later, Lillie emerged from the ship walking steadily, her gray eyes clear as her mind. She hugged Kella, still pregnant, and Keith. She listened as DeWayne and Spring filled her in on everything that Scott Wilkins hadn't already told her. She stood for a long moment in Mike's arms, neither of them needing to say anything about Hannah's death or their future. Then she went to find Cord, who had slept alone in the barn, who had refused to come anywhere near the house or the ship or any person, human or pribir.

He was at Dead Men's Arroyo, sitting on a boulder, staring at the mass grave of the marauders dug fourteen years ago. A flash flood had carried away the stone marker and the grave was indistinguishable from the scrub around it. You had to know where to look.

"Cord."

"Mom!" He jumped up, hugged her hard, blushed, and let her go.

"I'm fine, Cord. They repaired me."

"Are they . . . is anybody . . ."

"They're working, Cord. Doing what they came to do."

He couldn't tell anything from her tone. He burst out, "You were right, Mom! They're monsters!"

"Yes." She sat on the boulder, patted the place beside her. Reluctantly Cord sat down. He wasn't in the mood for anybody else's emotion except his own.

He said, "I should go check on Clari."

"You haven't thought about Clari in quite a while, it seems. She can wait a little longer. I want to talk to you."

But then she said nothing. Silence dragged on. Cord recognized this trick from his childhood; sooner or later the other person, unable to stand the silence, would tell Lillie whatever she was after. Not this time.

More silence.

He said, "They're horrible, Mom. They don't care about all the people dead in the war, or about your generation—" *only vessels* "—or about any human at all. They only care about our genes!"

"I know," Lillie said.

"That's why you hate them! And you're right!"

"No, that's not why. I don't hate them. But I don't trust them, because their goals aren't ours. Their goal is to remake humanity in their own image. Like gods. And our goal—" She stopped.

"Is what?"

"I don't know. I've never known. I don't know why we're here or what the purpose of life is. When I was your age, I worried about that a lot."

"But not anymore?" Cord had never, he realized, thought about "the purpose of life." He just lived it. This was a side of his mother he'd never seen, and it made him uneasy.

"Not any more. We've been too busy surviving. But I know this, Cord. The pribir know so much more than we do, but they can't . . . see. No, that's not right. Let me try again."

Cord waited, wishing he were somewhere else.

"The pribir have a vision of the infinite manipulability of genes. Using genes to create anything, to accomplish anything. But they have no vision at all to give the bodies that house those genes. They don't care about those bodies because they're temporary and genes are not. I don't even think they care about their own bodies. They're shaped like us—for now, anyway—to help their work. But their real shape is probably far different. Once, I saw—"

Cord stood up. He didn't want to know what his mother had seen once. He'd already seen enough himself, and none of it was what he'd imagined.

Lillie smiled. "Okay, Cord. This isn't your kind of conversation. That's all right. Help me back to the farm."

Alarm ran through him, followed by suspicion: His mother never asked for help. But she leaned on him as they walked the mile to the farm, and he didn't know if her grip on his arm was to ease herself or to lead him firmly, inescapably home.

PART V: LILLIE

"He who prepares for tomorrow, prepares for life."
—Ovid

CHAPTER 26

For the first few weeks, Lillie wondered what else the pribir might have done to her brain besides free it of the prions that were killing her. If they had changed her brain chemistry significantly, had altered her neurons or transmitters into those of a different person, how would she even know?

She seemed the same to herself. More significantly, how everyone at the farm treated her didn't differ from her memories of how they'd treated her before her illness. No one reacted to her as if she were acting out of character. Her memories of past years matched others people's recollections. And no amount of genetic tinkering could create memories, could it? Only erase them. So gradually Lillie began to believe she was still Lillie.

Whatever that might mean.

Maybe it meant only her memories. Maybe that's all the essence of a person was: what she remembered, and how she felt about those memories. The mind's eye, not the cell's DNA.

Certainly memories thronged around her thickly. Why not before now? For the reason she'd given Cord: she'd been too busy with everyone's survival. But now survival seemed to be in the hands of the pribir. So now, in the middle of a present tense with significant genetic futures, Lillie found herself caught by insignificant memories from a world past and gone.

Riding on the crosstown bus with Uncle Keith to the Museum of Modern Art. The feel of a cherry popsickle on her tongue. The smell of paste in art class at her elementary school on New York's West Side. The sound of planes shrieking overhead as they took off and landed at Andrews. Giggling with Theresa behind the Youth Building when they'd found someone's stash of illegal cigarettes behind a dumpster and they'd each taken a single disgusting puff. A dress Madison had once worn at Andrews, yellow and slinky, with tiny mirrors sewn around the neckline. A nurse she'd especially liked at Malcolm Grow, a big black woman with a huge laugh, whose name Lillie wished she could remember. Going to the movies, and trying to decode graffiti, and standing in the supermarket in front of seventeen brands of scented soap, trying to choose.

"Aunt Lillie," Taneesha said, "Mom wants you right away. Aunt Lillie? Are you listening?"

"Yes," Lillie said. Taneesha looked worried, her pretty brown face creased, an infant in her arms. A pretty child, and already a mother. Well, so had Lillie been.

"Mom says to come right away!" Taneesha said, and Lillie left the past.

"What does Sajelle want? Is Susie in labor?" Susie was the only one still pregnant, except Clari. All the rest had had healthy triplets. Once again the farm was overwhelmed with infants, and she, Lillie, had no business daydreaming over her work.

"No, Susie isn't going over the top yet," Taneesha said, and Lillie wondered if she knew the phrase had once belonged to men at war in muddy trenches with much different weapons than any war Taneesha had known. Probably not. "There's a man here!"

"A man? What do you mean, a man?"

"Somebody not one of us! The pribir want to take him inside the ship."

Lillie took off at a run. She was strong now, so strong that again she wondered what the pribir had tampered with while they cured her war-given disease. And what did they want to do with this man?

No one had come to the farm in at least three months. There were still pockets of survivors on the planet; Rafe monitored them on the Net. But each week the pockets were fewer, and no one had reported in from the rest of New Mexico. Which didn't, of course, mean they weren't out there.

Strength or not, Lillie was panting by the time she reached the ship. It was closed and no one was beside it. Lillie covered the short distance to the big house.

"They're at Dr. Wilkins's lab," said Kendra, looking frightened. She sat in a deep chair nursing two babies at once. "Aunt Sajelle wants you right away!"

Scott wasn't in the lab. Since the pribir had done something to his immune system, he could go anywhere again, despite whatever bioweapons might still exist. The pribir had done the same to everyone in Lillie's generation who would consent. Not everybody would. Next the pribir had started on her generation's children,

Keith and Kella and the rest. After that would come the infants; no one had forgotten that one of Angie's babies had died.

But now Pam and Pete were not escorting another sullen, frightened person into their ship. Instead they stood over a bed in Scott's lab, staring at the man lying there. Sajelle spied Lillie, blew out a breath in relief, and pointed.

"He came in an hour ago, from God knows where. Or how. And I don't even want to think about what he might be carrying. He was raving, and Dolly put him out."

Dolly, Senni's sulky daughter and Clari's sister, was the only other person in the room. Lately she had been helping Emily in the lab, cleaning up and running simple tests. She was the only woman on the farm between fifteen and twenty-nine who wasn't pregnant or nursing, and Emily had taken what help she could get. Everyone else was desperately needed to ensure food or to care for children.

Dolly said, "He needs a bath. He smells awful."

A bath wasn't all he needed. The stranger was so thin that his collarbones stood out like mountain ranges above the sere wasteland of his sunken chest. Forty? Thirty? Twenty-five? It was impossible to tell under the beard and dirt and sunburn. His shirt and pants were torn, probably by mesquite, and if he'd ever had a hat, he'd lost it. A purple skin cancer spread from the top of his forehead to under his hairline.

Lillie said, "Did anyone send for Scott or Emily?" and then realized how stupid that was. There was nothing Scott or Emily could do that the pribir couldn't do infinitely better.

Pam and Pete had been gazing at the stranger with interest. Pete said, "We need him in the ship. He's never had any engineering at all, not even the rudiments. He could be carrying really fascinating micros."

Lillie said, "Will you cure him of that cancer? And whatever else he has?"

"Sure."

Sajelle said, "We can each grab one end of that bed and carry it, he don't look heavy at all. Skinny as wire."

On impulse Lillie said, "Let Pam and Pete do it. I'm sure they're engineered to be stronger than we are. Aren't you?"

"Yes," Pam said absently, "but he's really one of yours." And the two pribir walked out.

Sajelle blew a raspberry. "Come on, Lillie. Grab that other end. Dolly, you scrub this room down with disinfectant and air it out good."

In twenty-four hours the stranger was back, cured and clean and sane, but still very weak. No engineered reserve strength, Lillie thought. He gazed fearfully at Lillie, Dolly, and Emily and tried to get out of bed.

"Lie still, please, I'm a doctor," Emily said. She'd already performed her own tests on the man while he was still drugged, learning what she could from whatever the pribir had done to him. *Picking up their crumbs*, Lillie thought, and hoped Emily didn't think of it that way. Pam and Pete had lost all interest in the stranger once they had their samples.

"Where . . . am I?" he said.

Dolly answered, "This is the farm," and Lillie realized that to Dolly, born here and seldom off the farm, that was sufficient identification.

Lillie said, "We're a group of survivors from the war who've been here many years before that. Who are you?"

"Martin Wade. Santa Fe."

Emily said, "Is there still a Santa Fe?"

"No," Martin said. Lillie saw the painful memories shadowed in his eyes.

Dolly said shyly, "Can we get you anything? Are you hungry?"

"Yeah, I am," he said wonderingly. Lillie understood. He'd been at the edge of death, body too ravaged to keep food down, and now he found himself hungry again and food offered. A miracle.

"I'll get you something!" Dolly said eagerly, and Emily's eyes met Lillie's across the bed.

Martin Wade proved resilient. He absorbed what he was told about the pribir without disbelief or horror. His body was too abused to recover rapidly, but he turned out to have a knack with babies and after he was moved to the big house, the harassed childminders were grateful to put one, two, or even three infants on the bed where he lay. He couldn't nurse but he could change diapers, rock fretting infants, even sing to them in a low tuneless monotone. Watching him handle a baby, Lillie knew that he had been a father. She didn't ask, and he said nothing about his past, ever. After Susie gave birth, the last of the triplets to be born, Martin was desperately needed.

Dolly developed a sudden interest in children. Whenever she could she helped Martin with his transient charges, considerably less skillfully than he. On a hot July night when Lillie couldn't sleep, she went outside onto the porch and found Senni and Dolly screaming at each other in whispers.

Lillie had been hoping to find Mike. Since she had become

well again they had said nothing, done nothing. But Hannah was dead, and Lillie knew that eventually, when Mike was ready, it would happen. She could wait. She had waited years already.

Instead of Mike, she blundered into mother-daughter anger. "—like some whore! Like those mutant whores, sleeping with just anybody, having their pups in litters!"

Lillie caught her breath. Senni never used this language around her, or around anyone else on the farm. She'd have been slapped down.

"He's not just anybody! He's . . . he's . . ."

"Like a girl, tending those babies! You sure he's not queer like Bonnie? Sure he wouldn't rather be with Rafe or Alex?"

The sound of flesh slapping flesh. A gasp and a scream, not whispered. Then Senni stalked past, giving Lillie a look of such deep contempt that Lillie was startled. She knew Senni didn't like her—hell, she didn't like Senni either—but Senni was Tess's daughter and for that reason alone, Lillie had been as kind to Senni as possible.

Dolly sobbed softly in the darkness. Lillie moved toward her. The girl said shrilly, "Who's there?"

"Aunt Lillie. Don't be scared. I overheard. I'm sorry."

Lillie had expected Dolly, usually a sullen seventeen-year-old, to either storm past or turn sarcastic. Instead, Dolly grabbed at Lillie's sleeve.

"It isn't fair! Everybody else has somebody for love and sex, even Clari, and she's two years younger than me! Nobody ever thinks about me, maybe I don't want to be alone, and when somebody finally comes along who wants me, that bitch my mother . . . it isn't fair!"

"No," Lillie said calmly, trying to calm Dolly, "it isn't."

Dolly peered like a frightened rabbit. "You . . . you agree with me? You think it's all right for me to be with Martin?"

"Do you like him, Dolly?"

The girl let go of Lillie's sleeve. "Yes. I do. He's sort of soft, not like Keith or Dakota or Bobby—" Lillie heard the resentment that none of those had chosen Dolly "—but he's nice. And I do like him. And he's cured now, not carrying disease like she said, and forty-two isn't that old! Bitch!"

"He likes you," Lillie stated quietly.

"Yes! He does, which is more than anybody else around here . . . oh, Aunt Lillie, is it so terrible to want what everybody else already has?"

Lillie blinked at the transition from resentment to genuine despair. Seventeen. For the first time, she liked Dolly.

"No, it's not terrible. Do you want to . . . I mean . . ."

"We want to get married," Dolly said fervently. "Not just be together until I get pregnant and then forget it ever happened like those whor . . . like some of the others. We want a real wedding, with a white dress and flowers and a party!"

Like she'd seen on old Net shows, Lillie thought, and wondered if that was what Martin wanted, too, or if this was Dolly's vision. Maybe she just wanted to one-up Clari, who had never actually married Cord. A wedding like that—any wedding—in the middle of the pribir's attempt to remake humanity: how ludicrous was that? But Dolly was Tess's granddaughter, and Dolly was filled with hope and pleasure for the first time that Lillie could remember. A white-dress antiquated wedding was no more ludicrous than anything else going on now. And maybe a wedding would . . . do what? Remind them all that they were human.

"You and Martin should talk to your Uncle Jody," she told Dolly. Jody was the only one with influence over his sister. "I'll bet he'll be on your side."

"You think so?" Dolly's young voice vibrated with hope. "We'll talk to him tomorrow!"

Poor Martin, Lillie thought. Tumbleweed in the gale. Well, Martin was gaining, too. Survival, for one thing, plus sex and probably devotion. Dolly seemed capable of complete, devouring devotion.

"Thank you, Aunt Lillie."

"You're welcome. Now go to bed. The mosquitoes are fierce tonight."

The next day, Dolly announced that she and Martin were getting married on October 5, at six o'clock in the evening. Martin said nothing. The date tickled at Lillie's mind. Only hours later did she realize that October 5 would have been Tess's sixty-eighth birthday.

"We have something to tell you," Pam told Lillie. The pribir had apparently decided that all their communication with humans would go through either Lillie or Scott, the only two humans who didn't scowl or draw away when an alien approached. Cord's generation had found the pribir of actuality to be too different from the pribir of imagination. They were grudgingly grateful for the genetic help, but awkward in talking to the helpers.

Lillie accepted the burden with resignation. So far, the pribir had not tried to do anything to any human without permission, or to smell to them in any way that manipulated human behavior.

So far.

"We want you to find Scott and Emily," Pam continued. "They need to hear this, too. It's important."

"I don't think Emily will come," Lillie said. Emily learned everything second-hand, from Scott. The old man looked and acted twenty years younger since the aliens had done to him . . . whatever they had done.

"Make Emily come," Pam snapped. "This is too important for her to miss."

The meeting was held in Scott's lab; Emily flatly refused to enter the pribir ship. Lillie looked around her curiously. She saw nothing that she could identify as a pribir machine, only the usual jumble of expensive, aging scientific equipment, none of which could ever be replaced again, with crude wooden boxes, vials labeled in Scott's careful hand, Sajelle's nursing equipment. This was also the hospital. Two neatly made beds stood against the far wall. On a separate shelf were Scott's handwritten records on his precious supply of paper, encased in plastic boxes against damp, rodents, and time. Records that no one was left to read.

Emily sat stiffly on one of the beds, Scott beside her. Lillie seated herself on the other. Pam and Pete stood between them, holding what looked like a clear container stuffed with a mutilated rabbit.

It *was* a clear container stuffed with a mutilated rabbit.

"Look at this," Pam said. "Just look at it! This is what you people have done!"

Emily's fist clenched. Scott put a restraining hand on her arm and said mildly, "Not us, Pam."

"Your species!"

Pete, upset but calmer than Pam, said, "The rabbit's genes have been damaged, in the germ line. It now carries a gene that expresses at death, making a kind of poison. The gene was adapted from plants that use poison to keep away predators. The gene turns on throughout the rabbit's muscles and flesh, triggered by the reduction in oxygen. If humans eat this rabbit, they will die."

Pete's statement electrified the room. Lillie stood shakily. "I have to tell that to Sajelle, the kitchen crew fixes rabbit stew all the time, we had it two days ago—"

"Those rabbits weren't poisoned or you'd already be dead,"

Pam said crossly. "Don't you listen, Lillie? And I already told Sajelle. The point is, you can't eat any more rabbit at all. This genemod is dominant, and it's coupled with other genes that confer a preferential evolutionary advantage on rabbits that have it. A nasty construction. Eventually every rabbit will have it."

Rabbits currently formed a mainstay of the farm's protein.

Scott said, "Are you sure, Pete?"

He looked surprised. "Of course we're sure."

Scott said, "Have you detected this gene in any other wildlife?"

"That's just the point," Pam said. "It's already transmitted, probably by transposon in a parasite, to those little rodents in the desert, the small quick ones that jump so well."

"Deermice," Scott said. "We don't eat those."

"But the transposon might keep jumping species. And we've also detected something strange in the mesquite."

In the mesquite. That meant *plants*. . . . Lillie was no scientist, but she understood that plants underlay everything, the whole food chain.

"It's not interfering with basic plant functions," Pete said, "photosynthesis, respiration, nitrogen fixing, all that. We're not even sure its expression could harm you, and anyway you don't eat mesquite. But it's a sign."

Lillie said, although she was afraid to hear the answer, "Of what?"

Pam said, "Of the complete changing of Earth ecology. Between what you've done to the atmospheric gas balance, what that's done to the climate, and what your perversions of the right way have done to the fauna and now even the flora . . . you people just aren't worth our trouble!"

"But you're our assignment," Pete said. "So we'll do what's necessary. However, you can't keep your current genome and hope to survive more than a few more generations. We gave you all the adaptations we thought you'd need, starting way back at your generation, Lillie, but it isn't going to be enough to protect you. We have to rebuild from the beginning."

Emily spoke for the first time. "'Way back at your generation.' You knew the human race was going to need genetic modifications to survive, didn't you. You knew it seventy years ago, when you started all this with poor deluded Dr. Timothy Miller. You knew it."

"Yes, of course," Pete said.

"Did you know a war with bioweapons was going to happen?"

"With a sixty-seven percent probability," Pete said. He flicked his hair off his sweaty forehead; the room was already stifling, and it wasn't even noon.

Emily repeated carefully, "You knew there would be a devastating biowar. And you didn't use us engineered kids to warn humanity, back in 2013, when it might have done some good."

Pete said patiently, "That's not the right way, Emily."

"And now you want to 'rebuild from the beginning.' You mean, you want to take human genes and create some creature that can survive in the new ecology, but won't look or act or function anything like human beings."

Pete and Pam looked at each other, bewildered. Pam said, "How could they not be human? They'll have mostly human genes. Of course they'll be human."

"Brewed up in some vat?"

Pam said, "Carried in human wombs, of course. It has to be a heritable germ-line rebuilding, you know that. Emily, you're being ridiculous."

Emily stood. "I'm being human. Which you are not. And before we'd let you turn our children into the kind of monsters you are, we'll all die first and the whole race with us." She walked past the pribir and out the door.

Scott said quietly, "What would the new ones look like?"

"We don't know yet. We'll try to preserve as much of your current appearance as we can, if you like, but, really, there are much better and more efficient designs."

Lillie remembered the . . . thing she'd glimpsed, for a brief almost-sedated moment, behind the wall of the garden on the *Flyer*. A shapeless blob, flowing toward her . . .

The future of humanity. And just yesterday she had been regretting the loss of the crosstown bus, cherry popsickles, movies, graffiti. All nothing compared to the losses to come.

Or else the human race could die out completely.

Pete said, "We wanted to tell you three first, before we tell the others." He looked proud of this piece of adaptation to local custom.

Scott said quickly, "Don't tell the others, please, Pete. Let me do it."

Pam frowned. "It's our—"

"Of course it's your project, your discovery, Pam. All the credit goes to you two. But just let Lillie and me present it to everybody else."

"Well, all right."

Lillie said, "I have a question."

"Yes?" Pam said. She even smiled. She still thought, Lillie knew, that she and Lillie had a special shared bond. It made Lillie's skin prickle.

Lillie spoke very carefully. "If the others don't like the idea of 'rebuilding from the beginning' . . . if they refuse . . . will you go ahead and try to do it anyway? Without our consent?"

As you did on the ship when you made us all pregnant. She didn't say it.

Pete said, "Why would you refuse?"

"If we do," Lillie said. No use explaining; Pete would never get it.

Pam and Pete were silent. *Smelling to each other*, Lillie knew. Beside her, Scott's body tensed.

Pam finally said, "This planet is our assignment. The sentient life on it is our project. You said that yourself, Lillie."

It wasn't an answer. And it was.

She said, "Tell me exactly how you would remake humans, all the survival advantages, so that I can tell the others."

"Well, we're not exactly sure yet of the—"

"Tell me what you can, Pete. It's important. I have to have positive arguments, and I have to present them to everybody before Emily gets to them."

Scott said, "Lillie . . ."

"I have to know, Scott. *We* have to know."

The pribir told them.

"Oh my God," Scott said.

Emily had had a chance to talk to no one yet. As she left the lab for the big house, Cord grabbed her to say that Clari had gone into labor. "She's screaming, Emily . . . I can't stand it!"

"Well, I don't know why not," Emily snapped. "*You're* not in labor."

"I'll go get Mom—"

"Don't bother. She's too busy with the pribir. Take me to Clari."

Cord did, then ran to fetch Sajelle and Carolina, and then ran to sit by Clari until she whimpered for him to get out.

So by the time Lillie reached the small house where Clari sat on the birthing stool Alex had built months ago, Clari was eight centimeters dilated. The girl squatted among the women, who wiped her face and gave her sips of water and held her hands when the pain came. "It's going to break me in two," Clari gasped. "Oh, save the baby if . . . if . . ."

"None of that talk," Sajelle said, but she shot Lillie a worried look.

Clari had a very bad time. It wasn't until midnight that Cord's son slid out from her torn body, amid a wash of blood. Scott and Emily immediately sedated Clari and worked feverishly to repair the damage. Lillie held her breath until she heard the tiny, high wail. Carolina, she of the gentle hands, took the baby to the tub of heated water to be bathed, crooning to him in Spanish. "*Primito, mi corazon . . .*"

"Can I—"

"You get out of here, Lillie," Sajelle ordered. "You never were any good at nursing." Gratefully, Lillie went. She leaned against the side of the house and gulped the sweet fresh air. A figure hovered there.

"You have a son, Cord."

"Can I—"

"Not yet. Scott and Emily are—"

It didn't matter. He had bolted through the door. Well, sterility was a thing of the past, anyway. The pribir adjustments to the immune system made it able to fight off anything.

No. Not anything. If that were so, there would be no need for the pribir to go on being here. And God, what a blessing that would be.

Lillie made herself stay awake until Emily emerged. Lillie said only, "Wait until morning?"

Emily nodded wearily, her shirt splattered with blood. "Both of us, then. To everybody at once."

"Okay."

Emily stumbled toward the lab, where she often slept. Lillie longed for sleep, but she went once more into the house to check on Clari and to see her new grandson. Cord was holding the sleeping baby, his face suffused with wonder. So he was parental, after all, as she herself had not been. Lillie breathed in relief. The baby would enrapture Cord, and Clari would see that, and the tension Lillie had detected between them during Clari's pregnancy might wither away.

Lillie dutifully inspected the infant. Clari's abundant dark hair, a standard baby face. Lillie wasn't sure she could have differentiated this child from Kella's dark-haired one. Or maybe even from any dark-haired infant on the farm.

But this one *was* different. If the pribir had their way, it would be the last human-looking child ever born.

CHAPTER 27

It rained that next, crucial morning, a steady warm thunderless gift of water that greened the desert, filled the cisterns, and slid gracefully down the glass windows. Rafe and Spring planned on going to Wenton, eventually, to scavenge for anything useful, including more glass windows pried from the deserted buildings. Once they were convinced the town was truly deserted, for good.

Lillie and Emily stood by the cold fireplace, facing everyone else seated or standing around the great room. All the infants except Clari's were in the adjoining den, with the childminders on duty hovering in the doorway between rooms. This early in the morning the room was at least cool, even with this many bodies packed in. It smelled of rain and cattle and babies and chicory coffee carried hot from the cookshack that kept cooking heat away from the big house.

Emily talked first, and Lillie had a sudden, useless flash of memory: Emily standing shyly alongside Rafe in the classroom aboard the *Flyer*, supplying Pam with the English words for genetic concepts. Emily blushing, proud of her ability to help these wonderful teachers in this most wonderful school.

Emily surveyed the tense faces in the great room and spoke with restraint. Lillie saw what that cost her. "—and the rabbit population *is* poison to us now, or soon will be. There may or may not be difficulties with eating some plants, and more difficulties might develop later. The pribir say we can't survive with all the changes that are going to happen on Earth. So they want to . . . want to . . ."

Emily licked her lips, and chose her words with care. ". . . to reengineer our genes again. To create embryos and implant them in fertile females, as they did aboard the ship fifteen years ago. But this time, the embryos will be much different from us. The pribir say they will have a different shape, different internal functions, different diets and . . . they're not sure yet of all the necessary changes. But one thing the aliens are very clear on. These offspring we will give birth to will not be human, and they will eventually replace humans on the planet."

There was stunned silence. Lillie stepped into it.

"Emily has told you the truth, but she's left a few things out. First, the alternative to the pribir plan is death to the human race, forever. The genemods we already have, that the last two generations have, aren't enough to let us adapt to what might happen to Earth. The bioweapons are too many and too persistent, and they're mutating. Also, climate changes aren't settling back down as we hoped they would. Rafe ran a computer simulation, and the global warming is caught in a feedback loop. All the sensors still transmitting from the upper atmosphere say the methane, ozone, and carbon dioxide are all increasing. Down here it's only going to get worse. Our choice is simple: we do what the pribir suggest or our descendants all die.

"Second, there's a big difference between this engineering and the last one. The pribir are asking our permission. They won't go ahead with any embryo implants in anybody without consent."

Scott stirred on his bench. Lillie met his eyes steadily, and held her breath. If he disputed that statement, the argument was over. Scott said nothing.

Rafe called out, "Lillie, you said 'what *might* happen to Earth.' Maybe the jackrabbits are the only thing that will be affected, and otherwise we can go on like we are now. Or the Earth's natural homeostasis might kick in."

"No homeostasis has kicked in so far. At all."

Sajelle said, "I'd rather take our chances with Mother Nature than with the pribir!"

"Me, too!" Alex.

"And me!"

"And me!" The calling came faster, louder, angrier.

Spring, the peacemaker, stood. "I'm no scientist, God and everybody else knows, but couldn't the pribir just . . . Emily said the rabbits and maybe the mesquite, couldn't the pribir just reengineer those things? Instead of us?"

Shouted agreements. Lillie held up her hand, but it was a long time before she could get their attention. She said, "The problem with that idea is that other genetic changes might affect other foods, and not even the pribir know which ones. There are some nasty transposons out there, splicing genes into many different living things. The pribir can't tell what will be next. The increased UV is causing a lot more mutations than ever before. Plus, the pribir are leaving soon, so they can't go on fixing things for us."

"Fucking things up, you mean," Robin called bitterly.

"At least they're leaving!"

"Maybe this time they'll stay away!"

No chance at all, Lillie thought. A few more months in space for Pam and Pete, a few decades gone on Earth, and they'd be back.

Senni snarled, "Lillie, why are you on their side anyway? Deserting your own race?"

She'd expected this. "No. Trying to help it."

Rafe stood, a far more dangerous opponent than Senni. "You hated what the pribir did to us as much as anybody. You were a major victim, remember? Rape, manipulation, experimenting on human beings . . . what happened to your outrage at those things, Lillie? Are the pribir manipulating you right this minute, with mind drugs?"

"No!"

"How would you know?"

Emily said harshly, "She wouldn't."

Julie stood. Julie, fearful, clutching Spring's shoulder for support. "I think . . . I think Lillie's right."

Everyone turned in amazement.

"I lost one of my babies, remember. Dakota and Felicity's sister. We don't even know what killed her. I held that little still body and . . . If the pribir can make it so no other mother loses a child . . . then it's worth it. It is! None of the rest of you except Angie know that because you haven't gone through it. But I did. It doesn't matter what your children look like, as long as they get the chance to live." She collapsed into her seat and buried her face in Spring's chest.

Ashley shouted, "It matters to me whether what I give birth to is human. If it's not, it's not my child."

Lillie said, "Who gets to define 'human'?"

"It's already defined!" Sam yelled. "If you can't see that, Lillie, you're a fucking idiot!"

Mike stood and started toward Sam. Only Scott's urgent hand on Mike's arm made him sit down again, glowering.

Emily said, "No personal attacks, Sam. I mean it. This is too important to decide that way. Put out reasonable arguments or leave."

Lillie glanced at Emily in admiration. Emily did not return the look.

Cord stood. "Clari's and my son has all the life-saving stuff the pribir built into my genes. Dr. Wilkins says so. That's good enough to survive a lot of climate dangers. I should know, it saved me during a sandstorm in the desert. Is Earth going to get worse than that? I don't think so. We already have enough genemods for our descendants to survive."

He won't look at me, Lillie thought. My son refuses to look at me. How had she and Cord changed sides? Once it had been she who feared the pribir and Cord who idealized them. Well, he'd met his ideal and changed his mind, and she was more afraid of the extinction of the human race than of the pribir. The pribir were bullies, tyrants even, short-sighted, selfish, uncaring. They were also the only antidote available to what humans themselves had done to their planet.

She tried to say all this, but the crowd had gone past lengthy, reasoned speech. They shouted and interrupted and no amount of calm orders from DeWayne or Scott or even Jody could stop them. Finally, Sam screamed for a vote.

"How many want to tell the pribir to leave us the hell alone?"

Every hand went up except four: Lillie, Scott, Spring, and Julie. And that was that.

Lillie, completely drained, left the big house to look again at her new grandson, sleeping peacefully beside Clari, unaware that the fate of his children and his children's children had just been decided for him.

Lillie wasn't present when Scott told the pribir of the farm's decision. He emerged from the interview gray-faced, saying only, "They say we're crazy."

"But—"

"I'm going to lie down now. Don't pull at me, any of you. All they say is that we're crazy." He stumbled down the hill toward the lab. Lillie, watching this old man bent and defeated, pushed down the impulse to offer him her arm. Scott wouldn't take it.

Sajelle, standing beside Lillie, said, "What are you going to do now, Lillie?"

Lillie knew it was a challenge: *Are you going to go on opposing your own? Stirring up trouble?* Sajelle waited, looking scarcely older than when they'd left the ship together fifteen years ago, although both she and Lillie were grandmothers. At twenty-nine, to Scott's sixty-nine.

Lillie said wearily, "I'm going to help prepare for Dolly's wedding."

"Good," Sajelle said.

The whole farm was caught up in the preparation. The activity had a desperate edge, the gaiety not forced but brittle. Everyone wanted, needed this distraction, and yet no distraction would have been enough.

Hannah's children played her music cube over and over, and every time Lillie heard it she was back on the *Flyer*, happy and excited, putting on Madison's make-up for that first "dance," making her way shyly to the ship's garden, dancing in Mike's arms. But she didn't ask Frank, Bruce, or Loni to stop playing the music. They were mourning their mother's death, even as they prepared for Dolly's wedding.

Lupe and Kezia, the best needlewomen, took time away from babyminding to sew every bit of clean white cloth on the farm into a wedding dress for Dolly. Spring and Jody slaughtered and barbecued a cow. Sajelle and the kitchen crew made everything good possible out of the garden produce. Forage, and judicious amounts of the hoarded stuff that could not be replaced: sugar, baking powder, rice. There was even a wedding cake, decorated with fresh flowers that Carolina's excited daughters picked by the creek.

The wedding was held at dusk, in the cool space between the dying of the wind and the dying of the light. The children had dragged every chair on the farm to the newly swept area between the big house and the barn and set them in rows on either side of a dirt-packed aisle. At the barn end, a table was draped with flowers, bright with candles. Dolly would come out of the big house, preceded by two little girls carrying more flowers, and walk to the table, where Martin waited with DeWayne, who would recite the ceremony. "Dearly beloved. . . ."

All of it off the Net, Lillie thought. Copied from countless old shows that had as much relevance to their lives now as the tribal rituals of Hottentots. And as for relevance to the lives they would be living ten years from now . . .

She kept her mouth shut. This was what Dolly wanted. And apparently few others thought as she did. Scott, maybe. Emily. DeWayne. Maybe even Cord, although he would never say so. The others were caught up, or made themselves be caught up, in the artificial excitement. Even Senni had been smiling the last few days, as she changed endless diapers or tended the pots kept constantly boiling outside to launder them.

"Dearly beloved, we are gathered here together . . ."

Pam and Pete had not been invited.

The night was lovely, clear and starry. Afterward everyone moved inside, escaping the insects, to eat and dance. No, Lillie thought, don't play it! But they did. *"Don't matter none to me, never really did . . ."*

One of the small houses had been cleared out for Martin and Dolly's "honeymoon." No other couple had had such a thing . . . but no other couple of Dolly's generation had come together slowly, voluntarily, free of pribir-engineered sex triggered at a pribir-chosen time and physiologically allowing no delay.

The day after the wedding, neither Martin nor Dolly emerged from the house for breakfast. Lillie happened to catch Mike's eyes. Something in her expression (What? She didn't know how her face looked) made his gaze deepen. He didn't look away. Lillie caught her breath. He was ready, then, enough over Hannah's death. She smiled at him, and the smile made her feel fourteen again.

Later. Soon.

Dolly and Martin didn't come to the big house for lunch, either.

"Something's wrong," Senni said to DeWayne. "I left some breakfast for them outside the door, and nobody touched it. This isn't just sex. I don't believe it."

Senni knocked on the door. When there was no answer, she pushed it open. She screamed.

Why screams? Lillie thought irritably. All she saw was that Martin lay asleep on the bed and Dolly wasn't there. Dolly could have been in the latrine, for all Senni knew. Senni never considered the reasonable explanation.

But Dolly wasn't in the latrine, and Martin couldn't be wakened.

"He's breathing normally," Emily said, after examining him. "Nothing has been damaged. He's drugged. Did anybody find Dolly?"

"Jody and Spring are still looking." But after an hour the news had spread and everyone was looking. Martin did not wake up.

Sam said grimly, "The fucking pribir have her. In their ship. And Martin's knocked out with the same stuff we always were on the *Flyer*—you telling me you don't remember?"

Lillie, along with the others, remembered.

She slipped away, to the pribir ship. It was undoubtedly impregnable, but that wouldn't stop Sam and the others like him from assaulting it. Lillie wanted to get there first.

She stood on the ship's far side, where she couldn't be seen from the big house. "Pam. This is Lillie. I need to talk to you."

Immediately Pam's disembodied voice sounded through the ship wall. "What do you want, Lillie? I'm busy."

"Pam, you can't implant engineered embryos in Dolly and

pretend she got pregnant by Martin last night. I mean, you can physically do it. But everyone knows what happened. Senni found Martin before he revived and before you could get Dolly back beside him. Everybody else will be up here soon."

"So?" Pam said.

"Scott will abort the fetuses. Or Emily will. Dolly herself will insist on it."

Silence. Lillie thought she'd lost, but then a door appeared in the ship and Pam erupted through it. "Abort? You mean she would destroy our embryos?"

"Of course she would, Pam," Lillie said. She struggled to keep control of her tone. "Scott told you we don't want it."

"But we saw! With your lot! Once the babies are growing inside the females, they let them grow! And after they were born, they nurtured them anyway! We saw it right here on this farm! You and Bonnie and Emily and Julie and Sajelle, and in the next generation Felicity and Kella and Taneesha and Angie and—"

"You didn't see everybody from the ship, did you, Pam? Jessica aborted her triplets, fifteen years ago. So did Madison, and she died of the abortion." All the memories back, after so many years not thinking of them. Tess's story of Madison lying ashen and dead in an Amarillo basement, her legs caked with blood.

"What's wrong with you people!" Pam screamed. "You refuse the only thing that will save your species, you piss on the right way, you disgust me! All of you!"

"Give Dolly back," Lillie said, and heard her own voice rise. "You can't succeed with this. Not against our will."

"You ungrateful, impotent, stupid stupid *stupid*—"

Pam was seized from behind and her arms pinned to her sides. Sam. And behind him, Alex and Cord.

Lillie said levelly, "Let her go, Sam."

"It's not a 'her.' It's a fucking thing, and she's not going to turn us into fucking things, too." He pulled a knife from his belt.

Not real. None of this was real. She made her tone stay calm. "Sam, think. If you hurt her—if you even *can* hurt her—Pete is in the ship and has control of machinery we can't even imagine. He'll fry you right where you stand, and maybe the rest of us, too."

Pam said, "Sam, you're stupider even than the rest. You always were." She flexed her arms and Sam went flying through the air, landing hard on the ground a few feet away. "Now, about Dolly and our embryos—"

Alex threw another knife. It hit Pam square in the back.

She gasped and fell forward, onto her knees. The humans stood frozen. *Now*, Lillie thought, now Pete would—now—

Pam collapsed and lay still, the knife still protruding from her back. The next moment Lillie fell to the ground. Her last thought was *Not Cord!* But it was too late.

She awoke in twilight, lying in the same spot on the ground, Cord and Sam and Alex around her like folded dolls. Lillie shook off as much grogginess as she could and crawled over to Cord. Breathing. He was alive.

She lay gasping, pushing the last of the drug out of her lungs, gulping in the sweet night air. A hawk soared overhead, oblivious. For a moment, it was limned against the rising moon. Lillie saw Pam sitting to one side on a sleek green chair molded to her body, watching her.

"Pam . . . Cord . . ."

"Oh, he's all right," Pam snapped. "See? It's just as I told you. You humans take care of your young, once they're born. Cord isn't anything like you genetically, but you nurture him. Dolly would nurture her embryos, too."

"Dolly? The others? Where—"

"Everybody's perfectly fine. And thank you about asking after me, Lillie. I thought we were friends."

Pam, too, looked fine. She stood, and the green chair dissolved, seeping into the soil. The last thing Pam looked like was a woman who'd taken a knife in the back.

Lillie sat up. "Pam, are you and Pete immortal?"

"Our genes are. So are yours, so are all genes, only the bodies that hold them change. Unless a species stupidly allows itself to become extinct, of course!"

"But . . . are you the same Pam who just took a knife in the back? Or are you . . ." Lillie couldn't say what she meant. Incoherent thoughts chased themselves through her head. Cloning, regeneration, what else?

"My genes are all on file with ship," Pam said crossly, and Lillie gave it up. The basic assumptions were too different. She said, "Dolly—"

"Is back in her primitive house with her mate. Everybody will be waking up soon. I wanted to talk to you first. At least you tried to warn me, Lillie. Thank you."

It was the first time Lillie had ever heard a pribir thank anyone for anything. And yet, at the same time Pam's lovely face wore a slight triumphant smirk, as if she were congratulating herself on getting it right, this strange senseless human ritual.

Pam continued, "Yes, the embryo is still implanted in Dolly. Now we'll have to engineer a permanent maternal virus to make the idea of abortion totally abhorrent to Dolly. Do you know how hard that is? Pete has the entire ship genetic library working on it, plus everyone in orbit. You people think it's easy to engineer behavioral changes. Well, maybe it is if you can keep pumping olfactory molecules into a closed space, but it's a lot harder to engineer a permanent brain change in behavior that doesn't also affect other species-specific behavior. You can't appreciate how difficult. We had no idea about Madison and Jessica. We had no idea how perverse and backward you people really are. Your males didn't even mate with non-engineered women, except for Cord, in order to enlarge the gene pool as much as possible. They just wasted a dominant genome by mating with females who already had it to pass on. I don't know why we even bother."

Pam was back on full rant. Lillie said, "The embryos are still in Dolly?"

"I said so, didn't I?"

"It won't work, Pam. Even if Dolly now wants to have your . . . your creation, the others wouldn't let her. They'd abort anyway. They'd think she was just being manipulated by you and Pete." Which would be the truth.

Pam was speechless. A first, Lillie thought, and rushed in while there was still time.

"Listen, Pam, you have an alternative. Remove the embryos from Dolly. You can do that, can't you? Don't force or manipulate anyone to carry them. That will simply never work. Instead . . . instead . . ."

Lillie faltered. She wasn't sure she could say it.

"Instead what?" Pam demanded.

"Instead you'll have a willing mother, without any weird viruses in her brain. We humans have voted against forced pregnancy. Well, that ought to mean we voted for unforced pregnancy. The others have no right to insist on abortion if the mother doesn't want it. And I think they'll see it that way. I really do.

"Take the embryos out of Dolly and plant them in me. I'll carry the babies, and 'nurture' them, and start your new version of humans.

"I'll do it."

CHAPTER 28

No one believed her. They believed that the embryos nestled in her womb; Scott had verified that. Three fetuses. But no one believed that Lillie's choice to carry them was voluntary. They thought, Emily and Sam and Rafe and DeWayne and maybe even Scott, that she'd been drugged, brainwashed into her decision. Lillie didn't tell them about the "maternal virus" the pribir had been trying to concoct for Dolly. Instead she pointed out that no pribir olfactory drug had ever been known to affect only one person; the molecules always affected everyone who smelled them. This was not a coerced decision. She wanted to carry these embryos. It was her choice.

"We all voted against it!" Bonnie said.

"I want to do it," Lillie said, over and over and over. "And when we voted, we didn't know how far the pribir would go to get this done. Look, people, say for the sake of argument that you're right. This is a different species, not human. That doesn't mean that the rest of you can't go on breeding normal humans."

Normal, she jeered at herself. Cord and his generation were already engineered so much they had once seemed monstrous to Jessica, to Madison. Too monstrous to give life to. Now Cord and the rest had become the norm. And so would this new child, at least to itself. Normal was whatever you yourself were.

There was no way most of them would see that. They didn't want to see it.

"So you breed your race and we breed ours, and the best species wins, is that it, Lillie?" Rafe jeered. "Evolution in practice?"

"It's a big planet, Rafe. And as far as we know, empty. You saying there's no room for another intelligent species?"

"Mom," Kella said, and her voice broke, "why are you doing this?"

Why was she? Because she was making herself a sacrifice, acting to save everyone from the kinds of coercion the pribir were capable of using if they were completely resisted. Because she was a pessimist, and believed the worst sim scenarios about where Earth was headed ecologically. Because she was an optimist, and believed that change could work out for the best. Because she was, and always had been, an outsider. Because she had always yearned for a mission in life, and this was one. How could you put all the reasons of a human heart into a few words?

She said to her children, Kella and Keith and Cord, "You never knew your great-uncle Keith. He was a wonderful person. He and I had a discussion once, a long time ago, about an orbiting nuclear power station. He said that unfortunately new technologies always seem to cost lives at first. Railroads, air travel, heart transplants. Probably even the discovery of fire."

"Was it worth it, Uncle Keith? Two people dead, and everybody else gets lots of energy?"

"We don't look at it like that."

"I see," Lillie's ten-year-old self said primly. And then, "I think two deaths is worth it."

Kella and Keith stared at her with incomprehension. But in Cord, Lillie thought she saw a flash of reluctant understanding.

Eventually, during the arguing and shouting, Lillie asked the key question. "What are you going to do about it? Tie me down and abort, against my will? How does that make you different from the pribir?"

Even Emily and Rafe, the quick-witted ones, had no answer.

Finally, DeWayne came to her when she sat alone on the bench in the cottonwood grove by the creek. She'd gone there hoping that Mike would join her. But he'd seen her leave, and he'd turned away tight-lipped, and Lillie knew he never would be joining her, in any way.

That was part of the price she was paying.

She sat in the cottonwood shade, watching a lizard bask on a sunlit rock beside the creek. Lillie wasn't much of a naturalist, and lizards interested her even less than jackrabbits or wildflowers, but it seemed to her there was something odd about this lizard. Its color? Shape? She didn't know. She looked across the creek at the strip of wildflowers hugging the bank, and she felt reassured. Purple vervain, blue gila, yellow columbine. Tess had taught her the names. The flowers all looked normal.

"Lillie?"

"Hello, DeWayne."

He sat down awkwardly beside her, pulling up the non-existent crease on his trousers—even, she thought, after a decade on the farm. Of everyone, DeWayne was the least comfortable out of doors. He said, "I think you know why I'm here, Lillie."

"Yes. I do. When do they want me to leave?"

"Not until after the . . . your babies are born."

She'd hoped for that. "Who's going with me?"

"Keith and Loni. Spring and Julie and all their kids. Roy and Felicity. Lupe and Juan and Alex."

Alex was a surprise. She said steadily, "Not Cord."

DeWayne didn't look at her. "He would have, I think. But Clari . . ."

"I know." Timid Clari, who always let Cord have his way. But not now, not when she had her son to, as she saw it, protect. Lillie understood.

"And not Kella, either," DeWayne said.

"I didn't expect Kella. I'm glad to have Keith." Always her most adventurous child.

DeWayne said, "You'll have enough people to survive if you go up toward the mountains. There are so few people left that you can probably have your pick of houses. Jody is more than willing to supply you with a few cattle, plus chickens and seed. Rafe thinks he can get you on-line with us, using that old equipment in the storeroom, and you can summon help if you ever need it. We'll do everything we can, Lillie."

"Except let me stay here. You don't want my kids around your kids."

"No," DeWayne said, and still he didn't face her. "We don't."

"It isn't your kids who will object to the new humans, you know. Kids accept whatever is around them as normal. It's you adults."

"I know," DeWayne said. He hesitated. "Do you know what they'll look like? Has Pam even told you?"

Pam had, but Lillie was not about to tell DeWayne. "No."

He burst out suddenly, "Lillie—how *can* you?"

"DeWayne, look at me." He did, reluctantly. She noticed for the first time how furrowed his brown face looked, as if it were he, and not Jody or Spring, who spent most of the time in the sun. Genes were strange things.

She said, "How can I? Because I have to. Or, rather, somebody has to, or we risk extinction. Like dinosaurs, like mastodons, like saber-toothed tigers. If I had another choice besides extinction, I'd take it. But I don't."

"Yes, you do. Go on adapting, the way we have been so far, maybe with a little help from the pribir. You don't know that the climate's going to make that impossible. You don't *know*."

I know, Lillie thought. The pribir, damn them, had never been wrong yet. Except about how human beings would behave, and Lillie wasn't sure she could blame them for that. Humans themselves weren't very good at predicting their own behavior.

Aloud she said, "Then call my choice an insurance policy. If humans in our present form go extinct, the new humans will take up where we left off. If we don't, then surely the Earth is empty enough to hold two strains of humans."

DeWayne said somberly, "It didn't once before. *Homo sapiens* killed off the Neanderthals."

So that was their real fear. Lillie could have told him it wouldn't happen that way, but she knew that was the one piece of information about which she absolutely must lie. Would he ask the question?

He did. "Emily wanted me to ask you something, and I said I would. If . . ."

"Spit it out, DeWayne."

"If they ever wanted to . . . will your 'New Humans' be able to mate with our descendants?"

"No," Lillie lied. And if Emily actually believed that, she was a fool. The pribir would not only ensure compatibility, they would ensure genetic dominance, and Emily knew it. But Lillie wouldn't give Emily that weapon for her arsenal.

Even DeWayne, no geneticist, looked unconvinced. He sighed heavily and stood. "I'm sorry about all this, Lillie."

She merely smiled up at him.

"They won't be human, you know. Your kids. No matter what you call them. There are limits."

"And can you say for sure where they are, DeWayne? The limits of being human include Cord and Taneesha, with all their genemods, most of which we haven't even seen expressed, but those limits don't include the next batch of genetic engineering? Who decided that?"

He said nothing, turned and walked from under the shade of the cottonwoods and over the rise to the big house.

Lillie stayed on the bench. Sometime during the human conversation, the lizard had quietly left its rock. She should feel somber, Lillie thought, but she didn't. Amusement flooded her like water.

All her life she'd wanted the universe to have a design, to make sense, and she herself to have a mission within that design. Now Pam and Pete, tunnel-visioned carriers of their own mission, had given her one: to save the human race. Or, at least, to play a part in that rescue. And it had nothing to do with any grand universal design anywhere.

Lillie had a sudden vision of the entire empty, depopulated planet, falling toward ecological ruin. Beyond it, the rest of the solar system, the galaxy, the local group . . . all that stuff they'd taught her in school. Huge unimaginable distances filled with an infinity of suns and worlds, and all of them were hurtling toward eventual ruin. Novas, burn-outs, maybe even—what had Rafe called it once? —she couldn't remember the word but it meant that everything in the universe would eventually run down and stop. Everything was going to go extinct, and in the face of that there *were* no missions in life. Humanity, old or 'new,' was just an eyeblink that hardly anyone except two egomaniacal aliens would even notice.

Oddly, this not only amused Lillie but refreshed her. It was comforting. She'd never needed a grand mission at all. All she'd needed was to live whatever life circumstances presented to her, and she was automatically a part of the universe. Nothing she did could ever make that part any bigger, not on the true infinite scale of things. That implied that nothing could make her part any smaller, either. She was already as counted in the cosmic census as possible, already part of whatever salvation was possible. Not the religious salvation her mother had believed in, but the salvation of the great march of evolution, the only point the universe had.

She rose, stretched lazily, and watched a jackrabbit tear across the open spaces and into the mesquite. She felt amazingly refreshed. She wished she could tell Uncle Keith; he'd have enjoyed knowing.

With the careful gait of pregnancy, she walked up the rise toward the farm.

"Breathe, damn it!" Pam said. "Breathe harder, Lillie!"

She managed to get out, "You should have . . . made the head . . . smaller."

"Can't do that," Pete said. "Not without loss of cranial capacity for intelligence. There are some design features we were stuck with, you know." He sounded put out.

"Breathe, don't push yet! Fuck it, Lillie, you've done this before!"

And it wasn't any fun then, either, Lillie thought, between waves of pain. But Pam was right. It was too early to push.

She lay inside the ship, but that didn't seem to make labor any easier. Pam had refused to give her any drugs. Surely the pribir could have created molecules to block pain centers in the brain without affecting the babies, but they hadn't. Why? Lillie hadn't thought to ask before, and now it was too late. Maybe they wanted to see how New Human births would go after the pribir departure.

Carolina put water to her lips. "Drink very small, *cariña*."

To please her, Lillie sipped the water. Carolina was the only person who had insisted on being present at the birth, although Lillie suspected that others waited outside to hear the outcome. Carolina had defied even Jody, unleashing torrents of Spanish and tossing her black hair defiantly until he had helplessly given up. Nothing could keep Carolina from babies, even non-human babies, or New Human babies, or whatever these three were going to be.

"Now push!" Pam commanded, and Lillie gratefully complied. She felt the equivalent of shitting a pumpkin, and gasped.

"Is it . . . alive?"

No one answered her. "Here comes the second," Pete said. "All right, push!"

"Is it . . ." She couldn't get the rest of the words out.

"Aaaahhhhhh," Carolina said, and Lillie fainted. A second later she was back, shocked into consciousness by some olfactory molecules from Pam, who said angrily, "Stay with us, Lillie! You're not done!"

Like a car still good for another thousand miles, Lillie thought. These children would never see a car. "Are they . . ."

"Push!"

The third one finished her. She passed out, or fell asleep, but not before the unexpected came to her, startling as snow in ninety degrees. *Oh, my God—*

She woke all at once, undoubtedly by design. No one was in the room.

But I smelled it, Lillie thought, with complete clarity. *I smelled them.*

No. They, her babies, had smelled to her.

"Pam?" she called, and instantly a door melted from the wall and Pete bustled in, carrying a wrapped bundle. Lillie smelled it again.

Her child, emitting olfactory molecules as Pam and Pete did, molecules that created an image in Lillie's mind. The image was fuzzy, mostly a smear of color, but the feeling that accompanied it was clear as spring water: distress. *Too cold, too bright, not the womb.* Her child, like all children, was protesting the birth experience.

Pete didn't ask how Lillie felt. "Do you want to see her?"

"Yes," Lillie said, and struggled to sit up.

Pete put the bundle on Lillie's lap and unwrapped it. Lillie gasped. She'd been told, but still . . . Pete didn't notice the gasp. He glowed with the satisfaction of the right way.

Pete said importantly, "The torso is tilted forward like that to relieve pressure on the vertebrae, and then the neck has that pronounced curve to counteract the tilt, so the adult form will still be able to face forward. The legs are so short in order to keep the center of gravity lower. Those short legs will be very strong. The knee bends backward like that to prevent the grinding and deterioration that you humans all get eventually. Including you, Lillie. This human will live about one hundred and sixty years, and we built everything to last. The bigger ears, of course, are better at gathering sound. We thought about eliminating the vocal chords, since essentially they're unnecessary, but in the end—"

"Be quiet," Lillie said.

Pete, unlike Pam, occasionally listened. He fell silent while Lillie studied the sleeping . . . baby.

A cross between a troll and a turtle, with the curved neck of a swan.

The baby's skin was thick, gray-green, scaly. Its body, with all the features Pete had so clinically described, reminded Lillie of an illustration in a picture book she'd had as a child, a drawing of a stunted gnome. On the child's back, however, was a very thin, flexible, hard shell, extending from tailbone to neck. The feet were webbed with more of the gray-green turtle skin. The hands had scaled skin, too, but ended in a mass of long, delicate tentacles.

Most awful was the face. The nose was a long snout. There was no mouth. Two eyes closed in sleep.

Pam bustled in. "Isn't that a good engineering job, Lillie? She can survive in sand, dust, rain, heat, go into estivation in the cold. And—"

"How does she eat?" Lillie faltered, and a part of her brain not in shock was amazed that she got the words out at all.

"That's the best part," Pam said triumphantly. "We saved it as a surprise. There's a slit just under the curve of the throat for conventional feeding; you can't see it now because it seals completely when not used. But in an emergency, she can also send a tubule into the earth for water and nitrates and then synthesize ATP for energy from sunlight. It's a limited function, only supplementary, of course, but an ingenious one. What Pete and I did was use halobacteria, which photosynthesizes not with chlorophyll but with retinal rhodopsin, and—"

Lillie scarcely listened. It didn't stop Pam, who went on about halobacteria and photosynthesis before returning to her tour of Lillie's child.

"That long nose allows for filters that should block nearly all pathogens before they get inside, but in case not, she's got an immune system like you wouldn't believe. She can also draw her entire body under that shell against really adverse conditions and just estivate for up to six months. Her—"

"How does she talk?" Lillie stared at the mouthless face.

"Why are you so interested in *that*?" Pam said, offended. "We almost didn't give her your primitive communication system, since she has ours. But if she wants to, she can tilt her head back slightly and talk through her throatslit. The vocal chords are intact, as Pete told you. And of course, her hearing is excellent and she can hear your speech just fine."

"Will she understand . . . is she . . ."

"She's a lot more intelligent than you are," Pam said. "Really, Lillie, don't you think I know my profession?"

Lillie unwrapped the baby's diaper. The baby had normal genitalia. Against the rest of her, the sight was terrible.

"Couldn't do much about that," Pete sighed. "The design has to stay cross-fertile with the old-style humans as long as they're still around. Although maybe we can fix that next time through here."

Lillie started to tremble. She was not this strong. She'd thought she was, but she made a terrible mistake, she couldn't do this, it wasn't possible, this thing was not human, oh God help me Uncle Keith—

The baby opened her eyes.

"There!" Pam said in triumph. "Our other surprise for you!"

Under a thick nicitating membrane, the baby's irises and pupils were a duplicate of Cord's, of Lillie's own. Deep gray flecked with gold, alert and bright. Human eyes. A smell came to Lillie, an image in the mind, a stirring in the heart. The baby looked at her.

Immediately, Lillie loved her fiercely.

A trick of the olfactory molecules.

So what? This was Lillie's child.

Pam said, "Do you want to see the other two? Bring them in, Pete. Lillie, what are you going to name them? Lillie?"

Lillie didn't answer. She gazed back at the baby, lost in the infant's eyes, its helpless need of her. She would do anything to protect this child. Anything.

And oh God, the baby was so beautiful.

CHAPTER 29

Rafe said, "It's a defense, isn't it. Built in. Like a skunk's bad smell."

"Not the best comparison," Lillie said acidly. They sat on chairs outside Scott's lab, in the early evening. To the west the sun was setting amid piles of gold and orange clouds. Lillie's infants were inside, being poked at by Scott, with Sajelle and Carolina in eager attendance.

Rafe continued, "When any of us are near the babies, we love them because they continuously send out pheromones to make us love them. It's only when we're out of that particular olfactory range that we remember what they really are."

"When did you become a biologist, Rafe? You're supposed to be our engineer." *Their* engineer. Lillie was leaving with her children in another two weeks. Jody had found her an abandoned vacation house at the foot of the El Capitan mountains, north of what had once been the city of Ruidoso. The place had, he said, a good water supply, insulation, stored canned food, fertile soil. She wondered if Jody had had to bury the bodies of its previous owners, and what bioweapon they had died of.

"I'm not a biologist," Rafe said. "Just an observer. The pribir can learn how we behave, even if they can't anticipate it. They built in their secret protective weapon in the little mutants' pheromones."

"Don't call them that," Lillie said sharply.

Rafe grinned at her ruefully. "Even when you're not smelling them, you can't see them clearly, can you. Well, you're their mother. I guess Pam and Pete couldn't risk you going to the latrine and just deciding to never return. Lillie . . . do yourself a favor. Don't ever be alone until Pam and Pete leave next week."

She started in surprise. "You mean you think the pribir might—"

"They want as many of these . . . offspring as they can get. They could easily impregnate you again."

Lillie considered. "No. It's too soon. They know I'm nursing three kids. The strain on my body would be too great. It would endanger both sets of kids."

Rafe looked unconvinced. He stood, gazing down at her. Abruptly he said, "You're very brave."

She said nothing.

"But, then, you always were. Even on the *Flyer*. Probably the bravest of all of us." He turned and walked away very fast.

Lillie went inside. Sajelle sat holding one of the infants, crooning to it affectionately. Carolina changed another's diaper. The third lay on Scott's lab table, her gold-flecked gray eyes fastened on his face. Julie fussed with baby clothes. The room was very crowded.

Scott, delighted, said, "She's smiling at me with her eyes!"

Lillie had been holding her breath, trying to assess her children objectively. Squat, gray-green, scaled hybrids . . .

"Scott," she said, not exhaling, "Did Pam use reptile genes along with human ones? Did she?"

Scott looked startled. "Why, yes, she did. Does it matter?"

Lillie couldn't hold her breath any longer. She let it out and gulped air, and with the air came the sweet baby smell.

"No," she said, "it doesn't."

Sajelle said, "Have you decided yet what to name them?"

"The boy is Dionysus. The girls are Rhea and Gaia. You're holding Gaia."

"I never heard of names like that," Sajelle complained. "What kind of names are those?"

"Very old ones," Lillie said. "Scott, what have you learned about their genome?"

"Not a whole lot," Scott said. "Four billion base pairs, a third more than we've got. I can only identify about twenty percent. Less than I can identify for your first lot of kids, Cord and Keith and Kella. We never even found out what all *their* genes can do, let alone this lots'. There's just no match in the database. Maybe I'll learn more over time. Here, take Rhea. I have to sit down."

He eased himself into a chair. Lately Scott's right knee had been bothering him. His hair was almost gone now, his face deeply lined. "Lillie, there's been some shifts about your move. Lupe and Juan aren't going."

Well, that wasn't unexpected. Neither Lupe nor Juan had built-in olfactory engineering. They never perceived the pheromones the babies sent out, and so their ridiculous prejudices must always be operating. The same was true for Martin and for Carolina, but Carolina was here anyway, calling Rhea "little cousin." Evidently some people were naturally nurturing no matter what.

Scott continued. "Roy and Felicity also decided to stay here."

Roy. The men weren't around the babies as much as were the women, all with babies of their own. Roy may have persuaded Felicity to not go. Felicity was Julie's daughter, did that mean—

"Spring and I aren't going, either," Julie said. She looked near tears. "I'm sorry, Lillie. But my own kids—"

"I understand," Lillie said. Julie's older children, Dakota and Felicity, and her six grandchildren would be here. Julie wanted to be near them.

"But," Scott said, "Keith and Loni are still going. So is Alex. And also Cord, Clari, and the baby."

Gladness flooded through her. *Cord.* "Did Clari—"

"I think it was actually her idea."

"I'm glad I'll have one of Tess's grandchildren along."

"You'll be fine," Scott said, wiping his forehead. He felt the ever increasing heat more than anyone except Robin. "As far as Rafe can tell over the Net, there's nobody left in a hundred square miles of where you'll be.

"And one more thing. I'm going, too."

"You?"

"Don't look at me like that. You neither, Sajelle and Julie. I know I look like an old wreck to you, but I'll be better off at a higher, cooler elevation than I am here. And somebody should document as much as possible of the gene expression of *Homo sapiens novus.*"

Why? Lillie thought. Her children were not going to be building sequencers and analyzers any time soon. When they did, the design and data would be all different. She didn't say this; she was too glad Scott was going with her. He was one of the few who could remember the world she had grown up in. One who could share those memories, that vanished life.

"I'm happy you're coming, Scott."

He said, "Emily can handle medical needs here."

Sajelle said, "And all the rest of us will visit often, Lillie, and you can visit here. We don't want to lose track of you, or these precious babies." She gazed fondly at the infant in her arms.

Scott and Lillie looked at each other, and he made a complicated gesture not even Lillie could read.

* * *

The pribir ship lifted off in the middle of the night. No one heard it go. When Lillie came out of Scott's lab in the morning, a knot of people stood behind the big house where the ship had been.

Lillie wasn't really surprised. The last time, Pam and Pete had just ceremoniously dumped the humans in the desert, hardly saying goodbye. Farewell speeches apparently weren't genetic.

She walked up to the group. A few people drew back, Sam and Senni and Kezia and, most hurtfully, Kella. Kella wouldn't meet her mother's eyes.

Lillie said, "Where's Jody?"

"Inside," Gavin said. "Do you want me to get him?"

They didn't want her to go inside the big house, even though she wasn't carrying any of the babies. A strange pain slid through her. "Yes. Get him."

Jody came out, a few minutes after the others had left. He looked embarrassed but stubborn. The look suddenly reminded Lillie of a very young Tess.

"Jody, I want to leave for the mountains tomorrow, not in a few weeks. There's no reason to wait. The children and I are more than strong enough to travel—" thanks to the pribir "—and I think we should go."

He looked relieved, and that, too, sent a pain through Lillie. He said, "Okay. Tomorrow is good. Can you be ready at four? I want to get there before the heat of the day."

There and back, he meant. But she only nodded. "We'll be ready. Send out Cord and Keith."

It was a caravan, the next morning, peculiar but probably no more peculiar than other caravans that had crossed this desert. Covered wagons, prospectors on mules, oil-seeking geologists, nuclear-waste trucks. Lillie had spent last evening using the old computer they were taking with them, seeking information on the site of her new home. She'd been shocked to see how little was left to access. Most sites had just ceased. The electricity had gone, the batteries had gone, the people had gone. How had the big libraries continued, with no one running them? Maybe someone was running them. Or maybe the machines were self-running by now, providing data and services endlessly for users who no longer existed. Lillie could have asked Rafe, but she knew she wouldn't.

Jody drove DeWayne's truck, still in good condition. In the ample truck bed, under tarps, rode Lillie, Alex, and Scott, each holding one of Lillie's triplets. Keith and Loni's three ten-month-old children were, miraculously, all asleep. Clari sat close beside

Cord, holding baby Raindrop. Keith's children were named Vervain, Stone, and Lonette. Cord and Clari, Keith and Loni had spent their whole lives on the isolated New Mexico farm. Conventional names meant little to them, mostly associated with silly Net shows. They named their kids after things that mattered to them. And, Lillie thought, "Gaia," "Rhea," and "Dion" were hardly more conventional.

Somewhere behind DeWayne's speedier truck, Taneesha and Bobby drove horse carts piled with bags of foodstuffs from the farm, kegs of salted or smoked meat, some of Scott's lab equipment. He'd apparently had an argument with Emily over what went and what stayed, but Scott must have pulled rank because it seemed to Lillie that most of it was here. There was also a precious box of weapons and ammunition.

"We don't want them," Cord said, but Lillie had spoken to him quietly and changed his mind. The mountains, too, had warmed and changed their ecology, although not as much as the desert, and it was possible they might encounter black bears, mountain lions, wolves.

Or leftover humans.

She didn't say this last to Cord. Her favorite child, still idealistic, still prickly. But all of them knew how to use a handlaser on a rattlesnake, and Alex and Keith could fire everything in that sealed box.

Somewhere behind the horse carts, Spring and Dakota rode herd on a few dairy cows that would be left with Lillie. So would two horses. Spring, Bobby, Dakota, and Taneesha would return with Jody at nightfall, in the empty truck. And after that Lillie would see them . . . when?

Not soon, she knew. Away from her newest babies, the others' memories of the children's monstrosity would grow. That's the way the human mind worked. Unless Lillie sent someone on horseback to fetch help, it might be a very long time before she saw the people she'd lived with for fifteen years, including her daughter.

Not Lillie's choice. But innocence never meant you were spared punishment.

"We're nearly there," Jody said from the driver's console. "Does everybody understand the route back?"

Lillie didn't answer.

Six thick-walled cottages, of roughly equal size. This place had been a vacation compound, maybe a tourist resort. Four of the cottages were guest houses, each with three small bedrooms, comfortable large living room, and spectacular glass-walled view. The roofs had working solar panels, although the windpowered electric generator was no longer functional. The fifth, slightly larger cottage was a communal dining room with the kind of kitchen Lillie hadn't seen in decades: steel appliances, smart ovens, servos. None of them worked. But the dining room had a woodstove and a huge fireplace, and water still ran in the sinks and toilets and tubs.

"Nice big tubs," Jody said, grinning without mirth, "and you should have enough water. It won't be as hot up here, either. Good thing, with those glass walls. Stupid building design."

There had once been air conditioning, Lillie thought but didn't say. Possibly Jody had never experienced air conditioning.

"Jody," Scott said, "why don't you all move up to the mountains?"

A reasonable question. Once, Tess and her husband had had to live where they owned land, and it was their good luck that it was in an area that the warming had made wetter rather than drier. Then, the farm people had huddled together for defense. After that, isolation from the bioweapons. But now there was no reason to stay in that exposed, hot, drying place. The world, or most of it, was empty.

Jody said, "Oh, we've always been there." To him, Lillie saw, it was a reason. His farm, his roots, his mother's grave.

"When are you starting back?" Alex said. There was some tension between him and Jody. Alex had always idolized the older man. No longer.

"Can't go until tomorrow," Jody said. "There's a big storm coming up."

"You should stay as long as you want," Lillie said deliberately. "You're always welcome with us." Jody looked away.

Everyone helped unpack. Lillie and Scott took one cottage, with Gaia, Rhea, and Dion. Keith, Loni, and their children took another, as did Cord and Clari and little Raindrop. Alex was offered the third bedroom in Cord's cottage but said he preferred to put a bunk in what they were already calling "the big house," the dining room/kitchen. Scott declared the vacant cottage his laboratory. The sixth remained what it already was, a storehouse bursting with supplies.

Did Alex miss Kezia? It was hard to tell. She had refused to come with him, and Lillie knew that unlike some of the men, Alex had never felt much personal attachment to Kezia or to the children that the pribir-mandated sex had given him. Kezia didn't seem to mind. For her, too, the driven interlude seemed to have been total hormonal. And maybe Alex simply wasn't very parental.

She had known, once, what that felt like. No more.

When everyone was settled, dinner over, and the infants asleep, Lillie went outside. Scott remained in their cottage, using the ancient computer. For a brief moment she let herself imagine what it would be like if Mike sat there instead. She suppressed the thought. Don't dwell on it. No use in pointless pain.

How strange it felt to be completely surrounded by trees again! Pine and spruce instead of cottonwood and cedar. But the ubiquitous piñons were here, too. The trees blocked sections of the sky, which Lillie was used to seeing whole and vast and limitless. Not here.

When she looked more closely, she could see that some of the trees were dying. The climate was starting to dry off, just as it was on the plains; the process just hadn't yet advanced as far. She didn't know which flora had migrated here when the warming accelerated and the rains increased, but those plants were probably again in retreat. How long would it take?

Lillie felt the wind rise: Jody's storm. It whipped tree branches this way and that. She didn't venture very far; she didn't know either the terrain or the area's vermin, and it was black as a pit in the windy dark. She stumbled back to the house and went inside. Two candles glowing in the living room, and Scott looking up from the computer with a weary smile, and, above all, the faint smell of her babies, asleep in the next room, as living and welcome as the scent of water.

At the end of October, three months after Lillie moved to the mountains, Spring and Jody and Kella visited overnight. Kella did not bring her triplets, Lillie's grandchildren. The visitors didn't bring much news, or carry any away, since the two homesteads communicated by computer almost every day. Kella exclaimed over how much her brothers' children had all grown. She didn't look at her mother's children, and Lillie saw that Kella was trying to stay away from them. It was a miserable visit.

It was another year before Spring returned, and Kella didn't come with him.

It was remarkably easy to live in the mountains. Crops grew easily. Water was more plentiful, although the growing season was shorter. Game was plentiful. Keith, Loni, and Alex learned to make snares. On the entire mountain, they never met another person.

Keith tended the cows, and Cord devoted himself to farming. Clari became pregnant again, and gave birth to a girl they named Theresa.

Scott grew frailer, but his mind was sharp and clear, mapping more of the children's gene expressions every year. At the farm, Robin died. Natural causes, Emily e-mailed; Robin's heart just gave out. Lillie wondered if anyone genuinely mourned. Angie bore another child, a single baby, not triplets. Evidently Pam had had some mercy. Susie had a baby; Felicity had identical twins boys. Kella had a baby Lillie had never seen.

In the mountains the four older children turned two, three, five. They ran barefoot through the woods and learned to trap, fish, farm, read, add, and write code. The old computer held out. "Cheap Japanese parts," Scott joked, and only Lillie understood what he meant. The real miracle was that the Net still functioned. It would, Scott said, as long as the telecom satellites stayed functional in orbit.

It had been three years since they'd seen anyone from the farm. E-mail came once a week, then once every two weeks, then maybe once a month.

Alex and Lillie became lovers in a detached, considerate sort of way. Neither risked passion, but they were kind to each other.

Gaia, Rhea, and Dion stuck together from the time they were toddlers. They didn't avoid the other children; they just preferred their own company. "They're smelling to each other, aren't they?" Cord said. "The way the pribir can. Even though they can talk normally. But this way, nobody else can listen."

"I think so," said Lillie, who knew so. Her hair had started to gray, pale strands glittering in the bright sunlight among the dark brown. She was thirty-four.

"Mom, I saw them eating something yesterday. A woody bush, not anything we can eat. They were nibbling the leaves and sort of laughing. I told Scott, and he said they're probably engineered to digest a big range of plants that we can't."

"I know," Lillie said. She'd observed it for a few months now, and had had her own talk with Scott. She had been concerned. Cord's tone conveyed something else: doubt and distaste.

"They play well with Raindrop and the others, though," Cord said, as much to reassure himself as anything. Then, "But they wouldn't ever . . . turn on the others, would they?" He and Lillie were having this conversation away from the children, which was the only way they could have had it.

"Of course not," Lillie said acidly. "Why would they? They're all cousins."

He didn't answer.

"Cord," Lillie said, "have you noticed that it's getting hotter, even up here in the mountains?"

Cord looked at her as if she were crazy. "Of course I've noticed. Everybody has noticed. Clari and I were saying just last night that the vervain have all but disappeared. It's drier, too. And the UV—we're going to keep the kids inside even more than we do."

His kids and Keith's kids, he meant. Not Lillie's.

Rhea, Gaia, and Dion went wherever they wanted, whenever they wanted. They were only five, but Lillie had spent an entire week following them, and she had seen that they were safe without her. She had seen it graphically, during a thunderstorm that had sprung up on what had been a quiet afternoon.

"Rhea! Gaia! Dion! Come on, we're going back to the house now."

Rhea materialized at Lillie's knees. Short and squat, her gray-green scaly skin blending in with the foliage, she could achieve near-perfect camouflage. She gazed up at Lillie from Lillie's own eyes set above a large snout in that mouthless face and smelled to her mother.

"Not yet, Mommy! We want to stay here!"

"No. It's going to thunderstorm. There could be flash flooding."

The feel of interest came to Lillie's mind. The triplets were interested in everything. Intelligent and curious, they had learned to understand language at a precocious age, and they smelled back increasingly complex ideas. They differed more from each other in their thoughts than in their appearance. Rhea was the gentlest, meditating on butterflies, seldom disobeying. Dion was the most adventurous, and also the most loving. Gaia was the brightest but had a temper. Sometimes Lillie wondered if Pam's own genes were in Gaia. She hoped not.

A surprise had been Gaia's intense interest in Shakespeare. Scott had bought a few actual books with him, antiquated volumes on acid-free paper, including a collection of Shakespeare's plays. Even before she understood the words, Gaia delighted in the rhythms as Scott or Lillie read to her. Lillie was startled by how quickly Gaia remembered and recited long passages. It was disconcerting to see a snouted, scaled five-year-old making mudpies and singing to herself:

"'Full fathom five thy father lies;
Of his bones are coral made:
Those are pearls that were his eyes:
Nothing of him that doth fade,
But doth suffer a sea change
Into something rich and strange' . . . Mommy! Dion's throwing mud at me!"

Where had Gaia's interest in Shakespeare come from? Lillie had never particularly liked literature, nor had Uncle Keith.

Often Lillie wished she could show Gaia, Rhea, and Dion to Uncle Keith. They were children any mother would be proud of. But they were still children.

"Come on, Rhea, the storm is coming. Where are the others?"

Gaia emerged noiselessly from the brush. "I'm here," she smelled. "I don't know where Dion is."

"Dion!" Lillie called, just as the first clap of thunder sounded. "Girls, smell to him, at far range."

"We are, Mommy," Gaia said. A second thunderclap, and two seconds later lightning split the sky.

"Where did he go?" she shouted. Gaia smelled her the direction.

Fear crept cold up Lillie's spine. There was an arroyo that way, and it could flash flood in an instant. "Go back to the house!" she shouted over more thunder. "Hold hands and stay together!" She started off in the direction Gaia had pointed.

The rain came, lashing against Lillie's face, making it difficult to see anything. She tried to run, clumsy against the wind, and stumbled over a dense knot of twisted vines. In less than a minute she was soaked to the skin. The solid sheet of rain blew almost sideways, warm and merciless, and she couldn't make herself heard over the wind.

"Dion! Dion!"

He could smell to her, even over the storm . . . couldn't he? Maybe not. She fell again, tearing open one pant leg. Blood ran down her calf, instantly sprayed off by the rain.

By the time she reached the arroyo, it was already flooding. Water tore along between the bare banks, washing down so much mud that the water looked like sludge. But it raced along at a speed no sludge could match, rising visibly as it was fed by countless flooding streams up the mountain.

"Dion!"

She saw him then, upstream on the opposite bank, a small,

squat, twisted figure watching the water. "Dion!" she screamed again, and he looked up, startled, and took a step forward. The bank gave way and he fell into the flood.

Lillie nearly jumped into the water but some native shrewdness stopped her. *Not here*, there was a place just a little ways down the arroyo where it turned sharply to follow the hidden rocks underneath. Dion would be slowed there, she'd have a better chance of getting him, his speed in the water would just about equal hers in reaching the place—

She thought all of these things, and none of them, even as she began to run. She reached the spot a few seconds too late. Dion's body shot past her in the torrent.

Lillie screamed and ran alongside the banks. Now she had no chance of matching his speed. She ran anyway, lurching and stumbling, flogged by the horizontal rain. Later, she could never remember how far she'd gone, or how long. When she finally reached a flat place where the water spread out into a slower flood plain, Dion was already bobbing in the shallows, inert.

She splashed in and pulled him out. He was dead, he must be dead, she'd seen his body banged against the rocks. . . .

He wasn't dead. His clothes had been entirely torn off, but his squat, fat-cushioned body had curled into a tight ball and the flexible thin shell on his back had curved around it. In the air he uncurled, opened his eyes, and smelled to her. "Hi, Mommy."

"Dion!"

"I'm not hurt." She felt puzzlement in her mind.

"I . . . see that," she gasped, but there was no way he could have heard her because thunder split the sky, deafening as an explosion.

His big ears closed against the din. She saw his throat slit open again, without shedding water because none had gotten in. The big nostrils in his snout also opened. Dion stood.

Gaia and Rhea burst through the underbrush, obediently holding hands as Lillie had told them to. Their pink play suits were torn and soaked. Dion turned toward them and Lillie knew they were smelling furiously to each other, with those olfactory molecules meant only for each other.

All at once her leg hurt where she'd fallen, and she was drenched and cold.

"Come on, Mommy," Rhea said, taking her hand. The little girl's unfurled tentacles felt warm and soft. "We'll take you *home*."

Gaia looked down at herself. She smelled in disgust, and then spoke aloud. "I'm not going to wear clothes any more. Stupid things! This pants got me caught on bushes!"

Dion clasped Lillie around the knees. "I'm not hurt, Mommy," he repeated, this time aloud.

"No," she said, and felt worn out by the gratitude, the strangeness, the sorrow that she was inevitably losing them and the sorrow that they were still hers to agonize over, a loving burden on her useless heart.

CHAPTER 30

They compromised on the clothes. The triplets agreed to wear tough canvas shorts to cover their genitals, which were both vulnerable to thorny bushes and embarrassing to the other children. Shorts, but nothing else.

Everyone else needed coverings from head to foot, as the UV increased.

That summer, the computer finally broke down for good. Neither Scott nor Loni could get it up again. This mattered greatly to Scott, but not, Lillie realized, to anybody else. When he wasn't carefully noting data about the triplets in a crabbed longhand, or reading to them, Scott sat quietly in an old chair under the cooling shade of an oak tree, doing nothing. He wasn't sick, he insisted. "I'm too old and it's too hot," was all he'd say. He ate less and less.

Rhea, Dion, and Gaia spent more and more time away from home, off somewhere on the mountain. The first time they stayed out overnight, Lillie was frantic. Oddly enough, it was Clari who reassured her. The young woman sat beside Lillie through the long dark hours, brewing chicory coffee, a wispy young figure in her brief white sleepgown. The cottage was slower to cool off these days, even though Lillie drew the curtains during the day. She could feel her shirt sticking to the small of her back.

"Rhea was talking to Vervain yesterday and I overheard," Clari said, and Lillie thought how easily they all used "talking" and "overhearing" to describe conversations that may or may not have been one-way audio and one-way pheromonal. "Rhea said they had found eighteen different plants they could digest, and were looking for more. Also that Gaia could build a good campfire in their 'special cave.'"

Lillie raised her hand helplessly, let it fall back to her lap. "Clari

. . . are they going to revert to cavemen? Hunter-gatherers? Foraging for plants and building fires in caves?"

Clari laughed. "Lillie, they're kids. Kids do that. Yours are just better at it than most. Besides, could cavemen solve square roots and recite Shakespeare? Scott says the triplets can do both."

"You have no idea," Lillie said, "how glad I am that you married Cord."

Clari blushed with pleasure. She ducked her head, and in the gesture Lillie suddenly saw Tess, a Tess younger than Clari was now, and infinitely less experienced. Tess at Andrews Air Force Base, glitter in her masses of black hair, embarrassed at a compliment from some boy.

Some boy. All at once Lillie wondered: Was Clari so casual about the triplets staying away from home because she genuinely believed that they'd be safe? Or because it meant they would be spending less time around Raindrop and the others as adolescence approached?

Probably both. That's how humans were, motives as knotted and twisted as mesquite. Anyway, adolescence was a long ways off.

Gaia, Rhea, and Dion straggled home the next afternoon, dirty and sleepy and hugely pleased with themselves. Immediately they fell asleep, and were still asleep when Jody rode up to the compound on horseback calling, "Lillie! Scott! Alex! Anybody home?"

"We're here!" Alex called from the big house, and Jody dismounted and threw his horse's reins over the porch railing. Everyone streamed out.

He looked much older. Sun lines, deep and deadly, creased even the skin on his thin cheeks. A purple carcinoma sat at one temple . . . did that mean Emily wasn't there to keep up with cancer removal? Lillie's chest tightened.

The five children at home, Keith's three and Cord's two, clustered on the porch behind their parents, peeping shyly. Lillie realized they hadn't seen a stranger in . . . how many years? It was so easy to lose track.

Jody said abruptly, "I've got bad news."

Keith said, "What? Shove it out, Jody."

"Some sort of microbe got to the farm. Maybe engineered, maybe naturally mutated, Emily didn't know. She said it might have lain dormant somehow, or jumped species, or anything."

Alex said steadily, "Who? How many?"

"Bonnie. Dakota. Two of Gavin's kids. Wild Pink." He looked away, and the flesh in his throat worked. "And Carolina."

Carolina. No engineering, no boosted immunity at all, nothing but her generous heart. Lillie felt more for Carolina's death than she did for Wild Pink, Kella's daughter, Lillie's own grandchild. She'd barely known Wild Pink.

Clari said gently, "Come in, Jody."

"No. I'm not staying. There's no way of knowing who's carrying what, Emily says. I just came to bring you this. It's her genetic analysis and some doses that seemed to prevent dying from—where's Scott? Is he dead?"

"No, no, just in bed. He feels his age."

"It's good he's not dead because you might need him," Jody said grimly. "Emily says if this can happen once, it can happen again, with a different micro."

Just as Pete and Pam had said. *"What your perversions of the right way have done to the planet . . . We gave you all the adaptations we thought you'd need, starting way back at your generation, Lillie, but it isn't going to be enough to protect you."* These days Lillie seldom thought of the pribir. They had said they'd return "soon," but to pribir that didn't mean the same thing as to humans.

She said, "Come in, Jody. We'll take our chances with you if you will with us. We're still family, and you look completely tired out. We have some very good stew left from dinner."

Jody hesitated, then clumped wearily up the steps. He halted at the children clustered behind the adults: Vervain, Stone, Lonette, Raindrop, little Theresa. Lillie saw his eyes scan them, then look beyond them down the length of the porch. His face relaxed when he didn't see her triplets.

He ate the stew greedily, the kids clustering wide-eyed around this new "uncle." As Jody ate, he filled them in on news of the farm. There were only ten head of cattle left, but those were healthy as long as they stayed out of the daylight heat. Two years ago Sajelle and DeWayne had had another child, which shocked and pleased them both. DeWayne was seventy-seven now, as old as Scott, but going strong. (Scott grimaced.) The farm had two new windmills, but the generator no longer worked and so the windmills drove crankshafts. Rafe and Jason had built a better irrigation system, which conserved water from the storms better and also kept flooding down. A few Net sites were still responding on the old computer, there were people left in the world, but not in Wenton where Dakota and Susie and Sam had gone and brought back a great find of useful objects, all sorts of—

Dion stood in the doorway of the big house, blinking in the candlelight after the dark path up from the woods.

Jody put down his spoon and stood. He said nothing. Lillie saw that he was holding his breath against any olfactory molecules, and that although he hated himself for doing it, he couldn't stop himself. Jody walked carefully past Dion, went down the porch steps, and mounted his horse. Several yards away he turned and looked at Lillie. "I'm sorry. I can't help it."

"Jody—"

But he was gone, from embarrassment and guilt and old, old anger. Probably Jody wouldn't try to get all the way to the farm tonight, in the dark. He'd camp somewhere not all that far from here, with the insects and vermin and possible rain, rather than be manipulated by scent into accepting Lillie's children.

"Who was that?" Dion smelled to everyone at the same time that Lonette said plaintively, "Why did Uncle Jody go away?"

No one answered either of them.

The climate changes accelerated. The pounding rains all but ceased. Streams went dry. The winds still blew fiercely, but with each year they carried less moisture. Certain wildflowers retreated to growing only along streams or in run-off pockets of moisture. Others disappeared altogether.

Scott, now mostly bedridden but still clear-minded, said, "It all goes back to the oceans. If we had the computer, maybe we could tell what's going on. But if the ocean gets warmer or colder in different places, or currents shift for any reason, then winds shift. If winds shift, everything else changes. Precipitation, evaporation, the whole nine yards."

Lillie tried to remember the last time she had heard anyone say *the whole nine yards*. When Scott's generation, which was also her generation, went, no one ever would again.

"Maybe the ocean currents will shift back," Cord said.

Scott smiled sadly. "Did you know that during the last ice age, glaciers extended as far south as Ruidoso?"

"Glaciers," Cord said wonderingly, and looked through the open door at the hot, parched pines.

Wildfires increased dramatically. Any stray bolt of lightning could start a fire. The first time one began several miles away, Lillie sat on the porch and watched the black clouds of smoke rise and blot out the sun. That fire didn't last too long. Afterward, the sunsets and sunrises were glorious. There was still some rain in some months, and she thought they were probably safe for now.

The next year, there were more wildfires.

The triplets were ten years old. With the other children, they hauled water and gathered firewood and hoed crops and pounded chicory nuts. Their long, soft tentacles, seven on each hand, were good at using tools: sewing needles, meat grinders, knives. Like the others, they could skin an animal and debone a fish. They were better than the others at learning everything Scott could teach them about genetics, everything Alex knew about building things, all the poetry and history and physics from their few precious books. They worked cheerfully, played happily, and, always, kept their private "conversations" private. Lillie had no idea what they smelled among themselves. She didn't even have any proof that they did, that any exchange of olfactory molecules existed except the ones that everyone could receive. No proof, but she knew it happened. She was their mother.

"I don't like them anymore," she once overheard Stone say to his sister.

"Oh, they're all right," Vervain replied. "They're just different. Look . . . what's that over those trees, up in the sky?"

Lillie's breath caught. She whirled to look where Vervain pointed, but it was only a trick of the clouds, the light, the shimmering heat.

One blisteringly hot day in June, Gaia, Rhea, and Dion had been sent out to fill in the old latrine and dig a new one. Lillie felt vaguely guilty about assigning them this chore. But they seemed to mind it much less than anyone else did; in fact, it didn't seem to bother them at all. Could they selectively close their receptors to certain odors? She didn't know. Nor did they mind the sun streaming down on them, and Scott said they didn't have to. Their gray-green scales, flexible carapace, and mysterious genetic cooling system meant they didn't have to wear so much as a hat, although Dion often did. He said he liked the look of hats, and he tried to persuade his sisters to wear them, but the girls refused.

It was all right to assign them latrine duty three times in a row.

No, it wasn't. It wasn't fair. The other kids were inside, doing unstrenuous tasks. Lonette was actually asleep. Lillie decided to at least take the triplets a plate of cookies. The "cookies" were a recipe Clari had invented, using pounded acorn flour and agave syrup to create a sweet, sticky confection. All eight kids loved them.

Lillie put on a hat with neck shades, a jacket with long sleeves, and her boots, now so worn that any minute they were going to develop another hole to patch. She covered the plate of sticky cookies with a light cloth against bugs and set out for the main latrine. Unlike the nighttime privy, which was conveniently close to the house, the daytime latrine lay down the mountain beyond a grove of pines, below the water supply and downwind.

It was relatively cool under the pines. Lillie paused a moment, balancing her plate, breathing in the sweet clean fragrance. Then she heard the noise.

Rhea stood beside the shithole she had just filled in. The wooden seat had already been moved, and another hole was partially dug. Rhea held the shovel in her hand, its handle shortened for her squat frame. Rhea's big ears had swiveled forward, and her mouthless head on its curving scaly neck jutted a foot in front of her forward-tilted body. Lillie smelled her surprise. Gaia and Dion weren't in sight.

The men had stopped beside a creosote bush. There were three of them, dressed in what Lillie recognized from a long time ago as military camouflage. They were unshaven, unwashed. They carried guns.

"What the hell is *that?*" one of them cried. He raised his pistol.

Laser? Projectile? Something Lillie couldn't even imagine?

She dropped the cookies and ran forward. Before she even broke cover from the pine grove, the other two men had leveled guns at Rhea. There was no sound, no flash of light. But Rhea dropped to the ground and a tree behind Lillie exploded.

Then all three men dropped their guns, shrieked in pain as they clutched their heads, and collapsed.

Lillie rushed to Rhea. The little girl, so flattened to the ground that she'd been nowhere higher than the thickness of her head, was already getting up. She smelled "Mommy!" and rushed to Lillie, clutching her mother's knees. Lillie snatched her up and was starting to run when Gaia smelled to her, "Stop. They're all dead."

Slowly Lillie turned with Rhea awkwardly, heavily in her arms.

Gaia stood over the three men. Dion was emerging from brush a short distance away. Lillie smelled both of their grimness, their anger. She put Rhea on the ground and walked over to the men, bent, felt for pulses in their necks. They were dead.

"What . . . what did you do?"

Gaia tilted her head back to say aloud with stout determination, "They were going to kill Rhea!"

"What did you do, Gaia? Dion?"

Gaia said defensively, "Rhea did it, too."

"No, I didn't," Rhea retorted. "Mommy was holding me wrong. Just you and Dion did it!"

"I don't care," Dion said. "They were going to hurt Rhea."

"Dion, Gaia," Lillie said, as carefully as she could manage, "what did you *do?*"

The two children looked at each other. Finally Dion said, "We noised them. Don't be mad, Mommy."

Gaia added, "We wouldn't do it if they weren't hurting Rhea!"

"I know," Lillie said. "What do you mean, you 'noised' them?"

"We made the stopping noise," Dion said. "Like bats do, except theirs doesn't stop anything."

"A very high-pitched noise," Lillie said, and was met with dumb stares, which she didn't believe. They understood pitch.

"If you did that," she said, still very careful, "if you noised the men's brains to make them fall over, why didn't it stop me, too?"

"We wouldn't hurt you!" Rhea said, shocked. She'd switched to smelling the concepts to Lillie, as all three children tended to do when emotional. "You're our mommy!"

"But why didn't it stop me?"

"We only aimed it at them," Dion said.

A directed signal, like bats used for navigation. Lillie could understand that. Too high-pitched for her to hear, yes. Very loud, high sounds could cause enough pain to stop the men cold, make them fall down, and then—

Rhea, watching Lillie from gray gold-flecked eyes, said, "I made the defense poison, Mommy."

Defense poison.

Dion said, "Don't look like that, Mommy."

Rhea smelled fearfully, "Are you mad at us?"

"No. No, I'm not. Those are bad men, they were going to kill Rhea—"

"Like Macbeth killed King Duncan," Gaia said helpfully, and through her confusion and shock Lillie thought again what a heritage her children were getting, what a terrible jumble.

Gaia said, "'By the pricking of my thumbs, something wicked this way comes!' It's my turn to dig, Rhea."

"I smell *cookies*," Dion said. "Did you bring cookies?"

"Under the pines," Lillie said, still shaky. Dion took off running. If the cookies were dirty from falling, it wouldn't matter. The triplets could digest anything.

Rhea, the most thoughtful, said, "We need to dig a big hole to bury those bad people."

"I'll start the big hole," Gaia said enthusiastically. "I like to dig."

"Well, have a cookie first," Rhea said.

Dion returned with the plate, its cookies covered with dried pine needles. The children ate eagerly.

"Mommy, do you want one?" Gaia said.

"No, I . . . no, I don't. I need to get out of the sun." She retreated to the pine grove and lowered herself, trembling, to sit on the fragrant ground.

What were her children?

Not human, Emily had cried once. Once, twice, an infinity of times, from everyone who had stayed at the farm. A few minutes ago Gaia, Rhea, Dion had casually killed, without weapons, without contact. Now they sat gobbling sweets like any human children from any place, any time. They learned Shakespeare, history, algebra, their intellectual heritage. They played games with Raindrop and Theresa, Lillie's grandchildren. They did their chores, sometimes grumbling, sometimes interested.

They had just casually killed three men. As casually as Alex or Loni killed game for dinner.

If they had to, if there was nothing else, would her children eat those three men for dinner? Why not? The men were another, lesser species.

No. Her children were human. The next step in humanity, yes, but human. What made them human was . . . was . . .

Eagerly Gaia began to dig a grave next to the three fallen bodies.

Not their genes. Not really. Everything on the planet shared the same DNA, base pairs and sugar phosphate spines and protein expression. Everything: bacteria and mesquite and gila monsters and Lillie. DNA didn't make her children human; God knows what DNA they had in their genome, anyway. Pete and Pam could have put anything in there. Pam and Pete, who also shared this same DNA, and whom Lillie no longer considered human at all.

Intelligence? Did that make for being human? No. There could be—probably were—all sorts of alien beings out there who were highly intelligent (an oozing glob behind the ship's garden wall, glimpsed for only a second . . .) Pam and Pete were intelligent, more so than Lillie, than Lillie's children. Not intelligence.

Love? Even animals loved. Dogs, cats. . . . No. Too sentimental an answer.

Culture? Gaia could recite whole sections of Shakespeare. Rhea loved the abstract puzzles of geometry. Dion had begun to read Scott's endless notes on genetics. But what if they couldn't do those things? If they knew nothing at all of the vast human heritage, nothing, would that make them less human? No. Kalahari bushmen isolated and ignorant of the rest of the world were—had been—fully human.

Evolution, maybe. Gaia and Rhea and Dion were human because they were born of Lillie, who was born of Barbara, who if you went far enough back would end up sharing a common ancestor with apes, and that ancestor was certainly not human. One thing evolved into another, different thing.

Which was what was happening here, in front of her very eyes, with help from those who had already gone ahead, taking charge of their own evolution and so becoming something else in the process. Could you start a new race with only three people? Lillie vaguely remembered learning something about an "African Eve," a single woman who had been the ancestor of everyone alive on Earth before the war. And Scott had told her once of a herd of feral English cattle that had had no new genes available to their tiny pool for over three hundred years, yet the herd had stayed healthy and growing.

And, of course, there might eventually be more than just Gaia, Rhea, and Dion to start this new race. The pribir had promised to return, and no one really knew what they could, or would, do next.

Maybe Emily and the others at the farm were right. Maybe Gaia and Rhea and Dion were *not* human. A new thought came to Lillie: Did it matter?

It was hard to accept.

How did you accept such rapid evolution, even if you yourself were causing it? Nations, states, villages had always had trouble accepting people who were "different." Outsiders. Foreigners. But never before in history had the biological outsiders been your own children, so genetically different that you were watching your own extinction right before you, all at once, in an eyeblink.

Not human.

But still hers.

She got up off the ground to retrieve the discarded plate from the cookies, take it home, wash it, store it away for more sweets, another day, to give her children. They were digging earnestly, "conversing" with each other without sound, feeling the warm sun on bare heads; even Dion had lost his hat. None of them noticed Lillie leave.

But all of them would look for her when, tired and sweaty and satisfied, they made their way home.

EPILOGUE: GAIA

"I believe that man will not merely
endure; he will prevail."
—William Faulkner

2083

Gaia emerged from the canyon, carrying an armful of prickly pear fruit she'd stripped off the cacti. Rhea loved juice wrung from the sweet, purplish fruit, and Gaia planned to pulp the pears and boil them into jelly for her sister. This was partly guilt; lately Gaia hadn't been spending much time with Rhea or Dion. She didn't know why, but more and more she wanted to go off alone to explore, to taste, to . . . what? Something. Now she was further from home than she'd ever been.

"I have immortal longings in me." Uncle Scott had taught her that, before she could read it for herself. Gaia had loved the old man more than anyone else on Earth, except her mother. He had been so good. The good should never die.

She dumped the prickly pear fruit into a pile and pulled a stoppered earthen jar from her backpack, the only thing she wore except for her shorts. One by one, she squeezed the fruit above the jar, every motion quick and strong. A bit splashed back, onto the new breasts which had suddenly started swelling on her chest a few months ago. Impatiently Gaia wiped the juice off with her tentacles.

Someone was coming over the rise to her left.

Gaia immediately flattened, ready to retract into her shell, but just as quickly she rose again. Her gray, gold-flecked eyes widened.

A stranger. A boy. Like her cousins, but it wasn't Stone or Raindrop. She smelled him advancing, not because he was sending her a greeting; he couldn't do that. Rather, she smelled his body on the wind. Instantly, without volition, Gaia was smelling back to him.

He could receive. He stopped cold and looked for her.

For just a second, so brief that later Gaia thought she'd imagined it, the terrible look appeared on his face, the one that Gaia saw sometimes on Alex's face until she got closer to him. She'd learned to accept it from Alex, although she avoided him as much as possible. But she couldn't have seen that look on this boy's face because the next moment he was striding toward her, his face with all those unnecessary holes more alight and curious and interested than Alex had ever been.

"Hi," the boy said. "I'm Troy Freeman. Who are you?"

"Gaia," she smelled to him, and his cluttered face contorted into surprise. Cluttered, but beautiful, especially his dark eyes, darker even than his skin, which was the color of rich, wet earth.

"How did you do that, Gaia? Make your name in my mind?"

"That's how I sometimes talk," she said. Her breath was coming faster. So, she thought, was his.

"That's cool," he said, and Gaia knew what he meant because Lillie sometimes used that word in that way. It made sense. Cool places were always good.

Troy's body was covered against the sun: long pants, long sleeves, hat with neck drape, poor thing. Gaia said politely, because the others always needed it, "Would you like to sit in the shade?"

"I'd love to sit in the shade with you."

They moved into the canyon and sat in the shade of a rock overhang, their backs to the rough stone. Troy offered her some water, and she took a few sips. She couldn't understand what was happening to her. Her body had never felt like this before.

She said aloud to him, "You're from Jody's farm."

His eyes widened. "You *can* talk. How do you know about our farm?"

"Only what my mother and Uncle Scott told me. My mother is Lillie Anderson."

He frowned. "I think I've heard that name, maybe somebody mentioned it once. . . but I can't remember who."

"She used to live at your farm, before some of us moved to the mountain. It's cooler there, or at least it used to be."

"We've moved, too. Pretty far away, the forest at Lincoln."

"I've never been there," Gaia said.

"You're almost there now. Want to see it? I'll show you."

"Yes," she answered, but neither of them moved. The feeling inside Gaia was stronger now, almost overwhelming. And she knew it was inside Troy, too.

He put his hand shyly, carefully, on her short, gray-green leg. "Gaia . . . I've never met anyone like you. You look so different, but you're so . . . so . . ."

She leaned over and "kissed" him.

Troy "kissed" her back, their arms going around each other. Ah, Gaia thought, so this was what she'd been looking for, roaming all over the mountains and plains. This was what she'd wanted, what Shakespeare had meant: "*Now join your hands, and with your hands your hearts.*"

"What was *that?*" Troy said. Abruptly he pulled away from her.

"What?" She hadn't heard anything. Her big ears swiveled questioningly.

"In the sky! Didn't you see it? A big silver thing, huge, flying overhead! I just glimpsed it over the canyon wall!"

And then Gaia smelled it. Clear images in her mind, unmistakable.

Troy said, "The pribir are coming."

"Yes," Gaia said. She reached for him again.

"We have to go find them!" Troy said. "They're calling us!"

It was true. Gaia felt it, the insistent command. Somehow it was in more than her mind, in her muscles and lungs. She slid toward the message . . . and stopped.

No. The pribir could wait. She wanted to stay here, "kissing" Troy.

Only they wanted her to go to the ship . . .

Gaia sat very still. This had never happened to her before. First her body driving her to Troy, and now the pribir pulling her toward them . . . she felt a stab of fear.

Except that the two things were *not* the same. Her body was hers, was her. If it wanted to "kiss" Troy, to mate with Troy, that was she, Gaia, wanting to do that. The call was inside her. But these pribir were not inside her, and she didn't have to do what they said, she wasn't *joined* to them, hand or heart. She could choose, even though they were trying to dictate her choice. Well, they weren't going to choose for her. She was.

Carefully, she tested her own mind. Could she not answer the pribir call? She considered the question. The cells of her body released chemical cascades she had never drawn on before, had not even known were there. Her brain fired patterns of new neurons. Her mind surveyed its capacities in ways unimaginable to the boy beside her. When all this was done, Gaia knew the answer to her question.

Troy was scrambling to his feet. She pulled him back down beside her. "Stay here, Troy."

"But we have to go!"

"No, we don't. Not really. Anyway, the message is dissipating now, don't you feel it lessen? In a minute it will be gone."

He said quietly, "It will come back."

"Maybe. But we still don't have to listen to it."

He gazed down at her. So big, so much taller than she, so beautiful. The most beautiful thing she'd ever seen. Maybe he couldn't resist the message—Raindrop and Lonette couldn't do things she could do, either. But she could resist the pribir for them both. She could choose, and she would choose everything good for Troy, everything he wanted or needed, always. And if the pribir wanted something different for him—well, too bad for them. The pribir didn't scare her. She had taken inventory of her own resources. Pribir didn't live on this world, and she did.

Gaia reached again for Troy. He responded eagerly, intensely. When the next message from the pribir came, a few hours later, Gaia held him tightly until it dissipated on the wind. No message could last too long outdoors, in the free hot wind.

Gaia was completely happy. The shadows in the bare stone canyon lengthened, and the steamy thick-aired night fell, and the few plants in sight gasped in the drying soil. And for Gaia and Troy, wildflowers bloomed and nightingales sang.

Five thousand copies of this book have been printed by the Maple-Vail Book Manufacturing Group, Binghamton, NY, for Golden Gryphon Press, Urbana, IL. The typeset is Electra, printed on 55# Sebago. Typesetting by The Composing Room, Inc., Kimberly, WI.